Trust No Man

Lock Down Publications
& Ca$h Presents
Trust No Man
A Novel by *Ca$h*

Lock Down Publications
P.O. Box 1482
Pine Lake, Ga 30072-1482

Visit our website at **www.lockdownpublications.com**

First Edition 2009
Printed in the United States of America
This is a work of fiction. Names, characters, places, and incidents either are products of the author's imagination or are used fictitiously. Any similarity to actual events or locales or persons, living or dead, is entirely coincidental.

Cover design and layout by: Marion Designs
Book interior design by: Shawn Walker
Edited by: Shawn Walker

Stay Connected with Us!

Text **LOCKDOWN** to 22828 to stay up-to-date with new releases, sneak peaks, contests and more…

Submission Guideline.

Submit the first three chapters of your completed manuscript to ldpsubmissions@gmail.com, subject line: Your book's title. The manuscript must be in a .doc file and sent as an attachment. Document should be in Times New Roman, double spaced and in size 12 font. Also, provide your synopsis and full contact information. If sending multiple submissions, they must each be in a separate email.

Have a story but no way to send it electronically? You can still submit to LDP/Ca$h Presents. Send in the first three chapters, written or typed, of your completed manuscript to:

LDP: Submissions Dept
Po Box 1482
Pine Lake, Ga 30072

DO NOT send original manuscript. Must be a duplicate.

Provide your synopsis and a cover letter containing your full contact information.

Thanks for considering LDP and Ca$h Presents.

Acknowledgments

When you've stomped the streets in my size tens from Cleveland, Ohio to ATL, where I put my hustle and gangsta down with the best of them. And as a consequence, been buried alive in prison for the past 26 years. Best believe, time has shown whose love is real and whose was flex. Most of y'all was only on my dick because I had the block on lock and you feared me.

Well, now I know who is who. To the few whose love has proven to be real, I sincerely thank you for holding me down. To the fake hobbies and females who counted me out a long time ago—I'm still pushing weight, fam, but now it's straight legit. And I'm putting the urban literary game in a choke-hold just like I did the projects back in the day.

On the humble side of things, I owe thanks to my Ma Duke, first and foremost. **Mama**, you're the only angel I've ever known. To my seeds—**Destiny, Keke, Kia, Shawt, Lil Cash, Cortez, Fred**—I love you all. That's why I've never given up. I do this for each one of you. To my son, whom I don't know, I'll find you one day. Only death can keep us apart.

Much love to my siblings, my nieces, nephews and extended relatives. When it comes down to the raw facts, family is all we got.

Last but not least, shout out to everyone associated with **LOCK DOWN PUBLICATIONS**. The authors, readers, and all of you that help make us a movement.

Special thanks to the Queen and COO of LDP, **Shawn Walker**. Black woman, you are one of a kind.

Peace.

CHAPTER 1

It was an unseasonably cool, late summer night in the ATL. The jackmobile came to a quiet stop two houses away from the targeted address. Lonnie and Shotgun Pete, dressed in all black, wearing ski masks and packing heat, quickly hopped out of the vehicle and rushed up on the porch of the house they had been casing out for the past two weeks.

Terrence aka Youngblood, who was a virgin in the stickup game, remained behind the wheel of the jackmobile, a plain, black Crown Victoria, ready to mash out as soon as his partners returned. He was only sixteen, but he was trained to go and was looking to make a name for himself on the streets.

Steve, a mid-level dope boy, was chillin' on the living room sofa with his wife and their newborn son when the front door came crashing in.

"Ahhhh!" Steve's girl let out a loud scream before the back end of Pete's shotgun wickedly slammed against her mouth, knocking out two of her front teeth and sending a spray of blood in the air.

"Make another sound, bitch, and I'll blow ya mafuckin' head off!" barked Shotgun Pete, standing over the crumpled woman.

Lonnie had his Desert Eagle trained on Steve, who had his hands up in the air as if he was surrendering to the cops.

"Pussy nigga, you know what it is. Where that money and dope at?" demanded Lonnie.

"I ain't got no dope, man," replied Steve in a frightened voice. "But I got a coupla thousand dollars."

Whop!

Lonnie smacked him with the burner. "Nigga, you better have more than a coupla racks or it's gon' get real ugly up in this bitch!"

"Fam, that's all I got! I swear to you, man!"

Lonnie and Shotgun Pete wasn't tryna hear that. They led Steve, his wife, and their infant into the kitchen, where they found the two thousand dollars inside a flour can.

Ain't no way this all the money this nigga got around here. Shotgun Pete frowned. "Nigga, you wanna play games? I bet this will make you come correct."

He snatched the baby from Steve's girl's grip and put it inside the microwave. He was so geeked up on powder it made him heartless.

"Nooo!" The woman screamed, but her shrill cry got drowned out by the loud sound of Pete's shotgun.

Boom!

Shorty's whole head disintegrated.

Steve lunged at Shotgun Pete and just as quickly Lonnie's Desert Eagle went off.

Boc! Boc! Boc! Boc! Boc!

Steve's body was lifted in the air by the succession of shots, and it came crashing down to the floor next to his wife's.

Kaboom!

Shotgun Pete blasted a hole in Steve's chest just to be sure he was dead. "Made me get blood on my shit!" he remarked, looking down at his shoes.

Lonnie took the baby out of the microwave and carried him back to the playpen in the living room. "Let's go!" he said.

"I would've cooked that lil' muthafucka," said a heartless Shotgun Pete as they hurried outside and walked briskly back to the car.

"Nigga, you're buggin'. I wouldn't have let you do no foul shit like that." Lonnie shook his head at his partner's coldness.

When they reached the whip, Youngblood questioned them. "What da fuck happened in there? I heard a—"

"Just drive, nigga!" Shotgun Pete snapped. He didn't really like Youngblood, but he tolerated him since Lonnie fucked with him.

Youngblood, felt that hater shit leaking out of Pete's pours like a toxic germ. He didn't know what that muthafucka's problem was but he knew he hadn't done a goddam thing to him.

Had Youngblood been able to see into Shotgun Pete's cold, black heart, he would've known that he was jealous of him because he peeped a thoroughness in Youngblood that he lacked himself.

Lonnie couldn't quite understand his boy's attitude toward the youngin', either. In fact, he was beginning to give him the side-eye about a few things, as of late.

Him and Shotgun Pete, who were both 27 years old, had known each other since their early teens. They had been robbing together for the past two years, but lately Shotgun Pete's snorting habit had become a serious concern. Lonnie felt that cocaine made his partner unreliable, so he took it upon himself to add a third person to their team.

"From now on, Youngblood is gonna rock with us," he'd announced two weeks ago without consulting Shotgun Pete first.

"Why? It's been just the two of us all this time, and shit been gravy. We don't need another nigga eatin' off of our plate!" Shotgun Pete complained.

But Lonnie didn't waver, and eventually Shotgun Pete conceded to his decision, though begrudgingly.

"I'ma roll with it, but Youngblood bet' not step on my toes. And if you ever cross me for that nigga, I'ma send both of y'all to meet Jesus!" he spat.

"Nigga, you'll meet Him before I would," Lonnie warned. And he meant that shit.

As they dropped Youngblood off in front of his girl's crib, Pete thought, *Well at least I'll get a chance to holla at his bitch. They say she got that bomb pussy and a fool ass head game.*

Pete's dick stiffened a bit as he imagined fuckin' Shan. He felt like she wanted to cut something with him as bad as he wanted to run up in her, but the timing had never been right for them to hook up.

But that's all about to change. Pete smiled wickedly as he watched his new partner in crime walk up on Shan's front porch.

***

Youngblood stood outside of the apartment door in Englewood projects in Southeast Atlanta, where he lived with his sixteen-year-old baby mama and her family. Before knocking on the door, he took off the black sweatshirt and stuffed the ski mask inside his pants pocket. He didn't want his girl all up in his business.

Shan's mother, Poochie, let him in almost as soon as he knocked. One look at her told him that she was geeked up, as usual. Her eyes were big like saucers, and she kept licking her dry lips.

"Loan me ten dollars," she begged as soon as he stepped through the door.

"I ain't got no money." He brushed past her.

"Yo ass ain't never got no damn money! You're gonna start paying some bills around here or you gon' have to move out. You and Shan ain't gon' just lay up in my shit, for free, making babies. I don't know what the fuck y'all think this is!" she cussed, mad because he wouldn't support her habit.

Ignoring her, Youngblood headed down the hall to the bedroom. When he got inside, he saw Shan's silhouette up under the covers on the bed. Quietly, he stripped down to his boxers and slid under the covers with her.

"You sleep, shawdy?" Youngblood whispered as he scooted closer and spooned their bodies together. A few seconds later, his dick was jumping and his hand eased between her thighs.

Shan came awake with a full attitude. "Don't fuckin' touch me! You think I'ma fuck you after you been out in the streets slinging dick all night? Nigga, you got me twisted!" She angrily scooted to the edge of the bed.

"Girl, you trippin, ain't nobody been out slinging dick. You must be creepin', 'cause you always accusing me."

"Whatever! Just don't touch me," she spat, but being the nigga that he was, Youngblood was unperturbed.

"Oh, it's like dat? You ain't my bitch no more?" he asked, pulling her back close to him. But she snatched away and scooted back to the edge of the bed again.

"If I'm a bitch, you a bitch nigga!" said Shan.

She was tryna start an argument so that she'd have an excuse to go hookup with her girls, Cita and them, tomorrow and go kick it with some ballers from the Westside.

Youngblood suspected her of being up to something shady. He knew Shan had a reputation for being loose with her pussy, but he tried not to judge her on her past. Besides, she had shown him love when his own mother hadn't.

While Youngblood was in the Youth Detention Center, his moms, Ann, had gotten married to a lame, ex-military nigga named Raymond. Youngblood hated Raymond on sight, and the feeling was mutual. Two weeks after coming home from YDC, he and Raymond butted heads over a curfew Youngblood flat out refused to respect.

"Nigga, you ain't my pops, and I'm not a lil' boy. You better get the fuck outta my face with that sucka shit before I put you in a body bag," threatened Youngblood.

Raymond didn't cower, though. He met Youngblood's fire with equal aggression, which led to a violent fist fight.

Ann and Toi, Youngblood's mother and little sister, was screaming and trying their best to separate the two, but Youngblood was intent on letting Raymond know that he wasn't to be fucked with.

"That's all you got, nigga?" He taunted after taking a punch in the face from Raymond.

Youngblood shook the blow off and countered with a four punch combination that buckled Raymond's knees.

Raymond wobbled but he didn't go down. He quickly regained his balance and charged at Youngblood like a raging bull. They wrestled around and went blow for blow until they were both bleeding and out of breath.

Afterwards, Raymond kicked him out of the house. Ann and Toi cried as Youngblood packed his few belonging and bounced, but Youngblood was glad to leave.

"Bitch ass nigga, you can get these hands put on you again! Anytime you're ready," he spat at Raymond right before slamming the door behind him.

Having no other family in the city, he went back to Englewood, where he had grown up. Those projects embraced him no matter what.

That same day he bumped into Shan, his little childhood sweetheart. Back when they were little snot-nosed kids, Shan had enticed him to put his weener in her bun. He'd heard that she was out there now—legs open all-night like a drive-thru. But when he saw her on her front porch, looking like a young Serena Williams, Youngblood discounted all of the rumors, he had to hit that.

Shan was game, too.

Laying up with him wasn't a problem. Crack had her mama in such a choke hold, she didn't care if her teenage daughter let boys spend the night, as long as they broke her off a few dollars or a rock or two.

Youngblood did both, and then he laid up with Shan that first day, got sprung on the pussy and never left.

Ten months later, she gave birth to his son Terrence Jr., whom they called Lil' T.

In Youngblood's eyes, that made Shan his girl forever, because he damn sure wasn't going to allow her to have his seed around no other nigga. So, whatever she was tripping about, she needed to get over that shit.

"Shawdy, you know you're my heart, don't you?" Youngblood asked, whispering in her ear while scooting over closer, reaching around and rubbing her nipples through the sheer nightgown she had on.

"Don't be touchin' me! That other bitch must wouldn't give you no pussy tonight."

"See, that's where you got the game all wrong. You're my one and only." One hand gently pinched a nipple, the other rubbed her thighs and his dick was pressed hard against that junk in Shan's trunk. He nibbled on the back of her neck and shoulders while his fingers spread her pussy lips. "Damn, you're hot, shawdy."

"Stop. I. Told. You..."

"You told me what?" He pressed two fingers down on her clit and rubbed in a circular motion.

"Stop—nigga," Shan tried to hiss but it came out as a pleasurable moan.

"Open your legs." She did so reluctantly. "Yeah, just like that." Youngblood breathed hard in her ear.

Shan's legs gapped open involuntarily as his fingers sent heat-waves through her body. "Ooh, you finna make me cum."

"And?" he whispered in her ear, still playing with her clit.

"I should've never taught you how to turn me on, now your ass use it as my weakness," she half complained while thrusting her pussy up to meet his touch.

"Shut up and cum for me."

"Okay, boo," she moaned.

"This my pussy, ain't it?"

"Yes."

"Tell me, then," he was rubbing her clit faster now.

"It's your pussy, daddy! I'ma make it cum for you," Shan cried. Then she came, shaking all over.

When her body stopped shaking, Youngblood said, teasingly, "I thought you wanted me to stop."

"Shut up!" Shan punched him in the shoulder.

"I'm just saying, baby mama, you talked all that shit then folded." He laughed.

"So! You got a bitch hot. Your black ass knew what you were doing. You gon' make me cum some more?" she asked in a voice thick with desire for him.

Youngblood smiled, he was really feeling himself. "Want me to eat your pussy from the back, like you taught me?"

"Yeah, you so nasty," she cooed, getting into position.

As soon as her ass went up and her face went down, Youngblood stepped to his business, eating her pussy like it was a Georgia peach.

He made Shan cum so hard, she saw stars.

After regaining her vision, she looked at him and ran her tongue over her lips. "Now, let me suck that dick."

"Come get it." Youngblood rolled onto his back.

Shan wasted no time. She crawled between his legs and covered the head of his pipe with her mouth.

"Ummmm!" he moaned as she proceeded to slurp in his pole.

Later, they smoked a blunt together and then fell asleep in each other's arms, fully satiated.

The next day, people in the hood was talking about Steve and his lady being robbed and killed. Steve wasn't from Englewood, but he was well known in the A because he was a flosser. Everybody in the projects was talking about the double murders, particularly, as it was reported in the news that the couple had been shot gunned to death.

The whole hood knew that the use of a shotgun was Pete's MO.

People whispered their suspicions, but Shotgun Pete didn't catch any heat from the po's.

A few weeks later, they donned their robbing gear again and struck for thirty bands and a quarter brick of crack.

For driving the getaway car, Youngblood got five G's and three ounces of hard.

He took Shan and the baby shopping and gave Poochie three-hundred dollars for food and bills.

Youngblood sold the crack to his homey, Murder Mike, at a low price, and then added that money to his stash. The plan was to stack $500,000. But with his and Shan's spending appetites and Poochie's drug addiction, the money began dwindling just as fast as he made it.

At least I'm balling, he said to himself as he made plans to cop himself a whip that would make muthafuckas gawk.

CHAPTER 2

The popsicle blue BMW 325i was phat. Youngblood had just picked it up from being customized and it was turning heads as he cruised back to the hood. Shan was in the passenger seat with Lil' T in her lap.

A coupla weeks ago, he and his stickup crew had done a home invasion that netted him 15 G's and a whole brick of coke. He flipped the dope for 30 racks bringing his stash to 45 bands. Lonnie and Shotgun Pete had split much more between themselves, but Youngblood wasn't tripping it. After all, his partners cased out the licks and ran up in the houses, all he did was wait outside in the jackmobile and served as the lookout.

In due time, he figured, he would set up a lick of his own and end up with the lion's share of the dough.

In the meantime, he was ready to floss. He wanted to drive through dope traps and show off his new ride and his two-month old son to his dope slangin' homies, but Shan wasn't down with that.

"Crazy ass boy, you ain't taking my baby in no drug trap."

"Why not? My lil' nigga ain't scared, he's gansta." Youngblood reached under his seat, retrieved a nine milli and laid it across the infant's lap, boasting, "You already strapped, ain't you, lil' man?"

"Boy, move dat gun off him! You so damn crazy." Shan punched him in the shoulder.

Youngblood just smiled. He could see in her eyes that she loved that thug shit that was embedded in him.

They were leaving Englewood, headed to Youngblood's mother's house in Hapeville, so that she could finally see the baby.

Enroute, Youngblood saw and honked his horn at Rich Kid, who was seated on the hood of a candy-painted '64 Chevy Impala.

Rich Kid was twenty-two and already Englewood-famous in the dope game and he was always tryna get Youngblood to slang dope for him.

Youngblood pulled up next to Rich Kid's whip and hopped out. "What it do, Big Homie?" He dapped Rich Kid.

"Getting this cream. When are you gonna get down with me? I'll have you slangin' more coke than Escobar."

"Nah, shawdy, I don't sling yayo, I slang hammers." Youngblood lifted his shirt to show the burner he kept on his waist.

"I feel you, but if you ever decide to switch your game, I got a spot waiting for you on the team," said Rich Kid.

Youngblood appreciated the offer but had no plans to accept it. Jacking niggas wasn't his hobby, it was his get down. "I'ma rob until I get rich or get killed," he vowed

"I hear dat, lil' pimp." Rich Kid looked over his shoulder and checked out his ride. In the process, he saw Shan posted up in the passenger seat, looking ghetto fabulous. "What's up, Shan?" he spoke.

"Hey," she beamed like a bulb.

Youngblood cut his eye at her sternly and Shan dimmed her smile a little. Rich Kid picked up on the silent admonishment but didn't comment. He desperately wanted to warn his lil' homie that he couldn't turn a ho' into a housewife.

But some things, a man has to learn on his own, he reminded himself.

He and Youngblood chopped it up for a minute, just talking about hood stuff before Youngblood said, "I'ma mash out. Be safe out here on the block."

"Always."

Youngblood climbed back in his whip and snatched the car in gear. As soon as he pulled off, he got in Shan's shit. "Fuck you smiling at another nigga for?"

"I wasn't smiling at him, I just spoke back. Damn, what's wrong with that?" She downplayed her flirtatious nature.

"Don't try to act like you all innocent and shit. I'm telling you, do that fuck shit again and I'ma punch you right in the face." Youngblood fumed as he bent a corner and left the hood.

"Pfff!" Shan brushed off his threat with a flick of her wrist.

They road in silence until they reached his mother's house. Youngblood hadn't even wanted to go by there, but Shan had kept badgering him to take the baby to see his moms.

The bass from his speakers thumped loud and hard as he pulled into the driveway.

"Don't you think you should turn that music down some? You said your mother's husband be tripping," Shan reminded him.

"Fuck that lame," he spat, bobbing his head to a Shawty Lo jam.

"Boo, can you just please turn it down."

Youngblood shook his head in despair.

Why she gotta always wrestle with me?

Sighing, he turned the music down. "You happy?"

"Yes, I am." She leaned over and gave him a kiss.

Youngblood kept a mean look on his face, causing Shan to laugh.

Why does he always have to be so hard? she wondered. It was irritating as fuck but sexy, too.

He turned the engine off and they got out of the car with Shan carrying the baby. "I'm telling you, shawdy, if Raymond comes at me sideways, I'ma cook his muthafuckin' cabbage today. I mean that shit," he said.

Before she could respond, they were met on the porch by Youngblood's mother and Toi. Ann allowed the front door to slam loudly behind them but not before they heard Raymond bellow. "That boy ain't allowed in this house!"

Youngblood looked at his mother to see how she would respond. As he expected, she pretended not to hear Raymond. He started to challenge her but decided to let it go.

Fuck it! She ain't gotta stand up for me. I'm good.

Toi gave him a look like she could read his mind and agreed with him 100 percent, their mother was choosing a man over her own child.

Ann sensed her son's discomfort. "Don't pay Raymond no mind," she offered weakly.

"I don't know how you put up with that nigga. But, oh well..." Youngblood swallowed the rest of what he wanted to say, and Ann quickly changed subjects.

She turned to Shan. "Chile, how old are you?" she asked reproachfully.

"Sixteen."

That's a shame! Ann thought.

She wanted to lecture her, but she was a teenager herself when she had Terrence and Toi. So, she shut up and looked hard at the baby, making sure it resembled her son, knowing young girls were quick to put a baby on a boy.

"I guess he looks like you," she said.

"Mama, be nice. That baby is his twin," remarked Toi. She took Lil' T from Shan and planted kisses all over his cheeks. "You so cute. Give auntie some of that sugah."

Lil' T smiled.

Just then, the front door cracked open and Raymond stuck his head out. In a firm voice, he commanded, "Ann, come back inside."

"Nigga, don't be bossing my mother around," Youngblood snapped.

Raymond ignored him but Ann followed his orders. "Nice meeting you, Shan," she said then darted in the house.

Youngblood's forehead wrinkled up. Toi recognized the look on her brother's face and moved to diffuse his anger before he acted it out.

"Let's go sit in the car. It's too cool out here for the baby."

"Nah, lil' sis, we finna bounce. You can hit me up if you need something." He gave her his cell phone number along with $300.

They hugged and then Youngblood bounced.

When they were headed back to the projects, Shan said, "Eww! Your stepfather is sooo meannnn!"

"That nigga ain't my stepfather. He's my mama's husband, but he ain't shit to me! Don't you ever say no fuck shit like that again. You understand me?" Youngblood's eyes were red hot coals.

The fierceness in which he spoke warned her not to say anything slick. To calm things down, she reached over and stroked his arm affectionately. But her touch did little to simmer Youngblood's boiling anger.

I hate that muthafucka!

His jaw was tight with fury, but eventually Shan was able to coax him out of the violent mood he had easily slipped into.

When they got back home, she put the baby to sleep and then sexed Youngblood until the incident with his mother was long forgotten.

Laying with her snuggled in his arms, he kissed her on the forehead. "You knew just what a nigga needed."

"That's my job." Shan smiled proudly.

The next day, Youngblood rewarded her for her tenderness. He took her to the mall and let her buy it out. With a pass to purchase whatever she wanted, Shan hit the stores hard, choosing designer jeans, bags, shoes and all.

Youngblood didn't trip about anything she bought, it felt good to treat his girl to an unlimited shopping spree, and he even grabbed a few outfits himself.

The spending didn't stop there. Over the next three days, he splurged on new bedroom furniture for them along with an expensive flat screen television and a room full of toys for Shan's three little brothers.

Now, it was time for him to ball without his girl, Youngblood decided. But when he got dressed to go out, Shan went ballistic.

"Oh, now you're about to go fuck with your other bitch!" She jumped up in his face and shoved him in the chest. "If you think I'm going for that shit, you got the wrong muthafuckin' one!"

"Shawdy, you're tripping. Man, I'm not going to fuck with no other female. I'ma hang out with my niggas," he said.

"You're a liar!" She swung at his face but Youngblood easily swatted her hand away.

"You better calm the fuck down before I get stupid right along with you," he warned.

"C'mon, black ass muthafucka, let's get stupid up in this bitch!" Shan walked across the room, grabbed a ceramic bowl off of the living room table and flung it at him.

Youngblood sidestepped the bowl and it shattered against the wall.

Poochie heard the commotion and came flying out of her room. "What is going on in here?"

"His black ass got another girlfriend!" Shan accused as tears ran down her face.

Knowing how dramatic her daughter could be, Poochie asked Youngblood was it true. "And don't lie. If you lie, you're getting out of my house," she threatened.

"Man, y'all are tripping!" He put his hand to his forehead. "A nigga can't even go out of the house without your crazy daughter thinking I'm creeping. I ain't got time for this shit!"

"Get the fuck out then!" yelled Shan.

"Shawdy, you ain't said nothin' but a word. I'm gone!" Youngblood snatched the front door open and stormed off to his car.

Shan flew behind him, cussing and crying. When she caught up to him outside she began wailing on him with both fists. Youngblood had seen his mother take beatings from men, so it took a whole lot for a woman to make him put his hands on her. He tried to shove Shan off of him without hurting her but she was a mad woman.

"Shan! Bring your ass in the house and let the boy go wherever he wants to go!" Poochie ran up and pulled her daughter off of him.

"Let me go, Mama. I'ma kick his no good ass tonight!" Shan tried to snatch free but Poochie had a tight grip on her. "I hate you!" She raised her foot and tried to kick Youngblood.

"Girl, you better go in the house before you make me knock you the fuck out. I ain't no bitch ass nigga." He was doing his best not to punch her in the mouth.

"Just leave!" said Poochie.

While she restrained Shan, Youngblood jumped in his car and drove off.

Angry at Shan, he hit the strip club and balled out of control. That night, he ended up at a hotel with a stripper named Luscious. For two days, they smoked weed and sexed each other like crazy. But by the third day, Youngblood had tired of her.

"Get dressed, I'm taking you home today, shawdy," he said.

"Why? I like chilling with you," she pouted.

"I gotta go out of town," he lied.

Luscious continued to pout as she got dressed and gathered up her belongings, but Youngblood ignored her. He barely said another word to her until they pulled up in front of her apartment.

"Am I going to see you again?" she asked.

"Of course. I'ma call you when I get back, okay?" He tried to sound sincere.

"Yep." Luscious didn't believe him. She got out of the car, slammed the door and walked off without looking back.

Bitches! Youngblood said to himself as he drove off and went back to the hood.

His Beamer drew the attention of all the young chicks as he cruised through the city. Even the older females sweated his ride. It didn't matter to them that he was a real young nigga, as long as he was getting money they were fans.

For days, he fucked with different females and chilled at the hotel. Shan was blowing up his phone and sending him back to back texts apologizing for acting jealous, but he didn't respond. He was determined to teach her a lesson about flipping out on him.

It was almost a week later when he finally answered one of her calls. And he did so with much attitude. "If you're not calling about my son I don't wanna talk," he said in a hard tone.

"Baby, don't be like that. I said I'm sorry," she cooed.

"Oh, now you're sorry? Fuck that! Your mouth too muhfuckin' greasy."

"Boy, you know I can't live without your black ass. Come and punish me for talking crazy to you," she said in her most seductive tone.

"Suck my dick!"

"I plan to," she laughed.

"Ain't nothin funny, shawdy. I'm fa real, you'll make a nigga tap that head."

"I want you to tap this pussy. She miss you. It's so wet right now."

Youngblood knew what she was trying to do but he couldn't resist. He continued to front like he wasn't coming back to her just to make her beg a little longer but then he gave in. "A'ight, keep my pussy wet for me. I'll be there in thirty."

"Okay, I'll be in bed naked, waiting on you," promised Shan.

Youngblood made a beeline for Shan's crib. He missed her just as much as she missed him and he planned to put a hurting on that pussy when he got there.

I'ma show her who runs shit, he said to himself as he exceeded the speed limit.

CHAPTER 3

Shan was waiting in bed naked, as promised. Though she had just had a baby two months ago, her young body showed few signs of childbirth. Youngblood looked down at her and instantly rocked up. *My shawdy bad.* He couldn't wait to get deep inside of her.

"I hope Lil T is sleep."

"Hey, baby. He is. You ready to get your pussy?" Shan made of display of spreading her legs wide and rubbed her lower lips.

"Hell yeah." He began discarding his clothes as he walked toward the bed. "Rub them titties for me." His voice turned raspy.

Shan did as he commanded, rubbing her breasts until her nipples stood erect and then she flicked her tongue across them. "You like that?"

"I love it. You sexy as fuck." Youngblood stripped down to his boxers. His dick poked out, stiff and long.

"Bring that pretty, black muthafucka here." Shan licked her lips and crooked a finger at him.

Youngblood loved when she talked that shit. There was never anything shy about Shan, in or out of the bedroom, and that was what had him so gone over her.

He stepped closer and Shan wrapped her hand around his hardness and slid it up and down. "Show a nigga you missed him," he said.

Shan didn't hesitate. She covered the head of his pipe with her mouth and stepped to her business like a grown woman. She got it sloppy wet, with lots of spit, just the way he liked her to blow him.

"You like the way your bitch suck your dick?" she asked, looking up at him as she took more of him inside her mouth.

"I love it," grunted Youngblood.

"Make me gag. Fuck my throat."

Youngblood grabbed the back of her head and pushed himself deeper into her mouth, stroking in and out. Shan gagged, pulled back a little and coated his wood with more saliva.

"That's right, shawdy, suck this muthafucka." "Ummm, I'm sucking it."

Before long, She had him rising up on his toes and moaning. She slurped and sucked and jacked his dick up and down until he groaned loud and bust a nut in her mouth.

"Arghhh!" He growled.

Like a young pro, she swallowed every drop and then showed him her tongue as evidence. Youngblood's knees were so weak, he collapsed face first on the bed.

Shan laughed, "See what you've been missing." She got up and laid on his back. "Boy, you better not go to sleep. I need you to beat this pussy up and put me in check."

"Hold up." He needed a minute to catch his second wind, but with Shan grinding her moist mound on the back of his thigh and sucking on his collarbone, it didn't take but a few minutes for him to rock up again.

"If you don't hurry up and give me my dick, I'm going to catch a serious attitude," she threatened.

"Nawl, ain't no need for that. I got you, baby." He rolled her onto her back and began kissing his way down her body.

Shan grabbed ahold of his head and stopped him from going down on her. "Boo, you can do all of that later. I need some dick."

Turned on by her aggressiveness, Youngblood moved up her body and eased his hardness inside of her soft, buttery cup. "Is this what you need?" He stroked in and out of her slowly.

"Go faster," moaned Shan, rolling her hips upward to meet his powerful thrusts.

Youngblood increased his pace until her pussy started talking to him. Then, he put her feet on his shoulders and started hitting the bottom of her well.

"Yeah, nigga, fuck me!" she cried.

Youngblood didn't have to be prodded any further. Her sex brought the beast out of him and before long, they were screaming each other's names as they erupted in climax together.

Lil' T woke up wailing just as their cries of passion simmered. Shan was as weak as a wet noodle and couldn't move.

"Boo, get your baby," she said on faint breath.

"A'ight, I miss my lil' man, anyway." Youngblood got up and slipped on his boxers and then picked his son up out of the crib and brought him over to the bed. "Daddy just blew Mama's back out," he bragged.

Lil' T smiled, like he comprehended. That cracked Youngblood up. He laid down beside Shan and placed the baby on his chest. Placing one arm around Shan, he held them both until all three of them were sound asleep. At that moment, everything was peaches and cream.

But would the peace between them last? He wondered.

***

Two days later

Youngblood was at the crib chillin' in the living room and high off of some bomb ass weed. He looked up at Shan through squinted eyes as she came into the room wearing tight stretch pants and a wife-beater.

Stopping right in front of him, she asked, "Are you still going to let me use the car to go to the mall with my girls?"

"Fuck no! Not dressed like that."

"Tsk! What's wrong with what I'm wearing?" She threw her hands on her hips and cocked her head to the side.

"I ain't gotta answer that shit. Go change into some jeans and a shirt that don't show your muthafuckin' nipples or your ass ain't going no goddam where." He snatched his car keys off of the table and put them in his pocket.

"You're a damn trip! Why you gotta be so fuckin' jealous? Eww! I can't stand you sometimes." She turned and stormed to the bedroom.

When she came back out she was dressed more appropriately.

"That's better. Now, go get Lil T. You're taking him with you or you can't go," he said.

"Why?" she complained.

"'Cause I said so."

Youngblood was hoping that having the baby with her would block her from getting with another nigga while she was out. He didn't really trust her with her friends, who he believed was always tryna hook her up with different niggas behind his back.

Besides, he couldn't forget Shan's reputation for having her legs open all night, like a drive-thru, before they had hooked up.

Shan gave him the evil eye before going to get Lil T.

This shit don't make no sense. If I wanna fuck a nigga, I'll fuck him with Lil T with me, she muttered to herself.

Youngblood knew he had pissed her off, but he didn't care. When he gave her the car keys, Shan practically snatched them out of his hand.

"Whatever, shawdy. Just have your ass home before it gets dark outside." He fired up another stick of weed and stretched out on the couch.

"Boy, bye." Shan left out of the door.

Hours later

Youngblood hadn't realized he had dozed off until he woke up and checked his watch for the time. Shan had only been gone a couple of hours so he tried not to let his distrust cause him to stress.

Fuck it! If she wanna creep, she gonna do it anyway, no matter how tight of a leash I try to keep on her.

Resigned to the fact that he couldn't watch Shan 24/7, 365, Youngblood pushed all concerns of her faithfulness out of mind. He got up and went to the bathroom to take a leak.

After washing his hands, he went to the bedroom, sat down on the bed and started playing a game on his PlayStation. The bedroom door creaked open, causing him to turn his head in the direction of the sound.

Poochie came into the room and sat beside him. "Youngblood, can you loan me $50?"

He could tell that she was already geeked up by the way she was looking.

The fuck if I'ma give her my bread to take to the dope man.

"I ain't got no money," he lied.

"Boy, stop being stingy and loan your mother-in-law $50. That ain't shit to you."

"I told you, I ain't got no money. Straight up!" Her begging was starting to irritate the fuck out of him.

Poochie realized that she wasn't making any ground, so she switched up her game. She got up and closed the bedroom door and then slowly walked back over to the bed.

Youngblood eyed her with suspicion. "Why da fuck you close the door?" he questioned her.

Poochie smiled, connivingly. "Because I'm about to suck your dick and I don't want Shan to walk to come home and catch us." She reached down and then rubbed his dick through his boxers.

"Yo, you trippin'!" He slapped her hand away.

"No, I'm not. Come on, let me make you nut in my mouth." She grabbed his dick again and stroked it with a skilled hand.

"Poochie, don't do..."

Before Youngblood could protest she had him inside of her warm mouth, weakening his resistance. Slurping his wood like it was a lollipop, Poochie asked, "Does it feel good to you?"

"No!"

"Nigga, don't lie."

Poochie took his dick deeper into her mouth, all the way to the back of her throat. She sucked him hard, and coated his meat with her spit.

Youngblood forgot all about what was right or wrong. He grabbed the back of her head and forced his wood in and out of her mouth, causing her to gag.

With money to buy crack at stake, Poochie sucked his dick so good, Youngblood busted down her throat in less than ten minutes.

"Argh!" he growled like a wild beast as she rubbed his balls to coax more cum out of his nuts.

When he had released every last drop, she opened her mouth and stuck her tongue out. "All gone," she said.

Youngblood couldn't do nothing but compliment her and smile. "You did that shit."

"Why are you looking at me like that?" she asked.

"Because I wanna fuck. You down?"

Poochie took a few seconds to ponder his question. Sucking his dick was bad enough. Fucking him would be the ultimate betrayal.

"Nah, I don't think we should do that." She desperately tried to hold on to some of her pride.

Youngblood, grabbed his pants off of the chair, where he'd placed them last night, and pulled a roll of bills out of the pocket. "I'ma give you $200," he offered.

Poochie's eyes lit up. With that much money she could buy twenty $10 rocks!

"What you gon' do?" asked Youngblood.

Poochie took off her top, and then wiggled out of her shorts and panties. "You bet' not tell my daughter."

"Never dat."

Youngblood's eyes roamed all over her body. For a basehead. Poochie still looked kind of good. Her titties sagged a little but she wasn't all skin and bones. She was slim but shapely, and her pussy stuck out from between her legs like a plump peach.

That muthafucka fat as fuck!

Youngblood boned up again.

"I swear, if you ever tell Shan, I'ma stab your ass to death," Poochie threatened as she laid down on her stomach, propped her ass up in the air, and spread her legs open.

Youngblood stared at her meaty pussy and quickly kicked his boxers off. "Ain't but three muthafuckas gonna ever know about this --- me, you and God!"

"Don't say that shit!" Poochie looked over her shoulder at him and scowled.

"Shut up, and take this dick.

Youngblood pushed her face down on the pillow and guided his engorged pole inside of her. As he began moving in and out, Poochie's pussy moistened. Before long, they were fucking like a couple.

After Poochie came crashing down from her high, she cried over her indiscretion. She'd vowed to quit getting high.

The past two nights, Poochie had dreams about smoking a rock as big as a baseball, with a glass pipe the size of a saxophone and she did well to fight it. But now, the crack jones was calling her, and Youngblood was offering her the means to answer that call.

"Like you told me a few days ago, you do something for me, I'll do something for you," he bargained. "I got a fiddy spot if you let a nigga see that monkey. And I'll break you off an extra $100 if you let me hit."

Poochie resisted his proposal, although it was a battle to do so. "Boy, get the fuck out of my room before I hit you upside the head." She grabbed a hairbrush and threatened him with it.

"A'ight, you got that lil bit." Youngblood threw his hands up and retreated out of the door without saying another word.

When he was gone, Poochie felt proud of herself for once. But that feeling didn't last long.

A short while later, Youngblood returned from a quick trip up the block to the trap. Poochie was sitting on the bed, painting her toenails, with the towel still wrapped around her.

Youngblood pushed the bedroom door open and strode in the room with a smirk on his face.

Poochie looked up. "Out!" She pointed to the door.

Youngblood ignored her demand. He walked toward the bed, flashing several small plastic baggies that contained Poochie's weakness. "Fuck with me and I'ma fuck with you," he said.

"No!" she spat. But her sincerity sounded weak.

"C'mon, Poochie," said Youngblood. "Move that towel. Let a nigga see what you working with. Shan ain't gonna find out."

"I said no, didn't I?"

"A'ight, I ain't gonna press you. Here you go anyway. This is just on the strength." He tossed one of the baggies in her lap.

"What's this for? I told you I'm not finna do nothing with you."

"It ain't even like that, Poochie. That's just on GP 'cause you a'ight with me."

"And I ain't gotta do nothing for it?" she asked, suspicious of his sudden generosity.

"Nawl, you good." Youngblood gamed, knowing that after she took that first hit she would do just about anything for the next one.

Poochie got up and went to her closet to retrieve the lone crack pipe that she hadn't broken up and thrown away. From there, she walked over to her dresser and grabbed a lighter and then she sat on the edge of the bed and surrendered to that monster that she had fought so hard to keep at bay the past few days.

As soon as she took that first hit and the euphoric high set in, she wanted to get higher. She looked up at Youngblood with bulging eyes. "You got some more?" she asked.

Youngblood smiled. "Yeah, let's work something out."

Poochie didn't respond at first. She sat there geeked and wrestling with the small amount of morals she had left. But those rocks had more power over her than her principles could fight off. In one last desperate hope to hold out, she said, "Are you going to really make me do this?"

"I ain't making you do nothing. It's all good. I'm out." Youngblood turned and acted as if he was about to leave.

Poochie sprung up off of the bed and damn near tackled him. "Come back! I'ma give you what you want, but you bet' not ever tell my daughter," she said.

"You ain't *een* gotta worry about dat," he promised as he slid another rock into Poochie's palm and began unbuckling his belt.

She accepted it and then she dropped her head in shame as she unknotted the towel and let it fall to the floor.

Youngblood pulled a condom out of his pocket and began undressing. When he was butt naked, he guided Poochie down on the bed and took her last bit of pride.

CHAPTER 4

The next night, Youngblood had put Poochie and pussy out of his mind and he was back focused on hitting licks. He was at Lonnie's crib leaned up against the kitchen counter smoking a blunt and discussing a planned robbery with his stick-up partners.

Youngblood's pants sagged off his boney ass the way young thugs sported 'em. Females always told him that he resembled Tupac, but as he caught a reflection of himself in the compact mirror that we lying on the counter, he didn't think so. His hair was braided in cornrows and his skin tone was two shades darker than Pac's. But they both were about that thug life, Youngblood had to admit.

He glanced up and looked at Shotgun Pete, who was sitting at the kitchen table snorting coke. He'd been at it for a minute. The powder he was snorting was so potent it had torn the skin inside his nose and blood ran from his nostril, but he was steady snorting more.

That nigga gon' end up being a muthafuckin' junkie, thought Youngblood as they listened to Lonnie lay out the plans before they rode out on a caper.

Youngblood kept tryna get one of them to switch roles with him tonight. He wanted to run up in the vic's house while Lonnie or Shotgun Pete waited outside in the car. But neither of them wanted to trust their life to him if something went wrong once they kicked in the door and ran up in the spot.

"Y'all niggas must think I won't bust this bitch," said Youngblood, slamming a clip in his Nine. "I wish a nigga would try to buck. I'll leave everything in that house stanking."

"I feel you, youngin', but it ain't all about that," said Lonnie.

Shotgun Pete looked up from the lines of coke in front of him. "Junior, you got a lot to learn. You're still a virgin in the jack game," he added with an undertone of derision.

Youngblood noted the affront but didn't speak on it. He stored it in his mind along with the other small shit Pete had let come out of hood mouth.

"I hear you talking," he said.

"You better do more than hear me. You better take heed 'cause one fuck up can put you in the penitentiary or in a pine box," said Pete and then he began recountung several of his own foul-ups that had almost turned out fatal.

When Youngblood went to the bathroom, Lonnie placed both palms flat on the table and leaned down in Pete's face. "Blood, that powder got you slippin'! If a nigga wasn't there, he don't need to know about that! I don't give a fuck how official he is!"

Win, lose, or draw, Lonnie never discussed capers once they were completed. To his way of thinking, what was done was done and the only thing that could come from loose lips was an indictment.

That coke is gonna be Pete's downfall, he mused.

However, he had to admit when it was time to pull out that steel and lay someone down, Shotgun Pete had never failed him.

"My bad, but that's your boy, ain't it?" Shotgun Pete offered in his own defense.

Lonnie didn't even reply because inside he was boiling hot. If he hadn't put so much time into scouting out tonight's lick, he would've called the whole thing off.

He looked at Pete and shook his head. "Dawg, don't let that white bitch bring you down," he said, referring to the coke.

Youngblood could feel the tension in the air when he returned from the bathroom. He looked from Lonnie to Pete and then back to Lonnie. "Everything good?" he asked.

"Yeah, let's roll out." Lonnie walked out of the kitchen to go gather up his gear.

Thirty minutes later, Lonnie knocked on the intended vic's side door. He and Shotgun Pete we're both wearing black ski masks over their faces. Lonnie knocked once more before stepping to the side, out of the vision of the peephole. If this ruse didn't work, they were prepared to do a kick door.

A few seconds later, a grandmotherly looking woman cracked the door. "William? That's you?" her timid voice called out.

William, her grandson, was the target of this lick.

A second after Lonnie heard the security chain rattle, he rammed his shoulder into the door and forced his way inside, knocking William's grandmother to the floor. Shotgun Pete quickly stepped in behind him and pulled the door up.

"What do y'all want?" asked the terrified woman.

Before either of them could reply, William's pregnant girlfriend came rushing in from the kitchen. When she saw the masked gunmen, she let out a loud scream.

Pete slapped her across the face with the butt of his shotgun. "Bitch, you better shut the fuck up if you don't wanna die!" he growled.

Holding both hand over her busted mouth, the girl whimpered into her bloody palms.

"Get on the floor!" Lonnie commanded.

Once she was down on the floor, they quickly duct tapped both women's hands and feet.

"A'ight, we can do this the easy way or the hard way?" said Lonnie. "Tell me where William keeps good stash, and we'll be out."

"There's no money or drugs here," the girl cried.

Whap!

Shotgun Pete cracked open her forehead. "Bitch, don't lie to me!" he warned.

Grandma got her old head cracked, too, when she claimed not to know what a stash was. "A'ight, y'all think this shit is a game?" Lonnie click-clacked a bullet into the chamber of his fo-fo.

"Yeah, dawg, kill those bitches," Shotgun Pete egged him on.

Granny heard those words and she started singing like Diana Ross. "Okay! I'll tell you where everything is! Just don't kill us."

After she gave up the location of the loot, Lonnie gagged their mouths, and then he went to search the house while Shotgun Pete looked out of the living room window, in case William unexpectedly came home.

Youngblood was on post outside in the nondescript Crown Victoria, blending in with the night. While watching the block, he was thinking about the way Shan's mama had put that pussy on him the other day. Though Poochie was a base head, she still had some bomb ass snapper.

Even better than her daughter's, Youngblood reminisced.

As he mind become occupied with lurid thoughts of Poochie, William pulled into the driveway in his SUV and climbed out of the vehicle. The sound of the driver's door shutting snapped Youngblood back to the present.

"Damn!'" he said out loud as he instantly went into action.

Youngblood quietly eased out of the car with his nine in hand and crept up on the unsuspecting dope boy. One false move was going to get the whole back of William's head blown off.

Inside that house, Lonnie heard a car pull into the driveway and hurried back downstairs to join forces with Shotgun Pete. They waited inside the darkened living room ready to surprise their prey. But, just as William put his key into the front door lock, he heard a rustle behind him and instinctively turned around.

Startled by the black-cladded figure that was moving in his direction fast, William dashed to his right, leaped over the porch banister and ran like hell.

"Fuck!" Youngblood cussed. He hadn't even squeezed off a shot. "Yo, dawgs! Open up, it's me!" he furiously banged on the front door.

Recognizing Youngblood's harried voice, Lonnie snatched opened the front door, dumbfounded. "Where'd he go?" he whispered.

Youngblood pointed toward the backyard.

Lonnie looked toward the two duct-taped and gagged women and instructed Youngblood to keep an eye on them.

While Shotgun Pete and Lonnie raced behind the house to search for William, Youngblood robbed the two women of their jewelry. He had just stuffed the jewels inside of his pockets when Lonnie ducked in and said, "Let's get out of here, shawdy!"

When they got back to Lonnie's girl Delina's apartment in the projects, Shotgun Pete was furious. He cussed and yelled at Youngblood so fiercely that they almost came to blows. Lonnie stepped between them but minutes later, they were at it again. Fortunately, Delina and her sons were away.

"Stupid ass, nigga! You fucked up the lick!" Shotgun Pete stormed.

"Fuck you, ugly ass mafucka!" Youngblood retorted. "I already said it was my bad. What you want, blood?"

"Back up, 'fo I dump on you!"

"We can do this, nigga!" they stood facing each other, cowboy style.

"Chill!" barked Lonnie. "Both of y'all niggaz gimme y'all burners before y'all kill each other."

"I ain't giving you shit, my nigga!" spat Shotgun Pete.

Lonnie turned to Youngblood to see if he could calm him down first. "Dawg, gimme your banger."

Youngblood shook his head back and forth. "I'm scraight, folks. Fuck that." He scoffed.

"Let's make this shit pop, then!" Shotgun Pete raised his sawed-off, chest high.

Youngblood's arm rose up, too, but Lonnie placed his body dead smack in front of him, shielding them both from each other.

"What both of y'all fools gon' do is chill!" he barked. "This shit is unnecessary!" He let out a sigh but stood between them until they both let their guns fall to their sides.

Once Lonnie calmed them both down, he explained to his young protégé how he had blown the lick, adding, "You should've just let William come on inside, we were waiting on him. I told you how to react in that situation before I took you on the first lick with us," he reminded Youngblood.

"I feel you, my nigga. It was my fuck up. It won't happen again." Youngblood apologized but he kept his face tight when he looked from Lonnie to Shotgun Pete.

For the moment, the rift between them was let go but Youngblood felt it was destined to come up again.

Days later, Shotgun Pete was still heated. Youngblood had blown a lick that had taken months to scout out. Had Youngblood not frightened him and made him run off, once William came inside the house, Lonnie and Shotgun Pete would've snatched him up and made him take them to his stash.

"Well, it's over now, dawg," Lonnie sighed, smoking a blunt. "William gon' be on alert from now on."

"He probably done moved out that spot already," guessed Shotgun Pete, laying out a few lines of coke on a mirror. "Man, that nigga Youngblood pussy! He ain't even bust his gun."

"Naw, man," Lonnie defended his protégé. "Shawdy just fucked up, that's all."

"I'm telling you, that nigga ain't 'bout it," he tried to convince Lonnie as the two sat on Delina's steps.

If Shotgun Pete really believed that their young partna was pussy or afraid to bust his gun, Youngblood squashed those concerns a few months later.

Since the night of his fuck up, Youngblood had driven the getaway car on two other small licks without incident. He even proved that he didn't bar gunplay.

Lonnie and Shotgun Pete had beef with Black Boy, a big brolic drug dealer from Thomasville Heights, the projects up the street from Atlanta Federal Penitentiary, not far from Englewood.

While Black Boy was away, a couple of years ago, doing a short bid, Lonnie and Shotgun Pete had jacked his girlfriend for five stacks and one of them thangs. Now, Black Boy was back on the bricks and telling people that he was gonna straighten the violation. But he was frontin', talking tough for the benefit of his street rep because if he was gonna kill something, he wouldn't have been telling people.

Still Lonnie and Shotgun Pete were planning to see about Black Boy real soon.

But they never got the chance.

Youngblood was sitting in his Beamer outside the Purple Onion strip club on Moreland Avenue when he spotted Black Boy coming out of the club and walking to his Yukon Denali. It was nearly 4 a.m. right as the place was about to close.

Damn! My dawgs would love to catch this pussy nigga slippin' like this, Youngblood thought as he watched Black Boy half-walk, half-stagger to his whip. *Fuck it, I'ma do this nigga myself.*

Black Boy wasn't stone drunk but he was a bit intoxicated. He had been throwing back Henny and Cokes and drinking Dom all night in VIP.

When he got inside of his ride, he rolled down the windows so the breeze would keep him alert as he drove home. But in reality, that would seal his fate.

Youngblood caught up to the truck at a traffic light two miles from the club. Black Boy glanced over at the car that was now side by side with his. When he pulled off, so did the other vehicle.

Suddenly, he was sprayed with a burst of gunfire from Youngblood's semi-automatic. Before Black Boy could react, he was wet up and the Yukon crashed into a utility pole.

Youngblood smashed out, hopping on I-20 West, heading back to the hood.

Two days later, Youngblood admitted to his two robbing partnas that he had killed Black Boy for them, just on the strength. "Y'all enemies are my enemies," he said from the heart.

"You wild, nigga," Lonnie said, with much respect for Youngblood's gangsta.

Shotgun Pete suspected that their young comrade was false claiming, though. Youngblood peeped the doubt in Shotgun Pete's face but didn't comment.

Fuck him, if he didn't believe it. Youngblood wasn't tryna prove anything no way. He had done for his dawgs what he'd expect them to do for him. Shotgun Pete was just a hater in his mind.

Lonnie was impressed with the loyalty displayed by his li'l nigga just as much as he was impressed by the sheer audacity of the fatal assault. It took true street love to straighten a beef that wasn't his to handle, as Youngblood had done.

Violence and drive-by's and other hood mayhem were a common occurrence in ATL, like most major cities. There were no eye-witnesses to the late-night/early morning murder of Black Boy and there was no due diligence on behalf of the police to investigate. It was just chalked up as just another black-crack murder.

The trio jack boys resumed their usual routine of laying low and indoors in the day and creeping up on vics at night.

For them money came fast and in lump sums, and that was how they spent it. Therefore, it was usually only a matter of weeks after a successful lick before they needed to strike again.

Now that Youngblood had bodied Black Boy and proved he would bust his gun, Lonnie promised to let him run up in a vic's house with him. That way Youngblood could get broke off equally when they split up the loot.

Youngblood could hardly wait to run up in a dope boy's spot and lay him down. He was anxious to get major dough.

Lonnie advised him to just chill, the next lick was on deck.

"I'm feenin' for it!" Youngblood admitted.

That ski mask shit was addictive as fuck.

CHAPTER 5

The eighty-five degree fall day felt like summer, and the trio's anxiety to hit another lick was sweltering. So later that night their appetites were fed and the victims were left duct-taped.

The lick had been a real sweet one, so they celebrated at the strip club, Magic City.

The next morning Youngblood woke up at the Comfort Inn with two strippers, Sunshine and China Doll, ready to serve him up one last time before they bounced.

"I'm wit dat," he said, lying between two of the freakiest broads in the Dirty South.

He ended up staying with them 'til three the next morning and Shan was hot as a tea kettle when Youngblood got home.

Shan wanted to argue and fight, but Youngblood had a hangover so he mushed her in the face and hopped in the bed and crashed out.

He'd only been asleep for ten minutes when he was startled awake with a face full of ice water. "Bitch, I'ma kick your ass fo' dat!"

Seeing the scowl on his face, Shan lost her nerve and broke out for the door. Youngblood caught up with her in the living room and slapped her weave crooked.

Poochie jumped up off the couch, and hit Youngblood with a broom.

Shan's little brothers came from their bedroom to watch, as if they were seeing some Jerry Springer drama. Just a year old, Lil' T was too little to know what was going on, but he watched on, as well.

When Youngblood caught a glimpse of his son, he decided not to let him see him hitting Shan. "Fall back, shawdy. Lil T is watching us," he said in a calm tone.

Shan's eyes drifted to their son, who was now crying. She stopped fighting Youngblood and went over to Lil T and lifted him in her arms. "Don't cry. Mama and Daddy was just playing," she lied and then kissed his tears away.

Youngblood walked over and put his arms around them both. "It's all right, little man," he cooed.

Within seconds, Lil T had stopped crying and everything was back to normal. Even Poochie was chilling.

Later that evening, Youngblood gave Shan some dick to make up. When they came out of the bedroom, Poochie said, "Y'all all right now, ain't you?"

"We scraight," Youngblood smiled. "You still ain't have to hit me with that broom, though," he frowned at her.

"Ah, boy, you ain't hurt. Gimme a hug," Poochie replied.

After they hugged and made up, she hit him up for some dough.

"I shouldn't give you shit," Youngblood replied in a playful tone, breaking Poochie off a hundred-fifty dollars.

"You love me, though," she smiled.

Youngblood smiled back at her as his thoughts turned sexual.

I ain't shit, he thought as his eyes followed her ass out of the room.

Grinning devilishly, he returned to the bedroom and did to Shan what he really wanted to do to her mama again.

Shan was happy with all of the affection Youngblood showered on her over the next few days. That weekend, she pestered Youngblood into taking her to Piedmont Park, where many people went to floss and be seen.

Something instinctual kept telling Youngblood not to go there but under her heavy plea, he did.

Dope boys had started linking him to his two notorious partners and he didn't want to run into any unexpected drama. But he fell weak to Shan's complaining. Plus, he was tryna make up for staying out two nights straight.

Shan wore see-through coochie cutters with a green thong, a sheer halter with a strapless bra that matched her panties. Around her neck was the thick chain and diamond encrusted pendant that Youngblood had given her a while back. On her wrist was a matching tennis bracelet. She loved rings and wore one on each finger and on two toes.

Youngblood rocked baggy jeans, a loose fitting jersey to conceal the heat tucked in his waist and beige Timbs.

They were sitting on the hood of his freshly waxed Beamer parked across from the park in a mini shopping center's lot, just checking out the crowd in the park. The boom in the trunk of the BMW knocked the other whip's sounds out the box.

Shan stood up between Youngblood's knees, letting bitches know that he was already claimed. She was sticking her phat ass out, making chicks jealous and niggas lust.

Youngblood knew many of the ballers who cruised by flossing, too. They honked their horns, acknowledging a young playa. Even cars filled with fly honies honked at him, sweating the Beamer as they drove by at a crawl.

The hood was dog-eat-dog and cats maimed cats. While dudes jacked for cars, loot and jewels, girls jacked each other for their man.

Shan was saying something, but Youngblood missed it. A super thick shawdy with more junk in her trunk than Shan had just walked by licking a lollipop.

"I seen you sweating dat ho's ass!" accused Shan.

"Ain't nobody paying dat ho no attention," Youngblood tried to lie. "She is on swole back there, though," he half joked, igniting Shan's jealousy.

Digging her nails deep into his arm, Shan hissed, "Don't act stupid, nigga!"

"Ouch! Crazy ass girl!"

"How would you like it if I was sweatin' that fine nigga over there?" Shan remarked, tryna fuck with his heart.

"You can't stress a pimp," popped Youngblood. "Anyway, you probably be doing more than sweatin' niggaz when you're with ya lil' ho ass girlfriends. I know how your peeps, Cita and Fiona, do it. Birds of a feather, shawdy."

"Nigga, don't nobody be creepin' on yo jealous ass."

"You the one who's jealous," Youngblood pointed out. "I don't trip that shit. Just don't get caught or I'ma split dat wig."

"You got a wig, too."

"Shawdy, you ain't hard," he laughed, kissing her on the nose.

Shan looked up at him from under thick eyelashes. "I ain't scared of you, boy."

Youngblood then diverted his eyes at Rich Kid and a crew of twelve young hustlers on his payroll pull up in four cars: a Chevy Blazer, a Jeep Cherokee, a Chevy low-rider truck with mad boom and Rich Kid's Benz 500 SL, all tricked out, parking haphazardly around Youngbloods' BMW.

The twelve deep crew got out of their rides and profiled along with Youngblood and everyone else.

A short while later, William and his lady, who was pushing a baby in a carriage walked by. Youngblood hadn't recognized William, the drug dealer he and his crew tried to rob or his lady.

As the fly honey pushed the baby carriage her ass jiggled like Jell-O. Dudes sweated her but didn't disrespect 'cause William had baller status in the game.

William's lady sweated the fuck out of Shan as they passed by. *Shan peeped it but felt confused. Why is the bitch eyeing me?*

She wondered if she knew the ho from somewhere but her face wasn't familiar.

"What up, money?" William asked Rich Kid.

"It's yo world, playa," Rich Kid hollered back.

After speaking to Rich Kid, William and his lady strolled by Shan and Youngblood again. Their eyes seemed locked on Shan. This time, Youngblood noticed it. When the couple was out of sight, Shan whispered to him, "Why dat ho and her nigga sweatin' me?"

"I don't know, but I peeped it, too," acknowledged Youngblood still not recognizing William.

Youngblood and Shan left the park soon after the couple disappeared into the crowd.

Traffic was bumper to bumper for a mile or so. They were on the Boulevard, just past Georgia Baptist when the po-po got behind them and turned on thier flashing lights.

"Fuck I do?" cussed Youngblood, thinking about pushing the pedal to the floor because he had a burner and an ounce of weed right between the seats, but traffic was too thick.

"Put that shit in your purse," he told Shan, handing her his weed and .9mm.

As soon as Youngblood pulled over, he was boxed in by three police cruisers, two of which seemed to appear out of nowhere. Guns were pointed in Youngblood's and Shan's faces and angry white cops ordered them out of the car.

Youngblood was thrown to the ground, roughly frisked, cuffed and slammed into the back seat of one of the police cruisers after po-po found a blunt in his pocket.

"What da fuck y'all doin' to him?" Shan cussed and fought the police, defending her nigga.

The cops cuffed her, too.

When they searched the car they found the ounce of weed and the gun inside Shan's purse. Youngblood and Shan were then arrested and the Beamer was impounded.

Youngblood and Shan were taken to jail in separate police cruisers and booked on a myriad of felony charges, including armed robbery and kidnapping.

William and his lady had recognized her stolen jewelry around Shan's neck and on her wrist when they passed by her and Youngblood at the park. The couple had found a police man and dropped dime on them.

Inside an interrogation room at Atlanta's Pre-trial Center, Shan was questioned by a detective. When she wouldn't give up the answers the detective wanted, in walked a female officer, pretending to be friendlier and more understanding than her partner.

She handed Shan a cold soda and a bag of chips, ingratiating herself to the teenager before sitting down next to her and placing a comforting hand on her arm.

It was all just a game, though. The two detectives played good cop, bad cop to perfection.

"Leave her alone, Detective Mitchell!" the female detective yelled at her partner. "Would you like for him to step out of the room, honey?" she asked Shan.

Shan wiped away tears and nodded *yes.*

"Please leave, Bill," Detective Sharon Johnson instructed her partner.

As soon as Mitchell stepped out of the interrogation room, Detective Johnson coerced Shan into admitting that Youngblood had given her the bling on her wrist and around her neck. Shan maintained that she knew nothing about Youngblood robbing anyone, even after the *good* detective flipped the script on her and threatened to charge her with armed robbery if she didn't turn canary on Youngblood and whomever his accomplices had been.

"I wanna call a lawyer," cried Shan. But by then, she had already said too much.

As a result of Shan's ill-advised disclosures, the detectives were able to obtain a warrant to search Poochie's apartment, Shan's and Youngblood's stated place of residence.

Initially the only evidence po-po had to connect Youngblood to the armed robbery was the bling that Shan had been wearing, both pieces had William's lady's initials engraved on the clasps.

But during the search of Poochie's apartment, police found $47,630 hidden in Shan's bedroom, two Glock's, three black ninja-like outfits, two black ski masks and several rolls of duct tape.

Inside Poochie's bedroom they found a crack pipe and numerous razors smudged with crack residue. They arrested her, too, and placed her three sons in a temporary foster home.

When Lonnie caught wind of what happened, he came through for his tightman and his tightman's peeps.

He bonded them all out of jail and Poochie got her sons back.

While awaiting trial, Youngblood continued jacking dope boys, tryna stack some cheddar in case he had to go do a bid.

For a minute he was salty with Shan for letting po-po trick her into saying too much, but he soon forgave her. She wasn't built for the life, like he was because when the detectives had tried to play good cop, bad cop with him, he had told 'em to suck his dick.

As fall turned into winter, the hard-hitting attorney that Youngblood hired worked out a plea bargain with the D.A. If Youngblood would plead guilty to robbery by intimidation, he'd be sentenced to a hard nickel—no parole. And all charges against Shan and Poochie would be dismissed.

"Fuck it. Tell them crackers to come on wit' it, I'll take the five years," he informed his attorney, though he knew the only evidence the state had against him was circumstantial.

William and his lady couldn't say that they'd seen any of the robber's faces. They'd all worn ski masks.

"We'll take it to trial if you want to," said the attorney. "But if you want my advice, I think you should accept the plea." He knew that the Georgia courts were quick to railroad a young black man.

"I'ma take the plea," Youngblood decided, just so his baby's mama and Poochie didn't get caught up in his troubles.

Fuck it, I can do a bid, he thought.

Later that day, they had rented a room at the Comfort Inn. Poochie was babysitting Lil' T for them. Tomorrow Youngblood would have to turn himself in and begin serving the nickel he agreed to, so he'd figured they spend one last night together.

They had been blowing weed and drinking Henny and Coke the whole time. But now they were lying naked across the bed.

Shan kissed her way down her man's body, caressing his balls along the journey. When she got to his dick, she licked pre-cum from the head of it and then let the head slide into her mouth.

"Do that shit, shawdy." Youngblood encouraged with his toes beginning to curl.

Shan was definitely Poochie's daughter. She could suck hella dick, too.

She turned onto her back and cooed, "Fuck me in the mouth."

Youngblood straddled her head and slid his hard dick back into her mouth. He pumped in and out, watching her as she practically swallowed the dick.

Shan was looking up at him from under fluttering eyelashes, making it hard for him to hold his nut. Her warm mouth felt like he was up in some pussy.

"I want you to cum all over my face," Shan mumbled with a mouthful of dick.

Youngblood didn't wanna bust yet. Tonight would be his last piece of pussy for five long years. He was gonna savor this night, instead. He pulled his hips all the way back and his dick left Shan's mouth with a plop.

"Un-uh! Give it back," she whined.

Ignoring her, Youngblood kissed his way down her neck, nibbling on that spot that always made her squirm and shiver.

"Ahhh!" moaned Shan, stroking his dick.

Youngblood put one of her taut chocolate nipples into his mouth, curling his tongue around it and then sucked it. Shan arched her back and pushed down on his head, anxious for him to go downtown.

When they had first hooked up Youngblood had virgin head. Shan, being the more sexually experienced of the two, had been the first to turn him out to eating pussy. Still, she was the only shawdy to have gotten head from him. She had taught him how to take his time licking and sucking the pussy, stimulating the clit. Now, he was adding his own moves, making her climb the headboard.

Youngblood rubbed her clit while sucking on her wet inner folds.

When he felt her knees squeeze the sides of his head, he eased a finger into her backdoor and slowly stroked it in and out.

"Ahhh—nigga! I'm—cumming!" Shan cried out. "Goddam!" she exhaled after a long, intense orgasm. Youngblood came up and stuck his tongue in her mouth. "You—

"You feel like riding?" he asked, fingering the pussy and nibbling on her bottom lip.

"Any way you want it."

Youngblood laid back and let her hop up on the dick. Shan slid down it only part of the way, moving up and down, sensually.

"Whose dick is this, huh?" Looking into his eyes as she let the full length of him slide up into her.

"Do dat shit, girl!" Youngblood moaned. Her pussy was soaking wet. Hot and gripping.

"Is this my dick?" she repeated.

"You know what it is, shawdy," keeping it G. "I ask the questions," throwing dick up at her.

"Mmmm."

"Reverse dat shit for me, boo." Shan turned around and straddled the dick reverse cowgirl. "That's what I'm talkin' bout," Youngblood said, gripping her ass and watching his dick go in and out. "Whose pussy is this?"

"Yours, baby."

"For how long?"

"For—ever," replied Shan, speeding up.

"You gon' hold me down while I'm gone?"

"Ahhh—Ummmm! Yesss!"

"Word is bond?"

"Uh-huh," she was bouncing up and down on the dick now.

Youngblood reached around her and messaged her clit while she rode him as if this would be the last time. After Shan came again, he flipped her over on her back and put in work.

They sucked and fucked all night.

Morning brought with it the painful reality that today Youngblood would have to turn himself in and begin serving the bid.

Deep down, he wasn't feelin' that move. But he knew that if he went on the run, it would mean not seeing his son again. He had grown up without a pops and wasn't tryna leave Lil' T ass'd out like that. So he had to do what he had to do.

"Peep this, Shan. Now you know a nigga 'bout to go behind them walls for a minute. What you gon' do, shawdy?" he asked as they drove to Poochie's apartment.

"What you mean?"

"Are you gon' hold me down?"

"Yeah. You ain't gotta ask me that," she replied with indignation.

"Fa real, girl. If you ain't gon' do this bid with me, let me know now, and I won't even be mad. But if you wait until I get into my bid and then turn your back on me, I swear I ain't fuckin' with you when I get out. You feel me?"

"Yeah."

"Fa real, shawdy," he repeated, reaching over and holding her hand as he drove. "I'ma be gone for a nickel so I ain't gon' even try to fool myself that you ain't gon' fuck somebody else."

"I'm not," Shan declared.

"Kill dat," retorted Youngblood, knowing better. "Just don't be all out there like a ho. Don't fuck niggaz I'm s'pose to be cool with and don't have no damn babies while I'm gone."

"*Tsssk*! I ain't gon' be doing nothing to have no babies."

"Whatevea, shawdy, just don't have no babies," he restated. "And don't leave a nigga hangin'. I'm leaving you my ride and my stash. Don't cross me."

"I won't," promised Shan.

Poochie, Shan, Lil' T, Lonnie and Shotgun Pete were present with Youngblood in court as he pled guilty to one count of robbery by intimidation and was sentenced to five years.

Shan cried as her baby's daddy was led from the courtroom in cuffs.

"Can I kiss my shawdy and my son goodbye?" Youngblood asked the bailiff.

"Escort the prisoner out of my courtroom!" barked the judge. "He should've said his goodbyes before now."

"I wasn't even talking to you!" Youngblood barked back to the judge. "Cracker!"

Youngblood was then quickly removed from the courtroom.

CHAPTER 6

Youngblood had spent eighteen months in a Youth Detention Center before, which was akin to serving a bid. So it wasn't anythang for him to adjust to serving this five-year bid at Alto, a notoriously violent state prison for males between the ages fifteen to twenty-one.

It took him nearly eight months to get the streets out of his system and settle into his bid. So far, Shan was holding him down, sort of. She was bringing his son to visit him at least twice a month. But she had moved from her mom's spot into her own apartment and was hardly ever at home when Youngblood tried to call.

Rumors made its way to Youngblood that his baby's mama was sleeping with different homies of his from Englewood, a violation Shan had promised not to ever commit.

Youngblood finally caught up with her on a three-way with Toi. When he confronted Shan with what he had heard, she straight up denied it, copping attitude.

"I might as well fuck them Englewood niggaz since you accusing me of it!"

"I tell you what, shawdy," Youngblood replied, "fuck whoever you want just take my dough to my sister and my ride, too."

"Nigga, please!" she screamed in his ear and slammed down the phone.

Toi said, "That bitch ain't no good."

But Youngblood wasn't ready to see that.

Shan hadn't been to visit him in months. He'd written letters to her but they went unanswered. Lonnie told him that po-po had snatched the BMW. Apparently, Shan had allowed some Grady Homes hustlers to use his ride during a drug deal that turned out to be with undercovers, posing as dope boys. The Beamer was seized when the Grady Homes boys were arrested.

"I'ma kick that bitch ass!" Youngblood fumed.

When Shan was acting up, not visiting him or sending money for commissary, Youngblood got so vexed that he stayed getting into trouble. Him and some homies from Southeast Atlanta jacked white boys for their commissary and stayed getting into fights with country niggaz from small towns in Georgia.

Kyree, the twins, Rafael and Rufus, Tony and Youngblood had each other's backs inside *The Toe*.

Youngblood was also vexed about his estrangement from his mother. Three months ago she had come to visit him with her husband in tow, like it was all good.

Youngblood disliked the monkey-ass nigga, so he refused to sit there and fake it. As soon as he saw that his mother had brought Raymond with her to visit him, Youngblood turned around and walked out. Ann hadn't been back to visit her son since.

Youngblood was stressing in the worst way. He was shooting dice with a group of Down South boys when a dispute began over Youngblood's point. When the fader refused to concede the bet, Youngblood punched him in the mouth. Blood spurted from the boy's grill as he fell back against a bunk. Kyree, Tony and the twins stood close by, ready for whatever. Like Youngblood, they had shanks hidden in their pockets.

"I'ma kill you, fuck ass nigga!" the country boy cried, running off to his bunk to get his shank.

Youngblood and his crew caught up to the country nigga before the boy could reach his bunk. They stabbed the country boy repeatedly in the back and shoulders, wetting him up.

When the boy crumpled to the floor, two of his homeboys ran up to try to save him from getting bodied.

Youngblood and his crew attacked, screaming, "Y'all hos want some?"

When it was all over, they had wet up all three boys. They were placed in the hole where all five remained for six months.

To pass time on lockdown, Youngblood wrote rap songs and perfected his rap skills.

Rapping was something he hadn't had an interest in until he fell on this bid and started kickin' it with the twins and them. All of his crew in *The Toe* was nice on the mic. But Youngblood, they agreed was a natural lyricist, with a Dirty South flow.

Also while in the hole, Youngblood wrote Shan a letter, trying to patch things up with her.

Dear Shan,

Shawdy, I really don't know where to begin so let me first say that I still love you. I know that shit has been messed up between us, and I've said a lot of foul shit to you. But we both were wrong, 'cause you did some things that really hurt a nigga. I hear so many rumors about how you're out there disrespecting, not only me, but yourself as well by fuckin' with a whole lot of different niggas. I gotta believe what mafuckaz telling me, 'cause you've damn sho' turned your back on me. But dig this, Shan, I still want you in my life. See, I can accept anything you do as long as you be real with me about it and as long as you don't fuck with anybody I'm s'pose to be a'ight with. And don't have no babies by whoeva you kick it with. Damn, shawdy, is that too much to ask of you?

I ain't even salty about you fucking up my money and getting my car took. Fuck it! I'll get all that shit again when I touch down. Just come back to a nigga, girl. Hold me down like you promised. Bring my son to visit me once in a while, and drop me a letter every now and then, just so a nigga don't feel like you don't give a fuck. Feel me?

Anyway, write back ASAP. And send me your new phone number so I can hit you on a three-way.

I love you, Shan, but I ain't gonna beg. If you still love me start showing it. Tell Lil' T that daddy loves him. I miss y'all like crazy.

Love,

Yo' baby's daddy.

Months after swallowing his thug pride and pouring his heart out to Shan in the letter, Youngblood still hadn't heard from her.

Stressing, he called Lonnie to see if his dawg had the 411 on Shan.

Lonnie gave it to him straight up. “Dawg, Shan fuckin’ with Shotgun Pete.”

“What?”

“Yeah, shawdy, and that’s some foul shit. I stepped to ‘em both about it, but you know how that shit went. Shotgun Pete told me that it ain’t none of my business. Said he would deal with you when you hit the bricks if you got a problem with it.”

“That bitch nigga said that?” Youngblood was heated. “What Shan say?”

“Shid, she was like fuck you. Said something about you fucked her mother. But that shit don’t justify what she’s doing, ‘cause the bitch was already fuckin’ with Pete before she heard about you and Poochie.”

“Who told her?” asked Youngblood, his face twitching from anger.

He knew that Shotgun Pete had to have dropped the dime because Lonnie and him were the only two Youngblood had told about him boning Shan’s mama.

“You already know who told it, dawg,” confirmed Lonnie, his one thorough partna. “That’s why I don’t fuck with that nigga no more. Feel me?”

“Uh-huh.”

“Shan got that nigga fucked up, and he got her snorting that dust with him. Both of ‘em ain’t shit.”

When Youngblood got off the phone, he had already made up his mind not to ever fuck with Shan again. As for Shotgun Pete, the love Youngblood had for him was gone, too.

For the remaining three years left on his bid, Youngblood harbored bitterness for all those who had crossed him. The only thing that helped him maintain while he marked off the three calendars was the love Lonnie and Toi showed. Also, his homie Kyree had hooked him up with his sister, Brenda, who was a thirty-four-year-old, bisexual ex-stripper.

At first Brenda didn't take Youngblood seriously, due to his youth and wildness. But after a few letters back and forth, and a couple of visits, Youngblood managed to get past all of that.

She began visiting him once a month and she sent money orders consistently.

On lock, Youngblood got mad props 'cause he had snagged a fly, older chick.

But he never bragged about it, 'cause that would've been disrespecting Kyree, and Youngblood didn't roll like that. Besides, Brenda had made it clear that she wasn't looking for a man. They were only friends, but she held him down much realer than lowdown Shan.

Despite having Brenda in his life to help ease the last three years of his bid, the bitterness Youngblood held against his baby's mama, Shotgun Pete, his mother,and everyone else who he felt had betrayed him festered like an infection. So when he walked out the prison gates after completing his bid, he walked out an angry young G screaming, *Mafuckaz gon' feel me or kill me!*

CHAPTER 7

Lonnie's spot was a two-bedroom townhouse in Roswell, Georgia, a quiet, little suburb north of Atlanta. Youngblood sat on the couch with a box of hot wings balanced on his lap. He licked the spicy sauce off his fingers. "That weed made me hungry as a mafucka," he said to Lonnie, who laughed.

"It's been five years since you smoked a blunt, lil' nigga. How it feels to be home?"

"Gooder than a mafucka! Shit seems strange, though. A lot of shit done changed. Like you not living in the hood no more."

Lonnie said, "I still roll through Englewood every day, but I got too many enemies to lay my head down there. You know how I get my loot, off the muscle, as always. Those bitch-ass dope boys be puttin' out contracts on a nigga now, or they take a warrant out on stickup kids. Like dude did to get you sent away." Youngblood shook his head. "That shit is foul!" he said in disgust. "Them niggaz livin' illegal, too. How they gon' run to po-po for help? That's some real bitch shit. Real niggaz settle they beefs in the street."

Lonnie rolled another blunt, ran the cigarette lighter flame across it to dry the spliff and then passed it to Youngblood.

"Well, niggaz don't play it like that no more. They get the stickup kids out the way however they can. Anyway, I know today is your first day home but what you gon' do? You out the game or what?"

"I don't know," admitted Youngblood. "I gotta eat, and I gotta get my own crib, so I gotta shake something."

"You on parole or probation?"

"Naw, I did all mine."

"True dat."

Lonnie went to his bedroom and returned with a .9mm Glock and two full clips. He tossed the gun, the clips and a small wad of money to his tightman.

"I ain't got much, dawg. But this ought to get you started. What's up with that older broad you were hollerin' at from prison?"

Youngblood explained that Brenda was cool, but they were just friends. He didn't want to step to her empty-handed. His plan was to hit a lick, get a car and a wardrobe before he went to see Brenda.

She knew he was due to get out of prison soon, but he hadn't told her exactly when. He figured her brother would call her and tell her he was out.

The grand in his pocket that Lonnie had just given him would last for a minute, long enough to carry him until he could find a mark. He'd crash at Lonnie's crib until then. But not too long, he didn't want to impose too much on his one true friend.

Later that evening, Lonnie took him to the mall to buy a few pairs of jeans and some Timberlands. Youngblood stole a couple of video games to give to his son. He assumed Shan had already bought the boy the latest Play Station.

Lonnie hadn't seen Shan in a few months, but he knew where she lived.

Youngblood said, "Let's go by her mom's crib first. Maybe she'll be over there."

They drove through Englewood, stared at people they'd known for years. No new faces, just older and more tired-looking. Some people were still doing the same old shit. Some of the kids were teenagers now, following the neighborhood blueprint: hustling, having babies and smoking dope.

Lonnie stopped the car in front of Poochie's apartment and waited in the car while Youngblood got out.

Knock! Knock! Knock!

The door opened and Youngblood stared in horror. "Damn!" he said, not meaning to let the words slip out.

Poochie stared back, looking like a skeleton with big eyes and dry lips. Crack was still kicking her ass, good.

"Well, look what the wind blew in!" she said, honestly glad to see Youngblood out of prison. Then, as if realizing she looked a mess, Poochie combed her disheveled hair with her fingers and licked her lips to relieve the dryness. But in ten seconds, they were dry again.

"Boy, when did you get out?" Poochie smiled and pulled Youngblood to her and hugged him. She was musty as hell.

"I got out today," answered Youngblood, holding his breath. He stepped back a bit. "Where is Shan and my son?"

"They live in Bowen Homes, in the front apartment building. I hope you ain't planning to get back with her. She's my daughter but she ain't right. Find yourself a nice girl and stay out of trouble," Poochie warned.

"I just wanna see my son."

"You need me to show you where they live?"

"Naw, I'll find it." Youngblood handed Poochie twenty dollars. He pitied her but he had love for her, too.

She stuffed the money in her pocket. "You ain't have to gimme no money, you just got out of jail." But she didn't offer to give it back.

"Don't trip," Youngblood said. "You all right with me." He gave Poochie a hug, and then he and Lonnie bounced.

A half hour later, they pulled into Bowen Homes. The first person they encountered directed them to Shan's apartment.

"'Preciate that, folks." Youngblood thanked the block boy before they headed around the corner to Shan's crib.

Not wanting any drama to jump off, Lonnie went to the door with Youngblood. He knew how hotheaded they both were.

Shan opened the door. She was seven months pregnant.

"When yo' ass get out?" she asked.

"Where's my son?"

"He sleep."

"Wake him up," Youngblood demanded.

"I ain't."

"Girl, wake my son up!"

"I said no!" Shan said nastily. So Youngblood pushed his way into her apartment, brushing against her bulging belly.

"Oww! You hurt my stomach, fool!"

As soon as Youngblood stepped through the doorway and into the living room, Shotgun Pete walked out of the bedroom wearing boxer shorts and no shirt. Their eyes locked. Neither one looked away.

Shotgun Pete, who was still bigger than Youngblood, was trying to intimidate him. Youngblood had gotten taller in prison, but he was still a skinny man, but he had mad heart.

The stare-down lasted more than a minute. Finally, Pete spoke. “What you want? Drama or what?”

“I came to get my son. I ain’t got nothing to say to you, nigga. I didn’t fuck you, did I?”

“Prison done made you tough, huh?”

“I been tough!” Youngblood boasted.

“You frontin’. You a bitch!” Shotgun Pete said, intentionally disrespecting.

“You see a bitch, kiss a bitch,” challenged Youngblood.

“You ain’t my type, too skinny. But I got the type of bitch I like,” Pete said, looking at Shan.

“Y’all don’t start no stuff in here! If y’all fools wanna fight, go outside,” Shan said.

Lonnie cut in. “Yo, Pete, I ain’t taking sides, but why you disrespecting Youngblood? He just came to see his son. You got a problem with a man seeing his son?”

“This ain’t got nothing to do with you, Lonnie,” Pete said. “If Youngblood got beef wit’ me, we can do it any way he wanna, knuckles or pistol play.” Pete moved toward the bedroom, obviously going to get his heat. Lonnie was packing heat himself, but he didn’t want to blast Pete in the back.

It really wasn’t his beef and Shan wasn’t worth dying over or killing for. Plus, Lonnie also knew that Younglood had left the .9mm he’d given him in the car.

“Yo!” he yelled and Pete stopped and looked over his shoulder.

“Y’all don’t need no pistol play. Y’all can step outside and settle the beef with fists,” Lonnie offered.

“I’m down with that!” Shotgun Pete didn’t hesitate to agree.

“Nigga, you ain’t saying nothing. I’ll whoop your punk ass up and down the muthafuckin’ block.” Being fresh out of jail, Youngblood was used to throwing hands.

When they stepped outside, he went straight off in Shotgun Pete's grill, busting his mouth. Blood poured down Pete's chin as he shook off the effects of the blow and charged at Youngblood.

They fought like Hearn and Haggler back in the day. Blow for blow, neither one giving ground.

They were still swingin', trying to knock each other's head off when the police arrived on the scene with their sirens blaring.

Since Youngblood and Shotgun Pete refused to press assault charges against one another, the cops locked them up for disorderly conduct and creating a public disturbance. Youngblood was released from jail hours later, after paying a $250 fine. But Shotgun Pete was held on traffic warrants.

CHAPTER 8
Youngblood

I stayed in the city jail for nearly five hours before they let me pay two and a half bills and bounce. But those five hours in jail fucked with my head worse than the whole five years I had just spent in prison. It made me realize that once po-po put the cuffs on a nigga, there was no telling when he'd see freedom again. I was at their mercy, and I didn't like that setup at all.

I made a vow, right in that city jail cell, that po-po would never lock me up again. Mad niggaz screamed that, just frontin' like they gon' hold court in the street. But I was dead-ass serious about mine. Not that I planned to square up and stop doing crime. Shit, what else was a young nigga with no legitimate skills gon' do? Doing crime was just the hand I'd been dealt. I damn sho' wasn't gon' go looking for a job.

It was real stupid of me to throw fists with Shotgun Pete. Number one, the nigga was mad bigger than me. Even if I would've busted the nigga up, his pride would've made him come at me with his heater, his gat. And I would've hunted him with my heat had he beat me down. So, the best thing for me to have done was to bust caps in his ass off the jump. Fuck a fistfight.

But after giving it some serious thought, my baby's mama wasn't worth the drama.

I was steamed 'cause Shotgun Pete was trying to regulate me seeing my son. If Shan had some respect for herself, she would've laid the law down to the nigga and made him respect me about mines.

But rats and chickens like her wasn't 'bout business. They loved drama. They were loyal to whoever stickin' dick in them at the time. Now, Shotgun Pete was older than me and Shan and he should've been up on himself. Instead of letting a chicken head put him at beef with me, a nigga he had robbed with and all. He should've figured that if Shan would violate me, her son's daddy, she would one day do the same foul shit to him. But young pussy had a way of fucking up those older cat's head. *Fuck it.* Next time the beef wouldn't be settled with fist.

A few days had passed and I was riding with my dawg, Lonnie. We ran into a dope boy named Freddie, a mafucka that pushed a little weight.

His real claim to ghetto-fame was that he had a project in East Atlanta locked. He was also one of those pretty boys and his uncle had mad juice on the streets. Niggaz knew that Freddie was semi-soft, but his uncle Hannibal wasn't to be fucked with.

Hannibal pushed major weight, had a crew of young killers who made niggaz disappear if they disrespected. Hannibal looked like a black ass Suge Knight, and he always rolled in a caravan of vehicles. He was so hard to touch and so violent that po-po didn't even fuck with him.

Anyway, Freddie got some respect from street niggaz just 'cause Hannibal was his uncle. We never saw them together, and I don't think Freddie got his dope from Hannibal, but niggaz wasn't really sure so they basically didn't fuck with Freddie. Meaning, they didn't bring drama to him. He rode the wave of his uncle's rep.

When Freddie pulled alongside us in his candy-apple painted Porsche Roadster with a dime ass bitch in the passenger seat, and motioned for Lonnie to pull over, it didn't surprise me one bit to see him showcasing like a star.

In the BP gas station lot, Freddie got out of his whip, came over to Lonnie's Cadillac Avant and leaned his wavy head inside the driver's window. I could see the dime bitch in Freddie's whip bobbing her head to the sounds coming from the Porsche's sound system.

Conceit was written all over her fly ass face, like it was her ride and she was just letting Freddie drive her around. *Dumb ho!*

I didn't have to know shit about her to know that bitches like her came a dime a dozen. I would've fucked her, though. I hadn't splacked any pussy since I got out. I could've went to see Brenda or fucked a rat out the hood, but my mind was on getting loot. Even a young nigga, like myself, knew to get the loot first. Everything else, especially the rats, follow the cheddar.

As Freddie spoke to Lonnie, he looked over at me like he couldn't place my face. I told him who I was and where I'd been the last five years. He still acted like he didn't know me. That kind of pissed me off, but I knew that it was just a matter of time before niggaz was gon' recognize my name. Then again, in my line of hustle it was good not to be recognized. Still, every street hustler, no matter his hustle, wanted niggaz to recognize and respect his name.

Lonnie got out of the car and him and Freddie talked in hush tones. I was eyeing the dime in Freddie's whip. She looked over and our eyes met. She made a face like I was throw-up, or shit, or something! I checked that in my mental file. Told myself I'd get with her when I came up, drag her ass for that nasty look she gave me. If not her, I'd drag other bitches like her. Atlanta was full of them ho's.

Out the corner of my eye, I saw Freddie hand Lonnie something. It looked like a roll of money. When Lonnie got back in the car and we were back in traffic, he showed me what Freddie had given him, a wad of big faces, loot. He told me what Freddie wanted us to do for him.

I said, "Bet that!" letting Lonnie know I was down with it.

He told me to split the loot in half, and he didn't even count behind me when I handed him his portion. He just stuffed it in his pocket. That was the way it should be with partners, mad trust. Not enough niggaz keep it real, though.

A week passed before Lonnie and I finally saw Jerrod, an up-and-coming hustler who was inching his crew into Freddie's territory.

Jerrod was from D.C. and hadn't been in ATL but a few years. I didn't know playa, but Lonnie gave me the 411 on him. Well, all that he knew, which wasn't much.

To sum it up, Jerrod was just another nigga from out-of-state who came to the Dirty South to get money and fuck southern bitches. Problem was, he was trying to get money in a spot that already belonged to Freddie.

Freddie wasn't a killer and he didn't really have a crew, so Jerrod probably didn't even blink before putting work down in Freddie's East Atlanta spots.

The niggaz Freddie fronted dope to wasn't gonna war for him, 'cause they had no love for him. Their arrangement with Freddie was strictly business. I would think that it would be in the best interest of *business* for the niggaz who Freddie fronted dope to *to* get together and put Jerrod to sleep. But for some reason, they were letting Jerrod get money that should've went in their pockets. My guess was they all were scared to catch a murder case.

Lonnie said they had an *every nigga for himself* mentality.

Whatever.

Freddie might've been scared to get a cold body but he had paid Lonnie and me to step to Jerrod. So, Jerrod was gonna get *stepped to.*

Funny shit about it, though. Freddie didn't want us to do the nigga. He had instructed Lonnie to just shoot him in the legs.

Yeah, right!

We tried to catch this fool, Jerrod, for a week or more. But playa didn't have a set pattern we could pin him down to.

We then saw him parked at a McDonald's drive-thru. *But how we suppose to shoot a nigga in the legs while he's sitting inside his car?*

"Yo, pull around the corner and wait for me," I told Lonnie as I got out the car.

"What you 'bout to do?"

"Just park around that corner," I pointed about fifty yards away.

"Be ready to pull off in the other direction when I get back to the car." I checked my gat before stepping out of the car and shutting the passenger door. I didn't wait for shit. I knew Lonnie would try to talk me out of what I was about to do.

I heard him say, "Nigga, you stupid!"

By the time I walked calmly across the street and set foot in the McDonald's parking lot, the sun had faded behind the clouds and the darkening sky provided cover for my mission. In addition, I pulled my baseball cap low over my eyebrows. My collar was up but I didn't tuck my chin. I was hoping to look cool, not criminal. Both hands were in my baggy jeans pockets, one hand gripping my heat. My jeans sagged; I was just a young nigga headed to McDonald's for a Big Mac.

I acted like I was checking traffic to be sure it was safe to cross the street, but I mainly was making sure po-po wasn't nowhere around.

I saw that two cars were ahead of Jerrod and three more behind him at the drive-thru.

Playa was boxed in!

I got right up to his passenger side and unloaded right through the window. Glass shattered. He tried to pull off but rammed into the car in front of him. I stuck my arm inside the shattered passenger door window and let loose some more.

I saw his body jerk with each shot, then it slumped down bloody and crooked. The stupid bitch in the car behind Jerrod's screamed. So I opened up on her old ass, too, before I dashed across the street and around the corner where Lonnie was waiting, engine running.

Once I got in, he drove off in a direction that nobody from McDonald's could see us.

We didn't chance driving all the way back to Lonnie's crib. It was damn near twenty-five minutes away. Instead, we drove to some bitch's house he knew.

I saw the shit on the news that night after Lonnie and I crept back to his crib. Jerrod was damn sure dead. I learned that the old bitch who had screamed got hit in the shoulder and the jaw, but they expected her to live. They showed a sketch of the suspect from witnesses account. The shit didn't look nothing like me.

I was a little nigga. The mafucka they described was six feet tall, 180 to 210 pounds. *I wish!*

The car we used was a jack mobile. Lonnie got rid of it with no trace or trip to him. Of course, it was only a few days before we'd step to Freddie and put the press down on him for some extra dough since I had bodied Jerrod.

What the fuck could he do but pay up?

Freddie came correct and told Lonnie he'd holla at him in the future. I was thinking how nice it would be to jack Freddie. But I put the thought on hold.

Lonnie only wanted 30 percent of the dough Freddie had just gave us. He said I deserved a bigger share ‘cause I did all the work. But I split it with him fifty-fifty. *I kept it real.*

Later, Lonnie told me Freddie asked him why we had murked Jerrod. Lonnie told him it just happened like that. Pay up and forget about it. Lonnie never asked me one question about it, either. He just said, “Boy, you wild as fuck don’t do shit out in the open again. You gon’ fuck around and get cased up.”

“I hear you, fam.” I chuckled, feeling invincible.

CHAPTER 9

I had some cheddar on my plate and was ready to unwind from the adrenaline rush I'd been on from the moment I told I Lonnie to park around the corner from that McDonald's.

Delina worked for a car rental company and was able to hook me up with a rental. I went shopping and bought the latest thug gear. I went in the hood and paid a rat to braid my hair in a fly style. I also stopped by Poochie's neighbor and dropped off some gear for her to give to my son.

I didn't trust Poochie, she was on the pipe too bad. I gave the lady a fifty-spot, and she promised she'd make sure Lil' T got the stuff. I didn't wanna take it to Shan myself, 'cause I knew I still had beef with Shotgun Pete. But I'd deal with him later.

Inside Poochie's crib, it looked like she had sold everything, but the rug. Damn, I hated to see her fucked up on crack like that.

I pulled out a stack, peeled of six twenty dollar bills, gave them to Poochie and hugged her.

"You want a blow job," she offered.

"Naw, Poochie. You ain't gotta do that. You're my son's grandmother," I declined.

"You still got a sweet young dick?" I just laughed and shook my head. Poochie said, "You need to take Shan's ass to court if she won't let you see your son."

I let Poochie's advice slide down my back. Gangsters didn't go to the court for help.

"I'ma catch up with you later." I turned and walked out of the door.

Outside, I got in the rental car and drove to the hotel where I had rented a room for the weekend. It was a plush room in the downtown area.

The receptionist on duty stopped me as I strolled through the lobby. I showed the white bitch my room key, told her I was in the music industry and let her see the back of my ass as I walked toward the glass elevator.

In my room, I sat my bags of gear on the bed, reached inside one of the bags and pulled out three jewelry boxes. I had bought some shine for my neck, a heavy platinum chain and some weight for my wrist. The bracelet was bling-blinging. The third jewelry box was a nice friendship ring for Brenda.

I had gotten to know Brenda pretty well through letters, phone calls and a few visits while I was on lock. She had showed a young nigga love when I was in the joint when Shan had got ghost. I hadn't called Brenda since I bounced from the pen but I hadn't forgot that she sent me loot and accepted my calls from prison when nobody else would. Well, nobody besides Lonnie and Toi.

I picked up the phone and dialed Brenda's number. It had just turned dark outside my hotel window.

"Hello?"

"Whud up, old lady?" I joked.

"Who is this?"

"The realest young nigga you know," I boasted.

"Terrence? Youngblood?" Brenda sounded excited.

"The one and only."

"Your ass has been home from prison! Why're you just now calling me?" She was no longer excited.

"I had to build my weight up, get some loot before I dialed you up."

"Yo ass going back to prison trying to build your weight up," she mocked, but I heard the excitement return to her voice.

"Can I take you out tonight?" I asked, trying to sound smooth.

"I don't know," hesitated Brenda. "Where are we going?" I told her my plans and she said she'd be dressed and ready in a couple of hours.

I didn't want to push the rental car. This was an occasion for style, so I splurged and rented a Range Rover limo for the night.

When Brenda stepped out of her door, she freaked out. She was too experienced to say anything to reveal her shock, but I saw it in those big brown eyes of hers.

I had told her to dress casual 'cause I was in baggy jeans, Fubu football jersey and Timberlands—casual, but blinging and thugged out.

Brenda was rockin' a leather dress that fit her fine ass like second skin. I had a dime on my arm that night.

We went to Red Lobster, ordered seafood, wine and some dessert. After we finished eating, I gave Brenda the friendship ring and said, "I'll never forget how you showed a nigga love when you didn't owe me shit." "Aww, thank you, lil' daddy," she named as she slid the diamond onto her finger. Then, she leaned over and gave a nigga mad tongue.

A short while later, we left Red Lobster and hit a few nightclubs, finally settling on a spot out in Buckhead where they had a live jazz band. It wasn't my style, I was a rap head but Brenda was good, so I was good. I wasn't the type of nigga who had to talk a lot on a date. *Shit, I had never been on a real date no way.*

So I just listened to the band and let Brenda lead the flow. "I'm really feeling you. You carry yourself like a real man," she complimented.

"What else were you expecting, with your sexy ass?" I leaned over and stroked her face.

"Don't get yourself in trouble."

"Nah, don't you get yourself in trouble. I'm just coming home from lock up. You can't handle this." I took her hand and guided it under the table.

"Damn!" Her eyes got buck when she felt my steel.

"You wanna go back to the hotel?"

"That sounds good to me. But it don't mean you gettin' the pussy, though," she warned, half-heartedly.

Of course, I was gettin' the pussy, even if I had to stay up all night seducing her. I was long overdue and the wine, Brenda's perfume and her sex appeal had my dick harder than prison bars.

At the hotel, again she was surprised to see that a young nigga was camped at a plush spot. Once I talked Brenda into the Jacuzzi, the rest had already been written.

Her shit was bangin'! Shawdy could work her pussy like a pair of hands.

I tried to get her to give me some head, but she politely said, "We'll save that for another day."

"Like when?" I damn near begged.

"I'll surprise you," Brenda cooed. Then she put one of her legs behind her neck and said, "Fuck me like this. You can get all the pussy this way."

That pussy looked so pretty, wide-open like that. I wanted to tell her to hold that pose while I jacked off. Instead, I got all the pussy, just like she promised I could in that position.

When I woke up in the morning I got my surprise. Brenda's head was that fi'! Just like the pussy. I had to grab a pillow and bite it to keep from screaming her name.

The rest of that weekend we fucked, sucked and ordered room service. We had to shower damn near four times a day and we managed to squeeze in a few hours of conversation when we weren't bent into pretzels. Brenda did most of the talking, and we didn't talk about any real serious shit, just everyday conversation. We didn't make each other any promises, either. Brenda said she knew I was just getting out of prison so she wasn't gonna crowd me.

"Just don't be a stranger. And be careful, whatever you're doing," Brenda warned when I dropped her off at her crib early Monday morning.

We kissed and I told her I'd call her in a few days. I slid her some funds to send to her brother who was still in prison. She accepted the loot for him, but she wouldn't accept the money I offered to her.

"You don't owe me nothing," she said sweetly. I stuffed the bills back in my pocket and said, "Whatever, shawdy." I kissed her again and asked her if she still thought I was a baby.

"Naw, nigga. You're all man!"

She then exited my ride and I watched her fine ass run up the stairs to her crib.

CHAPTER 10

I had paid for the rental car for a week so I still had four days before I had to return it.

It was like 10 a.m. and the streets weren't really poppin' yet, unless I rolled to the hood. But the hood wasn't really on my mind. I was thinking: *I gotta find a steady hustle because my bank was getting thin, or I need to hit a lick. A big one.*

Everything was good at Lonnie's crib. I was welcomed to stay for eternity, but I don't roll like that. I wasn't trying to crowd my dawg forever. I needed a spot of my own and some wheels.

But my stash wasn't strong enough to cop all that.

The other shit on my mind was my fam', Ma Duke and Toi.

My sister understood a nigga, but she had to play by Ma Duke's rules 'cause she was under Ma Duke's roof. It was actually my stepfather's crib, but I tried not to mention that buster's name, if I could help it.

Now, I hadn't talked to Ma Duke and Toi in a while, they probably didn't know that I was out of prison. It wasn't because I didn't love my mom, I did. But I had mad anger for her 'cause she chose her husband over me, her son. A mother ain't supposed to let nobody dis her kids. Nobody! She was supposed to tell Raymond that if I wasn't welcomed she wasn't either.

Then, Ma Duke, Toi and me would've left G.I. Joe in his mafuckin' house all by his lonesome. Ma Duke should've represented just like that, but she didn't. It was like she had said fuck me.

My reservations about seeing her were pushed aside 'cause I did wanna see my sister. Besides, I also wanted Ma Duke to see me looking good, then she'd know I didn't need no fuckin' body.

At age twenty-one, Toi was now a lady and she looked like one.

She hugged me tight as a mafucka and I saw tears in her eyes. I was her only brother, her love was real for me. I even let her talk me out of the new shine on my neck. But I could always hit a lick and buy another necklace. Besides, it was worth that big ass smile on Toi's face.

Ma Duke hugged me and then looked at me like she wanted to ask, *Who you done robbed?*

Raymond was at work, so I stayed for about an hour and then jetted. Wasn't shit to talk about.

I left there wanting to cry because deep down I missed the closeness we shared before she let a muthafuckin nigga come between us.

A few minutes later, my hurt turned to anger. I needed something or somebody to release my rage on.

I started to go find Shotgun Pete and pump mad holes in his ass! But that was just my temper hyping me up to do some dumb shit.

I checked my thoughts and drove aimlessly around the city until I had my mind together. I ended up in the hood, Englewood. Those projects accepted me win, lose or draw.

I saw mafuckaz I hadn't seen since I got back on the turf. Most mafuckaz was doing the same shit they'd been doing five years ago when I got knocked. Some were doing worse. Little girls were now fine ass teenagers, with mad ass and titties and attitude like they had the only pussy in the South. Lil' niggaz had grown up and was now pushing they own whips and checkin' paper.

Seeing them mafuckaz, all grown up and shit, made me feel old. And I was still a young nigga. I realized then that hustlers were getting younger and younger in the hood.

A few of us sat around an old car and puffed chronic and sipped Henny. I was higher than gas prices.

I bought a dinner from the Ribs Lady who lived in Englewood, right behind the dope trap, clockin' crazy loot by selling the best damn ribs right out her back door. The neighborhood dope boys was her most loyal and frequent customers, they bought barbeque ribs from her by the slab. But people came from all over to buy dinners from her.

She'd been selling those dinners since I was a little boy. Her fat ass had to be rich by now or at least well-paid. I figured she hadn't moved out of the ghetto 'cause it paid too well. Everybody in the hood protected her from would-be robbers 'cause her food was so mafuckin' good they didn't want anybody to chase her out the neighborhood.

I bought two rib dinners and a cold ass forty ounce. A barbeque dinner consisted of six to eight bones, baked beans, coleslaw, collard greens, two cornbread muffins and a piece of chocolate cake. The shit was so good it made my dick hard. And the barbeque sauce was the shit.

I drove up the hill to Poochie's spot. Poochie was glad to see me and thanked me for the dinner I bought for her. I sat on the couch in her empty ass living room eating my rib dinner with my fingers while Poochie just picked over hers. She told me how happy my son was when she gave him the gear I'd left with Poochie's neighbor.

"I kept his bad ass for Shan last night," Poochie told me. "She just came and got him a few hours ago."

Damn! I wanted to see my son.

I really didn't hear shit else Poochie was saying. I was wrestling with my temper. It was telling me to go blast Shan and Shotgun Pete, take my son and hit the highways.

I calmed myself again. I fired up a blunt and offered Poochie a toke. She shook her head. I looked at her like I couldn't believe she refused a free high. I was thinking maybe weed wasn't potent enough for a crackhead.

After I had smoked the whole blunt and chilled on the couch, doing nothing but thinking, Poochie started looking good as hell. I had to be fucked up, 'cause I swear Poochie looked like Toni Braxton!

Before I got high, she hadn't looked so good.

"Come sit on my lap," I said, lips dry as sheetrock.

"What?" Poochie said, caught off-guard. I repeated what I'd just said and Poochie came to me.

I hate to admit it, but I was so high I tongued her like she really was Toni Braxton. Yeah, I know Poochie is a base head and probably done sucked mad dicks. I went out bad.

But I blamed it on the weed and all the other shit that was circling in my head besides the chronic smoke. But on the real, Poochie still had some good ass pussy. I didn't just fuck her and jet out. I stayed all-night and hit that good pussy again and again. The pussy was so dope I was damn near hoping Poochie got pregnant.

I fell asleep on the couch wondering what the fuck them niggaz had put in that blunt. If I dreamed that night, I don't recall it. I do recall waking up the next morning with a piss hard-on.

I reached for Poochie, but she wasn't on the couch with me. I wanted some of her fi' head while my dick was like steel. So I walked around the sparsely furnished apartment looking for her, stumbling and calling her name.

I was butt-naked like a baby with a big dick. Poochie didn't answer and she wasn't in any of the rooms. I accepted the fact that I'd have to piss my hard-on off.

After pissing, washing my hands and splashing water on my face, I came out the bathroom and went back in the living room to put my clothes on. My neck and wrist felt naked.

That bitch creeped my shit! Reaching up I felt for my chain but it wasn't around my neck. Glancing down at my wrist, I saw that my bracelet wasn't there. I was close to panicking until I reached the living room and found my jewelry bling-blingin' on the floor next to the couch. I had taken it off last night during a break from fucking Poochie. I was surprised Poochie hadn't stolen it and run down the hill to trade it for some crack.

My money!

I reached in my pants pocket and pulled out my roll of bills, all the money I had to my name. A quick count and I was sure Poochie hadn't stolen no more than fifty or sixty dollar, but the rental car keys were missing and so was the car when I looked out of the window.

Before I could close the curtain, I saw Poochie drive up in the rental. She came into the apartment with two bags of groceries.

"You thought I had stolen that rental car, didn't you?" she asked.

"Naw," I lied. I followed Poochie into the kitchen and watched as she put the groceries inside of the refrigerator.

"I got seventy dollars out your pants pocket. I'll pay you back when my check comes if you want me to," Poochie explained with her back to me.

"You don't have to pay it back, I'm straight." After a pause, I added, "I ain't gon' lie, though, I thought yo ass had clipped me for my whole knot and went to buy some rocks."

Poochie laughed. "I wouldn't do you like that. I'ma quit fuckin' with that shit anyway. Get myself together and move away from these projects." She turned to face me. "You want me to cook you some breakfast?"

"Hell no! You might start thinking I'm your man." We both laughed like hell. Then somebody began knocking on the front door.

"Answer the door," Poochie said, like I lived there or something.

When I opened the door Shan and my son was standing there.

Shan said, with an attitude full of suspicion, "What you doing over here? Where my mama at?" Not waiting for me to answer either question, she dragged my son by the arm, right past me and came inside of the apartment calling out for Poochie.

It smelled like y'all been fuckin' in here!" The bitch said it just like that, in front of my son. A real project bitch!

Poochie found some baby powder and sprayed it up in the air in the living room, trying to freshen up the funk. She lied, telling Shan I had just got there. But I could see in Shan's eyes she didn't believe it.

She was sweating me like mad.

"Why your braids all loose and fucked up?" I ignored her ass.

I didn't owe that ho any explanation. I was tempted to admit I had fucked her mama last night, but I didn't wanna put Poochie at beef with her daughter. I had never admitted to fuckin' Poochie before I went to prison, but I knew Shan had found out somehow. Probably Poochie had blurted it out in one of her crack induced tirades. But I could stick to a lie forever.

Shan was cussing, accusing and telling Poochie she should be ashamed of herself for screwing me, the father of Poochie's grandson, who didn't know what the fuck was going down. My little soldier didn't even know who I was anymore. Shan kept accusing. Poochie kept denying, more like lying.

I kneeled down, face to face with little Terrence Junior. He was sporting some of the gear I had bought him. I was prouder than a mafucka, looking at a little me. He was almost six years old. I told him who I was and he looked at me like I was lying.

Poochie said, "Lil' T, hug your daddy's neck." He did, too.

My junior and I left Shan and Poochie arguing. Shan acted like she didn't want me to take Lil' T nowhere, but she could see that he wanted to go with me. She also knew I would've kicked her ass for old and new if she would've tried to trip. I couldn't believe that bitch had the mafuckin' nerve to say to me, "Don't take my son around none of your bitches!"

If my eyes were an AK-47, that bitch would've been dead as I spoke. That bitch was 'bout to poot out a baby any minute by a nigga that was supposed to be my partner in crime, and she got the nerve to try to regulate who I took our son around? The ho must've wanted me to punch her in her goddamn face. But like Eminem said *Temper, temper!*

I checked mine.

It wasn't easy to *not* snap on Shan. I mean, she had got ghost on me while I was serving the five-year bid. And she had kept my son away. I had every right to bust her ass up. The bitch just wasn't worth it.

She was telling me to have Lil' T back at Poochie's spot before dark. Like my son would have turned into a vampire after dark or something. I just flipped the bitch off. Her ass would be lucky if I ever brought him back.

The Atlanta Zoo wasn't but a hop and a jump from where Poochie lived, so my son and I started our first day together, in five years, there. The whole zoo smelled like a thousand funky crack-heads. The elephant pens were the worst, but Lil' T loved the shit.

The zookeeper let us handfeed the giraffes. They had long black tongues that grabbed at the snacks like flat bungee ropes. As we toured the zoo, my son told me all about his schoolteacher and classmates.

"Daddy, I got a girlfriend!" He said all excited.

"What's your girlfriend's name?"

"Penny," my son answered.

"Is Penny pretty?" As if we were having a real father to son talk.

"Oooh, man! She real fine!" Lil' T got more hyped the more he talked about his lil' girlfriend. I was laughing my ass off, wondering how a six-year-old girl could be fine. *Kids are a trip.*

"How old is Penny, if she so fine?" I teased.

"She twenty-four," my son answered, straight-faced as a mafucka.

I really cracked up then 'cause either Penny was a freak bitch who liked little kids, or my son had a mad crush on a twenty-four-year-old.

I pumped him for more information and figured out that Penny was some chicken head who lived two doors down from my son. She watched him sometimes. I figured Lil' T had a mad crush on Penny.

We bounced from the zoo after a couple of hours and I took him to Chuck E. Cheese. We ate pizza and played video games, and Lil' T played with some other little kids who were there.

I called Brenda from the pay phone inside of Chuck E. Cheese. I told her a lot about my son when I was on lock. I wanted her to see him.

She told me to come on over.

By the time we reached Brenda's spot, Lil' T was knocked out. His lil' ass was snoring. That shit even cracked me up.

I was enjoying everything about my son. I hadn't seen him since he was an infant so every little thing he did amazed me.

It was mad crazy 'cause he looked like a miniature me.

I had to carry him from the car to Brenda's crib, 'cause shorty was sleeping like a log. Once inside, I kissed him on the forehead before laying him down on Brenda's couch, in the living room. Lil' T woke up for a minute, realizing he was in a strange place.

I introduced him to Brenda and he said, "Hi," in a groggy voice.

Then he laid his head on my lap and was asleep again in seconds.

Probably dreaming about the animals at the zoo or the fun he had at Chuck E. Cheese. Maybe his lil' ass was dreaming about Penny, his grown twenty-four-year-old girlfriend.

I used Brenda's phone to call Lonnie to see what was poppin'. I hadn't hollered at him in a few days.

I was still living at his spot. Well, I was crashing out there until I could build my weight up and get my own. There was no pressure, though, Lonnie was true people. I was welcomed for as long as it took me to get on my feet. He understood that the money we had split from that Freddie job wouldn't handle all my needs. Shit, I was fresh out the joint, I needed every mafuckin' thing. Plus, Lonnie understood a nigga was gonna splurge.

I rapped with Lonnie for a minute, just shootin' the breeze. We never discussed business over the phone. Lonnie had been schooled me 'bout that. Besides, when I was locked up I used to read a lot of true crime novels and watch *Court TV*. It was bananas how many fools talked themselves right into prison by running their mouths on the phone. Anyway, once a caper was completed what the fuck was there to discuss any fuckin' way?

I hung up with Lonnie and talked to Brenda for a while. I could tell she wanted me to stay but she knew I had to take Lil' T back home. I didn't want to stay the night at Brenda's no way. I was shook about spending the night at bitch's cribs ever since some old nigga kicked in the bedroom door on Shan and me when I first started fucking her years ago.

The only reason I had crashed last night at Poochie's crib was 'cause that fi' pussy had knocked a nigga out cold. And, I knew that the only man who claimed Poochie as *his* was *crack.*

With Brenda I figured it was different. She was phat to death, had her shit together and had trick niggaz to give her some of their shit. Plus, she fucked bitches, too. Them dyke hos were way more jealous than any man, and I didn't want no unnecessary drama.

Another reason I didn't want to spend the night with Brenda was because we'd just spent the weekend together. I didn't want her to be all in love with me, and I didn't wanna be in love with her. The situation with Shan had taught me that love complicates a nigga'z life, especially if he was a hustler or a gangsta. A nigga don't need no bitch on his mind when he got that heater in his grip. So I kissed Brenda goodbye and me and Lil' T jetted.

In the car, my son asked, "Daddy? Is that your girlfriend?"

"Don't be so damn nosy," I said, smiling and rubbing the top of his head.

CHAPTER 11

A few weeks later my pockets were empty and my options were few to none. All I had was some gear, the bling-bling on my wrist, and thanks to my dawg Lonnie, I had somewhere to lay my head and some food for my belly.

I assumed Lonnie had a stash of cash he'd saved up from capers over the years, 'cause he damn sho' ain't have no job, yet he had no trouble paying his bills. But pride wouldn't let a young nigga like me keep accepting charity from friends

Lonnie was showing more love than the average friend would already.

There was plenty of room in the two-level apartment, but I felt like I was cramping the spot when Lonnie's girl, Delina, and her two sons came over for a few days.

Now, Delina was a down bitch, straight out the PJ's, Englewood born and raised. She had been Lonnie's girl even before I went to serve those five years.

While I was doing those five, Delina had served eighteen months on a pistol case to save Lonnie from taking another fall. To say Delina loved Lonnie didn't do justice to their relationship, 'cause when I pictured two people in love, I pictured a lot of hugging and kissing and all up under each other. That wasn't the way I saw their relationship. So I'ma just say Delina was down for her nigga 'til their caskets dropped.

Every hustler needed a bitch like Delina for their main girl. She'd kick a bitch's ass for Lonnie, and she wasn't all jealous and shit. She might not have known where Lonnie's dick went 24/7, but she knew where his heart was at around the clock, 365 days a year.

She'd hold money, guns, dope, anything for her nigga. No questions asked. She'd gone to court and lied for Lonnie. The eighteen months in the pen proved that.

Delina had two sons, one eleven, and the other nine. Kurt being the oldest and Kobe the youngest. The boys' father was a junkie named Blue.

Delina and Blue had been teenage sweethearts. Back then Blue had dreams of being a famous R&B singer. The streets said Blue used to sing like a mafucka. People in the hood said Blue had once gone to the Apollo in New York and won the talent show five straight weeks when he was only eighteen, but crack had stolen Blue's R&B dreams like a sub-way pick pocketer. He woke up one day and was a flat-out crackhead! Now, he could barely talk above a whisper, let alone sing.

Every time Lonnie ran into Blue in Englewood, he'd toss him a few dollars. Blue would then ask Lonnie how his sons were doing and then he'd run off with the money to buy a rock before Lonnie could answer.

Seeing Lonnie do shit like that, blessing Blue with some loot 'cause he was Delina's sons' father, made me look at Lonnie in a different light. Not many niggaz would do a thing like that, especially for their girl's baby's daddy.

It wasn't like Lonnie and Blue had once been partners. They knew each other growing up, like everybody knows everybody in the PJ's, but that was the extent of it.

So, the way Lonnie treated Blue made me realize Lonnie was above pettiness. I already had mad respect for him, but that only added to it. I was beginning to understand that Lonnie wasn't a dirty, cold-hearted nigga even though he robbed and killed. That was just his hustle.

Now, Delina was mad cool. Although she was stingy with words, she liked anybody who showed love and loyalty to her man. If you were Lonnie's peeps, Delina was cool with you, too.

Her and her sons no longer lived in the projects, they'd moved into a better neighborhood the day Delina had got home from prison. But their crib was nowhere near Lonnie's. I assumed they arranged it like that to keep whatever beefs Lonnie caught in his hustle from landing at Delina's doorsteps.

Delina's sons were cool, not rowdy like most of us that came from the PJ's. When they were over Lonnie's crib, I would play Play Station with 'em and go outside and toss them passes with a football. Sometimes they'd stay only one night, sometimes Delina and the boys would stay a weekend.

Anyway, I just felt like I was crowding their space when Delina and her sons came over to visit Lonnie. None of them made me feel unwelcomed. It was really as simple as this: a man needs his own spot.

I put word out in the streets that I wanted to hook up as a bodyguard/pistol man for a dope boy. I knew that would be a weekly salary, a few bonuses and would give me an inside to future licks.

My prospects were few, though, 'cause a few niggaz were whispering that I was a stickup kid.

Niggaz really didn't know my business, but they knew I was Lonnie's dawg. The whole world knew Lonnie was a dope boy's nightmare.

Niggaz in the dope game would be foolish to let a stickup kid get down with their crew, especially pulling rank as a bodyguard. Of course, there were plenty foolish niggaz in the dope game. The way I saw it they were all foolish.

Weeks went by and still not a single dope boy had contacted me concerning the services I was offering. *Didn't they all know they needed a real gangsta to watch their back at all times?*

Most of 'em had lieutenants in their crew watching their back, though the lieutenants probably wouldn't kill nothing or nobody. They fronted like they were killers, shooting at rival crews from the other end of the street when there was beef. And they slapped crackheads down in a minute. But few of the lieutenants I had peeped would explode a niggaz dome, point blank range, like I would. Them niggaz were mostly about flossing for the bitches.

I was even willing to get a body for free, just to prove I wasn't no studio gangster. But dope boys weren't feeling me or else they were scared of me. Scared that if they hired me, I'd explode their dome and walk away with their bank, which I admit was a real good probability.

While I waited for a hookup, I put on the ski mask a few times and robbed a couple of small time rollers. I struck for six and a half ounces of hard and about ninety-five hundred all together.

Now, with weight in my pockets, I was able to relax a little. Ain't a hustler alive who can concentrate flawlessly when he was broke. Empty pockets breed desperation, which led to a nigga trying a foolish stunt.

My grip was tight for the moment. I dropped the six and a half ounces of hard on a lil' hustler from around the way. He gave me twenty-five hundred.

I had no use for the crack cocaine, I damn sho' wasn't gon' stand out on the block and sell rocks.

So now I had a total of twelve G's in my grip. I didn't want to just run through the loot like a giant termite and be broke again in a few weeks. I had mad shit I wanted and needed to get, but twelve G's wasn't gon' get it all. I needed a crib and furniture, a whip to floss in, and a whip for business.

I wanted to buy my son some gear, maybe my sister, too. And if Poochie was serious about not smoking crack anymore, buy her a television and some decent furniture.

Lonnie wasn't home so the townhouse was quiet, just me and my thoughts. With twelve G's in my grip, I was no longer desperate. I knew I still needed a steady hustle, though, something a little easier and more consistent than preying on smalltime rollers.

Mafuckaz had been offering me hustles like starting off as a lookout in dope traps, paying me five hundred to seven hundred a week. I wanted to explode their dome for offering me a chump off like that! They could've at least offered to let me slang the dope, so I could've got paid decently. But the scary-ass mafuckaz was too spooked to trust me handling their dough.

I wasn't gon' accept no slangin' job no way. But damn! They could've offered it.

I'd wash cars or shine shoes before I let a mafucka put me on the corner like I'm a ho. Slangin' dope for a nigga was the same as a bitch selling pussy for a pimp. Wasn't no difference besides the product they were selling.

When I was locked up, cats with sales cases didn't wanna see it like that. They ass was just ashamed to acknowledge they got pimped.

Brenda had a neighbor who had a used Nissan Maxima for sale. I cried broke until the lady accepted four G's for it. It was clean, in good condition, and it was dark blue.

All good. I just needed a business whip. I'd get something fly to floss in later.

I spent eight bills on a platinum watch for Toi. I called her from a pay phone and was glad she answered the phone instead of Ma Duke or Raymond.

"Come outside. I'm on my way over," I instructed Toi after identifying myself.

"What's up? Where you at?" she asked.

"Girl, just come outside, I got something for you. I ain't coming inside, I don't wanna see those other folks."

"You don't wanna see Mama?" Toi sounded disheartened.

I said coldly, "I ain't got no mama!"

When I drove up, Toi was outside waiting by the curb. I told her to get in and she dashed around to the passenger's side.

I pulled off. Toi wanted some KFC, so I took her and bought her a three-piece chicken dinner. I gave her the watch on the way back. She started crying.

"I love you." It was the first time she'd ever said that to me. I mean, I knew she loved me 'cause I was her brother. But we never said it to each other before. We just knew it.

"I love you, too," I said.

While parked in front of the house, Toi was trying to tell me that Mama did love me, she just didn't like my ways. And that Raymond wasn't really all that mean.

I cut her off. I didn't wanna talk about them.

Toi had just finished some computer school and Raymond was gonna buy her a new car. As a reward, I guess. I asked my sister why she still lived at home with *those folks*. She said, "*Those folks* is our mama and her husband, our stepfather."

"Not mine!" I spat back.

"Anyway, I'm getting my own place once I start working full-time and save up some money."

"I hate it for you," I half-joked.

As soon as Toi got out the car and shut the door, I honked the horn and jetted.

I had seen Mama peeking out the door, waving at me before I bounced but I kept pushing as if I didn't.

I dipped over to Englewood projects, stopped in the dope trap to holla at a few homies and to buy some blunts and check on my wire. to see if anybody had been looking to answer my offer to be their bodyguard.

Still no takers.

I went to cop a couple of dinners from the Ribs Lady. When I got there, two Atlanta cops waited on the porch for their barbeque dinners. She handed the cops' dinners to this little girl she'd adopted from a crackhead and then the little girl handed the cops their dinners.

Of course, the Ribs Lady's hustle was illegal, too, because she was clocking loot and not paying any taxes. But cops would turn their heads the other way to that type of hustle.

I collected two dinners and paid the Rib Lady. Then I drove up the hill to Poochie's, the hot sweet aroma from the rib dinners licked at my nostrils and tempted me to dig into them as I drove.

It was absolutely unbelievable that the Ribs Lady had put her two adult children through college from the sales of her dinners.

When I got to Poochie's crib I had already eaten three bones out of my dinner. I had sauce all over my mouth and my shirt.

When she opened the door, I gave the unopened dinner to Poochie and flopped down on her couch to devour the rest of mine before the roaches smelled the aroma and attacked.

Poochie did the same.

"I see you got a new television?" I noticed.

"Yeah. I got it from Rent-A-Center," Poochie said with pride. "I pay a little on it every month."

"You're *comin' up*, ain't you?" I joked, with a mouthful of food.

Poochie said, "I told you, I ain't getting high no more. I'ma get myself together and get out of these projects. I might even get my sons back from their daddy. I haven't seen them in a year. They live in South Carolina with him and his wife and other kids." Her tone and facial expression told me that Poochie missed her little boys and regretted that crack had dragged her so low she'd had to call their father to come get the boys and move them in with him.

I already knew the deal, but I hadn't really thought twice about Shan's half-brothers. I hoped Poochie could stay off crack, but I didn't really believe that she would.

I told her that I would help her move out of Englewood as soon as I built my weight up strong, and providing that she stayed off of the pipe.

Poochie claimed she hadn't smoked crack in a month, which was a long time for a crackhead. She claimed to have done it without having gone to a rehab center or nothing.

"Just woke up one day tired of being a crackhead," Poochie told me. She said she'd been to rehab several times over the years and it hadn't stopped her from smoking crack. She believed an addict couldn't kick their habit unless they wanted to do it themselves.

I gave Poochie five hundred dollars and made her promise to go buy herself some clothes. I wrote my pager number on a napkin that came with the rib dinners and told Poochie to page me whenever Shan dropped Lil' T off over there so I could dip by and see him.

"Page me if you need me for anything," I said sincerely and told Poochie which code to use so I'd know it was her.

She didn't have a phone but her neighbor did.

I drove around for a while looking for apartment vacancies. I had no job, credit or rental history, so I was hoping to run into an apartment manager who would take a few C-notes under the table and rent to me without running a credit check and all that mumble-jumble.

I struck out at all five apartment complexes I tried that day and ended up at a game room where a lot of hustlers hangout, shooting pool and profiling for the chickens and hood rats who came there trying to hook up with a baller.

Normally, I wouldn't grace that spot with my presence 'cause it was where mad dope boys frequented. And I was a stickup kid. It was like the eternal beef between lions and hyenas.

Dope boys and stickup kids were natural enemies. Put us in the same spot for too long and it was bound to be violence.

It was a territorial thing. Dope boys got uncomfortable when a stickup kid was around. They just figured we were there to stalk, rob or kill them.

Of course, their fears are well justified.

CHAPTER 12

I had neither beef nor caper in mind as I walked into the game room. My mission was to convince one of those high rollers that he needed me to watch his back. I spoke to a few niggaz I knew, grabbed a stool, sat down and checked out the happenings.

Niggaz were draped in all sorts of platinum and ice, tatted-up and rockin' Timbs and other fly gear. A dozen or so chickens were on the scene, hair bangin' and clothes tight and skimpy. A few of the chickens stood between ballers knees as the niggaz sat on a stool grippin' the chicken's ass with one hand and holding a pool cue in the other.

To someone from a different set it might have seemed crazy that bitches got all dressed up just to hang in a game room. But in the hood, chickens get dressed up just to sit out on the porch. They stayed ready to catch a major playa.

The vibe inside the game room was peace. I didn't feel like an outcast, I guess 'cause I didn't really yet have the label of a stickup kid. I wasn't well-known outside of Englewood, which was a blessing at this point.

I tried to holla at a thick, red bitch who was parading around begging for attention. But I had no rep and I didn't look like big loot, maybe she had seen me roll up in the Maxima. So shawdy brushed me off like lint.

I took it all in stride, I knew how the game went. Hos like Red ain't got no rap for a nigga with no juice. I was like *fuck it* and called next on a game of pool.

I held my own on the pool table, but got bored after a couple of hours and lost about $350 to a dude I should've easily beaten. I called it quits and found a stool. I was hoping Rich Kid would come through there.

The game room was where he usually met up with his crew and checked their weekly agenda. I hadn't seen Rich Kid in years, but he still had niggaz serving on the regular in Englewood.

That was how I found out Rich Kid came through the game room every week. Rich Kid had always tried to give me a package to push for him or a spot in his crew back in the day. I'd always refuse, but I knew he wanted me to get down with his team.

He was a Big Willie now so maybe he needed a full-time bodyguard.

I didn't run into Rich Kid that day in the game room, but Freddie and a few of his disorganized posse showed up. They pulled up in whips that turned heads. We could see the parking lot through the game rooms huge front windows. Rap music thumped loudly from Freddie and his posse's whips announcing their arrival. They all wore mad shine and came into the game room like they owned the world.

Freddie had a different chicken with him than the dime piece I'd seen in his Roadster a few months ago. Though she looked to be jail bait, this new girl was a dime piece, too. I had to give it to Freddie, though, the nigga had supreme taste. An artist couldn't have drawn a badder bitch than the young honey that was with Freddie. Shawdy was so pretty and fine niggaz stopped shooting pool just to look at her. The bitches in the game room, their whole posture changed. They all knew they didn't compare to shawdy.

Freddie gave dap to the two or three major ballers on the scene and ignored the head nods offered by small time hustlers dressed like they were major. He spotted me sitting on a stool against the wall and came over to dap my hand. We exchanged *whud ups* and Freddie asked how I was doing.

"I'm maintainin', playboy," I rapped. "But it's your show, I'm just in the crowd." Freddie's new dime piece was all up under him. She seemed to smile when I gave her man props.

Freddie countered with, "Naw, you da man, yo. I'll switch hands with you any day."

Bullshit.

I laughed. "If you switch hands with me you'd be sitting on this stool alone, and I'd have your dime on my arm."

"You like her? Her name is Pudding. Just say the word and I'll give her to you." Pudding looked scared to death, hoping Freddie wasn't serious. "I ain't frontin', yo. She's yours if you want her." Freddie was talking loud, making sure the whole game room could hear him.

"Give my folks a kiss," Freddie told Pudding. She hesitated for a minute, making sure Freddie was serious. Then she leaned into my space, fixing her sexy red lips to kiss me.

My hand went up and blocked Pudding's approach like the basketball player, Dikembe Mutumbo, wagging my index finger and the whole nine.

"No disrespect, Pudding, but you ain't my type."

The whole game room got ill. Niggaz cracked-the-fuck-up! The bitches now felt equal to fine ass Pudding. She was just a prettier version of a chicken.

Her contempt for me was written across her face but I didn't let it bother me. *Fuck you and every bitch like you,* I thought.

Twenty minutes later, she was still staring daggers at me. I flashed her a cocky smile, and then pushed her nothing ass out of mind.

Later, Freddie pulled me off to the side and asked if I my pockets was straight.

I told him I was neither rich nor poor. But I didn't accept the loot he offered me. See, Freddie and I both knew what I had did for him, but I'd already been paid for that. Freddie didn't owe me shit. It would've been foul for me to lean on Freddie for some more cheese. He had never brokered the deal with me in the first place. Freddie had done business with my dawg, Lonnie. Lonnie had put me down with the move. So to lean on Freddie would've been violating the trust he had in Lonnie. It would've been blackmail, and I don't roll like that.

I told Freddie, "I'm out."

When I bounced out of the game room, niggaz seemed to be looking at me with new respect. Maybe they respected how I had checked that lil' shit with Pudding. Maybe they thought I had juice 'cause I'd been kickin' it with Freddie. Or maybe I was just imagining they looked at me differently.

Before I could get into the Maxima, the chicken head, Red, I'd tried to holla at earlier came up to me and gave me her digits. Then she ran back inside the game room still hoping to get chosen by a bigger baller than me. I guess I was for a rainy day.

A week more passed before my luck began to change for the better. I found an apartment manager willing to rent me a one-bedroom unit on a month-to-month basis. She didn't even charge me not to run my application through the normal credit checks.

I paid first and last month's rent and a $250 security deposit, which wasn't bad for a one-bedroom in Decatur, just outside Atlanta. Decatur, also known as *The Dec'*, it used to be a suburb of the ATL, but it was becoming rundown like the inner-city. Still it was a spot away from the projects where I'd be more comfortable laying my head.

I went and bought a king-size mattress and linen and placed the mattress on the floor in the living room. I knew a dude who worked at Circuit City. He gave me a hookup on a big screen TV for $750.

The apartment came with a refrigerator and stove, that was all the furniture a young G like me needed. My spot wasn't no mansion, it wasn't even a condo, but it was my own shit. A nigga couldn't hate on that.

Just as my loot was getting thin, Rich Kid paged me. I had left my pager number with one of Rich Kid's workers in Englewood and told the worker to tell Rich Kid I needed to holla at him.

I called Rich Kid back from a pay phone, and he agreed to meet me in front of Poochie's apartment in an hour.

Forty-five minutes later, I pulled up to Poochie's apartment and three carloads of niggaz were waiting there. Rich Kid wasn't one of them.

I recognized the worker I had given my pager number to give to his boss man, Rich Kid.

"Whud up, Youngblood?" another one of the dudes asked.

"What you wanna talk to Rich Kid about?" A big black ass nigga joined in. These fools were acting like I was there to meet up with the president.

I tried not to look at those fools like they were a comedy team. I said, "I know y'all down fo' Rich Kid, but I don't think it's too wise for me to tell y'all my business or his."

"You strapped?" The big black ass nigga asked.

"I stay strapped, dawg. But my gat is in the car." He patted me down anyway, then he pulled out a cell phone and punched some numbers.

Ten minutes later, Rich Kid pulled up in a silver and black Escalade, rimmed-out and sparkling. He stepped out of the fly whip, oozing confidence like a mafucka.

"He clean?" Rich Kid asked the big, black nigga.

"Yeah, I patted him myself, boss man," Big Black Nigga said.

I didn't know if Poochie was home or not. I hadn't seen her look out of the window or door.

Rich Kid's crew gave us some space to speak privately, but they covered his back from all directions and the big, black nigga eyed me like a hawk. Rich Kid had security like a mafia don.

He had to be checking crazy flow to roll like this, I thought.

I calmly told him what my interest was, but it was clear Rich Kid didn't need another bodyguard.

He said, "Youngblood, you're down with Lonnie. I thought your game was jackin'? What would make you wanna change your stripes? Better yet, what would make me put an ex-stickup kid on my team? That's like paying a wolf to watch the sheep."

I told Rich Kid that I've gotten loot through many different hustles, but never have I taken it from a friend.

"I got principles that I live by," I said honestly. "Unless you know I'm not the nigga I claim to be, I feel like you're insulting my character."

Rich Kid laughed.

"Youngblood, I ain't worried about you doing harm to me. I've always liked you, young nigga. I just don't wanna have to kill you. And I would if you crossed me. Nah mean?" He looked me dead in the eyes. Neither of us blinked. "I can guard my own body," continued Rich Kid, "but I got plenty of niggaz to watch my back as it is. I got other work for you, though. Steady work that pays well. I'll page you in a few days."

After Rich Kid and his crew bounced, I knocked on Poochie's door. I got no answer. The lady next door told me Poochie was at work, she had gotten a job cleaning office buildings.

Damn! I guess Poochie was serious about staying off the pipe.

The apartment complex where I laid my head was quiet, mainly because no children were allowed to live there.

The tenants were all mostly young couples just starting out or single people with moderate incomes. I noticed a few honeys checking me out as I came and went, but I wasn't scouting for a bitch, I was still on the come up.

When my nuts got hot, I invited Brenda over or I dipped over to Poochie's crib and knocked her boots. I was also boning Poochie on the regular, but still on the low. She was thickenin' up, getting fine since she had got off crack. We were real careful not to let Shan bust us. She would've kept Poochie and me from seeing Lil' T.

As it was, I only got to see my son 'cause Poochie would page me when she had to babysit him. Shan had pooted out her newborn, and though I hated to give the ho props, she was right back fine again. I wasn't sweating her, though. To me, Shan didn't exist.

I wasn't trying to lock down no ho. Brenda had starting paging me on the regular, but I didn't see her but once every other week or so. I don't think Poochie or I would've classified our thing as this or that, we just did what we did, whenever.

It was a Wednesday night. Two weeks had passed when Rich Kid paged me. I had begun to think I wouldn't hear from him.

"Meet me at the game room," he said and hung up.

Outside of the game room, Rich Kid ran down his spiel to me. I said I was down with it and accepted half of the money he agreed to pay me up front.

Late that night, I drove over to Lonnie's crib and filled him in on what Rich Kid had hired me to handle. I wasn't putting Lonnie in Rich Kid's business for no ill purpose. I just wasn't sure if I could completely trust Rich Kid, so I wanted Lonnie to know the deal if I came up missing. I knew Lonnie would serve Rich Kid the same fate.

The big, black nigga's name was King, like he was meant to be a Rottweiler or some other big ass dog. I didn't yet know his rank in Rich Kid's crew, but he obviously had Rich Kid's trust.

I rode with King in a rental car down to Montgomery, Alabama. We stayed in different flop houses for ten dollars a night, for almost two weeks. That was how long it took us to find Richard.

Apparently Richard was getting dope from Rich Kid on consignment and was delinquent on his payment. He owed Rich Kid eighty grand and had been ducking him for two months. I had been paid to go to Montgomery and collect the eighty grand and/or Richard's hands.

King came along to show me around Montgomery and to point out the target. Also, to watch my back and, I assumed, to watch Rich Kid's money if I collected any.

After locating Richard, we watched and followed him for three more days trying to put together a good plan to kidnap him and force him to take us to his money stash.

Richard didn't know it but he was a dead man walking. There was no way I was going back to ATL without the eighty grand or both of Richard's hands.

There was also no way I would let Richard live to testify about it either.

While we were casing this fool out, I wondered what had pumped up his nuts to the size that he would stag on Rich Kid's loot? Didn't this idiot realize that if Rich Kid could afford to front him eighty grand worth of coke, Rich Kid could also afford to send a hit squad after his ass?

Some mafuckaz sentence themselves to death.

Richard had moved from Tallahassee, Florida, where Rich Kid knew where to find him, to Alabama trying to run from death. But a little money spreaded around had got Rich Kid the information he was able to use to track Richard to Montgomery.

Richard didn't know it, obviously, but Rich Kid and King had been to Montgomery, Alabama a half-dozen times over the past months. They'd watched Richard enough to know where he laid his head, and that he'd opened up a car wash in Montgomery. That was all explained to me by King on the ride down.

As we cased him out, Richard appeared to be a nervous man. I couldn't believe he had the nuts to sell coke, let alone runoff with eighty grand. Maybe he seemed nervous 'cause he knew he was living on borrowed time?

Richard had something else going on besides ducking Rich Kid. Even though King knew exactly where he lived and where he operated his car wash business, it took us a week to locate him.

King suspected Richard traveled back and forth between Tallahassee and Montgomery still pushing weight, just too greedy to cough up the cheese he owed Rich Kid.

It didn't add up to me, but I wasn't in town to solve math problems. I followed Rich Kid's instructions to a T on how to grab Richard and get him to tell me where he hid his loot.

King couldn't have pulled this caper off because Richard knew him, making my hustle necessary.

It was time to make my move. I bought a lawn mower and a weed-eater and went up and down the block where Richard lived asking to mow mafuckaz lawn for twenty dollars. I told 'em I was trying to make money to pay for my last year college tuition.

My young looks and preppy attire made it easy for them to take the bait. For three whole days, I mowed big ass front and back yards for only twenty dollars a fuckin' pop! And at the end of the day, I was tired as a mafucka.

I made sure I stayed on the block cutting somebody's grass until Richard came home each day. I wanted him to get used to seeing me in the neighborhood.

I wasn't worried about people being able to identify me, I was from Atlanta, and I didn't know a soul in Montgomery.

I'd give the lawn owners a fake name and I never removed my work gloves. Not even to drink a glass of soda they always offered. I knew that being an ex-con, my fingerprints were in the FBI fingerprint data-base, worldwide.

As soon as Richard pulled into his driveway and got out his car, I stopped him and solicited my services.

"Cut the front and backyard and then the hedges. I'll pay you twenty-five dollars," Richard bargained.

The idiot had just negotiated his life away.

CHAPTER 13

It was already early evening when I sat the gym bag down I was carrying and started on Richard's lawn. After a couple of hours of work, it started to get dark.

I knocked on the back door.

When Richard appeared I said, "I have to come back and finish in the morning. Can I use your phone to call my mother to pick me up?"

Not giving it much thought, Richard said, "Sure, come on in. Sit your gym bag down, the phone is in here." He then turned to lead the way.

"Would it be okay if I left my lawn mower and tools inside your garage? I'll be back bright and early in the morning to finish up."

"Sounds good to me."

With his back to me, I smacked my .9mm across the back of his head. When he pitched forward and hit the floor head first, Richard rolled over on his side and looked up. The big chrome heater with a silencer attached was inches from his forehead.

"One sound and you're a dead mafucka!" I said without a trace of leniency.

I made him duct tape his own mouth. Then I made him lie on his stomach and stretch his arms straight out above his head like po-po do a nigga. I managed to get his hands cuffed behind his back and then I took the heater from against the back of his head and rolled him over on his back.

"Richard," I whispered in a real menacing voice, "I came to collect that eighty grand you owe my man. Now, unless you owe more than one person eighty grand, I'm sure you know who I mean?" I pulled a machete out of the gym bag and ran the sharp blade across Richard's sweaty forehead. Blood trickled down immediately.

I said, real calm-like, "Now, Richard, I'm either leaving here with that eighty grand, or I'm leaving here with your head inside this gym bag. One or the other. I'm not taking you anywhere to get the money so don't insult me like that. For your own sake, the money better be here inside this house. You get one chance, only, to tell me the truth. You tell me where the money is, I'll take the eighty grand you owe my man, plus ten grand for making me come to collect it like this, then I'll leave. You live.

And we never see each other again. My man just wants his money, that's all. One lie, you a dead mafucka, you understand? I'ma remove this tape just enough so I can hear you. Richard, don't be stupid. I *will* kill you." I placed the gat, the heater with the silencer against the idiot's forehead. "Time to tell the truth." I said in a sing-song voice. I was betting that Richard kept a stash of loot inside of the house.

Sweat dripped from his forehead and his lips quivered when he replied. "I'll tell you where the money is at. Just don't do me dirty," he cried.

"Talk muthafucka," I growled menacingly.

"I'ma talk, man. Please don't kill me, though." He was so nervous his voice came out in a shaky whisper.

I leaned closer to him in order to hear his response.

After he divulged the whereabouts of his stash, I chuckled. "I lied about letting you live. Blame it on my upbringing."

I placed the banger against his head and squeezed the trigger twice. With the silencer, the gun barely made a coughing sound, but his blood splashed all over me. I ignore the sticky mess and rushed to retrieve the loot from where Richard said it was hid. If he had lied, I'd just have to search the entire house or take Richard's hands back to Rich Kid.

We didn't get back to Atlanta 'til four thirty in the morning. I went straight to the crib and crashed the fuck out. I had already showered thoroughly at the flop house in Alabama, so I was good on that.

I guessed that King went to report in to Rich Kid. And I figured since Rich Kid had my pager number, he'd page me when he was ready.

I slept 'til noon, woke up and went outside to a pay phone to call Lonnie. I let Lonnie know I was back and okay but I didn't mention anything about what had gone down.

I just said, "Everything is good."

"True dat," Lonnie replied. We hung up. I'd get at him later.

I went back to the crib and handled my hygiene, threw on some fresh gear and grilled two boneless chicken breasts on my George Foreman grill. I guzzled down a forty ounce with a grilled chicken breast sandwich.

I had stashed the upfront loot Rich Kid gave me in the freezer part of my refrigerator, inside several TV dinners. I retrieved all my loot and hit the streets ready to stunt.

I stopped by Brenda's and she wasn't home. At least that was what the dyke-looking female who answered the door said. I wasn't trippin' it. I ain't have no locks on Brenda.

I then dipped over to Poochie's thinking I'd jump up and down in her guts right quick, but Shan, my son, Shan's newborn brat and pussy-whupped ass Shotgun Pete was over there. Shotgun Pete was grilling me hard, like he wanted to test my hands again.

I stared him in the eyes and said, "Nigga, you don't want none of this." I lifted my shirt and gave him a glimpse of the tool on my waist.

Before things could escalate, Poochie pulled me aside. "Don't go back to prison over his punk ass," she whispered.

"I will if he make me. Fuck that lame!" I made sure my tone carried over to where he stood.

"Nigga, you're just bumping your gums. You know how to get at me if this is what you really want," he challenged.

"Oh, your time is coming. You can bet dat!" I said, and then I turned my attention to my son. "What's up with you, man?" I had Lil T a big smile.

"Nothing, Daddy." He smiled back.

I talked with my son for a few and jetted. Poochie hit me up an hour later and told me the coast was clear. I went back over there and fucked Poochie's ass damn near to death.

I bailed from her crib about midnight, stopped at the bottom of the hill on my way out of Englewood and bought some weed. Then, I went to my crib and got high by my damn self. Fuck it, I'd stunt some other night.

The next morning, the sound of my pager woke me up. The clock on the TV displayed 10 a.m.

Who the fuck is paging me so early?

I walked to the pay phone in the apartment complex in the same gear I had on yesterday. My braids were fucked up.

"This Youngblood. Who paged me?"

"Hey, baby. This is Brenda. You came by yesterday?"

"Where you paging me from?" I ignored Brenda's question to ask my own 'cause I hadn't recognized the number she was calling from.

She said, "I'm at home. I got a new number."

"Why you change your—nah, strike that," I said. "It ain't my business."

"Naw, it ain't even like that. It is your business. I just wanted a new number," Brenda lied, I assumed.

Why the fuck would anybody just want a new phone number? Whatever. I didn't own her ass.

Brenda stuttered something about why the girl answered her door yesterday.

"Yo, playgirl. I ain't keeping tabs on you. It's all good, you don't owe me no testimony."

"That's the problem!" Brenda cried. "I want to owe you an explanation. I need more from you than just sex and a phone call! Where you been the last few weeks? I been paging you and you don't call back. If all I'm going to ever be to you is a hole to stick your dick in, we might as well not see each other anymore!"

This bitch had caught me all off guard and hit me with a flurry of emotions.

"Slow down, shawdy." I said, hoping Brenda would pause and calm down. "Where all this drama coming from?"

Brenda snapped some more. “I was good to yo’ young ass while you were locked up! Is this how you repay me? You think all I need is to get fucked once in a while? Is that what the fuck you think makes me happy?”

This bitch is bananas. I hung the phone up on her ass.

As I walked back to the crib I laughed so hard I was crying.

Mafuckaz outside probably thought I was crazy. What I was really trippin’ on was that the only sure pussy I had now was Poochie. My baby’s mama’s mama. A forty-year-old crackhead trying to stay clean.

Ain’t life a bitch?

Rich Kid paged me later in the day and told me he’d be at my spot in thirty minutes.

Twenty minutes later, I answered the knock on my door and let in Rich Kid and King. The mattress I slept on in the living room was stood up against the wall, the way I kept it in the daytime.

I had no furniture so I couldn’t offer Rich Kid and King a seat, unless they were gonna sit on the big screen television.

Rich Kid made no comment about my empty apartment. He must’ve figured I liked living grimy or I’d furnish the crib when my pockets got heavy. The three of us stood in the living room, just us and the big screen, and the king-size mattress propped against the wall.

Rich Kid acknowledged that I’d done a good job in Alabama.

I’d brought back both the loot and the hands!

Acknowledging it now, I could still remember the feel of Richard’s blood and bits of his wrists bones splattering up in my face as I hacked his hands off with the machete.

Rich Kid handed me the rest of the money he owed me out of his pocket. A wad held together by a thick rubber band. I didn’t bother to count it. The nigga was too large to have to short me. I put the wad in my pocket. Rich Kid nodded at King and his loyal, big, black ass, right hand man tossed a brown shopping bag at my feet.

“That’s yours, too,” King said. He had a voice like a Rottweiler that matched his name and his face.

Rich Kid explained that the money I got from Richard had been way more than eighty grand. I had counted close to 200 stacks when I found it exactly where Richard told me it would be.

Rich Kid was saying, “You’re entitled to everything over the eighty grand you were paid to collect.”

“What about King?” I asked, wondering if King was entitled to a portion of the extra loot.

“He’s straight,” Rich Kid said. “I blessed him well.” King nodded down toward the shopping bag. “It’s all in there, everything over the eighty G’s.” I held my excitement in check while Rich Kid told me he’d be in touch soon.

The only thing I was thinking about was all that money inside the large shopping bag. I kinda wondered what Rich Kid had done with Richard’s hands, but I wasn’t about to ask him.

I walked Rich Kid and King out to the car. They were rolling in a plain whip today, keeping it low-key.

As soon as they turned out the complex’s parking lot, I dashed inside of the apartment to count the loot inside the shopping bag.

It came to fifty-three thousand dollars. Fifty-three neat stacks of a thousand dollars each.

I should’ve been gassed up, right? Fuck no! I was steaming. Rich Kid had said I was entitled to every dollar over the eighty grand he’d sent me to collect. Those were his words, not mine. And I held a man to his word.

Well, Rich Kid or King was full of shit. One of ‘em was shorting me. And they claimed I was the stickup kid? Rich Kid or King had just robbed me! I wouldn’t have sweat it if Rich Kid hadn’t said I was entitled to all the extra loot. I hadn’t expected anything more than what he’d originally agreed to pay me. I figured every dollar I recovered from Richard was rightfully Rich Kid’s loot since he’d spent mad time and cheddar looking for the idiot and had paid me, not knowing if I’d recover a dime of the eighty grand he was owed. But since Rich Kid said all extra was mine, I wanted my loot, all of it!

But which one of them had shorted me, Rich Kid or King?

One thing I was mafuckin' sure of: There'd been close to two hundred stacks of money in Richard's dryer in the basement. If all the stacks were a grand each, subtracting Rich Kid's eighty grand and the fifty-three grand they'd just given me, I'd been shorted about sixty thousand dollars.

Niggaz just won't keep it real. A'ight, they wanna play it like that!

I'd let it ride until I could figure out exactly which one of them niggaz had played me for a fool. I knew that if a nigga tried me once, he'd try me again. I'd be on point next time and the guilty one will find out that Youngblood don't take no shorts.

I packed the money inside some shoe boxes and stuck them inside the closet in the empty bedroom. My pockets were still swole with all the loot Rich Kid had paid me, as promised.

I dipped to Winn Dixie and bought two large boxes of frozen fried chicken, two half gallons of Minute Maid, some bread, ketchup and some more shit. I grabbed a notebook tablet, a small tablet of carbon paper, a box of envelopes and a Bic ink pen.

After paying the cashier, I stopped at the stamp machine and bought five postage stamps. On the way back to the crib, I stopped at Majik Market and filled up my gas tank, went inside and bought 5 five-hundred-dollar money orders. The cashier sweated my knot all the way back in my pocket.

At the crib, I put the groceries on the kitchen counter and pulled out the two boxes of frozen fried chicken. I popped six big pieces into the microwave and set the timer. I emptied the other pieces of chicken out the box into a large freezer bag. I did the same with the second box of chicken.

Then I went into the bedroom and got the money. I stuffed twenty-six stacks into one chicken box and closed it.

The other twenty-seven stacks of loot went inside the second chicken box. I took all the food out the freezer, put the two chicken boxes in the back of the freezer and then replaced the other frozen food back in front of the chicken boxes.

While the chicken in the microwave heated, I arranged carbon paper between four sheets of notebook paper so I could write five identical letters at once. I was just keeping my word. Keepin' it real.

Before I left prison I had promised five of my homeboys I would send them some loot as soon as I built my weight up on the turf. They were Brenda's brother, Kyree, the twins, Rafael and Rufus, two real soldiers from Bankhead serving elbows life for drug-related murders, a fool ass nigga from College Park named Tony, that sick nigga kept me trippin' the whole five-year bid and my lil' homie, Shortbread, who had life with no parole for killing and raping a white girl.

I had promised them I'd do something for 'em. I hadn't promised nobody else in there shit.

I began to write:

Yeah Nigga,

Whud up? I know y'all fools been draggin' my name in dirt (don't front!). You thought I was like those other fake niggaz who got out and didn't remember his dawgs still on locks. I told y'all I don't roll foul like dat. It took this long for me to get at you 'cause a nigga had to start from the ground up. Here's $500 to give you a little grip in there.

I ain't gon' tell you not to gamble with it, 'cause we all gotta do our own thing. Feel me?

I'm not rich out here, I ain't gon' even front like I am. I'm gonna maintain, though. I haven't even explored the rap thing. Fa real, as soon as I touched down I forgot all about becoming a MC. Shit, you know how I get down.

I didn't send no flicks 'cause I avoid cameras at all cost! Y'all know my steelo. I'm good, though.

I wish I could tell you I been fuckin' hos left and right, but that shit ain't a priority to me. I hit some guts, here and there, but for now I'm on a paper chase. I can't say when or if I'll holla at you again, dawg.

You know how uncertain the streets is. I just wanted to keep my word and do something for you. I ain't got no phone or address to give you to contact me. I got my own spot but I ain't putting that info on paper!

The address on the envelope is mad fake.

Yo, I'm 'bout to fuck this chicken up I just microwaved. I'll holla when I can. No more promises, though. You know how I roll. I might be dead tomorrow. Put blood on thi,s though, I ain't ever coming back there. From now on, court gets held in the street. Ya heard! I'm out.

Peace,
Youngblood.

On the letter addressed to Kyree I wrote:

P.S. Dawg, your peeps snapped on me! We gon' work it out, though. She's good people.

I took the chicken out the microwave and let it cool off, it was piping hot. I then found my five dawgs on lockdown info in some papers I kept in a leather pouch inside a pair of socks. I filled out the envelopes and put a letter and a five-hundred-dollar money order in each. I sealed each letter and put a stamp on them. After I finished eating, I took the five letters to the mailbox.

Now niggaz on locks couldn't say I was fake like the other cats that bounced and never kept their word or sent their homies in the joint shit.

I had kicked it with Kyree, the twins, Tony and lil' Shortbread every day in the joint. I knew they were bailed up with time and couldn't count on their fam' to always send them loot for commissary. The six of us put pain on some niggaz, so I couldn't just renege on my word to them.

Now my pockets were laced and my weight was up for the time being, but I wanted a fly whip, furniture and some other shit. Maybe I could afford to chill for a minute since money wasn't a thang. If Rich Kid hadn't brought me in on that work, I would've been hunting niggaz who slung rocks on the corner, trying to touch them for their lil' pocket stash.

My first inclination was to go to the rent office and pay my rent for about a year in advance. That way if hard times came, at least I'd have a place to lay my head, but I squashed that idea, though, 'cause how a stickup kid know if he'd still be alive in a year? Fuck it. I wasn't gon' jinx myself.

CHAPTER 14

Poochie got a three-bedroom, Section Eight apartment out in East Point. The neighborhood was slowly becoming ghetto, too, but for now it was way better than Englewood.

She told me her sons would be coming back to live with her after the school year, so I bought her new bedroom and living room furniture and gave her money to get a phone installed. I got a discount on her furniture 'cause I also bought furniture for my apartment.

I fixed up the one bedroom in my apartment for my son Lil' T, for whenever he came over. I would sleep on the couch in the living room. It costed me less than ten G's for all the furniture, Poochie's and mine. It wasn't like a nigga went furniture shopping out in Buckhead, at Haverty's or someplace like that.

After showering, I went by Lonnie's. There, I offered him some grip, but he said he was straight. "Keep your bread, fam. I'm sure you got plenty of shit to spend it on. I'm good."

"I feel you. But if you need anything, you know I got you. Anyway, I need to cop a whip. Something real nice," I told him.

"I know just the place you need to go. Let me hit my girl up and let her know the business so she don't be worried about a nigga. Then, we gonna take a ride," said Lonnie.

An hour later, we were on the highway.

We rode down to Fort Lauderdale, Florida to a DEA auction and I bought a Lexus truck for a bargain. It was silver with white interior and already rimmed-out. We took Blue, Delina's crackhead ex, with us to put the truck in his name. Then we hooked up the papers when we got back to Atlanta, like Blue had gave me the Lex truck as a gift.

Blue was just happy to get $250. None of that would've fooled the feds had they wanted to track the ownership of the truck. Blue would've certainly told them the deal had they stepped to him. But for now I was pushing a fly whip. The papers were all in my name.

Everything was proper if po-po ever pulled me over. It had cost over ten grand and they made Blue sign all types of shit. In Atlanta, he just transferred the title to me.

By now, Shan was letting Lil' T spend the night with me from time to time, depending on her mood. She'd just drop him off at Poochie's and I'd snatch him from there. I didn't go to Shan's crib and I didn't want her or Shotgun Pete to know where I laid my head.

Shan could see that I was comin' up, pushing a fly whip and shit. A few times she made little comments like she wanted to get with me, but I squashed that shit. ButWhenever I brushed her off, the dirty bitch wouldn't let my son spend the night with me until she was no longer mad.

I should've chin checked that bitch, but I wasn't trying to go there with her. When I beefed, somebody usually died. Shan wasn't worth that, I had paper to chase. Shit to accomplish.

That bitch had got on that powder, her and her nigga was strung-out on that raw. I wasn't letting two powder monsters bring me down. I was already killing them two fools, Shan and Pete, by comin' up and not letting 'em figure out how.

Small drama was trying to invade my space but I kept stiff-arming it away. Brenda came at me sideways, complaining that I never had time for her. I tried to handle her with kid gloves 'cause she was Kyree's peeps and even though he was locked down, I knew he talked to his sister regularly. I didn't want Kyree in the joint thinking I was out here draggin' his fam'. I had told him I would never get down like that. And if Brenda didn't force my hand, I planned to keep my word.

A coupla days later, she was all apologetic for snapping on me, telling me she had been stressed. I let her excuses roll off my back. I wasn't trippin' it. But I wasn't feelin' her anymore, either. She wanted some dick that night, but I wasn't going out like that. I knew if I started back fucking Brenda, I would see her jealous side again.

She was screaming that since I got my crib hooked up and my new whip I thought I owned the world.

"When yo' ass end up back in prison don't call me!" Brenda ranted and raved.

I squashed her anger with calmness. "Yo. What I owe you?" I reached in my pocket and pulled out some big faces and handed them to Brenda. "That oughta cover the loot you sent me while I was locked up." I was sincere.

Brenda went loco on a nigga. She threw the money back at me, started crying and cussing like that chick in the Exorcist.

"Yo, calm down." I reached for her shoulders.

"Don't fuckin' touch me!" Brenda screamed.

I had enough of playing Mr. Nice Guy. Kyree was my dawg, but his sister needed checkin'. I slapped that bitch so hard she did the snake. I backhanded her and she hit the floor.

"I ain't no weak nigga," I said calmly but with force, a tone a bitch respects. "I don't wanna cave yo' face in, but you can't come out yo' mouth anyway to a nigga." Brenda was holding her jaws in her hands, sniffing and looking dazed. I waited for her head to clear. "Damn! What's your problem?" I asked after she'd calmed down.

We talked for two hours. The bitch had issues only Jerry Springer could relate to.

CHAPTER 15

Lonnie put me down on a gambling house lick he was planning with two cats I didn't know and didn't wanna know. I trusted Lonnie, though. He could outline my role without me having to make friends with the other two dudes. Actually, it was four other cats, besides Lonnie and me, down on the lick. But two of them would be inside of the house gambling when the shit goes down. They were our key to getting into the house. So, only four of us would rock ski masks.

We ran up in that spot at two in the morning on a Saturday morning. Lonnie had a nine and a German Luger. I had a 12-gauge in my hand, to put fear in their hearts

Before we got everything under control in the house, a nigga tried to break for a mad dash to a back room, but Lonnie let the heater speak, stopping him in his tracks.

He busted dude in the back and watched him crumple to the floor. Walking up and standing over the bleeding man, Lonnie let his eyes case the room. "Anybody else wanna run!"

I then shot a fat man in the ass with buck shots just to let everybody know that at least two of us niggaz in ski masks would pull the trigger. I just hoped I hadn't shot one of the niggas who had helped set up the lick.

The two niggaz with us in ski masks started to take the jewelry off of the people in the gambling house. I shook my head at 'em, I had taken a fall for a move like that before.

I sliced at my throat, signing for them to kill that, but they took some jewelry anyway, despite my signal. *Fuck it!* They didn't know me and I didn't know them to really give a shit.

We had to move fast 'cause there weren't any silencers on our heaters. The gunshots might've been heard. So we were out of there in five minutes or less. I was sure we'd left some money behind, but we had to get up outta there.

The loot got split six ways evenly.

The next morning, I was back at my crib counting my cut. I had $4,950 and six books of food stamps. I'd give the food stamps to

Poochie later. I put three thousand in my freezer and I put the rest in my pocket with my other walk-around-with flow.

From there, I popped three boneless chicken breasts on the George Foreman grill and zzz'd out afterwards.

When I woke up later that Saturday evening, I took a shower and threw on some fresh gear and thought about some pussy. I could do that now. My freezer stash was a'ight. I still had loot left from that Alabama ordeal, plus the three G's I put with it earlier today. My pockets were laced, and I had a fly whip.

Who could I go fuck? Poochie, of course, but I wanted some new pussy—a young bitch with hard titties and a flat ass stomach. I dug around the crib until I found that red bitch's phone number I had met at the game room that day.

I looked on the piece of paper and found out her name was Cheryl.

I jetted to the pay phone.

"Hello?" A girl's voice. Mature. Probably a woman.

"Is Cheryl there?"

"Cheryl! Come get the phone! Hurry up. I gotta make a call!" I heard the phone being passed.

"This Cheryl. Who is this?"

"Youngblood," I answered.

"Youngblood? Where I know you from?"

I ran it down to her, explained when and how I had met her. The bitch met so many niggaz at the game room she couldn't remember me. She said, "Who you be with?"

"I be by my mafuckin' self. Who I need to be with, shawdy?" I was 'bout to blow.

"What you whippin'?" she pressed on.

"What?"

Cheryl smacked her lips like I must be stupid. "What kinda car you got?" She explained. I knew what *whippin'* meant, but I hadn't heard the bitch clearly.

"I ain't pushing nothing but a Lex truck," I understated.

"You got a Lexus truck?" Her interest soared. "What year is it?" I laughed.

"It's last year's," I admitted. "What? That ain't good enough fo' yo' ass to ride in?"

Cheryl laughed at that. "That's cool," she said. "I was just making sure you wasn't no buster."

I asked Cheryl if we could hook up and she told me I could pick her up in twenty minutes. I was like *whoa!* "That's too soon. I gotta go get my hair braided."

"Just c'mon, boy. I know how to braid hair."

Cheryl gave me her address and directions on how to get there. I still didn't think she knew who the fuck I was.

Cheryl stayed in a nice subdivision neighborhood, so her family had to be at least middle-class. As soon as I pulled in the driveway, Cheryl, with her fine red self, came out of the house and bum-rushed my whip. Cheryl got in the front seat.

"Hey," Cheryl spoke to me.

"Whud up?" I spoke back.

Cheryl wanted to swing by the game room but I wasn't having that. She wasn't about to sport me like a new pair of shoes. Ain't no tellin' how many niggas up in the game room had boned the bitch. They wasn't gon' be laughing at me. I'll fuck with the biggest slut in Atlanta, but I wouldn't sport her in public.

I didn't mind fucking a bitch with a ho's rep. Poochie wasn't Virgin Mary and Shan wasn't either when I was holding her down. It's all good to me.

We rented some movies from Blockbuster; I drove to the hood to cop some weed and grab a coupl'a rib dinners and then went to the crib.

I smoked two blunts with Cheryl while she braided my hair and talked my ears off.

This bitch claimed to know everybody. She was dropping names left and right.

Do you know such and such shot such and such over a bitch? Freddie and his crew almost got into it with some niggaz from New York in the game room last week. John Henry from Godby Road ran off with a block of Bay Bay's dope.

And on, and on, and on…

"You know Rich Kid?" Cheryl asked, not stopping for breath.

"I don't know nobody, shawdy," I said. My ears were smoking, begging for her to shut up.

"You don't know Rich Kid? Them boys you bought that weed from in Englewood work for him. He got that spot locked with weed and crack. He got spots all over."

"Do your mouth ever close?" I asked sarcastically.

Cheryl shut up for a minute and kept braiding my hair. The silence was killing her ass, so she broke the silence after a while.

"Well, if you don't want me to talk, you say something, then."

"Something."

"Oh. You trying to be funny?" She pushed me in the back of the head.

"A'ight, you gon' get beat down?" I said jokingly.

"I ain't scared. As long as you fuck me good after you beat me up." That fucked my head up more than the weed. Cheryl was cool, she just talked too much.

When my braids were hooked up, we finished smoking another blunt, then Cheryl heated the BBQ dinners in the microwave, making herself at home.

While we were fucking the ribs up, Cheryl said, "That was you talking to Freddie that day in the game room when he was gonna make that girl kiss you."

Her ass finally figured out who the fuck I was, I thought.

"Yeah, that was me."

"You clowned the heck out of her," she laughed, laying her head on my shoulder affectionately.

"Nah, she clowned herself."

"Tsk!"

"That's exactly how I feel."

"I bet you do." Cheryl smacked her lips.

"Gimme some of those juicy ass lips you're smacking," I said.

"Nope, I wanna watch TV." She played hard but I knew I would break through her tough act.

We watched half of a movie and then just like I thought, I was all up in Cheryl's guts.

I busted quick, but I was ready to go back again.

"I gotta pee," Cheryl said, making my dick deflate. She got up and headed to the bathroom.

Almost fifteen minutes passed and she hadn't returned, which seemed a little strange to me.

I went to check on her, and Cheryl was all off in the bedroom I had fixed up for my son.

I crept up behind her and asked, "What you doing?" She didn't even flinch.

"Making sure don't no bitch live here with you!" Then she pressed her naked body against mine.

"C'mon. Do it to me against the wall," Cheryl whispered before sticking her tongue down my throat. She felt between my legs. "Can it get hard again?"

"You gotta help it," I hinted.

"You trying to get me to suck yo' dick," Cheryl cooed before going to her knees.

The sun was just coming up when I took Cheryl home. On the way to her house, she talked me out of fifty dollars to get her hair fixed. I was too tired to refuse her. I would've paid her five hundred just to shut up. The way I saw it, I saved $450.

Before she opened the door to leave, I promised to get with her again later in the day.

"I'ma page you this evening. Don't be taking all year to call me back, either!" Cheryl said.

"Just page me. I'll hit you right back, shawdy." I was tired as hell.

She had drained a nigga. She leaned over and tried to tongue me before she got out the car. I turned my head. "Ain't neither one of us brushed our grill," I reminded her.

"You trippin', boy! Dag." She got out the car. "Don't forget I'ma page you later. You better call me right back, nigga! My code is three sixes."

"I know. Just like the devil," I said.

"Bye." I guess Cheryl hadn't heard my fly remark.

"I'll get at cha later, shawdy." I dipped.

Later that evening, I was rolling incognito in the Nissan when Cheryl paged me. I pulled up to one of those pay phones I could use without having to get out of my car.

"Yo. Who paged Youngblood?"

"It's me! Cheryl! Who the hell else put 666 in yo' pager?"

"What's up, shawdy," I laughed. "Where you at?"

"I'm over my friend's house in College Park. You know where the K-Mart at?"

"Yeah."

"She live in the apartments across from K-Mart. Building L. I'll be on the porch. Hurry up, don't have me waiting on yo' ass all day! So tell that other bitch her time is up."

"What other bitch?" I laughed.

"The one that can't fuck like I can," Cheryl said.

I heard a bunch of girls laughing in the background.

"I'm on my way, shawdy."

"You can't be 'cause you still on the phone," Cheryl jammed.

I couldn't do shit but laugh. I couldn't even front, I liked that pretty, red bitch. Not enough to lose focus on business and shit, never like that, but I liked her.

I pulled up in front of the apartment where Cheryl and a bunch of girls were standing and honked my horn. They strained to see who I was. I guess Cheryl was expecting me to be pushing my Lex truck.

When she realized it was me in the Maxima, she came over to the car oozing mad attitude.

"Why you ain't driving your truck?" Hands on her hips.

I said, "'Cause I'm driving this. I can't drive two cars at once. I'm bad, but not that bad."

"Why you always trying to be funny? Dag. I wanted my girls to see your whip," Cheryl admitted with no shame whatsoever.

I hunched my shoulders as to say, *Oh well.*

Cheryl told me she'd be right back and then she ran back over to her girls and told them something. I couldn't hear what she was saying, but I was betting she had explained to them that I'd left the Lex truck at home. Probably putting it in a way that left her girls thinking I pushed some kind of different whip every day and the Nissan was just for when I was handling business.

I knew Cheryl's kind. She probably bragged all day to her friends about my Lex truck, even probably hyped me up a little to make it seem like she had snagged a major baller. Cheryl had probably told her friends everything, and then some. That was, everything except that she had gave me some head last night. Then again, she might've told 'em that, too.

Cheryl talked the entire ride to my crib.

Once we were inside of my apartment and chillin', I asked her why she had got weave put in her hair. She hadn't had any weave last night.

"It's just a hairstyle. Dang."

"But it makes you look ghetto. All that different color shit. I liked your shit natural." I meant that.

"You want me to get the weave took out?"

"Nah, you ain't gotta do that. But I don't understand why shorties like you, from the suburbs, be trying so hard to look and act like y'all from the hood? Who told you it was glamorous to be a hoodrat?" I asked, hoping to get Cheryl to check herself.

Cheryl wasn't feelin' me, though. Or else she was just committed to being a hood rat, like I was committed to the robbery game. She smacked her lips, pulled a small compact mirror out of her Coach bag and checked herself.

"Ain't nothin' wrong with my hair. Anyway, why you always got something smart or negative to say? Yo' ass wasn't complaining when we was fuckin' last night." Fuck it. I figured the hood ain't the only place that bred rats.

Cheryl was red, thick and fine, sucked mean dick and moaned like my joint was a baseball bat when I fucked her. I couldn't judge Cheryl, though, my baby's mama was a rat, too.

Playgirl was cool to kick it with, and we hung out every day over the next few weeks. Cheryl wasn't like most rats in one way, though.

She wasn't always beggin' for cheese, which was fine with me.

CHAPTER 16

Rich Kid hadn't got at me, yet. And although I still had a nice stash in the freezer, I was itching for another lick.

A few nights me and Lonnie cased out this dope boy named Money Mark, but it was hard to follow him 'cause he always rolled with a crew, four cars deep.

The car with Money Mark in it would turn off from the other cars unexpectedly and then the rear car in the caravan would damn near come to a complete stop, making sure no other cars could follow Money Mark until he disappeared.

I recorded his movements in my mental, and then sat robbing him on the backburner for another day. When I wasn't plotting a jack move, chillin' with Cheryl or rollin' with Lonnie, I'd go by Poochie's spot and play house with her. We had that kind of uncomplicated understanding.

Poochie was staying off the pipe, working mad hours and getting her shit on point. Some days I'd wanna get with Poochie but she'd have to work, so I'd hit a quickie and drop her off at her job. I'd watch her walk away from my car, and I'd be thinking she really was starting to look like Toni Braxton. *For real.* And I hadn't been high on weed.

One day my pager started beeping and I recognized Rich Kid's code. I dipped to a pay phone to hit him up.

"Yo. Whud up, Money?" I asked when he answered.

"Youngblood?"

"It sho' ain't the Easter Bunny," I cracked lamely. Rich Kid let my attempt at humor roll off his back.

"Meet me in Englewood," Rich Kid said with the air of authority his major dope boy status gave him in the hood, and amongst niggaz like me, looking to come up.

This time there were no King and other niggaz from Rich Kid's crew awaiting my arrival. None of that patting me down routine, etcetera, etcetera.

Rich Kid and I arrived in front of Poochie's old apartment at the same time. I was in my truck. Rich Kid was the passenger in a big boy Benz. A fine jet-black honey was pushin' his whip.

Rich Kid stepped out, walked over to my truck and got in. I guess he trusted me after the job I had done for him in Alabama.

Still, I could see the print of a heater in the waistline of Rich Kids pants, under the silk shirt he wore untucked. I peeped his profile: Rich Kid stayed sharp everytime I'd seen him. He didn't rock baggy jeans, big jerseys, Timbs or other b-boy, rap gear. Rich Kid rocked silk, rayon and shit foreign to me such as 'gator belts and shoes and mad Sean John hookups. Even Armani and other fly shit that exclamated his major baller status.

Rich Kid was only five years older than me, but he had the presence of a nigga twice his age. Some people were just born *grown*. Plus, he had blown up so large while I was in prison, his success just hyped his style even more. I wasn't all on his dick, though. I despised jock riders. Yet I was not a hater, I gave props to any nigga that mastered his game. The streets was a dog eat dog. The Big Dog ate first and left the scraps and crumbs for the puppies. Rich Kid was already a Big Dog, regulating shit. I had to give him his props.

"Whud up, lil' nigga?" he greeted me.

I said, "You tell me. You da Big Dog, toss a puppy a crumb."

"Big Dogs were once puppies themselves, Youngblood. Stay real with those who are real to you and you'll grow. Bet blood on that," Rich Kid shot back.

"True dat," I agreed.

"Pull up your shirt," Rich Kid said, matter of fact, though I digested it as an order.

I hesitated, not because I didn't understand what Rich Kid was stressing, but he had come from out of left-field, catching me off guard.

"Pull up your shit, lil' nigga," he repeated. When I did, he looked me over and then patted me down, running his hands over my body, making a nigga uncomfortable. "Just making sure you ain't wired," stated Rich Kid.

It blowed me to know that dude could even consider me capable of being an informant, especially after what I'd done for him already. Not to mention I'd done juvenile time and time in the pen, never rolling over on anybody.

"Let's get one thing straight," I said, feeling like I'd been disrespected. Big Dog or not, this nigga was out of bounds. "I ain't never snitched or informed on friend or enemy!" I continued angrily. "If you think I'm suspect, we got no rap for each other."

"Calm yourself, Youngblood," Rich Kid responded without any change of expression or demeanor. "A nigga in my position can't afford to take things for granted. I get caught slippin', I fall and bust my head."

Rich Kid went on to explain that many boss hustlers were in the Feds doing stiff time because those they trusted had turned informant.

He further explained that he hadn't seen me in months and I could've gotten knocked and was willing to rat my way out of going back to prison.

"If Sammy the Bull can turn on Gotti, anybody can turn informant," Rich Kid reasoned. I saw his point but I wasn't no goddamn snitch. "Don't trip it, lil' nigga. If you ain't got nothing to hide, you should never be vexed if I ask to check. Feel me?"

"I guess," I relented.

"Anyway, let's step out the car and rap about a lil' business." Rich Kid told me that he wanted me to slump this dope boy who was dropping weight in some of his territories and making the block hot 'cause the dope boy didn't have an organized crew.

He just fronted dope to niggaz and let them go for self. Slangin' crack wasn't my hustle, but I understood what Rich Kid was stressing and how dropping weight on a block, without a crew handling it, could fuck up the scene. See, when a crew was holding down a hood, the game was in check.

All the dope on the block was the same quality, same size rocks. The sellers are usually working on a weekly salary, so there' was no beef over who a crackhead brought from. All the loot ended up going to the same Big Dog anyway.

But when niggaz rolled solo on the same block with a crew of slangers, there was gonna be mad beef. The niggaz rollin' solo gotta slang hard, 'cause their pay was predicated on how much they sold.

They tried to short-stop customers before they get to the regular crew slangers. That led to pistol play, which brought the heat, the cops.

And that was only one of the problems independent slangers caused a crew. There was a list of others.

Of course, independent slangers had their problems. They lacked the protection a crew offered. It was a simple case of numbers. A robber would rather draw down on one nigga than a gang of 'em.

I knew Rich Kid could solve his problem by ordering his crew to ride dirty on the solo niggaz go to war, wipe them out one by one until the others were afraid to show up on the block. But turf wars brought around-the-clock heat from the po-po, which meant loot couldn't be made. Rich Kid wasn't having that. So he'd decided to eliminate the dope boy who was supplying the solo slangers. Smart move.

"You'll probably need a partner," said Rich Kid. I immediately thought of Lonnie. "You can use Lonnie. Y'all still cool, right?" h

"No doubt," I confirmed.

"Don't tell him I'm involved, though. Our business ain't his." Rich Kid said with emphasis.

I nodded in agreement.

Rich Kid looked me in the eyes. I guess he was trying to read me on whether I'd tell Lonnie who had hired us or not. I would give Lonnie the heads up, but I doubt it showed in my eyes. Shit, I trusted Lonnie more than I trusted Rich Kid, or anyone else in the world.

"Who's the lucky fellow?" I asked, wanting the name of the nigga who was about to die but didn't know it.

The nigga was probably somewhere planning shit for next week, next month. Maybe even for next year, while we plotted the termination of his life in a fifteen or twenty-minute meeting.

"You know that nigga Freddie?"

"Which Freddie?" I asked, to be sure.

"Freddie who's supposed to be kin to Hannibal," Rich Kid clarified.

My head dropped. There went a lick down the drain.

"I can't do it," I said clearly.

"Huh?"

Rich Kid looked at me like he didn't comprehend.

"I can't do it," I repeated.

Without divulging any details of the thing I'd done for Freddie, I explained to Rich Kid that I had put in work for Freddie in the past and I never did dirt to a man I've done work for, unless that man did dirt to me first.

It was like this: I considered it foul to hit somebody for Freddie and then turn around and hit Freddie for someone else. I'd be eliminating future business if I smoked Freddie. But more importantly, it went against my principles. Rich Kid had to respect that, 'cause it also meant I wouldn't hit Rich Kid for anyone, unless he did me a bad first.

"I feel you," he said, respectfully. "I didn't know y'all were like that."

"We ain't like nothing, but business." I could see the wheels turning in Rich Kid's head. Finally, he spoke. "I wouldn't want you to tell Freddie what's in store for him.

"Freddie's a big boy, he has to look out for himself." And I meant that. It wasn't my beef.

"Good." Rich Kid nodded, wheels still spinning. "What if it was me?" he asked. "Would you tell me somebody was gonna hit me?"

I didn't have to think about my answer, I spoke up quickly, "Nah, you're a big boy, too. You can handle whatever comes your way."

"Most definitely." He dapped me up and we parted ways.

As I drove back to my crib, I shook my head at the fickleness of life. How the pieces and players came together; how a nigga could be on death row and not even know it. I wondered what possessed Freddie to drop weight in Rich Kid's territory. Was it greed? Probably. Was it stupidity? Definitely. Unless Freddie thought Rich Kid was slippin', growing soft.

Sometimes too much ghetto success did that to a nigga. He started figuring he had too much to lose to kill a nigga over turf. That was usually when he got killed himself, if he stayed in the game.

I didn't know what made niggaz choose the dope game years ago, and I still didn't have the answer.

All I knew were three things: the dope game still wasn't for me. Freddie was living on borrowed time and I was 'bout to go by Poochie's and get my fuck on.

CHAPTER 17

When I called Poochie from the pay phone, she told me she was waiting on a cab to come take her to the hospital.

Shotgun Pete had jumped on Shan and beat her up really bad.

"Where's Lil' T?" That was my only concern. *Fuck Shan!* I couldn't care less if she died.

"Shan's neighbor is keeping him," Poochie said.

"Call them and tell 'em I'm coming by to get my son."

"Okay. But don't go over there and get into it with ugly ass Pete," Poochie warned.

She could've saved the wind it took to say those few words. That was the last thing in the world on my mind. But I didn't say that to Poochie. Shan was still her daughter. Besides, I was struggling not to laugh.

I shot by Cheryl's and scooped her up before going to get Lil' T.

Back at my crib, all of us were eating McDonald's, Lil' T said, "Daddy? You got a bunch of girlfriends."

"Boy, shut your bad ass up!" I told him, laughing my ass off. I didn't know where he got that shit from, he'd only met Brenda and Cheryl. And Brenda was history.

"Don't tell him to shut up 'cause he telling on yo' ass. What's your daddy's other girlfriend's names, Lil' T?" Cheryl fed him some of her French fries, trying to make my son snitch.

Lil' T ate her french fries, although he had his own. Then he said, "I don't know. He ain't got no other girlfriends." Flippin' the script on Cheryl and playing the bitch out of her fries.

Cheryl and my son fought for my attention through two movies I'd rented. Lil' T wanted to sit on my lap and tell me about his mommy and Pete fighting. Cheryl wanted to lay her head on my shoulder and tell me everybody's business.

Finally, Lil' T went to sleep. I carried him back to the bedroom, undressed him and put him to bed. I'd make him bathe in the morning.

As soon as I came back in the living room and sat on the couch, Cheryl was all on me, like chest hairs. I kissed her lil' hot ass. I wanted to fuck, too.

She said, "I love you." I tried to play deaf. "Did you hear me?" she whispered, looking up at me with big, brown doe eyes. "I said, I love you."

"Damn! Why you gotta go there?" I didn't know what else to say.

"'Cause I do love you," she insisted.

I covered her mouth with my hand. "Don't tell nobody," I whispered, but Cheryl wasn't letting me out that easy.

"Do you love me back?" she prodded.

"Let's discuss it when my dick ain't so hard. I'll say anything while my nuts are hot," I laughed, hoping to change the vibe.

"You always trying to be funny. Dag," Cheryl pouted.

"I can't get none of that good stuff?" I rubbed between her legs.

"Tell me you love me." She rubbed between mine.

We went back and forth like this for what seemed like forever.

Finally, my dick was about to break, it was so hard. Our clothes were unbuttoned.

"I love you," I submitted. By now we both were damn near naked, so I couldn't hold out any longer.

"Show me," Cheryl purred, low and sexy as hell. She lay back on the couch and opened her legs wide.

I hadn't eaten her pussy before, but I was hungry to do it tonight. I was pretty sure Cheryl hadn't been spreading it around since we'd hooked up. Pretty sure, but not absolutely, 'cause a nigga never knew 'bout a bitch. You could keep them locked in a bathroom, and they'd fuck out the window if they wanted to fuck around.

I gave the pussy the *stinky finger* test. It passed so I proceeded on.

I kissed my way down that pretty red body, taking my time so Cheryl would be good and wet and hot when I got down to that pussy and the magic little button. Shan's bitch ass had taught me that.

I licked and teased until Cheryl was moaning and pushing my head. I teased her some more. She tried to force my mouth down to the pussy. But I skipped right by it and licked the inside of her thighs.

She was damn near crying.

"Pleeeaaasse! Stop teasing me, baby!" Cheryl moaned.

I stopped teasing.

Cheryl screamed so loud she scared me. But it made me feel ten-feet tall. The bitch wasn't faking, either. Her legs were shaking and she was crying, mumbling crazy shit.

"Why you doing me like this? You gon' leave me and break my heart. Oouuu—Ahhhh—Damn!"

I stuck my finger up her ass and sucked on her clit. Her knees clamped my head like a vise grip.

"I'm cuming!" she moaned. "Ahhh—Ahhh_Ahhh—Shit—Ahhh!"

When Cheryl calmed down, my face felt like a glazed doughnut.

After she regained her senses, I came up and kissed her. She tapped me on my shoulder and said, "Look."

Lil' T was standing there looking at us!

"Daddy? What you was doing between her legs?" I didn't know what else to say, so I told him Cheryl was sick and I was checking her temperature.

"What?" he said like his lil' ass didn't believe me.

"She got a fever. I had to check her temperature," I lied again.

"Oh," my son said. Like he hadn't heard me the first time.

I just hoped Shan or Poochie never caught a fever and told Lil' T. He might ask to check their *temperature*.

Lil' T wouldn't go back to sleep for shit. I knew his lil' ass was sleepy.

I was 'bout to die! So Cheryl got a blanket, laid her head on my lap and covered herself with the blanket so my son couldn't see what she was doing. I distracted Lil' T by pretending like I was watching TV with him while Cheryl gave me some head. That had me busting in five minutes. Then I went to sleep on both of them.

Two days later, when I dropped Lil' T off at Poochie's crib, Shan was there with her little baby. Shan's face was fucked up! Both her eyes were black and her nose was fractured. Her lips were swollen so big they looked like a baseball catcher's mitt. She tried to turn her head away from me and Lil' T when we walked into the apartment.

I didn't say shit to her. I spoke to Poochie.

With her head turned away, Shan mumbled through her bubble lips, "Why didn't you let him stay with you 'til my face went down? I didn't want him to see me like this." Sounded like she was crying.

I said, "Yo' face might never go down."

"If it do, that nigga gon' swell it up again," Poochie added. Shan couldn't say shit.

Lil' T went to his mama and hugged her. Shan was a stank bitch to me. To Lil' T, she was the world.

Poochie took the little baby from Shan and tended to it. Honestly, I didn't even know if that baby was a girl or boy. I damn sho' ain't know its name. It was Lil' T's sister or brother, but it was zero to me. That's just the truth about how I felt.

Lil' T was asking Shan a hundred questions, trying to touch her black and blue face. She was crying, head down.

I wanted to laugh.

After leaving Poochie's apartment, I stopped at the corner store to buy some phillies. It tripped me out when I ran into one of Shan's dope boy-chasing girlfriends, and she had the nerve to ask me if I was gonna step to Shotgun Pete 'bout beating up Shan.

"That ain't my biz," I said. "Shan chose the nigga. Now she is getting what she gets."

"She still yo' baby mama."

"So! She got a baby by Pete, too," I reminded Shan's friend.

"He only be jumping on her 'cause he know she wanna leave his ugly ass and get back with you," the friend claimed.

I laughed. "I'll stick my dick in a pit bull's mouth before I fuck with Shan again," I made it clear.

"Why you trippin'? Everybody makes mistakes. That girl still loves you, she tell me that all the time."

"Too bad. I don't love her."

"Youngblood, you got a lot of nerve being mad at Shan. You fucked her mama." She said like she was there.

I can lie with the best of 'em, though. "Bitch, you done bumped yo' head! I wouldn't fuck Poochie wit' yo' dick!" I swore, straight-faced.

"I don't have a dick, nigga! But you fucked Poochie wit' yours!" She fired right back at me.

"Where you and Shan get that shit from?"

"Pete told Shan about it. He said you used to tell him and Lonnie about it all the time," the friend confessed.

"Like that nigga tongue is notarized!" I was pissed that Shotgun Pete would go that route to get Shan.

What else would he tell to get what he wanted? I knew I would kill that nigga one day; I just didn't know when.

I really didn't hear the rest of playgirl's rap, 'cause she could politic for Shan forever, but I wasn't taking that bitch back. A nigga had to have principles he wouldn't break for nobody, but Shotgun Pete wasn't built like that. His bitch ass was flawed to the core.

It's cool. Ima deal with his ass before it's all said and done, I promised myself.

A few days later, I ran across Shotgun Pete at a BP gas station. The nigga looked bad. He'd been ugly from day one, but dude was rawed out. I mean, he damn near looked like a crackhead. He was putting gas in a beat up, old Impala with only two hubcaps. I was pushing my Lex truck with Cheryl riding shotgun, looking like Beyoncé from Destiny's Child.

As if on cue, Cheryl got out the whip and strutted inside of the gas station.

I saw Shotgun Pete sweating her on the low.

Without provocation he said, "You got beef with me?"

I mean-mugged him for a full minute before I spat back. "If I had beef with you, you wouldn't have to ask me. Bet blood on that." My voice didn't waver. I was strapped. I assumed he was, too.

He got in his hooptie and drove off. Probably going to swell Shan's face up again, taking out on her what he wished he could do to me.

I wasn't a bitch, though. He knew our next encounter was gonna end with one of us dead.

I don't know what Shotgun Pete's problem was. It couldn't be jealousy. I didn't have shit he couldn't get with one good caper.

Well, I had one thing Shotgun Pete didn't have and couldn't get with a pistol.

I had principles.

I wouldn't snitch on my partner to get his bitch. Pussy come and go. True dawgs were blood in, blood out, which proved to me Pete wasn't true.

Niggaz told me as soon as I caught my bid, slimey ass Shotgun Pete began checkin' for my bitch. Well, him and Shan deserved each other, they were two peas in a pod. Neither one of them were fit to be on my team.

Snake bastards!

CHAPTER 18

Everywhere I went niggaz were talking about one thing, and one thing only. It was all over the news, too.

Freddie La Mint DeFabio, a woman named Erline Brown, and her four-year-old son, Joshua Brown, were found shot to death, execution style in Erline's house. Police suspected robbery as the motive.

The streets did, too.

Rumor had it that Freddie's uncle, Hannibal, was offering big loot for the identity of his nephew's killer. I didn't like hearing that 'cause I wasn't sure if Rich Kid believed he could trust me not to drop a dime on him for the dough. But he could. I didn't roll foul like that.

But did Rich Kid believe that? That was the million-dollar question. Whether, it was a life and death situation, Rich Kid's ace, King, knew where I laid my head and I wasn't hard to find in the city.

My comfort was in knowing I was true to my principles and hoping Rich Kid had no doubts about that after I'd refused a fat payday to hit Freddie because I'd once done work for him. I hadn't even warned Freddie his life wasn't worth a crackhead's credit. I was out of it from both ends.

When I hooked up with Cheryl that night she was like CNN.

"You heard about Freddie?" She hadn't been in the car two seconds.

"Naw," I lied, of course.

"They found him dead! They say somebody blew his whole head off. He gon' have to have a closed-casket funeral. And the girl they found dead with him, they shot her in the head three times. She wasn't but nineteen years old! They even killed her four-year-old son!

"That's a shame. You think Freddie's uncle, Hannibal, gon' find out who did it and do the same thing to them? I hope he do, 'cause whoever did it should'na killed that girl and her baby. They ain't sell no dope."

I didn't say shit.

Cheryl said, "What if somebody killed me 'cause you be selling dope?"

"You ever saw me sell any mafuckin' dope?" My words had acid on 'em.

Cheryl came right back at me. "Nope, but I ain't ever seen you go to work, either."

"So," I said. "Tommy ain't have no job, and he wasn't sellin' dope."

"Tommy who?" Cheryl asked.

"Tommy on the Martin Lawrence show," I countered, trying not to laugh.

"What?" Cheryl said instinctively before catching on. "Aww, shit! Why you play so much? That was a damn comedy show! I'm serious. Dag."

Niggas said, *"Freddie's funeral was da bomb."*

Ain't that a bitch? Only fools out the hood would say some ill shit like that, mostly bitches.

Dude was dead. Gone forever. His peeps probably crying and mafuckaz all they can think to say was *Freddie's funeral was da bomb* 'cause he was buried in an expensive casket with mad flowers around it.

The church was packed with fly hos and many players, big and small. Outside was a car show—Benzes, mad custom SUVs, Acura's, tricked-out Lexus' and a few double Rs. Freddie's babies' mamas were trying to outcry each other. Two of them got into a fight at the cemetery. But a third girl was five months pregnant with another one of Freddie's kids.

I heard all of this from Cheryl first, her nosy ass wouldn't have missed the funeral for shit. But the streets were saying the same thing.

I shook my head at it all. Niggaz in the streets got killed so often it didn't phase mafuckaz anymore. The shit was damn near like a movie, entertainment. I wondered why people had funerals at a church when the mafucka laying in the casket hadn't gone to church since church came to him.

Is there a heaven for a G? I wondered.

Several days later that thought was still on my mind. Me and Lonnie were headed down to a little country town in South Georgia called Valdosta to do a reverse caper on some country ass dope boys.

Usually, a stickup kid robbed a dope boy by pretending he wanted to buy some weight and then he jacked the dope boy for his product. But in a reverse caper, the stickup kid pretended to be the dope boy selling the weight and did the robbery from there.

I didn't know how Lonnie found his marks because because he never told me anything I didn't absolutely have to know. All I knew was we were headed to Valdosta in a fly ass whip that didn't belong to either of us. The Porsche we were pushing couldn't have been a rental 'cause it was tricked-out, chrome rims and all. A fly whip was necessary to convince the country dope boys that we were big-time dealers from the city, which really was some backwards shit.

We were rockin' ice, fly gear and carrying cell phones all arranged by Lonnie. We looked like the absolute perfect picture of kingpins.

But if that was really the case, would we roll into a little country spot like Valdosta broadcasting it by our appearance?

No.

We'd roll low-key, not wanting to attract attention, but most dope boys didn't see it like that. They figured the nigga with the flyest whip and most bling-bling had to be true in the game or he wouldn't have so much shine. It was like the average nigga wasn't gon' trust a man to hook him up with a honey if his bitch was wack. Lonnie understood that mindset and he played on it.

When we reached the motel in Valdosta, Lonnie's girl, Delina, was already there. She let us in the room, gave Lonnie the room keys, and jetted.

Boxes and bags were stacked in a corner. Later, I watched Lonnie open those boxes and bags, and he pulled out rolls of wide red tape, squares of drywall, a triple-beam scale and other shit needed to hook up dummy kilos of cocaine. It took hours.

Lonnie made sure each *kilo* weighed precisely one thousand grams and wrapped perfectly. He made six perfect kilos. Then he reached under the bed and pulled out a bag that contained the one real kilo of cocaine. The bait.

Lonnie used the cell phone to call the marks. I was sure the cell phone wasn't registered to Lonnie or anyone who could be traced to him and would be destroyed as soon as this caper was over.

"It's on for tomorrow," Lonnie said after he ended the call.

He ran down the caper again, explaining what we'd do if different situations developed. If we handled it correctly, the worst that could happen was the marks might not bite because we refused to let them inspect all of the kilos. But if shit went smoothly, we'd get $126,000.00, eighteen G's per kilo, which would be a sweet lick for Lonnie and me. But a bad day for the Valdosta dope boys. They'd have one real kilo and six kilos of drywall and lactose powder.

The plan was to meet with the Valdosta dope boys outside at a park or in a small parking lot. That way we all would feel comfortable by the casual passerby. A robbery planned by either side was less likely to go down in a public place, in the light of day, where there would be dozens of witnesses.

Most sell-and-buy robberies took place indoors, but we didn't want the Valdosta boys to know we were at the motel and we definitely didn't want to invite them to our room and try to jack them from inside. No doubt they'd come strapped. At least two of them would want to come inside while others would probably be parked outside, ready to blast anyone coming out the motel room without their Valdosta partners.

Taking the money from niggaz wasn't but a third of the game. The other two-thirds was getting away from the scene with the loot and not getting hunted down and killed over it later. The last part being more difficult, in this instance, 'cause we wouldn't be wearing ski masks. We were gonna jack these country niggaz without using a mask or a gun.

Of course we weren't gonna use our real names, and they wouldn't know where to begin looking for us in Atlanta. If they just came to the city asking a bunch of questions, describing Lonnie and me, we'd find them before they would find us.

I had to hand it to Lonnie, he had it well planned out. I just hoped the one real kilo would make 'em bite.

The next morning, we cleaned up the motel room, checked-out and met the Valdosta dope boys at a restaurant in a mall. I didn't know if there was more than one mall in Valdosta, but Lonnie found it with no problem.

There were three dudes waiting for us inside of Piccadilly's. We sat at a table in a corner, all of us. Lonnie introduced me as *Popeye.* I already knew the Valdosta dudes thought Lonnie's name was *Tennessee.*

The dude doing the talking for the Valdosta crew said his name was Disco. I wondered if he was gonna break out with some John Travolta shit.

We all ordered burgers, just to not look suspicious.

"Everything all right?" Disco asked Lonnie.

"I got seven pretty ass pit bulls in my trunk," Lonnie said. "You got the paper?"

Disco bit into his burger and chewed and talked at the same time. "Yeah, I got the loot. But I'm 'bout ten G's short."

Lonnie stood up from the table and said to me calmly, "Let's go, Popeye." He then turned to Disco and said. "Get in touch with me when your paper is proper, like we agreed on. I came a long way for nothing, I guess." We both started to walk off.

"Tennessee!" Disco called Lonnie back to the table. I followed.

"Loosen up, playboy. I got the whole one-twenty-six." Disco smiled. A mouth full of gold.

The Valdosta crew ate their whole orders. Lonnie ate most of his.

I was too amped-up to eat. I just sipped on a Sprite.

After eating, we all walked out together to the parking lot. The biggest nigga out of the Valdosta-three stayed at our car with us, while Disco and the other one went to get their car and pull it around next to ours.

The two pulled up in a Ford Expedition, followed by a third dude in a small black car. He stopped four or five car spaces away from us all, their last line of defense.

We were outnumbered four to two.

Lonnie popped the Porsche's trunk and then reached in the trunk and unzipped a tennis bag, displaying the seven kilos. I stood shotgun, hands folded over my waist, inches from my heater.

Disco peeked inside of the trunk at the kilos.

"Can I bust one of 'em open?" he asked Lonnie.

"Do it fast, I don't wanna get jammed in y'all lil' country town," Lonnie said with cool. Then he reached in the tennis bag and handed Disco one of the kilos.

I touched my heater, just in case Lonnie had grabbed one of the fake kilos. Disco leaned over into the trunk to keep from exposing the kilo of cocaine to any passing shopper. He dug a hole in the side of the kilo and his finger came out crystal white. He tasted the substance on his finger and then nodded his head. The car that had been five spaces away slowly approached. The driver handed Disco three bags out the window, and Disco passed them to Lonnie. I was missing not a move by no one. Neither was Disco's crew.

Lonnie peeked inside of each bag, sticking his hand inside each to feel through the money. There was no way he could count it out there in the parking lot, which was perfect for Lonnie and I, 'cause it also meant there was no way Disco could check each of the seven kilos. That's why Lonnie wanted the sell to go down outside. In a motel room, Disco would've checked each brick.

Lonnie tossed the bags of money inside of the trunk and handed Disco the tennis bag with the kilos in it.

He said, "I'll call you if the loot ain't proper."

"It's proper," Disco answered Lonnie.

"Peace, then."

"Peace."

And that's how we robbed them Valdosta niggaz without ever pulling out a heater. Now we had to make it back to Atlanta with all that loot in the trunk of a Porsche. Two young black niggaz in a tricked-out Porsche traveling I-75 cocaine lane. Po-po would be itching to pull us over.

Lonnie didn't take I-75 back to Atlanta, he drove back-routes and shit. It took twice as long for us to reach the ATL, but we made it.

Lonnie, me, and $126,000!

Lonnie had paid twenty G's for the real kilo of cocaine, so, after he deducted that expense plus some others and broke Delina off a little something, we split ninety grand down the middle. I put thirty-five grand in the freezer and ten in my pocket. I got in fresh gear and went to scoop up Cheryl. When I got to Cheryl's house, her mother answered the door and asked me to come inside.

"Cheryl's upstairs. She'll be down shortly," her mother politely informed me.

It was my first time meeting Cheryl's Ma Dukes and I could see where Cheryl got her body and looks from. Her mom was a dime, beautiful and fine like that old broad Pam Grier. Moms was so pretty it didn't matter if she had kids with an ape, the kids would come out good-looking.

I knew from Cheryl that her father had been a doctor before he was killed in a car accident. I saw pictures on the end tables and mantel of an older man whom I assumed was Cheryl's deceased father.

In the pictures, the man had his arm around Cheryl's mother. He looked to be at least twenty years her senior. I also knew from Cheryl, that her father had been dead five years. And that Ma Dukes and Cheryl were provided for by the large insurance policy Cheryl's mother had collected on.

Cheryl came down the stairs, not her usual hyped self. She sat down next to me on the couch, her mother sat in a chair to our left, smoking a cigarette.

"Cheryl has something to tell you," her mother said in a tone that made me brace for the worst.

Cheryl looked at me and blurted it right out. "I'm pregnant." Cheryl gave me the news raw dog just like she'd given me the pussy.

Her mom hit me with the next punch.

"Cheryl ain't but fifteen years old. How're y'all going to raise a child? She's still a child, herself."

Now I was really buggin'. I mean, I never asked Cheryl her age, but fifteen? *That's bananas!* And now her mother was sitting here telling me Cheryl was just a child? It seemed to me, the bitch should've mentioned that when she was allowing her daughter to spend nights with me. Or she should've made sure Cheryl was in school instead of the game room!

The way I read it, Cheryl's mother was so busy trying to find an old man to replace Cheryl's father and pay the bills, she hadn't kept an eye on her fifteen-year-old *child.* The situation really was no different than when I had gotten Shan pregnant with Lil' T. Except I hadn't gotten Cheryl pregnant in her mom's crib.

I looked at Cheryl. "What do you wanna do?" I asked with genuine concern.

Her mom's spoke for her. "Oh, we don't believe in abortions."

I wanted to say, "*We?* Bitch, I ain't get *you* pregnant!"

Cheryl's mother interrogated me for the next hour, asking me my age, place of residence, family history, level of education, place of employment, criminal history, everything but if I loved her daughter.

I lied about everything but my name. Fuck her! I should've been interrogating her for failing to supervise *her* daughter.

"Damn, shawdy. I didn't know you were just fifteen," I teased Cheryl as we drove to the mall.

"You should've asked." Not sounding ashamed.

"Yo' fast ass would've lied, anyway," I told her.

"Lied for what? Nigga, you wouldna cared! Age ain't nothing but a number, no way."

I guess she was right. It didn't matter none now, she was carrying my seed.

Cheryl was mad cool about the situation. She didn't try to overcrowd me all of a sudden, or blow up my pager any more than she did before she got pregnant.

She was like, *Look, I ain't 'bout to be acting all crazy like other girls do over their baby daddy. I know a man gon' be a man, just tell your other bitches to respect me when I'm with you. And anytime you don't want me no more, I ain't fixin' to be trying to hold you down just 'cause I got a baby by you. As long as you do what a man supposed to do for his child. I ain't gon' ever be mad at you.* Cheryl wasn't but fifteen, but she had understanding way beyond her age.

CHAPTER 19

Summer kicked in like somebody had turned on a big ass oven in the sky. I stayed in the crib most days until evening, just to avoid the heat.

My bank was solid still, 'cause I really didn't splurge much. I had got two small televisions installed in my Lex truck, but I hadn't had to pinch my stash to pay for that.

Rich Kid had sent me to Kentucky to help King and other members from his crew to lay down the law and establish dope traps up there. Of course, I was part of the muscle. It took a month to get shit established. Rich Kid paid me decently and I touched a few Kentucky niggaz for some change during the process.

I had to admit I was a little spooked to meet with Rich Kid and then go to Kentucky with King. But the way I figured it, if I didn't meet with Rich Kid when he paged me and asked me to, he might've thought I had a reason for ducking him. And if they were planning to take me to Kentucky and kill me, well, Rich Kid could have easily put out a hit on me right in Atlanta.

That was why I didn't trip it when I got in that car with King to go to Kentucky and help establish shit for Rich Kid. Besides when it was my time to die, I would be out, like every other nigga whose number came up. I wasn't trippin' death, no matter how violent mine came. See, I could kill a bunch of mafuckaz, but mafuckaz could only kill me once.

I kissed Cheryl and then rubbed her pot-belly.

"Did you miss me, shawdy?"

"Yeah. Boy, yo' ass done got black! Dag." Cheryl observed with her usual dinginess.

Though she would sometimes surprise me with cleverness. She had a way of keeping a nigga off-balance like an Allen Iverson crossover.

"Wanna see something?" Cheryl beamed.

"Whud up?" She pulled down her T-shirt and exposed the top of her left breast. A tattoo read *Youngblood's Bitch* in fancy writing. I just shook my head.

I had been away from Atlanta for a little over a month, so after spending my first few days back with my shawdy, Cheryl and I hooked up with Lonnie and we cruised the hood in my truck. We blessed different spots with our presence, stopping to spit raps with niggaz I knew, avoiding those spots where Lonnie had enemies.

Hos were all on my dick, they're pussies getting wet just from seeing the televisions I had installed in the whip. One of the TVs was a seven-inch screen that was built in the passenger sun visor. The other television came down, by remote from the truck's ceiling. It was a twelve-inch screen, with a Play Station II hooked up to it.

We whipped through Englewood and grabbed a coupla' rib dinners from the Ribs Lady. We didn't hang down there long 'cause po-po was rolling deep, fucking with all the dope boys.

Blue was in the area and when he saw us, he flagged us down like his life depended on it. Blue looked bad. His eyes were like golf balls and his lips were white like powdered doughnuts. The nigga stank so bad I told him to back up from my whip! He stood back from my truck and talked to Lonnie.

Blue bullshitted around for a minute or two, asking about Delina and his sons before he got to what he'd really waved us down for. Lonnie took a knot out his pocket and gave Blue *five* twenty dollar bills. He also handed Blue his rib dinner.

Lonnie said, "Open the dinner and eat it right now."

"I'ma eat it later," Blue conned, anxious to run off and buy some crack.

"Naw, I wanna see you eat it now. Yo' ass so little you could hide behind a broom."

Blue sat down on the curb and started grubbing. He didn't have an appetite for nothing but crack, but he did as he was told. His junkie-ass was struggling to eat the ribs. I offered Blue an orange drink before his dry-mouth-ass choked to death. He hadn't eaten but one rib and the orange drink was ghost. I was about to laugh when Blue bent over at the waist and vomited.

I said, "Fool! You need to leave that crack alone!"

"I'm trying, Youngblood, I'm trying," he gasped as he wiped vomit from his powdered lips.

Lonnie told him, "Get yo' self together, man, and I'll bring your sons to see you."

We jetted from Englewood and went to get some weed in Thomasville Heights, the PJs, a few minutes away. We copped some trees and then I drove through the drive thru at KFC so Lonnie could get some eats to replace the rib dinner he'd given to Blue.

Lonnie knew that after we rolled a few blunts and got high, he would have the munchies. My nigga knew without being told that I wasn't gon' share my ribs with him. We could rob together, kill and die together, even fuck some hos together but when it came down to the Ribs Lady barbeque, I rolled mafuckin' solo.

At my crib getting high, I asked Lonnie why he be showing Blue so much love.

Lonnie told me when he was in junior high school, he had put his hands on some dude his age. The next night, Lonnie was on his way back home from the store when the lil' dude he had beaten up and two of the lil' dudes' older brothers chased Lonnie down and cornered him.

It was dark out and Lonnie didn't have a weapon to defend himself against a three-on-one. He was 'bout to get banged up. That's when Blue and Delina turned the corner, hand in hand, young lovers. Blue had peeped what the situation was immediately. He told the brothers they weren't gonna gang-bang Lonnie, not unless they wanted to fight him, too. Then Delina pulled out a switchblade, down for her man, Blue. The older brothers backed off and made the younger fight Lonnie head-up.

Lonnie spanked his ass again. Lonnie hadn't never forgot that Blue done him a good deed, when Blue could've just walked on by. So now, Lonnie never just walked on by Blue.

Though I was only away from the ATL a month, a lot of shit had happened in the lives of those connected to me directly and indirectly.

Poochie sons had come back to live with her now that school was out for the summer and Poochie had months of drug-free living under her belt. She was still holding down a full time job and going to church on Sundays. She'd even joined a drug-recovery group.

I was glad for Poochie but her sons living with her put a stop to my occasional sex life with her. But the boys moving back with Poochie wasn't the sole reason our secret affair ended. Poochie had gotten herself together and was being more responsible and self-respecting, couple that with the church yelling religion in Poochie's ear and holding sin and God's judgment over her head, my rap just wasn't strong enough.

Poochie admitted that sex with me was good, but she was now convinced it was wrong. She told me she loved me in one breath and snatched away my keys to the pussy in the next.

I wasn't mad, though. In fact, I had to respect it. I had mad love for Poochie 'cause she had always been on my side in the beefs I went through with her daughter. I let Poochie know that I would still continue to stop by and check on her and if she ever needed me, I was just a call away.

"You can also page me if you get lonely at night," I added half-joking.

"Go on! Boy, you the devil," but she smiled.

I guess for a split-second she was remembering our fucking and sucking, wondering how the Lord was gonna put out the heat between her thighs those nights she wasn't in church feeling the holy ghost.

I knew when I left out of Poochie's apartment that day that I would never rip those guts again. *Damn!* She was looking finer than Toni Braxton now. If Poochie could stop smoking crack, she could damn sho' stop fucking me.

I still had Cheryl for a steady fuck, and I enjoyed kickin' it with shawdy. Cheryl was peace. Plus, I knew some hood rats who would come off the pussy just to ride in my whip. I had crazy phone numbers of bitches I hadn't even called. I wasn't trying to get with all them hos, though, 'cause pussy had a way of fuckin' up a nigga' focus. Too many hos equaled too many problems.

One day, Shan paged me and told me my son was crying for me. I hopped in the whip and jetted over there. Shotgun Pete was doing county time for violating his probation when he'd jumped on Shan.

The probation violation was all they'd been able to pin on him, 'cause Shan refused to cooperate with the D.A., who wanted to charge Shotgun Pete with felony domestic abuse or domestic violence, whatever the fuck they called it when a nigga chin-checked his bitch these days.

I didn't know for how long Pete would be in the county, but the streets were whispering that Shan's legs had been open all-night, like a restaurant drive-thru, since Shotgun Pete had been in the county.

It wasn't any skin off my back. Shan was my son's mama, but I wasn't holding her down no more. Her ho-hoppin' was her ugly-ass nigga's problem.

Word from the street had made its way inside the county jail and had Shotgun Pete ruffled, anxious to get out and beat Shan silly.

It just wasn't my biz, I didn't know why people kept reporting Shan's activities to me. As long as none of Shan's trick niggaz didn't harm Lil' T, I was cooler than the other side of the pillow with whatever Shan did.

I pulled up in the apartments where Shan lived and mad honeys were sweatin' a young nigga's profile. My whip was freshly washed and waxed, rims sparkling in the sun and Jay-Z booming from the system.

As soon as my Timbs touched the ground, I felt bitches' eyes caress me from the ground up. My baggy jeans were crisp and brand new, I was rockin' a Fat Albert T-shirt, a blue studded bandana tied around my forehead, and I had just got a platinum grill put in my mouth the day before.

I smiled and the sun reflected off of my grill, blinding bitches. My neck and wrists were iced. I was a fly ass young nigga, braided up thug style.

"Where Lil' T at?" I asked Shan as soon as I stepped in the apartment.

"He gone to the park with Mama and the kids." I just noticed that Shan was pulling her T-shirt over her head. That left her with nothing on but a thong and a string bikini top.

"I just wanted you to come over so we could make up. You look good with that grill in your mouth." I ignored the compliment and Shan's flesh. "Can we be friends?" Her tone was pleading.

"We can't be nothing but Lil' T's parents," I said.

Before I could back away, Shan's hot body was pressed against mine and she was unbuckling my jeans. Her hands found what they were after and her lips sucked my chest through my T-shirt.

I was thinking about all the dirty shit this bitch had done, all the drama she'd put me through: having a brat by Shotgun Pete and…

She had me in her mouth. I was getting hard despite my dislike for the bitch. Her mouth sucked and her hands fondled my nuts. I grabbed the back of Shan's head and tried to make her choke. She pulled back a little and started using her tongue. My knees got weak.

Shan took me out of her mouth completely, but her hand took the place of her mouth. She began talking in a low, soft tone.

"Baby, I know I messed up bad. But I still love you, and I wanna make it up to you. Not just like this, but in every way." Her hand moved up and down my dick.

"I'll do anything you want me to do," Shan continued. "I know you're mad at me, Youngblood. You wanna cum in my face, treat me like a ho to punish me for messing up? I'll do *anything* to get you back. I'll sell pussy if you tell me to. *Anything.* Just as long as I can have you again." Her mouth went back to work.

I heard crying coming from her bedroom. Shan had to hear it, too, but she ignored it, that was until the baby's crying got loud and persistent.

"Let me go give her a bottle. She'll go right back to sleep." Shan stood up and pulled the string, releasing her bikini top. Two big titties promised me bliss. Then Shan wiggled out of the thong. She ignored the baby's cries while my eyes feasted on sweet memories. "I'ma give you all of this when I get back. Don't go nowhere. I'll be right back," Shan promised.

As soon as she disappeared into the bedroom, I dipped.

Five minutes later, my pager started blowin' up. I saw that it was Shan so I ignored it. *Fuck that bitch!* She'd tried the oldest game in the book: give a nigga some pussy and he'll forgive anything. Not Youngblood.

I'm game-tight.

I had no intention on fucking the bitch before her brat started crying. I was gonna bust in her mouth and then spit in her face. I knew the consequences would be me going through drama to see Lil' T, but I could always scoop him from Poochie's crib.

Shan paged me for two hours straight, non-stop. As I whipped around the hood showing off my new grill, I let the rings mix in with the music coming out my sound system.

A number I didn't recognize showed on my pager. I was hoping it was this bitch I'd met at Wendy's the other day. I stopped at a pay phone to see who it was.

"Anybody there paged Youngblood?"

A female's voice said, "Is this Youngblood?"

"Yeah. Who is this?"

"Hold on." I heard the phone being passed.

"What?" I figured it out too late.

Shan asked, "Why the fuck you play me like that!?" I slammed the phone on her desperate ass.

The next day Cheryl, Lonnie, his lady, Delina, and me was chillin' at my crib listening to the Outkast CD. We were high off weed and eating pizza. I told them about the stunt Shan had pulled to get me over to her crib and everything that had went down once I got there.

I acted the scene out like a comedian. I didn't put any cut on it. I repeated what Shan had said while sucking my dick, how she said it and all that. When I told the part when I dipped out her crib, Lonnie was crackin' the fuck up. I was all over the floor, too. Delina was smiling, shaking her head like Lonnie and I were some silly niggaz

But she busted a laugh, too.

Cheryl said, "I bet she felt stupid when she came out the bedroom and yo' ass was gone. Dag."

Delina hit the floor! Now she was laughing harder than Lonnie and me. Probably because of the way Cheryl had said it. Or maybe Delina thought Cheryl was too stupid to get mad at me for letting Shan slob my knob. But that wasn't the way I read Cheryl.

To me, Cheryl just didn't trip the small stuff. She was born not giving a damn. Her dinginess was just youthful innocence. It kept mafuckaz off balance, even me.

Cheryl looked at us laughing all over the floor, and she said, “What’s so funny? Dag.” We damn near laughed ourselves to death.

After Lonnie and his lady bounced, me and Cheryl were hugged up on the couch, my head on her belly trying to feel the baby move.

“It ain’t big enough yet,” Cheryl said, as if she’d had a child before.

She asked me if I had wanted to fuck Shan after she’d sucked my dick. I told her, *Hell no!*

Cheryl said she believed me and she didn’t blame me for dissin’ Shan, ‘cause Shan was lowdown for gettin’ with Shotgun Pete, knowing we were friends.

“I would never do nothing like that,” Cheryl swore.

“That’s what you say now. But if I went to prison ain’t no telling who you’d get with,” I insisted.

“I wouldn’t get with none of yo’ friends, that’s for sure. That would be disrespecting myself.”

Cheryl stayed the night with me. When I woke up in the morning she was pulling shit out of the freezer, looking for something to cook. I stopped her before she got to the chicken boxes where I kept my loot stashed.

Instead, we dressed and went to Denny’s for some breakfast. Before we’d left the apartment complex, I had called Toi and asked her to meet me at there. I knew my mother’s husband had bought Toi a car by now.

By the time Toi arrived at Denny’s, Cheryl and I had already been there twenty minutes. We hadn’t ordered yet, though. I introduced Cheryl to my sister and the three of us fell into easy conversation.

Toi was surprised but happy to hear that she was about to become an aunt again. She commented that Cheryl didn’t look pregnant and asked Cheryl if she was hoping for a girl or a boy. Cheryl said that I already had a son, so a daughter was her choice, although a healthy baby of either sex was what she was praying to deliver.

My sister filled me in on family gossip, telling me about out-of-town relatives I hadn’t seen in years and didn’t care if I never saw again. Toi stayed away from discussing our mama and Raymond at length, knowing I had no desire to hear about either of them. She also probably didn't want Cheryl to hear my opinion of Mama.

The love between me and my sister was quiet, but strong. Since Toi still lived at home with Mama and Raymond I didn't call her or come around much. She had my pager number but didn't use it often.

But I believed Toi knew that if she ever needed me or just wanted to see her brother, I would be there in a heartbeat.

My ill feelings toward Mama was something that kept wrinkles in my relationship with my sister. The few times she'd paged me, she would always try to play peacemaker and get me to talk to Mama on the phone. I'd threaten to hang up if Toi passed the phone to Mama.

Now talking over breakfast, I could tell it was eating Toi up not to at least try again to get me to forgive Mama and accept Raymond.

Cheryl's presence protected me from that reoccurring plea by my sister. Toi was too proud to discuss family problems in front of outsiders.

When our plates were clean, I paid the waitress, blessed her with a two-dollar tip, it wasn't like Denny's was high class. Then we dipped out of the restaurant shortly after Cheryl and Toi exchanged numbers.

"I wanna name the baby if it's a girl," Toi said.

"Okay. As long as you don't try to name my baby no crazy shit I can't even pronounce," Cheryl told Toi, laughing like she could imagine Toi wanting to name the baby Ooga Mooga or something.

I hugged my sister and watched her get into her Toyota Cressida and drive off. I dropped Cheryl off at her house and went to find something to get into. I knew Shan would still be in a foul mood over my dissin' her, so going to get Lil' T and kickin' it with him wasn't an option.

Our son was the only tool Shan had to use against me, her only assurance that I'd eventually have to make peace with her. That was, if I wanted to see my son. The bitch knew I wouldn't take her to court, and she knew I wouldn't kick her ass for holding Lil' T hostage away from me and risk going back to prison over some bullshit. So she was milking it dry.

If push came to shove, I could always flip the script on Shan and act like the reason I wouldn't get with her was because she be trippin' when it came to letting me see my son. That would entice her into letting me see Lil' T, at least until the scandalous bitch figured out I was just leading her on, and wasn't no Youngblood dick in her future.

But I despised Shan so much it would kill me to even let the skunk *think* I'd get back with her.

Anyway, I still had Poochie. I could always scoop my lil' man from her spot. The only wrinkle in that option was that Poochie worked evenings, the hours Shan usually took Lil' T over there and hit the streets. I didn't know who babysat for Shan when Poochie wasn't available. As was the case right now, which meant that Lil' T wasn't at Poochie's. So I dipped through Englewood to see what was poppin'.

Besides the usual dope slangin', bitch parade, little bad, dirty-ass kids ripping and running, and po-po cruising through trying to put a dent in the hood's natural flow, wasn't much happenin'.

I drove up the hill to the basketball courts. Fools were ballin' in mad heat, sweating like runaway slaves. I counted three pairs of Jordans, two pairs of Allen Iverson's latest kicks and some other fly sneakers that had just hit the stores.

On the side of the basketball court, a crap game caught my interest. I put my heater against my waist, under my Braves short-sleeve jersey, just in case a fool put some ill shit in the craps game.

"Yo! What his point is?" I asked, nudging myself into the circle, my fist grippin' a knot of twenties.

"His point six."

"I bet six or eight, twenty," I said, meaning I wanted to bet $20 that the shooter would roll a total of six or eight before he crapped out.

"I bet he don't," somebody challenged me, dropping a twenty-dollar bill on the ground next to mine.

Two rolls later, the shooter crapped out, losing my twenty.

"Who next on the dice? I'll buy your turn," I yelled. Forty dollars got me on the dice. I checked them to make sure they weren't loaded, fixed to crap out.

"The dice straight," some nigga said.

"Fool, let me put insurance on my money." I saw that the dice were good so I laid down twenty dollars as an opening bet and rolled the dice against a wall.

An hour later, I added eleven hundred to my pocket stash. The losers were mad when I quit.

A big bully-ass nigga named Charlie was the maddest.

"Nigga, you ain't gon' gimme a chance to win my money back!" His tone was threatening, as he followed me.

I turned around about halfway to my whip and lifted up my T-shirt, letting the fool see my heater.

"It ain't yo' money no more, nigga!" I spat back.

Charlie peeped I was strapped. He stopped in his tracks and yelled out some stupid shit just trying to save face. I let his studio-gangsta words bounce off of my back. Fuck him! I had his loot in my pocket, no need to bust a cap in his ass just to prove something that niggaz already knew—I would light a spark in a nigga!

Anyway, I knew that Charlie was just running off at the mouth 'cause he was stupid like that.

I dipped, eleven hundred richer.

That night I put on some fresh gear and headed to a shake-a-booty club called The Passion Palace. The club had just recently opened. I'd heard advertisements on the radio and the streets were giving it thumbs up.

Once inside, I saw that The Passion Palace was a little too upscale for my taste. I was more comfortable in a grimy, hole-in-the-wall joint, where bitches acted exactly like what they were: *shake-dance hos.*

The vibe inside of The Passion Palace told me that these shake-dance hos thought they were movie stars or divas, which meant conversation wouldn't even be free. I had won eleven hundred shooting craps easy come, easy go. But I wasn't paying just to rap to one of them fine bitches, so I gave a tall, white, blond honey a hundred dollars.

"Keep dancing 'til that runs out," I told her as she began giving me a table dance.

I sipped Yak, and watched Blondie grind what her mama gave her. Blondie moved slowly and seductively, leaning two big perfect titties down six-inches from my face. Blondie shook her shoulders, but her titties didn't budge.

Silicones.

Her blond pussy was perfect, too, but unlike the titties it was 100 percent real. Blondie turned her back to me and bent over and grabbed her ankles. Her legs were spread, allowing me to see all up in her world. I tipped her an extra ten-spot.

When the hundred dollars had been used up, I gave Blondie another c-note, flashing my knot.

"Keep dancing."

"Anything you say, sugar," cuffing the c-note in her palm.

An hour later, Blondie had hustled me for three hundred and sweet-talked me into buying *us* a bottle of Dom Perrigon for $130.

She said she needed to go freshen up and disappeared down some stairs. I wasn't green, so I assumed Blondie had gone down to the dressing room to talk with some of the other girls and get the 411 on me.

She'd seen my knot and that I was bling-blingin', the bitch wanted to know who I was and how much of that knot she might be able to seduce me out of with that perfect pair of silicones and that beautiful, blond pussy.

I knew Blondie would come back upstairs with the same info on me she'd had when she left—none. I didn't know a single one of the bitches in there, nor would they know me.

"I'm back, sugar. I had to go freshen up my cat." She had a perfect smile, too. "What's your name, sugar?" asked the blond dime.

"Popeye." It was the first shit that came to mind.

"Is that your name for real?" Blondie giggled.

"All year long." Straight-faced.

Blondie felt my puny biceps. "They must call you Popeye 'cause you're strong?" The bitch was jeffing.

"Naw, 'cause I keep plenty spinach." I flashed three rubber banded knots, letting her sweat the real green before returning the spinach back inside of my pocket.

"What you gonna do with all that money?" Whispering in my ear and her rubbing twin silicones against my arm.

"I plan to share it with you," I said, like a lame.

By the time I had tricked eight bills on Blondie, other hos had peeped the scene and wanted in on the action. It was as if the dee-jay had announced, *Trick at table seven, in the back!* because G-stringed and butt-naked hos came around like vultures.

Blondie whispered in my ear. "Tell them you came to see me personally." I felt her wet tongue.

I repeated what Blondie had told me to say to more than a dozen money-hungry bitches. Some took the rejection in stride, while a few had to be rejected twice before going off in search of their own trick.

"Variety is the spice of life," one dark stallion tried.

"Oh, you gon' let the white bitch make all the money!" a butt-naked sister said bitterly, not even whispering so Blondie couldn't hear.

"I got jungle fever," I snapped back.

Blondie smiled. Another four hundred dollars later, I had laid out my spiel. I told Blondie I was an A&R for a major record company that was opening an office in the Dirty South and about to come out with some new talent from Atlanta and other rappers from around the South.

I told her I was really at the club to scout females to put in a video I was directing for a rapper whose name I couldn't mention. I told Blondie not to mention any of this to the other dancers 'cause I didn't want them all bugging me to be in the video.

"If they find out I'm scouting for video girls, they'll stop acting natural and start auditioning."

"My lips are sealed," Blondie said, gesturing with her hand.

Then she immediately started telling me how she always wanted to be in a rap video, but didn't think rappers used many white girls in their joints.

"I might be able to put you in this video I'll be releasing in a few months."

"Don't be bullshitting me, Popeye."

I talked to Blondie for another thirty minutes, gave her two more C-notes and asked if she'd come home with me after the club. I flashed the *spinach* again and promised her a lead role in a video.

"I'll think about it," she promised. It was her time to go onstage.

I had no doubt she'd accept the offer, 'cause even if she hadn't believed the hype about the video role and me being an A&R for a major record label, I still had big knots in my pocket.

That wasn't a lie. Her blue eyes had seen the green. The white bitch already had fourteen hundred of my loot in her grip, I was sure she was greedy for more.

Before Blondie went away to think about my offer, I asked her about different dancers, as if I was interested in putting them in the video.

Blondie dropped salt on three of them bitches.

CHAPTER 20

Onstage, Blondie looked like a big-tittied younger Madonna.

She'd changed into a leather S&M type outfit complete with whip and chains. She worked the pole like the pro she obviously was.

Tricks stood in line to put their hard-earned or hustled loot in her garter. She was one of the only two white dancers working at The Passion Palace, at least this particular night, which made Blondie a different, if not special, treat to the predominantly black male patrons.

There were about twenty black dancers, all of them decent or dimes. But niggaz fucked sistas daily, white pussy was still an oddity to me and obviously to the other black dudes stuffing dollars in Blondie's garter like she was the ride back to Africa.

The bitch was tight, though. Her pussy trimmed so pretty God woulda licked it. She worked the crowd into a testosterone frenzy, an act that was hot even before the other white girl joined Blondie onstage to simulate a lesbian S&M fuck.

Niggaz grabbed their dicks like, *Damn!*

Other dancers were performing personal dances at private tables, but their trick eyes were glued to the stage. Those two snowflakes had mad fuck moves.

Blondie made eye contact with me as if to say, "*See what good pussy you might get if you're talking enough spinach?*"

I'm sure my look said, "*You can have my car, too.*"

There was a tap on my shoulder. I jerked around. Immediately I thought, *Fuck! My heater's in the whip!*

Rich Kid flashed a smile down at me. Relieved, I stood and we dapped hands. His main man, King, was a few feet to Rich Kid's rear, mean muggin' the whole joint.

I nodded to King, but I didn't really like that nigga and not just because I suspected him of cuffing some of that extra loot I took from that Richard idiot in Alabama. I'd also seen small but shady signs from King when we'd put in work for Rich Kid in Kentucky. The nigga just felt suspect to me. I don't know why Rich Kid couldn't feel the bad vibe coming off of dude. Still, it wasn't my job to wake Rich Kid up.

King ignored my head nod, but I was sure he had seen it. No biggie, the nigga would play himself sooner or later. At which time I would peel his cap just for the sport of it.

"Whud up, lil' nigga? I didn't know you like strip clubs," Rich Kid greeted me with respect and friendship.

"Yo, what man in his right mind don't?"

"Check," Rich Kid agreed. "You wanna roll with us in VIP?" I noticed a team of Rich Kid's crew headed toward the glass enclosed VIP room.

"Nah, I'm good. Thanks anyway." Then I told Rich Kid that my name was Popeye if any of the dancers asked him about me.

I told him the spiel I'd gave Blondie so he'd know how to cap it off. Rich Kid smiled, shook his head and bounced to VIP to join his crew. King followed behind like a loyal dog, though I wasn't convinced.

Blondie finished her stage routine and hustled downstairs to change outfits, I guessed, and stash our trick money wherever them hos stash their loot during the night.

While she was away the vultures attacked again. I shook 'em like the basketball player, Kobe, on a fast-break. They weren't too disappointed, plenty more tricks were waving them over for private dances. And the VIP room was now jumpin'.

I could tell Rich Kid was well known and respected at this club, 'cause a man in an expensive tailor made suit came from a back office to go in the VIP room and shake Rich Kid's hand. I had the expensive tailor made suit pegged as the club's owner. I tend to notice everything around me because my game required it. A potential lick could be missed if I wasn't on point. Or worse, an enemy might get the drop on me.

Blondie emerged in a different outfit, her titties pressed against my neck.

"Hey, sugar. Did you miss me?"

"And you know this," I shot.

"So, you know Rich Kid?" Blondie asked. When I didn't answer, she said, "I saw you guys talking while I was onstage."

"I thought you were concentrating on your girlfriend up there?"

"Oh. That's just an act when we're onstage. I still can see what's going on in the club."

I guess Blondie figured out I wasn't going to acknowledge her question, so she told me she had to go around and thank everyone who'd tipped her while onstage. Plus, she had to perform personal dances for several of her regular customers.

"Go do your job, baby."

"Don't let any of these girls steal you from me while I'm gone." She stuck her tongue in my ear. "Oh, I'm thinking about your offer, too."

A waitress brought two bottles of Cristal in a bucket of ice to my table and told me the guy in VIP had sent and paid for it. I could see Rich Kid and his crew being entertained by naked, dancing bitches through the thick glass enclosure. King leaned against the glass wall nearest where Rich Kid was seated on a couch. It appeared to me King was paid not to ever enjoy himself.

For the next hour, bitches came up to my table pandering private dances. I was just chillin', though, waiting on my young Madonna.

I saw her in the VIP room showing other niggaz the inside of her world. I wasn't vexed, the bitch was working. I saw her maneuver up close to Rich Kid a few songs later. Rich Kid nodded to King, letting him know it was cool. I had my head down like I was somewhere else, but I saw Blondie pointing at me.

Both of Blondie's fists were full of loot when she came back to my table. I didn't see any dollar bills, either.

"Rich Kid told me to tell you his little cousin is ready for a record deal. And he wants to know if you changed your mind about joining him in VIP?"

"Tell him I can't. I'm scouting dancers for a video. I'm trying to blend in with the crowd." While Blondie was off delivering my message to Rich Kid, another dancer slid into the vacated seat next to me.

"I know I ain't supposed to know this, but would you consider me for the rap video?" the chocolate, honey whispered conspiratorly. I felt her hand on my dick.

"I'll check you out. But don't tell anybody else." I knew she would. Shit, that was what I was counting on.

The rest of the night, stripper bitches was sweating me like I was Jay-Z, Hype Williams, Spike Lee or somebody of major importance. And after Blondie made her rounds, she stuck to me like skin.

I saw a big nigga enter the club surrounded by a flock of niggaz, all smaller than him. I recognized the kingpin, Hannibal. I didn't know him, but I knew who he was. My ears stayed to the streets and I knew the names of all the major dope boys, most of them I knew by face, too.

I knew all of their names and where they ranked in the game. Of course, the structure could change at any moment. The dope game was frailer than a mafucka.

Hannibal and his crew shared the spacious VIP room with Rich Kid and his posse. I didn't see the two crews interacting with each other, though. And if Rich Kid and Hannibal knew each other, I couldn't tell by watching them through the glass.

I never saw them speak or even acknowledge the other one's presence. Their crews were seated on opposite sides of the VIP room, roped off from one another.

Sensing there were more big spenders in the joint, the dancers swarmed Hannibal and his crew. Most of the girls were entertaining either Rich Kid's posse or Hannibal's in VIP. Only a few were moving amongst the regular customers and one was on stage making her ass jiggle on command. Blondie was stuck like skin to me. I guess she figured, *a trick in hand beats a room full in VIP.* Plus, I was her ticket into rap video stardom. But I wasn't trying to block her hustle. I told her to go make some money, I would wait on her 'til the club closed.

An hour later, the disc-jockey announced, "Last call for alcohol."

The crowd had thinned out considerably by now. Mafuckaz had spent their paychecks and went home broke and horny or had got wise and dipped before they went home broke and horny.

I was standing at the bar talking to Blondie when Rich Kid stopped to holla on his way out.

"I still might wanna use your blue Benz in a video," I popped.

"Just call me. And, dawg, you need to sign my lil' cousin. For real, though," Rich Kid sweetened my plot before he and his crew dipped, King right on his heels.

Hannibal and 'em left shortly after that when the club's lights came on. The dee-jay announced it was closing time and thanked us for coming out. Blondie told me she'd decided to accept my offer to spend the night with me.

"Popeye, I gotta go downstairs and change into my clothes. Wait for me in the parking lot, I won't be long. I hope you know how to treat a girl. I mean, I like *a lot* of spinach."

"I'll treat you right," I promised.

A few other niggaz were parked in the lot waiting to spend more money for all night dates or just to get a look at shake-a-booty bitches in clothes. Security was outside to make sure we didn't snatch the girls and take our money's worth.

I was parked so Blondie couldn't miss seeing me. She came up to the passenger side of my whip, the other white dancer at her side.

Blondie leaned her head in the window.

"If it's not a problem, whatever you're going to give me, could you give it to me now? Not that I'm charging you, but since you offered."

I told her to get in for a minute. We talked quickly, and I handed Blondie a small knot. It looked phatter than it was 'cause it was small bills from the crap game. Blondie put the knot in her purse and then handed her purse, with my knot, out the window to the other white girl.

"I should be home by noon," Blondie told her.

"Call me and let me know you're okay," her roommate worried.

I was sick watching Blondie's friend walk off with Blondie's purse, with my knot and probably all the other money she'd juiced out of me and other tricks tonight inside of it. I started replotting my game.

After we stopped to get something to eat, I let Blondie choose which hotel we went to. Of course, her gold-digging ass chose a hotel with a nightly room rate of $250. I gave her the money and let her sign the registrar.

In the room, she wasted no time stepping to her business. "Now that we're alone, let me show you how good I can make you feel," Blondie said.

She took my hand and led me straight over to the bed.

"You gonna be able to handle all of this?" I asked as I unzipped and pulled up my pipe.

"Oh yes, daddy." She covered the head of my dick with her mouth and began slowly bobbing up and down.

"Yeah, do that shit!" I pushed myself deep down her throat until she gagged.

She pulled back a little, then she slurped loudly on the steel, coating it with lots of spit. I gripped her head with both hands and fucked her mouth until I shot all down her throat.

"Ummmm," she moaned while swallowing every drop.

I laid there thinking, *It ain't no myth. White hos really suck dick better than sistas.*

At least, Blondie was the best I had ever met. I wanted to taste that pretty white pussy, but I stayed strong and kept my tongue in check. I put on a jimmy hat and fucked that white ass and I do mean the *ass!* Then I hit the pussy 'til the sun came up.

We slept for a minute, woke up and got busy one last time before hitting the shower.

While Blondie was getting dressed, I picked up the phone and dialed the number to a pay phone near Englewood. I used that pay phone regularly and knew the number by heart. I also knew nobody would be at the pay phone to answer it so early in the morning.

I talked so Blondie could hear me.

"Yo, this is Popeye. I checked out that club last night and you were right, they got some fly honeys up in there. Yeah—yeah," I said to no one, but a ringing pay phone. "We need ten girls, but I don't wanna use ten from the same club. I'm with one of the dancers from last night now. She's a real fine snow

"Hell yeah, they'll be able to make it. Where else can they make fifteen thousand for a few hours of dancing *and* be in a rap video? All right. I'll bring five girls from the club last night. We'll pick five other dancers from a club in Miami when we get there. Send two limos to drive the girls down to Miami. Yeah, I know. Don't—" I was running my spiel so strong I hadn't realized someone had answered the ringing pay phone on the other end.

"Man, who are you? And whud da fuck is you talkin' 'bout?" A lady's voice screamed into the phone. "This is a goddamn pay phone you're calling, dumb mothafucka!"

I kept right on talking like I hadn't heard a word the woman said.

Blondie was listening to my every word, smiling and eating my game up. The bitch who had answered the pay phone cussed me out some more and then slammed the phone in my ear.

I said, "I'll see you in Miami tomorrow. Peace." Then I hung up the phone before it started making that sound a phone made when no one was on the other end.

"You got me the lead role in a video, sugar? Oh, thank you, Popeye! I can't believe I'm gonna be a star!" Blondie covered my face with kisses. Her excitement turned her white face reddish pink.

She had a thousand questions: *Who was the rapper? Blah, blah, blah...*

"I'll explain all that in the car," I promised. "Right now I need to drop you off so I can take care of some other business before we leave for Miami tonight."

On the way to Blondie's crib, I put the finishing touches on my game. I told her to call the three dancers I had asked her about last night, and to tell them and her roommate that I'd chosen the five of them, including Blondie to be in a rap video and we'd be leaving at 8 p.m. tonight.

They were to all be at Blondie's apartment by 7:30. They'd need proper ID, several G-string outfits, lots of jewelry since it was a bling-bling-type video, $750 for an acting permit, which would be non-refundable.

She was to report that they'd be in Miami for three days, all expenses covered by the record label except for shopping expenses while there, and they'd each get fifteen thousand dollars at the end of the last day of the video shoot.

"You'll be paid twenty-five grand and get to stay with me at my house in Miami while we're there," I told Blondie.

Standing in Blondie's living room, with her roommate from last night present, I delivered the clincher. I gave Blondie the other two knots of loot out of my pocket.

"Hold onto this for me, baby. I don't like to ride around with a lot of money. I'll use my American Express card if I need to buy anything." I saw the roommate's eyes sweating the two thick wads of cash.

The trap was set.

"I'll call you at seven. Make sure all the girls are here. Remember, they can't bring boyfriends or friends along. They'll meet plenty of men in Miami on the video set." I kissed Blondie and dipped.

I went straight over to Lonnie's crib. Delina and her sons were over for the weekend, but they dipped to the mall so I could rap to Lonnie in private. I ran the game down to him, from start to finish.

"You had all this shit planned before you went to the club last night?" He was smiling.

"Hell no, dawg! I was just making it up as I went along."

"What if she has your license plates number?"

"She don't. I was watching her to make sure she didn't look at it." We went over some more *what ifs* and what we'd do if we got to Blondie's crib and more people were there than I expected, particularly men. We even had a plan for if no one was there, how I'd get my loot back from Blondie.

Later that evening, we arrived at Blondie's apartment about seven o'clock. I called to let her know I was on my way.

I was in fresh gear, carried a tennis bag over my shoulder and a briefcase stuffed with blank typing paper.

Lonnie carried a large tennis bag, too.

By seven-fifteen all three girls that didn't live there had arrived.

One was dropped off by a butch bitch who had to be explained the whole situation before she jetted. She was afraid that me or Lonnie was gonna dick her bitch in Miami.

After the butch bitch bounced, I told the dancers the limo would arrive by 8:30 P.M., it was running a little late. In the meantime, I needed to know if they each had the $750 for their acting permit. They did.

"Cool. I'll collect it from y'all when we get to Miami," I said in a professional tone.

"Let's all of us decide what outfits you'll each wear in the video. Y'all go into the bedroom and put on your favorite costumes. I'll let y'all know if it's straight for the video or if you'll have to choose something else. None of y'all can wear the same colors." I told Blondie we'd buy *her* something special to wear in the video when we got to Miami.

She stayed out in the living room with me and Lonnie while her roommate and the other three dancers rushed to the bedroom to change into their favorite stripper outfits.

As soon as they were out of sight, Lonnie drawed down on Blondie, like the pro he was. One hand choked wind out her windpipe while the other pointed a big heater in her face. Lonnie and I had decided that he should throw down on Blondie since she felt like she knew me and might try to buck.

Lonnie was choking that white bitch red! We had her mouth, hands, and feet taped in record time. Lonnie had carried her into the kitchen in case one of the girls came out the bedroom while we were tying Blondie up.

We pulled on ski masks and gloves and bum-rushed the bedroom where the other four girls were changing. Of course, they all had seen our faces already. The ski-masks were just to frighten them. Masks made us look more sinister and maybe confused them for a second, having them unsure if it was us, or not, under the masks.

The sawed-off got their attention fast! Blondie's roommate opened her mouth to scream and Lonnie knocked it back down her throat with the barrel of his heater. I was surprised the gun didn't discharge.

The snow crumpled to the floor.

"One sound and I'm killing everybody!" Lonnie said forcefully.

"Let me kill a couple of 'em," I added for effect.

We got all four bitches taped, tied and on the floor and then Lonnie went to get Blondie to join the party.

Two slaps with the heater and she told us were she and her roommate kept the money in the apartment. Lonnie put the tape back over her mouth and went to search the closet. *Bingo!*

The roommate's stash was under the mattress in the other bedroom. We robbed the other three bitches of their $750 each, plus whatever other money they had with them. I found all three of my knots inside Blondie's purse, plus a wad of other money she had probably made last night. We took all those hos' jewelry, though I didn't usually fuck with that anymore. But these bitches' jewelry wasn't custom made or engraved, all jewelers sold identical shit as what they were rockin'. Besides, Lonnie would keep all the jewelry and sell it to a fence he knew.

We put all of the loot inside of the tennis bags, wiped off anything we may have touched in the apartment, took off our ski masks and headed for the door.

When I opened the door to leave the apartment, the butch bitch was just about to knock, her knuckles were still in the air.

"Where's—"

"Come on in. They're all in the bedroom," I said politely, cutting her words off.

The butch bitch came in and closed the door. We drawed down and robbed her ass, too. We tied her up with tape and kicked her in the ass, just for being stupid enough to invite herself to a stick up.

We didn't get rich off this caper, but I got all of my trick money back plus me and Lonnie split a nice lump of those bitches' loot. They had more than we would have thought.

I wasn't worried 'bout them getting my real name from Rich Kid. He'd say he only knew me as Popeye. I hadn't told him I was gonna rob the bitches, but it wasn't no loot out his pocket and Rich Kid wouldn't rat. I'd done major work for him. The only drawback was I couldn't go back to The Passion Palace.

CHAPTER 21

Summer and its suffocating heat passed along until finally school started up again. I took Lil' T shopping for school clothes and supplies, making sho' my lil' man had all the freshest gear out for little kids. Shan was still mad at me, but she was never too mad that she'd refuse me buying things for my son. Her reasoning was simple: *if I bought it, she wouldn't have to.*

I also went and blessed Poochie with a little dough to help her with her sons' school things. She was looking good and doing fine. So far, Poochie was outrunning the crack pipe. I looked around her crib and saw that nothing was missing and the place was clean and tidy.

We talked for a while, just shootin' the breeze. I wanted to make a play for one last time in the bed, but I respected the new Poochie too much to step to her like that.

She told me not to be a stranger before I dipped.

School was about to start for Cheryl, too. Her mother had signed her up to attend an alternative school for pregnant teens. I wasn't against Cheryl going back to school and finishing her education, but I wasn't looking forward to picking my girl up from high school. That shit sounded whack like I was Chester the Child Molester.

I was living on Easy Street right now. My freezer was tight and my name wasn't hot on the block. Niggaz couldn't figure my steez, they just assumed I robbed 'cause I rolled with Lonnie. Still, I had no beef with cats in the hood, I hadn't jacked none of them.

I was living day to day, maintainin' until I ran up on that one big lick all stickup kids lay on. I was good for a minute, a young G with my own whips and crib, a shawdy with my seed growing in her stomach and I was doing what a nigga was supposed to do for his son.

I didn't own the world, but the world didn't own me, either. I could've got out of prison and tried to blow up in a hurry, but when a nigga be speedin', he'd eventually crash. I was a long way from Big Willie style, but I had patience on my side.

I picked Cheryl up from school in the Nissan. I hadn't been whippin' the Lex truck lately, just in case those shake-a-booty bitches had po-po, or one of their trick, dope boy-boyfriends on the lookout for it.

Blondie might not know my tag number, but she could damn sho' describe my whip down to a T.

"Hey," Cheryl greeted me, closing the car door.

"Hey, you." I leaned over and kissed her.

"I'll be glad when I have this baby!"

"Why? You should've kept your legs closed," I joked.

"Shut up! Dag. I'm getting fat, and my back hurts," Cheryl complained.

"You'll be a'ight, shawdy."

"Hmmph! You ain't the one pregnant."

I went over Cheryl's crib and chilled with her for a while and then dipped. Her mom's wasn't at home, she hardly ever was.

Now that Cheryl was back in school, she couldn't hang out all night with me and get up in the morning on time for classes.

Occasionally she'd stay over my crib and I'd take her to school, but not often 'cause she'd hated to get up in the morning after we'd been fucking all night. So we agreed Cheryl would only stay with me on weekends. I didn't wanna fuck up her school plans.

On weekday nights, I would call Cheryl from the pay phone to make sure she was peace and then I'd hit the streets looking for something to get into, usually some bitch's panties. I wasn't tryin' to claim no bitch but Cheryl, 'cause when a nigga put his tag on 'em, they expected him to pay their bills and lace their purse. And I wasn't goin' out like that. I'd bless Cheryl, but those stray pieces of pussy didn't get nothin' but some dick, maybe a burger and fries.

Most niggaz hustled for bitches and didn't even realize it. For the most part, they wanted big houses, fly whips and bling-bling 'cause it attracted mad hos. If there weren't any bitches in the world, niggaz wouldn't really be on a mad paper chase.

I admit *a part* of why I hustled was for the same reason, but not entirely. I had to look good for my damn self. Then I had Lil' T to provide for. Plus, as long as money made the world go 'round, I might as well get as much as I could. Enjoy life while I'm here, 'cause tomorrow wasn't promised. I could be sharing dirt with

Freddie in the time it takes to squeeze the trigger. That was the life I lived. I didn't lie to myself. I didn't wanna live to be old and wrinkled, wearing diapers like a hundred-year-old baby, no mafuckin' way.

Months passed by without me puttin' in any work for Rich Kid or hitting a lick on my own. The chicken boxes in the back of my freezer were still full 'cause I wasn't splurging, and my trick days had been over since I was a juvenile. So, I wasn't pressed for loot, but I was getting vexed 'cause I hadn't added to my stash in a minute. Without a regular hustle, a nigga could go through his stash like *whoa!* And not being mad-laced with dough kept a nigga from ballin'.

Around Cheryl's seventh month of pregnancy, Toi moved out of my mama and Raymond's house and into her own crib. Toi invited Cheryl and me over for buffalo wings and drinks, really just to see her apartment, and she wanted me to meet her boyfriend. He wasn't living with Toi, but she'd told Cheryl he'd bought the furniture and was gonna pay her rent, which was expensive 'cause Toi moved into a condo out in Buckhead, an affluent suburb of Atlanta.

My mama and Raymond had strongly been against Toi's moving out with the help of her boyfriend whom she'd not known very long.

They threatened to take back the car Raymond had bought for Toi, but that didn't stop Toi from moving out or continuing to date dude. He offered to buy Toi a better car if Mama and Raymond carried out their threat.

Toi told me none of this. Cheryl told me all of it, of course.

My sister's condo was plush. Every room was like some shit out of a magazine. She even had a bar that sat off from the living room, stocked with mad bubbly, some I had never heard of.

It was obvious Toi's new boyfriend had spent a lot of dough decorating her crib, which put me on alert, 'cause it wasn't like he lived with her. So, off the rip I was wondering what his crib looked like 'cause unless he was the sweetest trick in the Dirty South, I figured he wasn't gon' lace Toi's crib better than his own. I was also wondering what type of job he had to be able to afford trick bills like this. And, what the fuck my sister did to get a nigga to bless her so lovely?

Just as I was thinking all of this and stuffing my face with hot buffalo wings, Toi's trick daddy walked into the crib. Partner might not live with Toi, but he had a key to the condo.

"Hey, baby," he said to Toi when she went up to greet him.

He looked at me and Cheryl like we were aliens. Toi hugged him like they hadn't seen one another in a while, then she read his expression.

"Oh, baby. This is my brother, Terrence, and his girlfriend, Cheryl."

"Hi," Cheryl offered.

I nodded and mumbled, "Whud up?"

"What's up?" he responded. "My name is Glen, but everybody calls me Big G."

"They call me Youngblood."

Cheryl was looking at us like she wanted to say she had a nickname too.

"You want some buffalo wings?" Toi asked Glen.

"Naw, I'm straight. I ate a little while ago." Glen said. "Step back here in the bedroom. I need to holla at you right quick."

When my sister came back into the living room she mumbled some bullshit about Glen and her having to go somewhere.

Now, I wasn't no blocker and my sister was grown, so, if it was a matter of dude wanting us to bounce so him and Toi could get nasty, I could swallow that with no water. But that's not the vibe I was getting. It just seemed like dude simply didn't want us there. *Period.* The scene was so uncomfortable I didn't even finish the wing I was biting on. I dropped it back on the plate and wiped my hands with a napkin, balled it up and tossed it at Cheryl.

She said, "Dag."

"Let's go, shawdy. I know when I'm not welcomed somewhere."

"Aww, it ain't like that. I gotta go somewhere with Glen. I'll invite y'all over again next week." My sister tried to placate me with a hug.

I hugged her. "What's yo nigga's problem?"

"Dag, I feel too fat to stand up," Cheryl said.

"I'll call you, girl." Toi then turned to me and said, "Don't be trippin', Glen is cool."

"Whatever."

Cheryl and I left. It was the weekend, so Cheryl was staying at my crib. Her fat, pregnant self-went to sleep five minutes after we got there. I was playing Play Station II while listening to an Outkast CD and mentally sizing up Toi's boyfriend. What really had me curious about Glen besides him coming into my sister's crib like he owned the world was the whip I saw parked outside the condo when I bounced. A 600E Mercedes Benz, that Toi told me he owned.

The whip by itself didn't label Glen as a hustler, some niggaz with a good job and even better credit pushed Benz's or other fly whips.

But his mad spending on Toi, his attitude and persona had me suspicious. Whatever Glen's occupation was, it really was my sister's ball to bounce. My only concern was that she didn't get hurt or used in the process. I knew the dope boy's game on a green, unwise female. They hooked up the female in a fly crib that she can show off to her friends and family, but couldn't afford without the dope boy. That made the female dependent on the nigga if she wanted to maintain that lifestyle.

And once a female got a taste of luxury and style, she gotta be knocked off that high horse. She wouldn't voluntarily step down.

Usually, the female wasn't even the dope boy's main woman; whether she knew it or not, she was his side bitch.

I wasn't trying to see Toi be no nigga's bitch.

If Glen was a hustler, I hadn't heard of him. He damn sho' wasn't no rapper or entertainer or professional athlete. I had him pegged as a nigga doing well with his own business. But I stored it in my mental to watch dude until I could peep his profile. I had to make sure he wouldn't put Toi in danger.

While Cheryl slept, I popped in Tupac's CD into my stereo, cued *All Eyez On Me* and then put on the headphones while I played Play Station.

It wasn't no secret that listening to Tupac put a young G in the mood to do some thug shit. 'Pac was the realest nigga to ever bless a mic, no doubt.

My pager vibrated on my hip. I checked the number and then headed out the front door to the pay phone. I didn't go to the pay phone in the apartment complex, 'cause I planned to jet down to Englewood and cop a bag of weed and grab a bottle of Henny.

I stopped at the liquor store, first, bought some Henny and a six-pack of coke and then used the pay phone outside of the store.

"Hello?" A bitch's voice. Mad noise in the background.

"Yeah, this Youngblood," I said to the voice.

"Y'all hos be quiet, I can't hear!" The background noise lowered a little.

"Hello?"

"Yeah, this Youngblood," I repeated. "Somebody page me from there?"

It was a freak bitch named Fiona from the hood. Shorty was a dime, but her rep was zero. Shit, she was a straight ho, had fucked more niggaz than the justice system.

I had boned her a few weeks ago in the back seat of my whip while parked outside of her aunt's crib. The pussy stanked like dead dogs and like forty fat bitches! I'd had to get my interior washed and shampooed in a hurry. *Ain't no way Fiona gettin' anymore of Youngblood's dick.*

"Why you ain't call me?" she complained.

"For what?"

"Oh, it's like that?"

"What it s'pose to be like, playgirl?" I shot back.

Fiona caught a quick attitude. I could hear it in her voice. She spat, "Nigga, you ain't all that! So don't even try to act like you're sex on the fuckin' beach!"

"Why yo' mouth so fly?" I asked. "Ya nigga must don't beat you right."

"I ain't got no nigga. Why you trippin', Youngblood?" Fiona copped dueces, bowed down.

I told her I wasn't trippin' until she started trying to check a nigga for not calling her, like I owed her a phone call 'cause I had hit that stank pussy.

"My pussy don't stank, boy!" Feeling dissed.

"Whatever, playgirl. On the real, yo. Maybe you should go get a check-up. Your stuff smelled like dead dogs."

"Fuck you, bitch ass nigga! Your lil' bitty dick stanked!" I heard the phone slam down.

I cracked the fuck up, but Fiona's pussy was foul for real. I was sure she would certainly drop salt on my name in the hood before I could salt her name. That was the way punk hos rolled. Like that comment about my *lil' bitty* dick. Yeah, she'd probably tell her friends my wood was mad small. I wasn't trippin' it, though, 'cause the hos in the hood who'd been boned by me would squash that rumor. They knew first hand my shit was a long way from being little.

I was almost at my whip when a short, dark skinned dude got out of his car and approached me.

"Your name Youngblood?"

"Naw," I lied, sensing beef. I didn't recognize dude.

I opened the truck door quickly, but nonchalantly, hoping dude would swallow my lie. At least until I could reach my gat. *Damn!* I had left it in the glove compartment 'cause I didn't want to take it inside the liquor store.

Now, if I was reading dude right, there was beef and he had the drop on me. *Shit!*

I saw the heater in his hand before I heard it blast. Then I felt a fire explode in my side. I knew that if I tried to reach in the Lex' and go for my heater in the glove compartment, dude would shoot me in the back. I didn't wanna be a paraplegic, a young G in a wheelchair, so I turned to face the nigga. Fuck being paralyzed and wearing a shit bag. I'd rather die.

I grabbed at dude's arm, the one spittin' lead at me, point blank.

He jerked away and stepped back, still firing.

Pow! Pow! Pow! Pow!

My body jerked and I fell against my whip and slid down to the ground.

"That's for my sister. Bitch ass nigga!" Dude stood over me and shot me one more time. Then he spat on me.

I tried to record his face in my mind, in case I didn't die. He would see me again, and it wouldn't be to talk. My blood poured out while dude drove off. For some odd reason, Tupac came to mind as I thought, *they shot me six times, but real niggaz don't die!*

My whole body felt like it was on fire, and the pain became unbearable. I saw blurred faces run out of the liquor store and stare down at me before I passed out.

When I woke up, I was in a hospital room, hooked up to mad machines. I was so drugged up I couldn't recognize faces, only voices. They said I didn't wake up again for six days. I was so weak I could barely open my eyes. When I finally did open them and gain some sense of where I was at, Cheryl was in a chair by my bedside. She stood up and leaned down over the bed.

"Hey, you," she said, smiling through tears.

I couldn't speak back because I was still groggy, hooked to machines with a tube stuck down my throat.

Cheryl left out the room, quickly returning with a nurse. The nurse was a short, squatty, white lady with a nice, concerned voice.

Nurse Squatty checked my pulse and then the machines hooked up to me. A doctor then came into the room, followed by younger looking doctors. One of them checked my eyes with a little hand-held light.

The doctors huddled together discussing my condition, I assumed, and then left out without telling me if I was gonna live or die. Not that I would've understood whatever it was they could've told me, I was conscious but incoherent.

I knew I'd been shot and was in a hospital, but I didn't know which hospital or how long I'd been there. I knew I wasn't dead, unless heaven or hell was a hospital. If I was in thug heaven, I wondered where 'Pac was? I didn't see him. And if I was in hell, why hadn't any of my dead homies come to kick it, yet? Surely, I wasn't the only young G in hell. If that's where I was at. And why was Cheryl here?

A few days later I was much better, no longer hallucinating. I was moved from the intensive care unit and put into a private hospital room. While checking my vital signs, a male nurse explained that I'd been shot six times, had gone through emergency surgery and was lucky to be alive. To add insult to injury, I had been fitted with a shit bag. *Fuck!*

"It's only temporary," he explained.

He had the voice and the mannerisms of a bitch. When his bitch ass left out of the room, Cheryl came in with a smile on her face, her belly was like a blimp.

"Hey, boo." She came over to the bed and kissed me on the forehead.

"Hey," my voice was scratchy.

Later I learned the scratchiness of my voice was a temporary result of having a tube down my throat to help me breathe for a few days.

Cheryl said, "Youngblood, you sound like a frog! Dag." But I could see in her eyes she was just happy I was alive and talking, no matter how my voice sounded.

A few hours later, Lonnie and Delina showed up to visit me. I was still being given drugs for pain, so I hardly knew they were there or when they'd left. Cheryl told me my sister and my mama had also come to the hospital, but I was heavily sedated so they'd left.

They returned the next day. I tried to tell Cheryl I didn't wanna see my Ma Dukes, but Cheryl either didn't understand me or ignored what I'd said.

Ma Duke tried to kiss me, but I turned my head. Then I closed my eyes and refused to even look at her. I heard her crying, but I still kept my eyes shut until she left out of the room. I opened my eyes when I heard my sister's voice.

"Terrence? You okay?" Toi asked, her voice laced with concern and uncertainty.

"I'm good," I answered in a whisper. I sounded like a frog, for real.

"Why wouldn't you even look at Mama?"

"I ain't got no mama," I declared.

Toi was getting me vexed and shit, and the machine hooked up to me started beepin' and making other noises. I was feeling like I was 'bout to die.

A nurse came in and checked the machines and then told my visitors they'd have to go. After that, the nurses kept close tabs on who visited me. I told them I only wanted to see Cheryl, Toi, and Lonnie, which is why they'd refused to allow Shan and Lil' T to visit when they came.

I didn't want to see Shan no way, but I would've been glad to see my son. The nurses said children weren't allowed to visit patients on the floor I was on 'cause kids carried too many germs that might infect the patients. So I didn't see Lil' T the whole time I was in the hospital.

Poochie was able to talk her way past the nurses to see me. I was okay with that. She brought me a card my son had made for me, and a message from Shan. I let Shan's message roll off my back, but I kept my son's card on the stand beside my hospital bed.

Cheryl visited me every day after she got out of school, her mother never once visited. I wasn't trippin' it, though. I wasn't the one to care about nobody that don't care about me.

I was getting much better after three weeks in the hospital, but I still had to wear the shit bag. The doctors said I'd be discharged soon, but I'd have to wear the shit bag for a few more months. I wasn't too happy about that but at least a nigga was still alive. I was anxious to get back on my feet and find the nigga who'd tried to take me off the shelf. I'd remember his face 'til the day I splattered it with lead.

"That's for my sister!"

Pow! Pow!

"Bitch-ass nigga!"

I could still hear his words and the sound of the heater. Time would tell who the real bitch ass nigga was.

I had no idea who the nigga was, or who his sister was. She couldn't have been Fiona, the stank pussy bitch I'd dissed on the phone that night I got shot. It could've been any one of the black stripper bitches I'd jacked. But how had they found out my real name?

Or maybe dude's sister was any one of the many rats I'd fucked and forgot? Though that wasn't a good enough reason for a nigga to try to kill me. I was puzzled.

Now to add more drama to the situation, a day before I was to be discharged, po-po came to my hospital room and read me my rights before telling me that I was being charged with possession of a firearm by a convicted felon. A charge that was the result of po-po finding the heater that was in the glove compartment of my Lex truck the night I'd been shot.

I was placed under arrest in the hospital room, my ankle shackled to the bed rail, and a sheriff stood guard outside the room. Whenever I was discharged from the hospital, I'd go straight to the county jail.

Ain't that a bitch?

I cussed the sheriff's ass out. How the fuck they gon' arrest me? *I'm the mafucka who got shot.*

A detective had come to my room and questioned me about the shooting. I told him I didn't know who had shot me or why.

"Was it one of your drug partners?" The po-po questioned.

I told the fool I didn't sell no fuckin' drugs and I wasn't answering none of his questions so he might as well quit asking and step.

"You're going back to prison on that gun charge unless you cooperate!" the detective mean mugged me.

"Whatever," I said calmly. "I still ain't got no rap for you!"

Fuck po-po and the law. I wasn't telling shit. Real niggaz didn't run to po-po to settle beefs for shit that happen in the game. I wasn't letting nobody, but *me*, deal with partna that shot me.

The po-po's bluff to send me back to prison didn't have me shook, either. I had vowed to never return to prison, but I knew I could handle it if fate played out like that. I also figured I'd make bail before ever going to trial on the gun charge and once I was out on bail, po-po would have to bring ass to get some.

When my shawdy came to visit and saw the sheriff outside of my room and learned of the charges against me, she snapped.

"How the fuck y'all gon' lock him up and he's the one who got shot?" Cheryl screamed at the old ass sheriff, her thoughts mimicking my own.

"Ma'am, I'm just doing my job," the old bastard said meekly.

I had already sized him up and felt I could beat his old frail ass and take his gun from him if I could get him to remove the shackles from around my ankle.

Even though I was still weak from surgery and had staples in my side and a shit bag, I figured I could beat po-po's old ass and make a break for it. But the situation wasn't that desperate yet, I knew I'd get a bond and make bail. Besides, medically I was in no shape to go on the run. I had to just go with the flow.

The sheriff stood at the door while Cheryl visited with me.

"Yo, wipe away those tears, shawdy," I told her. "You can't help me if you're gonna fall apart. Look, it ain't no trip. I'ma be a'ight." I explained what I wanted Cheryl to do.

Cheryl whispered, "Dag. Why you keep your money in the freezer?" she asked after I'd finished telling her how to handle everything.

"Lonnie will take you to the lawyer's office and to the bail bondsman once I get a bond." The sheriff told Cheryl she'd have to leave, she stared holes through him. "Go on, boo. Handle biz and I'll be home soon. Take care of my seed." I patted Cheryl's big belly. She smiled, trying hard to be a soldier fo' a nigga, but I could see Cheryl was about to cry again. "I thought you was street tough?" I teased.

"I am," my shawdy said.

About midnight, two other sheriff officers rousted me from my sleep, read me my rights and the charges against me again and took me to the county jail. I was booked and placed on the jail's hospital floor.

A few days later, I was arraigned. The attorney I'd told Cheryl to hire was present along with Cheryl and her mother. Bond was set and a few hours later, I was in the car with Cheryl and her mother, on my way to the crib.

The ride to the house was mostly silent other than Cheryl's few questions about what had happened in court earlier. Her Ma Dukes didn't ask or say shit. I had the feeling she didn't like me too well.

Fuck it!

When Cheryl's mother dropped us off, I was all up in them guts. Cheryl was 'bout eight months pregnant, so I had to hit it from the back 'cause her belly was so fat.

Afterwards, Cheryl fell asleep. I went to the freezer to fix a bit to eat and to check my stash. Neither the lawyer's retainer fee nor the money Cheryl had paid the bondsmen to bail me out put a dent in my pocket. But I knew it would be a minute before I was in enough shape to go on a lick. I'd have to live off of my savings. I also needed to get my whip out of impound, but that wouldn't cost but a few C-notes.

I wasn't really hungry so I just ate one of them boil-bag soups.

Plus, fuckin' Cheryl had me weak as hell. The doctors had told me not to have sex until they removed the shit bag and gave me the okay, but a nigga wasn't studyin' that shit.

As long as my dick got hard, I was gon' use it. I'd just be careful not to bust the shit bag while I was fuckin', 'cause an open shit bag stink like a mafucka.

Cheryl was soon to find that out.

I stood over her while she was asleep on the living room couch and opened the shit bag on my side, letting the stink hit Cheryl square in the nose. She jumped out of her sleep, her hand immediately went to cover her mouth and nose.

"Oooooh! You stank, boy! Dag!" Cheryl cried. She got off of the couch and ran from me. I was cracking the fuck up, chasing her through the apartment with the shit bag opened and smelling foul.

Cheryl locked herself in the bathroom.

"I ain't coming out!" she vowed. Her ass was laughing, too. I promised not to open the bag anymore, so Cheryl finally cracked the door, testing the air. Her nose was still scrunched up.

"Stop playing, Youngblood. You gon' make me and the baby get sick."

"How the baby in yo' stomach gon' smell it?"

"It ain't gotta smell yo' stank self! If I get sick, it gon' make the baby sick."

Fuck that! I opened the shit bag one more time. Cheryl wouldn't come out the bathroom for a long time after that. When she did finally come out, I had fell asleep.

The next day while Cheryl was at school, Lonnie took me to get my whip out of impound. While we went through all the hassle and waited for the impound attendant to bring my whip to the checkout point, Lonnie asked if I had any idea who'd shot me. I'd already told him how the shit went down and what the nigga had said while pumpin' lead in me.

"It might've been some other reason dude tried to smoke you," Lonnie said. "Maybe he just made that shit up about his sister to throw you off?"

"What sense would that make, dawg? Shit, dude tried to send me to my maker. He wouldna been worried about throwing me off unless he wasn't trying to kill me."

"True dat," Lonnie had to agree.

"Anyway," I said, "I'ma find that nigga if it's the last mafuckin' thing I do. It ain't no way I can be at peace until I know who shot me and light a spark in his ass that the doctors can't fix. Nah mean?"

"I feel you, nigga."

Lonnie asked me if my bank would hold me until I was well enough to pull another caper. I let him know I was straight and I appreciated his concern. Shit was always real between Lonnie and me. He didn't have to tell me that he'd ride with me when it was time to revenge the six shots I'd taken. I knew we was tight like that. Still, Lonnie told me he'd put his ear to the ground and see if the streets were talking, maybe the fool who shot me would brag to the wrong person.

After that, I dipped to the crib and waited for Cheryl to come by after school.

I'd let her push the Nissan 'cause I wasn't trying to be in the streets too much, not with a shit bag.

Cheryl was sixteen and had gotten her driver's license. Well, a permit, allowing her to drive with a licensed driver in the car with her. But neither of us was concerned with following the law.

I went to the pay phone in the apartment complex to call Shan and see if she'd let Lil' T stay with me for the weekend. Her attitude was foul 'cause she hadn't been allowed to visit me in the hospital.

"I see yo' bitch was allowed to visit but not me and your son, huh?" Shan spat.

"Yo, it ain't like I made the rules," I said.

"You're a lie, nigga! The nurses told me *you gave* them the names of the only people you wanted to see!"

"Like nurse's tongues come notarized?"

"Why they gon' lie? Huh?"

"Check it, Shan. I don't know why they lied, and it don't much matter now. You gon' let me come get Lil' T tomorrow or what?" I was tired of the verbal wrestling, but Shan obviously wasn't.

"Ain't yo' bitch 'bout to have a baby?"

"Yeah. So what?"

"So, let the baby in her stomach spend the weekend with you. That's so what, nigga!" The phone slammed down in my ear.

Baby mama drama.

I let it slide off my back. See, if a bitch found out she could get a nigga vexed with all that dumb shit, she'd do it on the regular.

My pager vibrated and I dialed the number that appeared on the tiny screen. The woman who answered the phone identified herself as a nurse.

Then she said, "Your wife is in labor. You better come to the hospital, you're about to be a father."

Damn!

I somehow remembered to verify which hospital and jetted off in that direction. Ironically, Cheryl was at the same hospital where I'd recently been a patient.

I made it to the delivery room just in time to hold Cheryl's hand as she screamed, cried, pushed, pushed and gave birth to a healthy seven-pound girl.

The doctor asked if I wanted to cut the umbilical cord.

"Nah, a nigga ain't wit dat!"

So, Doc' did what he was paid to do. After the cord was cut and tied and my daughter had been washed off, the doctor handed her naked butt to Cheryl. The love in Cheryl's eyes was instant. So was the love in mine.

We kept our promise and let my sister Toi name the baby, with my input, of course.

Though barely a day old, my newborn daughter, Eryka Unique Whitsmith, was already a dime. Toi had come to the hospital to name her a few hours after she came into the world. Cheryl's mother was there by then, too. So were Lonnie and Delina.

CHAPTER 22

Little Eryka was born with a head full of pretty brown hair like her mother's. She had the best features of Cheryl's and mine.
If there was ever been a prettier baby girl born, one could never convince me of it. Yeah, my lil' girl was all that and a bag of chips.

Cheryl's bedroom at her mother's spot had been decorated into part-nursery for Eryka Unique, since that's where they'd be living.

Children weren't allowed to live in the complex where I lived. However, there were no rules preventing them from visiting and staying over a few nights at a time.

I was feelin' Cheryl and I had instant love for Eryka, but I would-na wanted them to live with me no way. I rode dirty and lived too dangerously to do it like that. Cheryl and the baby were safer living at Cheryl's mother's crib. I'd go by there to see them and they could always come and stay a few nights at my crib.

Cheryl was on maternity leave from school, the teachers mailed her assignments to her so she didn't fall behind in class.

Cheryl tried to be the perfect mother to our daughter, but she had no experience with babies and struggled with a lot of shit I'd seen most young mothers do naturally. Her Ma Duke wasn't much help, either. She barely was home long enough to hold her first grandchild.

Though she tried hard, I was better with Eryka than Cheryl. So, I usually fed Eryka and changed her diapers when I was with them. If the baby seemed agitated or sick, Cheryl would call my sister for advice. They'd always end up calling my Ma Dukes on a three-way, 'cause Toi didn't know shit 'bout babies, either. Besides, Toi's man kept her isolated from friends and family most of the time. Or at least that's how I read it.

In a pinch, I could call Poochie for advice or even Shan. *Yeah, Shan.* We were getting along fine for the time being, but I hadn't dicked Shan down. However, I had led her to believe I would as soon as I completely healed from the gunshot wounds. Of course, that was just game to see my son. The only way I'd fuck Shan again was if my dick was a bomb. Then I'd just be doing it to watch the punk bitch explode into pieces when I bust a nut.

By the time Eryka was a couple of months old, Cheryl was damn near going loco. Delina said it was some shit called postnatal depression, a chemical change in a woman's body after she gave birth that caused some women to go through temporary but severe depression.

Whatever it was called, Cheryl was buggin'. She was quick to cry or to get frustrated with Eryka. So much so that I was almost afraid to go home and leave Cheryl alone with our daughter. Some nights I'd take Eryka home with me and leave Cheryl at her Ma Duke's. I tried to keep my cool and understand Cheryl's mood swings, but she was really buggin'. Plus, I had other shit on my mental.

For starters, I still hadn't found out who had shot me and the streets weren't saying nada, which had me off-balance 'cause somebody usually knew something about whatever went down. Most niggaz couldn't keep their mouths shut.

I was vexed, not only 'cause I wanted revenge, but also because it was hard to watch my back when I don't know who was aiming at me. Then, I was always vexed when I was spending loot instead of stacking loot.

On top of all that, I was getting bad vibes from my sister's situation. I didn't know what was up with her nigga, but I knew he was blocking our communication. But why? It was like he had Toi imprisoned in that condo. I wasn't feelin' that shit. *But what could a nigga do?*

The first thing I had to do, before I dealt with any of the shit that was on my mental was check into the hospital to have the shit bag removed and the last of the staples in my stomach taken out. I was in and out of the hospital in two days, no more shit bag, no more feeling like a young convalescent. Time to take to the streets and get cheddar, revenge and respect.

I still had the gun charge hanging over my head and my mouth piece was screaming for big dollars to keep my ass out of prison. I had emptied one of the chicken boxes in my freezer paying bail, the lawyer's retainer and other shit over the past months. It was time to stack some more bank.

After I came home from the hospital from having the shit bag removed, it felt damn good to be able to sit on the toilet and take a regular shit.

I took a long, hot bath and tried to focus on my next move. As far as finding out who had shot me, I had no idea what would be the best move. I had fucked and dissed a handful of bitches, but not in a way worth murdering me over. That was why my mind kept going back to those stripper hos I'd jacked. But there was no way they'd know my true identity.

I'd talked to Rich Kid since getting out of the hospital. He said he hadn't been back to The Passion Palace since that night we'd ran into each other, and I'd already pulled his coat not to ever reveal my info to those hos.

I knew Rich Kid wouldn't drop a dime on me, but I couldn't say the same for his flunky, King. Though we'd done work together, it was no doubt in my mind King didn't like me. Maybe he saw me as a threat to his position in Rich Kid's crew? Had the nigga asked me, I would've told him that I had no aspirations to become Rich Kid's puppet. So King didn't need to fear losing his spot to me. But if I ever found out for sure that King had dropped my identity to those stripper hos, he would be wise to fear my brand of reprisal.

For now, I had to let the nigga live, 'cause I wasn't sure he'd dropped my real name to those hos. I didn't know when, or for what reason, but I knew I would eventually blast King. He was a hater supreme. No matter how much faith Rich Kid had in him, something didn't feel right about that nigga.

While Cheryl was at school, a neighbor of hers watched Eryka throughout the week until about three o'clock when Cheryl got home.

I usually picked her up from school, stunting in my truck, but these days I scooped her up in a rental because the Lex' was in the shop having the driver's door and side panel repaired and a brand new paint job. If a mafucka was looking for a nigga pushing a silver Lexus truck, I would have him off-balanced when my whip came out of the shop painted money-green.

After picking Cherry up today and dropping her off at the crib, I was rolling incognito in the Nissan rental, just checkin' the blocks for the latest hum. Niggaz hadn't really seen me since I caught six shots, so they were giving me smiles and dap like I was returning home a war hero, which wasn't too far from the truth. The street is a war zone.

I saw through those with false smiles, envy, and hate. Most hood niggaz were glad to see me still standing, but I knew a few had been squeezin' their nuts, hoping a nigga was face-up in a box. I could easily recognize the haters, though. That shit was written all over their faces.

I hung out in Englewood PJs for an hour or so, just kickin' the bobo and lettin' niggaz see I was hard to kill.

It was a Friday so the ghetto was jumpin': young hustlers gettin' their grind on, fiends out in flocks. Po-po cruised in and out, but they would've had to arrest two out of three people they passed by if it was crime they were out to stop today. So po-po just cruised on past, knowing they couldn't' stop the drug dealing juggernaut that was the hood.

Four morbid hos wanted to see my scars, so I lifted my shirt and let 'em get their rocks off. The next day I planned to get a tattoo around the scars.

"What your tattoo gon' say?" Angel, one of the morbid hos, asked.

"Hard 2 Kill," I explained.

"How it feel to get shot?"

"Shit, shawdy. It feel like yo' insides on fire."

"Did you almost die?" her friend wanted to know.

"Who? Me? Hell naw!" I popped. "How a real nigga gon' die? I could live with no head, shawdy! You don't know?" I had them hos swingin' on my dick.

"Where yo' whip at?" Cita asked. She seemed to be the ringleader of the crew. I knew her from the PJs.

"I'm resting it fo' a minute. Why? You wanna get fucked in the back seat while watching TV?"

She laughed. "Nigga, I don't fuck in no car! I got Peachtree Plaza pussy. You ain't heard?" Her friends giggled and gave her some dap.

I countered with, "Yo' ass got some on the ground, behind a dumpster pussy. That's what I heard."

"Oh, you wanna go there? I ain't gon' talk about yo' lil' bitty dick." Cita and her friends started laughing.

I had to pop back. "Ho, my shit bigger than your arm! You betta ask somebody."

"That ain't what Fiona going around screamin'," two of them said in unison.

Fiona? Who the fuck is—

"You mean stank pussy Fiona?" I laughed, remembering the bitch in question. I had pegged the rotten pussy bitch right. She had dropped salt on me in the streets.

When hood rats wanted to slander a niggaz name, they spread one of these three rumors: He got a little dick. He ate their pussy or he can't fuck.

Fiona had probably screamed all three, lying like a mafucka. My wood wasn't little! I wasn't no porn stud, but I'd make a bitch sing the woo-woo song in bed, so they couldn't say I couldn't fuck. And I might have ate a little pussy, but I fo' sho' didn't eat Fiona's stank stuff.

I didn't know if she had dissed a nigga's name like that or not, but a few playaz had walked up and was hearing the hype these hos were repeating.

I was like, "Aw, shit. You know how ya'll hos be lying and slandering a nigga's rep 'cause he put y'all on permanent timeout. Fiona just mad 'cause I told her *her* pussy smelled like dead dogs and canceled her subscription to this dick."

The niggaz who'd gathered around started laughing and adding their jabs at Fiona's foul rep.

A young grinder named Murder Mike said, "Yo, dawg, I hate to admit I fucked that bitch, but you ain't lyin', her coochie do smell foul as a mafucka."

Two other niggaz co-signed our remarks. One busta-ass nigga was just lying to kick it. He was as busted as a high-top fade. Fiona was a slut, but she only fucked niggaz with mad rep or ghetto riches. The hos around tried to take up for Fiona, like her word was bond.

I said to one of them, “I tell you what, shawdy. Come feel this dick. If it’s little, I’ll kiss yo’ ass in front of my niggaz.”

“Boy, I ain’t feelin’ yo’ dick!”

“Aw, ho, don’t front,” Murder Mike jumped in. “You done felt everybody in the hood dick, one more ain’t gonna kill you.”

“I woulda felt *yours* when we was fuckin’ that time, but it’s so goddamn tiny,” Cita countered, trying to slander Murder Mike.

I said, “See how y’all hos do it? Now, you doin’ the same shit Fiona did, dirtying a nigga’s name ‘cause you’re mad.”

“I ain’t *mad*. Ain’t nobody studyin’ Murder Mike. I bet he be knockin’ on my door as soon as he come out the trap tonight,” boasted Cita.

I stood around and kicked the bobo for a few more minutes, and then dipped. When I pulled up in front of her apartment, Fiona was sitting on the porch steps reading *The Source* magazine.

“Yo, whud up?” I said as I walked up to where Fiona sat.

“What you want?” Her tone matched her eyes—unfriendly.

“Oh, it’s like that now?” I rubbed her thigh.

“Don’t touch me! How you gon’ try to play me after all that shit you said”? Fiona snapped.

I told her I was just trippin’ that night, and I had planned to come over her house and get with her later on, surprise her, but I’d gotten shot. I spat some more slick shit in her ear.

I had dissed the fuck out of Fiona that night on the phone before some sucka opened fire on me, but I could see she was still feelin’ me, and all it would take to reel her in was persistence. The lil’ bitch swallowed my rap like she was thirsty for some slick shit. I was lying like a mofo, but Fiona ate it up.

“You forgive me, or what?” I could tell my rap had worked.

Fiona nodded.

“Cool,” I said. “Now what’s all this yak your girls talkin’ ‘bout you said my dick was little and shit? Why you slander a nigga’s name?”

“I ain’t tell nobody that!” Fiona lied, faking an attitude to make it more believable.

“Why Cita and ‘em gon’ lie on you?” I pressed on.

"Them hos just like to gossip and start shit," Fiona swore.

I told her to get in the car. We were about to go down the hill where her girls were at and straighten this shit out and see who was lying. Of course, the bitch tried to buck on that.

"Why you gotta prove something to them triflin' hos?" she asked. "That's lil' kids shit."

Fuck that! It ain't no lil' kid shit when hos spreading false rumors that I got a lil' kid's dick

I told Fiona if she didn't come with me down the hill and check Cita and 'em, I wasn't fuckin with her again.

"You trippin'." she said. But she liked the dick and didn't want me to cut her off completely, so she got her stank-pussy ass in the car.

When we got down the hill, Cita was sitting between Murder Mike's knees on a parked car. Her girls were standing around kickin' it with other block hustlers as they slanged rocks. They knew some ill shit was up when they saw Fiona get out of the car with me.

Now, Fiona was a known slut, but she was fine as hell. A nigga from another hood, who didn't know her rep' in Englewood, would think he had a star in Fiona. She looked like a younger version of Jennifer Lopez, phat ass and all. Cita and her crew could spend a year in a beauty parlor, and Fiona could just be waking up in the morning and she'd have 'em all fucked up in the looks department. Plus, Fiona had fucked all the ghetto fabulous niggaz so she had hood props Cita and 'em couldn't claim. So around them, Fiona had mad attitude.

She said, "Cita! You told Youngblood I said his dick was little?" She was trying to keep a straight face.

Murder Mike cracked up. The shit was funny the way Fiona just spat it out, no prefacing it.

"Ho, I know you don't call yo' self checkin' me 'bout that bull-shit," Cita responded.

Fiona said, "I'm just saying, why y'all spreadin' stupid shit like that? Y'all some silly hos."

"Aw, bitch, you the one who told us that shit," Cita said, laugh-ing.

I made Fiona admit that she'd spreaded the lie because she was mad at me for dissin' her.

"I don't know why you let that shit vex you no way," Fiona said to me in front of everybody out there. "Nigga, you lay good pipe."

She was stroking my ego.

Cita's friend, Angel, said, "Shan already told us you was *all dat* in bed. Why you think Fiona was all on yo' dick?" The hos started laughing, like they'd played me for a fool.

The busta ass nigga, who'd claimed he'd fucked Fiona, too, laughed with them. I started to slap his wannabe ass. Instead, I asked Fiona if she'd ever fucked him.

"Hell no!" she screamed, and the busta dropped his head.

Me and Fiona got in the car and dipped. She asked where my truck was, and I told her the same shit I'd told Cita. I was resting it.

I pulled into a Starvin Marvin and sent Fiona in the store to get some rolling paper.

"You got some weed?" the dumb bitch asked.

"Why else would I need some papers?" I asked.

As soon as she went inside the store, I pulled off and left her ass.

I checked my wrist and realized it was time to pick Cheryl up from school. In fact, I was running late.

Cheryl got in the car oozing attitude. She didn't ask why I was late. She didn't say shit, which for her was a first.

I wasn't gon' kiss her ass, so I dropped her off at the neighbor's crib who watched Eryka in the daytime and dipped. I didn't even go inside to see my baby girl. Shit, I can act ill, too. Besides, I had too much shit on my mental agenda to be going through drama with a bitch. It wasn't like the world was gonna end 'cause I was late picking her up.

The next day I went and got tatted and then picked up my truck from the paint shop later that evening. My whip was phat! The money-green paint job was slammin'. I traded in my rims for a new set of dubs they were selling,and when I pulled off the lot, I felt like I was pushing a brand new whip.

I dashed by Shan's to show off and to drop her some loot for Lil' T; they were going to White Waters amusement park with some more people Shan knew. I stayed and played catch football with my son for a minute, but Shan spoiled our fun, crying about Lil' Terrence getting his clothes dirty. *Leave it to Shan to ruin the simplest fun for a nigga.*

I'm convinced the bitch just hated to see me happy. That was probably why hos closed their eyes when they kiss a nigga—they couldn't stand to see us happy.

So, I bounced from there and went to find something to get into.

My dawg Lonnie wasn't home, so I decided to pay my sister a surprise visit, hoping her nigga wasn't around. Toi wasn't home either, so I got on the Interstate and headed back to the hood.

While I was in route to the game room, Cheryl paged me but I ignored the calls. I'd teach her ass about trying to catch an attitude with a nigga.

At the game room I shot a few games of pool and spit flava at a honey named Inez. I was just shootin' the shit, really, 'cause Inez was this nigga named Fat Stan's baby mama.

Inez was 100 percent eye candy. A real dime with that attitude like she knew it, too. The kind of bitch that'd make a nigga kick off in her ass.

I wasn't no hater, but keep it real. Fat Stan didn't deserve Inez.

She was more than his fat ass could handle. She looked just like that sexy actress, Stacy Dash. On the other hand, Fat Stan was bigger and uglier than the Notorious B.I.G. However, like the late Biggie, Fat Stan did have some game for a bitch. But with Inez it was mostly the loochie that kept her down for him.

Big Boy wasn't no major baller but he stayed on the grind and clocked decent figures, most of it finding a way into Inez' purse. I guess Inez figured it was wiser to fuck with Fat Stan and get *all* of his cheddar than to get with a boss hustler and only get small pieces of his.

See, a nigga didn't have to look good to get the flyest bitch; all he had to do was get money and respect from the streets and a fly ho would be down.

A bitch, though, she had to look good to lock down a balla, 'cause to street niggaz, it was all a show: Who pushin' the flyest whip? Who rockin' the most bling? Who holdin' down the baddest bitch?

Ugly bitches didn't stand a chance with a boss hustler, unless she sucked mean dick. Then she might get him to make a booty call, but never would she get showcased in public.

Anyway, I knew Fat Stan from way back in YDC. I only knew Inez from seeing her around. Yet, I was up on her situation with Fat Stan. I knew that Inez had that killa pussy. Meaning, Fat Stan would kill a nigga over Inez. Now, the creed of the streets dictated that a nigga was out of bounds if he brought the ruckus to another nigga about fuckin' his bitch, 'cause a nigga couldn't fuck what was really his. But some niggaz didn't respect the creed, or, perhaps, it was that some bitches got pussy so good a nigga lost his perspective. Whatever, it was well known that Fat Stan would heat a nigga up about his bitch.

Occasionally, niggaz would test him when his heater went warm, but he always met the challenge. So, any nigga with love for life avoided Inez like a modern-day plague. But it had already been documented that I didn't bar death. So when Inez got all up in my grill like a dentist, I did what any real nigga would do. I took her to the crib and dicked her down.

Lying in my arms, Inez told me that Fat Stan had caught a nickel in the state pen while I was convalescing from being shot. So he'd been gone about four months and already Inez had her legs open. I was laying there thinking: *Bitches ain't shit!*

A nigga be going all-out to give them the best jewels, gear, bling and shit and then as soon as he took a fall, those hos disrespect by fuckin' another nigga before their man could go through classification and get a prison number.

The game was mad crazy. Damn near everything about it was disloyal. That was why a hustler has to put money over bitches, M.O.B., and he couldn't love them hos, 'cause they damn sho' didn't love us. They loved what we represented, ghetto fame.

"What did Stan fall fo'?" I asked, both of us butt-ass-naked.

"He copped out to an aggravated assault. They dropped a dope charge and another assault," Inez told me. She didn't have to tell me that Fat Stan's agg' assaults were on niggaz who'd tried to holla at her, I knew the deal.

I asked, "You gon' stay down for him while he's on locks or what?"

"I'ma look out for him and take his daughter to see him while he's in there, but he already knows I'ma be kickin' it with somebody until he gets out," Inez explained.

"He's cool with that?" I asked.

"He ain't got no choice but to be cool with it. He gotta do five years. I ain't no nun, and I ain't gonna lie to him."

"True dat," I said. "But Fat Stan mad loco about you. I can't believe he just accepts it like that. He strikes me as the type of nigga who tries to control his bitch from the pen."

Inez propped her head up with her hand. "Let's get one thing straight, nigga!" She said, "First of all, I ain't no bitch. Don't get it twisted 'cause I'm in bed with you. It's just sex and ain't but four niggaz ever got it from me. If you're gonna play me like that, you won't be gettin' no more."

"Damn, shawdy! Don't get bent, I didn't mean it like *that*. You know a nigga just used to talking like that. Nah mean?"

Inez accepted my half-apology and told me not to disrespect her in that way again. I guess she was used to handling Fat Stan, but I was on another level, wasn't no bitch gonna handle *me. How the fuck she gon' demand respect when her nigga was doing a bid and she was doing my dick?* I can't respect that! I bit my tongue for the time being, I'd show my weight later.

I told Inez about Cheryl and Eryka, Shan and Lil' T, letting her know that I wasn't no pussy-whipped nigga like Fat Stan. She was cool with it, but she claimed not to fuck two niggaz at the same time.

"You ain't never cheated on Fat Stan?"

"Nah," Inez swore, but I didn't believe her.

"For what?" she said. "Stan might not be the best looking nigga around, but he treated me with respect and I didn't want for nothing."

"So that's what you're about, huh?" I stared straight into the bitch's eyes so she wouldn't get my words twisted. "Well, I ain't no cake daddy like Fat Stan. All I'ma give you is the same thing you give me, sex. When it's time to get your hair done and your nails fixed and go on shopping sprees, it ain't gon' be Youngblood's money in yo' grip."

"Have I asked you for some money?" Inez asked with a hint of indignation.

"I'm just letting you know, shawdy."

"You don't have to let me know *that!* 'Cause I don't want no money from you. Some female must've really played you for some big loot, 'cause you're paranoid as hell." I laughed.

"Never," I popped. "I'm way too clever."

Inez told me that if she hadn't learned anything else from fucking with Fat Stan, she had learned how to hustle and make her own loot.

"What you know 'bout hustling, shawdy?" I said.

"I know that loose lips sink ships," Inez said without hesitation, surprising the fuck out of me.

I liked her style.

"What else do loose lips do?"

"Do you really wanna know?" Her voice grew as husky as mine.

I felt her hands caress my scars and then her tongue followed. I gently pushed down on the top of her head, but she wouldn't go down. Fuck it. Some hos tried to front like they didn't suck dick, but they all did it.

It was just a matter of time.

I didn't force the issue. Inez' pussy was good enough to please a nigga, minus the brains. I climbed between her legs and gave her some more of this thug passion. In no time at all, she was bucking up against me and screaming, "I'm cumming!"

She was one of those bitches who made a lot of sexy moans and faces when she came and since I laid mad pipe, I had her face twisted and her moans plentiful.

The next morning, I dropped Inez off at her crib and told her to page me later.

"You know where I live," she said.

I assumed she meant she wasn't gonna page me and if I wanted to see her again, I'd come by her crib.

Whatever.

A week passed and Inez hadn't paged me yet. I was calling her bluff and I guess she was calling mine. I wasn't gon' front, though, I was thinking about her, especially because Cheryl was gettin' on a nigga's nerves.

If it wasn't one thing or the other, it was everything. Our daughter was almost four months and Cheryl still hadn't lost any of the weight she'd gained while pregnant. I told her if she didn't go on a diet, she was gonna end up looking like a sumo wrestler. Still, she ate up everything in sight.

She no longer was show-off material, so I never took her out anywhere, and I didn't like fucking her anymore. So I was mad as fuck when Cheryl told me she was pregnant again.

We had a heated argument. I threw a roll of money at her and told her to either get an abortion or forget about me. She was crying like a fat baby when I walked out.

Cheryl's mother paged me later that night pleading her daughter's case. I wasn't tryin' to hear that shit, though. So I ended up cussin' Cheryl's mother out. She told me they'd see me in child support court and slammed the phone in my ear.

Fuck it, I wasn't gon' let them vex me. But neither was I gonna let them play tug-o-war with my daughter like Shan did with Lil' T. I had no love for Cheryl's moms, so I wouldn't hesitate to go thug-style on her ass. *How the fuck she gon' step in and try to regulate shit between Cheryl and me when her ass was seldom seen?*

Lonnie kept telling me to let it ride, Cheryl and I would get an understanding once I accepted that she just wasn't gettin' an abortion.

I wasn't feelin' him, though. *Shit! What a young thug nigga need with three kids?*

I looked in the rearview mirror at my reflection and thought about some ill shit Jay-Z said on one of his records *How stress would give a young nigga an old face.*

I probably would've gone by Cheryl's crib and blasted her and her mama, took my daughter and got ghost if Rich Kid hadn't paged me and told me he needed me to do some work for him.

I had no beef about providing for Eryka. I loved my lil' girl and I owed her whatever I owed myself and my son Lil' T.

My beef with Cheryl was about the seed growing in her stomach. I could already tell there was nothin' between Cheryl and me no more, at least on my end. So, I wasn't feelin' her having a second child by me.

I couldn't really explain why the feeling I'd once had for Cheryl had disappeared like a crackhead's dreams. Before Eryka was born, Cheryl and I got along good, and she stayed lookin' fly. Now, she had turned into a lazy, fat chickenhead, hardly ever getting her hair done and always accusing and nagging me.

I thought back to when Cheryl had first found out she was pregnant with Eryka, and how she'd swore she wasn't gon' be trippin' on me like most young hos be trippin' on their baby daddies. Now, Cheryl was doing the very shit she'd sworn she *wouldn't* do. I began to think this second pregnancy was a trap, Cheryl's way of handcuffin' a nigga.

If having Eryka had turned Cheryl into Miss Piggy, what would she look like after having another baby?

I wasn't tryin' to imagine myself in a fly whip with a fat baby mama on my arm. *Fuck dat!* A thugged out, young nigga in a fly ass whip deserved a fly ass bitch on his arm.

I put Trick Daddy's CD in the deck and turned up the volume while I drove to meet Rich Kid.

As usual, Englewood was jumpin', niggaz on the grind, bitches tryin' to come up, lil' kids watchin' and learnin', po-po one step behind and the Rib Lady servin' 'em all.

I found Rich Kid parked up by the basketball court, sitting on the hood of his whip, a black Viper. The whip was tricked out, 20 inch rims and all, reflective of Rich Kid's ghetto fabulous status.

Two of his street soldiers stood guard, silently protecting the hand that fed them. I didn't see his watch dog, King, the big ugly nigga who was usually at Rich Kid's side 24/7. That was unusual.

Though it was almost sixty degrees outside, niggaz were playing ball and a huddle of niggaz were shootin' craps nearby.

"He's cool," Rich Kid said to his two soldiers, stopping them from patting me down. "Whud up?" he said to me.

"That's what I'm here to find out?" I said, skippin' the small talk.

We walked a few feet away from the others and I listened as Rich Kid talked in a whisper. I didn't ask a question or say a word 'til he finished explaining why he had wanted to holla at me.

Then, all I said was, "I'll handle it. You can count on it."

A day later, I was riding with Lonnie, explaining to him what Rich Kid wanted me to do. If Lonnie ever turned rat, the goods he had on me could send me away for life, but Lonnie was one hundred percent real. I wasn't worried about him ever flippin' on me. I trusted Lonnie with my life. Therefore, I didn't worry about him betraying my secrets.

Though Lonnie had never been put in that predicament with me, it was well known in the hood that he'd kept his mouth shut when the heat came down on him and some other niggaz, years before. Keepin' it real wasn't a badge of honor for Lonnie, it was just the way he lived.

I witnessed it with the way he treated his girl, Delina, and her children. Even the way he treated Delina's smoked out ex-boyfriend and the way he handled the beef between me and Shotgun Pete.

Sadistic torture couldn't get Lonnie to turn rat. So I had no reservations about letting him know what was on my agenda, especially when I wanted his opinion on the matter. Otherwise, I just played by the rules of the streets and kept my business off my lips. But this was one of those times I wanted to hear Lonnie's opinion.

He said, "I guess you're changing your steelo from stickup kid to hitman?"

"Nah, dawg. Really, the two go hand-in-hand."

"Not really," Lonnie disagreed. But I didn't see it that way.

I told him it was all a hustle. The same toilet, different shit. I was down for any hustle involving the gat, as long as the pay was proper and I could control the risk. Besides, I was itching to blast the nigga, Rich Kid, wanted eliminated this time. Not to mention I hadn't added to my freezer stash in a while. I had no targets to rob at the present, and Lonnie didn't have anything scoped out. So Rich Kid's offer was sweet music to my ears. It would take time to get the drop on the target and catch him alone and vulnerable. But like I said before, when a mafucka wanted you dead bad enough, wasn't no escaping it.

The only unknown was will the nigga who pulled the trigger get away with it or not.

Lonnie didn't say it directly, but I got the impression he wasn't feelin' my hitman steelo. It could've been that Lonnie didn't agree with my cleaning up Rich Kid's mess all of the time. I knew that my dawg had little respect for niggaz like Rich Kid, who would put a hit on a nigga in a minute, but wasn't apt to pull the trigger themselves.

Lonnie wasn't a hater, but his respect went out to the street soldiers more than it went to the nigga behind the scene calling the shots.

I was my own man, so Lonnie didn't try to change my mind about doing hits for Rich Kid. Instead, he was kind of short on words.

Still, he said, "If you need me to watch your back, just holla when it's about to go down."

I knew he'd ride with me outta love, not for the cheddar to be made for the hit. Though that somewhat confused me, 'cause a while back when I was fresh out the pen, Lonnie and I had settled a beef for a kid named Freddie.

Same toilet, different shit.

I just figured Lonnie didn't like or trust Rich Kid, 'cause the nigga Rich Kid wanted me to slump was King, his ever present right hand man. Lonnie reasoned that if Rich Kid would have King whacked, I could one day end up on Rich Kid's hit list. Maybe.

But I wasn't worried about down the road, the future. A street nigga wasn't got nothing but today. Nor would I give Rich Kid a reason to want me dead, as King apparently had done.

The way it was told to me, King had quit Rich Kid's crew and started his own. He'd also taken along a dozens of Rich Kid's young soldiers and had them working traps that competed with a few of Rich Kid's. A major violation and dis'.

I assumed that Rich Kid feared that King was building his weight up and then would make a power move to knock Rich Kid off of his throne.

Obviously, King had intimate knowledge of how his ex-boss operated. Perhaps King knew Rich Kid's suppliers and stash spots.

Probably knew Rich Kid's weaknesses, too. Had probably been skimming money from Rich Kid for years, waiting for the opportune time to make a break and start up his own crew.

What puzzled me was why had King not made his break with Rich Kid's blessings? Why'd he put dope in spots to challenge Rich Kid? What weakness had King seen in his ex-boss that led him to break away and challenge Rich Kid? Or was it pure and simple greed?

I wondered if Rich Kid felt threatened by the secrets King knew.

No doubt, King knew where the bodies were, and could always use that info to barter with po-po if he ever caught a major case. That was indeed something Rich Kid had to worry about.

I strongly suspected King was shady in money transactions. *But was he suspect to snitchin?* My own experiences have taught me that if a nigga would steal from you, he'd cross you in every other way, too.

Or it could be the simple fact that he just didn't like not having King under his thumb. Most dope boys were like that. They wanted to forever control a nigga. Like a pimp controled his hos.

Well, King had played ho for years for Rich Kid, jumpin' whenever Rich Kid snapped his fingers. He'd reaped the rewards, if that was what it was called. But now he would have to pay the piper for betraying his pimp. I had no qualms about it. Shit, I was the grim reaper. The last mafucka King would see before going to see his Maker. That was the game. It spared no one.

My day would eventually come. I was peace with that. But as long as my number hadn't come up yet, I wasn't lettin' no nigga put me in his crew and pimp me on the block. Put me on Front Street while he laid back and got fat.

Even as a shorty, I wasn't down with that. Fuck a nigga taking me to the mall and buying me gear and kicks. Or taking me to trick loot at a strip club and then having me slang dope all day, every day of the week, winter, spring, summer, fall.

Yeah, I'd let the pistol bark for Rich Kid or any other nigga who needed work done and could afford my price, but I was independent. I wasn't under anybody's thumb.

King's days were numbered. I knew I'd slump his ass one day, way back when he'd shorted me on that loot.

CHAPTER 23

Locating King wasn't easy. The dope spots his crew operated wasn't in the ATL, they were in Kentucky, where I had once went with King to help establish some dope traps for Rich Kid.

Hitting King in Kentucky had its advantages. One being he would not be expecting me up there, nor would anyone there know me.

However, by me not knowing my way around the city was a major disadvantage, which was why I told Rich Kid I'd rather wait and catch King when he came back and forth to Atlanta.

How did I know King would return to the ATL eventually?

Robbing dope boys was my bread and butter, it wa my steelo to understand their habits. A nigga that went out of town and blew up, would eventually return home to show off. I had no doubt King would soon return to Atlanta to style and profile, show niggaz that he was his own man now, no longer Rich Kid's puppet.

It was just a matter of patience and keeping my ear to the streets.

In the meantime, I had other shit to deal with. Scout out future capers, find the bitch nigga who shot me, check on my seeds and my sister; shine on jealous niggaz and fuck with mad hos. Everyday G shit.

I was whippin' the Lex' truck when my pager started ringing. I pulled into a convenience store parking lot to use the pay phone

"Yo. Anybody page Youngblood?" I asked when the other line was answered.

"Yeah, I paged you," the sweet voice said. "This is Inez. What's up with you?" *Fat Stan's baby's mama.*

"Oh. I'm good, shawdy. What's on yo' mind?"

"Can I see you?" She sounded seductive. Hopeful. But it was time to make her beg, establish who needs who, at least who *wanted* who.

"That depends on how bad you wanna see me," I said.

"Why don't you come over and find out?" She sounded like she was already naked.

"Peep this, Inez. Let's not play games with one another. You're fly as hell and you got da bomb sex. But a nigga like me be on a paper chase and too much good pussy just gon' slow me down. Fat Stan spoiled you and maybe you deserved everything you got from him, but I'm not the one. I like big faces…"

"Just come over," Inez interrupted. "I'm gonna show you how much I want you and it ain't gonna be about sex."

I got quiet for a minute as I contemplated her offer. Curious about what she wanted to show me, I finally agreed to roll through and holla at her.

"A'ight, I'll be over there in a half hour, or so."

"Okay, baby. I'll see you then. Bye."

"Bye."

When I got to Inez' crib everything was proper. In fact, the atmosphere was lovely. R. Kelly was crooning out of the system in Inez' living room.

"You can have a seat," she said, directing me to a plush white sofa.

The living room was fly, snow white sofa, loveseat and chair with overstuffed pillows, glass end tables, cocktail table with powder blue designs. African art decorated the tables and walls along with an assortment of pictures in blue frames of Inez and, I assumed, her and Fat Stan's daughter. I didn't see a single picture of Fat Stan, though.

I took off my jacket and Inez hung it on a coat rack in the corner.

My gat was poking me in the thigh when I sat down, so I removed it from my waist and put it between my feet on the carpet.

"You want me to put that up for you until you get ready to leave?" Inez asked. I guess a nigga packin' heat wasn't new to her.

"I feel more comfortable with it within reach," I said. And I wasn't frontin'.

"That's cool." She placed a bowl of weed on the cocktail table and some sticky brown rolling papers. "Roll one for me, too," Inez said. "I'm gonna finish cooking. I hope you ain't ate yet."

"What you cookin'?"

"Chili. Unless you want something different."

"Chili is cool." I watched Inez walk toward the kitchen.

She had on a pair of jeans that grabbed her phat ass like a pair of hands. The oversized T-shirt she wore was tied up in a knot at her navel. She had on her *chillin' at the crib* gear, accentuated by bling around her neck, wrists and on her fingers.

Fat Stan had treated Inez well.

I looked around and wondered where their daughter was. I was thinking Inez had sent her off to a babysitter so we'd be alone.

Anyway, I rolled two fat stickies' and then I thought about what old heads said about bitches putting roots on a nigga. Puttin' a curse on him by putting their period blood in chili or spaghetti.

So I went into the kitchen and watched Inez prepare the pot of chili.

I doubted if a bitch could really have a nigga'z head fucked up by putting her period blood in his food, but I still didn't want a slick ho trying no trife shit like that.

I leaned on the kitchen counter, smoking the joint with one hand and holding my heat with the other. I held the joint to Inez' lips while she busied herself with tomatoes and ground beef and other ingredients. She choked on the smoke, turning her head away from the ingredients and pulling away from the joint.

"Why you gotta hold your gun in my house? You don't trust me?" Inez asked, a little annoyed.

"I don't trust nobody," I firmly stated.

"You're too paranoid. You must do a lot of dirt to a lot of people." I let the remark rise up to the ceiling with the weed smoke and then the only sounds in the kitchen for the next fifteen minutes was of Inez adding the ingredients to the pot on the stove. When she was finished, she washed her hands and dried them on a towel. "Follow me," she said. So I did, gat in hand.

After we'd gone from room to room, upstairs and down, checking closets and underneath beds, we returned to the living room.

"Now you know ain't nobody here but us, maybe you can put that gun up and relax."

I checked the front and back doors, peeked out the window and saw nothing out of the ordinary. I sat back down on the sofa next to Inez and slid my heat up under the coffee table.

"Nigga, you a trip," Inez said, shaking her head.

"Don't take it personal. I don't know you too well, and I don't trust people I don't know. You've been with a hustler before. You know if we get caught sleepin', we end up with our dick in the dirt."

"Baby, I got something way better than dirt your dick can end up in. I'm not with all that cross out stuff. I'm trying to choose you, not *set you up.*"

"I'm listening," I said, cool-like. "Spit yo' game." Inez ran it down to me, precise. Like she'd rehearsed it for weeks.

Inez told me she had a major weed connection and to maintain her lifestyle while her trick nigga, Fat Stan, was doing time she was selling much weed, OZs and up. She needed a nigga to hold her down, claim her as his, so niggaz wouldn't be too quick to try to rob her or disrespect her spot.

Her crib was in a middle-class hood, away from the inner city mayhem. But since a lot of her clientele were street niggaz, Inez feared that someone would eventually cross her.

Needless to say, niggaz were quick to try a bitch on some robbery shit.

If they knew a thug nigga was holding Inez down, they'd hesitate to run up in her spot.

My rep' wasn't large on the street, but niggaz who knew me knew I'd let the pistol bark. And then some only knew me from rolling with Lonnie.

Still, they knew Lonnie wasn't to be fucked with, which gave me props by proxy. Regardless, I saw no drawbacks to holding Inez down. She'd do all the weed selling, all I'd do was be her nigga, letting niggaz know the bitch had muscle behind her. For that I'd get 40 percent of her profits. I was good with that.

The real clincher came when Inez went upstairs and came back with a shoe box.

"Here." Inez handed me the shoe box "I'm choosin', so here's my choosin' fee." I removed the lid from the box and estimated about four grand inside.

We talked and got high for an hour and then the chili was done. I ate two bowls of chili and three thick slices of hot garlic bread, drank some beer and counted my blessings. Sometimes loot just fell in a real niggaz' lap. I was sure if I hadn't handled Inez the way I had a few weeks ago, she would've never chosen me.

I suspected Inez had come to the game room that day looking for a real nigga to hold her down. I was sure this weed hustle of hers wasn't new. Bitches like Inez got game, too.

I stayed over Inez' crib for three days, only leaving to go get a change of clothes.

I watched mafuckaz come by and cop ounces and bigger weight from Inez. She had a steady clientele and strict business hours, noon 'til 6 p.m. *No exceptions*. The only flaw in her setup was that she had to invite the clients into her crib to serve them. This made her easy bait for a robbing, which I guessed was why she needed me to hold her down. Still, if somebody felt there was enough loot inside Inez' crib, my holding her down wouldn't stop serious stickup kids from plotting.

Inez' defense against that possibility was to only deal with people she knew and somewhat trusted, which was no defense at all. 'Cause *nobody* could be trusted where there was enough loot around. Shit, I was even wondering if I should just rob the bitch and get ghost, to hell with holding her down.

I decided to let it play itself out, for a while at least.

I saw a few niggaz that I knew come by and cop from Inez. Before long, the streets would know she was my bitch now. I guess that was the point of me being present while Inez served them.

I fucked Inez in every position and in every opening known to man for those three days, especially the third day, making sure I busted a nut in her mouth. 'Cause I knew she was going to visit Fat Stan in prison the next day. If he kissed her, he'd be sucking dick by proxy.

Let me back up. Inez told me a lot about herself over those three days and nights. I listened, but I didn't store it as fact, knowing a bitch would lie to make a nigga see her the way she sees herself, which wasn't never the true picture.

But I hoped that time would show that Inez was a real one, true to her claims. Of course. there was no way to know that then.

Her daughter was living with Fat Stan's mother. "I don't want my baby around while I'm selling weed," Inez told me. I respected that.

Three days had me feelin' the bitch. Her style was so on point I couldn't understand why she had fell for Fat Stan, other than the dough he'd given her.

In just three days, I knew he hadn't deserved the bitch. See, the way I was taught, a nigga wasn't no better than the bitch that represented him and vice-versa. If Fat Stan was a trick and Inez claimed him as *her* nigga, then *she* was a trick bitch.

Only, her style contradicted that.

I'd wait and see if these three days were flex.

So far, though, Inez seemed like a down bitch. If her profile changed, I'd still hold her down long enough to case-out some of her clientele and maybe her weed supplier and then I'd jack 'em all. After they'd copped some weed, it wouldn't be too difficult to get Lonnie to follow them from Inez' crib. Maybe they'd unsuspectingly lead Lonnie to their money nest.

The way I saw it there was no way I'd come out a loser by fuckin' with Inez. I hadn't paid it much attention before this come up fell right into my lap, but the streets were flooded with down-ass bitches looking for a real nigga to hold 'em down.

The dope game and thug living had claimed so many lives and sent mad niggaz to prison. Now the streets were short of real niggaz, true players and thugs a bitch could respect. That was probably why mad hos were dyking these days, not enough real niggaz to go around. I guess bitches figured they'd rather get with another bitch than get with a bitch nigga.

But, being a jack boy, true and true, the way I processed everything concerning Inez, her hustle and her clientele was mostly from a stickup kids point of view. Had I been a dope boy I probably would've thought in terms of expanding Inez' weed business or using her to push some hard white for me. Had I been a nigga with a tender head on my dick, weak for a bitch with good pussy, I might've wanted to replace Fat Stan forever. But I was all about the come up. Inez, with her good pussy and all, was no more to me than a hustle. The way I saw it, I would be robbing the bitch at her insistence.

The bitch had much about her a nigga could lay his hat on. If nothing else, Fat Stan had taught her how to get on the grind. I doubted that Fat Stan had ever actually sat Inez down and schooled her on the hustle game. He was too much of a *Captain Save a Hoe* type nigga to deliberately school his woman about the game. He'd rather risk his own life and freedom than put Inez in harm's way one single time.

I presumed Inez had learned the game simply by observing. Instead of banking on finding another trick to take care of her while Fat Stan was on locks, she was wise enough to go for hers.

Atlanta was full of players, niggaz who weren't tryin' to lace no bitch's pockets. Still the tricks outnumbered the players twenty-five to one.

Which meant it would've been real easy for a fly bitch, like Inez, to replace one trick with another one. So I guess she deserved some props for choosing a real nigga like me and hustling to maintain on her own.

Nevertheless, I understood the game, all of it. Inez was Fat Stan's *woman*. She was my *bitch.* Sitting on locks, his fat ass might not have understood that, but I did. My bid in the pen had force-fed me that reality back when I was behind bars and Shan was on the turf fucking other niggaz.

When a nigga was on locks, no matter how good he treated his girl before he got popped, she was gonna give another nigga some pussy. Trife hos like my baby mama, Shan, used a niggaz past transgressions as an excuse for their fuckin' around while he was on locks. But that shit was just an excuse they used to be the ho they were all the time.

When a bitch was 'bout business and had mad respect for her nigga, she did what she had to maintain, but she fucked on the down low. 'Cause above all else, she knew that her nigga had pride. And if she disrespected his rep in the streets, the bitch was on timeout forever.

Like Shan.

Well, Inez was trying to do the right thing by the code of the hood, but in my eyes, Fat Stan's rep didn't deserve respect.

CHAPTER 24

Just when a nigga's life was beginning to look sweet, things got even sweeter. I had dropped in at my lawyer's office to hit him with a coupla' grand for the case still hanging over my head. After pocketing my loot, he told me that he'd be able to get the charges against me *dead docked*, which was good with me. To have a criminal case dead docked meant that the DA agreed not to prosecute the case if the accused stayed out of trouble.

Just another way of puttin' a nigga on probation. I agreed to it just to get the charges from hangin' over my head. Though it was mad stupid for them crackers to wanna charge me with gun possession and I was the mafucka who got shot!

A few days after I'd gone to my lawyer's office and dropped that loot in his grip, I met him at the courthouse to sign some papers and make the dead dock deal official.

If he hadn't guaranteed me that there was absolutely no chance I'd end up in cuffs, there wasn't no way I would've walked inside of that courthouse. I was not frontin', my next trial was gonna be held in the streets, gangsta style.

When I bounced from the courthouse it was still kinda early and the streets weren't jumpin' yet. I whipped over to Inez' crib and let myself in with the door key she'd given me.

"Hey?" she said, rubbing her eyes.

I noticed the sexy negligee, the way it accentuated her figure and barely covered that phat ass when she walked back upstairs after realizing it was just me coming in her crib.

"What's up?" I said, sitting on the edge of her bed. She was already back under the covers.

"Nothing," Inez answered. "I was asleep."

"You want me to leave and come back later?"

"Naw, get in bed with me."

I undressed and slid in bed with Inez. Her back was against my chest and her ass craddled against me like we were two spoons. I kissed the back of her neck and reached around to play with her nipples, they were long and always hard, like root beer-colored Jolly Ranchers.

She moaned. "Ummm," and wiggled her ass against me.

I pinched Inez' nipples hard.

She loved that shit. My tongue slid down between her shoulder blades. I felt her body quiver and heard soft moans. I rolled her over onto her stomach and continued teasing with my tongue. Her legs spreaded and her ass rotated, inviting my tongue to taste her pussy from the back.

I'd been holding Inez down for a few months now, and I was confident she wasn't slutting around. I hadn't eaten her pussy before, but I most definetly get down like dat. I just tried to be selective as to who I gave the tongue to.

Inez was doing everything a down-ass bitch was supposed to do for me, so she'd earned a little freaky deaky.

I gave the pussy the stinky finger test before sampling it with my tongue. When my mouth sucked her wet pussy lips and my tongue found her clit, Inez' body shook. I licked her to a hard orgasm and then turned her over onto her back so I could eat her pussy real good.

Twenty minutes later, she was screamin' my name, pulling me up and sucking my tongue. Tasting her pussy, I guessed. Then she wanted my dick in her mouth. Of course she got that, too.

Inez sucked mean dick. Mad noise and a lot of spit and a lot of *umms*. She could make me bust real fast but this time, I held out. I wanted my joint rock hard when we got to the fucking.

"Damn! Don't make be bust, girl."

"Why not?" Inez muttered, mouthful of dick.

"I wanna save that for another hole of yours," I said.

"Umm! Which one?"

Inez liked to get fucked in the ass, hard. I was wit' dat.

By the time I shot mad cum up in her ass, Inez had promised me everything but eternal life.

Afterwards, we slept like two freaky ass babies.

Sometime later, a face full of chronic smoke awakened me from a deep, good-pussy-induced sleep.

"You gon' sleep your life away?" Inez smiled at me, holding a spliff.

She had that radiant look that was on a bitch's face when she'd been well-fucked.

"What time is it?" I asked, accepting the spliff from Inez and sat up.

"Why? You gotta be somewhere at a certain time?"

"Naw, ma. What, a nigga can't ask what time it is without having to play *a thousand questions*?"

"Where that attitude coming from?" Inez shot back. "I was just fuckin' wit' you, nigga. Bounce if you got somewhere to go. It ain't like I'm gonna be like Toni Braxton, wondering if I'll ever breathe again, just 'cause you got somewhere to go."

I laughed. "I just don't want you tryin' to check my schedule. I ain't Fat Stan, all pussy-whipped and shit."

"There you go with that shit again. What does Stan have to do with anything?"

"I'm just lettin' you know who wear the pants, shawdy."

"Nigga, you a trip. Pass me the spliff." Inez defused the potential conflict before it began.

We laid in bed gettin' high and kickin' it. Inez had already told me her story, from childhood to the present. I had told her little about my childhood, but not much about my present. My steelo was to disclose very little about myself.

This particular morning, though, the weed and Inez' warm body loosened my tongue. I got introspective and deep, we talked about things on a level no other female I'd ever met could relate to.

Inez didn't agree with all of my opinions, but neither did she take me to combat over them. Instead, she gave me an opposing view to consider. She told me I shouldn't let the drama between me and my baby mamas keep me from spending time with my kids.

"But, really, that's just an excuse," Inez said. "The streets be keepin' niggaz from their kids. They don't have time."

"Not me," I countered. But deep down I knew Inez was spittin' the truth.

I loved Terrence Jr. and Eryka, and I knew I'd love my third child when it came into this world, even though I was pissed at Cheryl for not having an abortion. Still, the streets demanded most of my time and my children got little of it.

Paper chasin' ruled a nigga's every minute, so it seemed. And the little time that wasn't spent chasing loot was spent inside of some pussy. A nigga like me needed forty-eight hours in a day.

Of course, a day wasn't but twenty-four hours long. So my seeds saw less of me than the streets and the bitches. Truthfully, though, I was living too dangerous to have my kids in tow when I whipped the streets.

Inez had a nigga feelin' guilty, like I needed to hit the brakes and go spend time with my young ones. Her ass had a lot of nerve giving out advice. She wasn't raising her own child.

I told Inez about Cheryl and the drama we were going through. "So, you broke up with her 'cause she got fat? You ought to carry a baby for nine months. I bet you would get fat, too," Inez defended Cheryl.

"It ain't just that. She went loco after she had my daughter, now she's pregnant again!"

"Well, you shoulda wore a condom."

"You got that right," I agreed. Inez read my thoughts.

She said, "Nigga, you don't have to worry about me getting pregnant. I ain't tryin' to have no more babies."

I fucked Inez in the shower and then we dressed and went downstairs and ate microwave pizza.

About five mafuckaz came to cop OZs from Inez. She was pushing that hydro weed, had a kick to it like a mule.

I checked an OZ and a G-note from her stash and told her I'd be back later. I wasn't gon' lie, that shit had a young nigga feelin' like a thug-style pimp. I was checkin' the bitch for paper just like pimps who get their loot from the womb. But I wasn't disillusioned, I knew that my bread and butter was jackin' niggaz for their loot and leavin' 'em with their heads in their lap.

I left Inez' crib with a mind crowded with conflicting thoughts.

The streets were me, no denying that.

Was it possible to be a street nigga and a good father to my seeds?

I didn't want my seeds to grow up without a father, like how me, Toi and most other mafuckaz in the hood grew up. Nor did I want them growing up calling another nigga Daddy. I wanted to hustle and give my kids all of the things they wanted and deserved. And if hustling sent me to an early grave, so be it. I was born to die, anyway. Like every other mafucka. At least Lil' T, Eryka, and my baby growing inside of Cheryl's womb would know that pops laid his life on the line for 'em.

Feeling a strong urge to see my children, I dipped over to Shan's crib to kick it with Lil' T, but nobody was home.

In the parking lot, one of Shan's neighbors was all on my dick like foreskin. Honey was slim, with a gap between her legs wider than a baby's head. I sat inside of my whip and played with her mental for a few minutes, but I wasn't trying to get with her. Her type came a dime a dozen, I'd catch up with her or a bitch just like her when I had nothing else to do. I gave her my digits and bounced, heading to Cheryl's crib to see Eryka.

When I got there, Cheryl's mom was fussin' at her about not cleaning the house and leaving pissy pampers lying around.

My showing up didn't help the atmosphere at all. But Cheryl's Ma Dukes cut the argument short and started cleaning up the house herself.

Occasionally I'd catch her staring bullets at me.

I didn't like her ass, either. The feeling was mutual, but the mood inside of their crib didn't vex me.

I picked up Eryka out of the playpen and kissed her fat cheeks. She squirmed and smiled, showing much love for her pops.

I stayed over there long enough to play with Eryka, feed and burp her, change her pamper and then rock her to sleep. I said little to Cheryl, just watched her stuff her pig face.

In less than a year after having Eryka, Cheryl had gone from sugar to shit. It was even crazier how we had gone from being close to being strangers. I gave Cheryl some loot and told her to spend it on my daughter.

"Did you have that test done to find out what you're having," I asked her.

"You mean the sonogram?"

"Whatever it's called."

"Yeah. I'm having another girl.

I didn't comment. Not that it too much mattered that she was having another girl as opposed to a son. I already had a junior to carry on my name after the streets put me in a box.

Since Cheryl had decided to not have an abortion, another daughter was cool with me. The talk I'd had earlier that day with Inez had made me accept Cheryl's second pregnancy. *After all, why should I trip the inevitable?* For as long as I breathe, I would love all of my seeds equally, regardless to the drama I had to go through with their mamas.

When I left Cheryl's crib, I went by my apartment and grabbed a change of clothes and whipped over to spend another night with Inez.

Shan paged me as I was closing Inez' front door.

"I need to use your phone."

"You know where it's at," Inez said.

Shan answered on the first ring. I told her I hadn't wanted nothing important, I'd just stopped by to see Lil' T and to drop off a little loot for her to get him a few things. Shan told me I could bring the money now that she was home.

"I'll drop it off tomorrow," I promised. "Let me holla at my son."

"He's spending the night with my mother," Shan said.

I told Shan I'd fall through there whenever Lil' T. came home, and I ended our conversation without saying bye, just a click in her ear.

I planned to go by Poochie's crib early in the morning and scoop my son up from there. I hadn't told Shan that because I knew she'd try to be at her mother's crib when I showed up to scoop my son, instead. Whenever possible I tried to avoid seeing Shan, which was really why my spending time with Lil' Terrence was becoming so infrequent.

I was beginning to understand how a lesser nigga could let his kids' mother push him to the point where he'd abandoned them totally. I hadn't reach that point with Shan or Cheryl, 'cause if push came to shove, I would've put a bullet in both of those hos' heads. I'd leave 'em somewhere stankin' before I'd let 'em push me out of my seeds' lives.

After disconnecting my conversation with Shan, I dialed Lonnie's number to see what was poppin'. While talking to my dawg, Inez' phone beeped.

"Yo, playgirl," I called out to her. "Your other line is ringing."

"You can answer it."

I told Lonnie to hold tight.

"Hello?"

The voice operator announced a collect call from Stan Montgomery. I pushed the button to accept.

"Hello?" I repeated.

There was a confused pause and then he said, "Uh—what number is this?"

"You tell me, playboy, you're the one who dialed it."

"Is Inez there?"

"Yeah, she's here." I knew a man answering his woman's phone was fuckin' with Fat Stan's mental, especially while he was in prison. I'd been in his shoes before and niggaz hadn't showed me no mercy. I was just gettin' some revenge.

"Who is this?" Fat Stan finally asked. His voice sounded like it was about to crack.

"I guess you should ask Inez that, my nigga," I said. Then, loud enough for him to hear me: "Yo, Inez, baby. Come get the phone. It's some nigga calling collect from the pen."

Inez gave me a stiff look when I handed her the phone. But not a disrespectful gesture or I would've slapped her in the mouth. Just to reinforce who was holding her down now.

I wasn't dissin' Fat Stan. It wasn't like we were dawgs, the way Shotgun Pete and me had rolled together before he got with Shan while I was on lock. Inez may have owed Fat Stan respect and loyalty, but I didn't owe him shit. I sat back and listened to Inez' end of the conversation.

She said: “Hello?” That was followed up with, “That was a friend of mine. Call me back tomorrow, okay? I don’t feel up to arguing with you.” Then she was silent for a while. Fat Stan must’ve been snappin’ at her on the other end. Finally, she asked him, “Why you wanna know his name? What difference does it make who he is?” There was a long pause. “I’m not telling you his name, so quit asking.” Whatever Fat Stan said to that really pissed off Inez. She snapped, “I ain’t gon’ be too many more bitches and sluts! I’m trying not to disrespect you on the phone, but I’ma cuss yo’ ass out if you keep talking to me like that!” Another pause. Then she snapped, “Yeah, I’m fuckin’ him! So, what? What da fuck you want me to do, masturbate fo’ five motha-fuckin years!?” *Damn.*

“So what! I didn’t put yo’ ass in jail. Yo’ ass was sellin’ dope when I met you, so don’t try to blame me for you being locked up! I didn’t tell you to shoot that boy!”

Pause.

“I told you I wasn’t fuckin’ with that boy, he lied!” She calmed down, adding “I’m handlin’ my bidness. I don’t know why you trippin’. I ain’t gon’ stop living ‘cause you’re locked up. No matter who I’m kickin’ it with, I’ma keep your commissary straight. I’ma do that ‘cause I ain’t no dirty bitch. You took care of me when you

Another pause.

Then she said it. “Naw. His name is Youngblood, since it’s killing you not to know.” Her voice was agitated.

Pause.

“I don’t know if he hangs with Lonnie or not. I don’t know no Lonnie.” There was hesitation in her voice when she said, “Why you wanna speak to him? Inez covered the receiver with the palm of her hand, turned to me and said, “He wanna speak to you. You wanna see what he got to say?”

“Fuck no!” I snapped. “I ain’t got no rap for that nigga! That’s between y’all.”

“He don’t wanna talk,” Inez said into the phone.

Fat Stan must’ve hung up on her ass, ‘cause Inez didn’t say another word after that. She just handed me the phone and told me whoever I’d been talking to on the other line must’ve hung up. I called Lonnie back and told him I'd whip through his spot later in the week.

Right away I could see that the conversation Inez had with Fat Stan had left her in a foul mood, probably regretting that she'd had to spit the truth and break his heart.

I'd been on the other end of the phone before. I knew that Fat Stan was probably in his cell, madder than a mafucka, ready to fight officers and inmates. All because his baby mama was gettin' dicked down while he was doing time. Though I knew the feeling, I still wasn't compassionate toward the nigga. The streets was dog-eat-dog, I didn't have no love for the other side. Mafuckaz, other than Lonnie, didn't have no love for me when I was in Fat Stan's predicament.

What had me peeved, however, was Inez' foul mood. Fuck sitting around the bitch while she was brooding over another nigga. I stood up.

"Yo, I'm 'bout to bounce."

"Why're you leaving?" complained Inez.

"Bitch, you think I'ma sit here while you get teary eyed, 'bout to cry over another nigga?"

Inez came and hugged me. "Don't go, please. I ain't fixin' to cry."

"You a lie! Why yo' eyes watery?"

I didn't hear her response. I was out of the door before she could spit it out. I went home and chilled for a few hours, bored like fuck.

Inez was blowing up my pager.

Fuck her. Let her ass suffer.

I wasn't calling her back until I was good and ready.

There were three things I have never seen: A UFO, a mafucka I was scared of and a bitch that I couldn't do without.

I took a shower, threw on some fresh gear, some bling and whipped to the nightclub. The parking lot was packed with fly whips sitting on dubs. It was winter and too cold for mafuckaz to be hangin' outside of the club, so only the whips were on display.

Niggaz were showcasing like usual. Bitches, too. Mafuckaz were dressed like they were at The Source Awards.

I was rockin' a camel skin jacket with a fur hood, starched khakis, a wool plaid shirt and a fresh pair of Timbs. I stayed thug gin'. My neck was iced and my wrist was frozen. My khakis were saggin', pockets laced with big head Benjamin's.

I bought a bottle of Alizé from the bar and took it to a table near the back of the club. Most niggas liked to floss where everybody in the club could see them. Not me. I was a robber, paranoid by my profession.

I prefered to sit where I could observe, without being observed.

I was drinking Alizé straight out of the bottle, just peepin' the scene, nodding my cranium to the beat of the music. Trick Daddy was rappin' from the speakers. The dance floor was crowded with fly honeys with phat asses, mad weaves and bling a nigga had went to prison trying to buy for 'em. The pretty boys, playaz and bustaz were dancing with the fly hos. The real ballers and the true thugs never danced.

Murder Mike came to my table and hollered at me. He had that hood rat, Cita, with him. She was looking like a movie star, even though her ass was project, born and raised.

I spoke to them and turned up the Alizé. Some dribbled from the corner of my mouth. I wiped it away with the sleeve of my camel's hair jacket.

Cita said, "Your girl, Fiona, is around here somewhere."

"My girl?" I asked. "Ha! Fiona ain't my girl, she belongs to the whole hood!"

"She's looking good, dawg," Murder Mike declared.

"Shit, she always looks good. The problem is she don't smell good once she takes her clothes off." They cracked up.

"You a trip," Cita said. Her look said she wanted to get with me.

She winked her eye, on the sly.

"Yo, main man," I addressed my homey, Murder Mike. "You need to check Cita. She choosin' me with her eyes, while she on your arm."

"What?" Cita damned near screamed.

"You heard me, shawdy. Bitch, don't front. You know I ain't lying." I looked her in her scandalous-ass mug. "Don't be disrespecting my homey."

"Whud up, bitch?" Murder Mike asked Cita. "You choosin' while my head is turned?"

"Naw! I ain't did no—"

Murder Mike slapped Cita's lipstick crooked.

"Get somewhere, bitch!" he barked.

Cita started to stand there and try to lie her way out of it, but she knew Murder Mike would turn into Mike Tyson and beat her half to death. So she walked away crying and holding her hand over her lip.

Murder Mike sat down at my table and I passed him the Alizé. He turned it up.

An hour later, we left the club with two fly bitches. They weren't hood, though. They were college girls, slumming it, thirsty for some thug passion, I guessed.

I couldn't even recall those hos name. I could recall that Murder Mike and me took them to the motel and made them fuck each other. Then we fucked them both, switchin' up on them hos like tag team wrestlers. Of course we both wore jimmy hats. Shit, Murder Mike was my homey, but I wasn't stickin' my dick in his cum. And I was sure he felt the same about me.

The two college girlies didn't bar nothing, though. Big time freaks.

Though she'd blown my pager up on the daily, I didn't call Inez back or go by her crib 'til a week later. When I finally went by her crib, I let myself in with the key she'd given me. I had the bitch eating out the palm of my hand.

I made her suck my dick 'til her jaws hurt, and I wouldn't fuck her, not that day. Some real mack shit. I guess it was in my blood line. Mafuckaz always told me my pops was a dog nigga to a female before he got planted in dirt.

I never knew my pops. He caught two slugs in the chest way back when I was still sucking on Ma Dukes titty. So the world couldn't blame my pops for having a bad influence on me when it came down to how I treated females. Unless he passed his *drag-a-bitch* traits on to me through DNA.

More likely, though, the streets influenced the way I dealt with bitches. I had seen their disloyalty and treachery up-close and personal, and I was convinced I couldn't trust them as far as I could pick 'em up and throw them. Therefore, I had little respect for the girls I came across and hooked up with.

Inez had much a nigga could use in his corner, but she wasn't wifey material, not in my eyes. So far, I hadn't met one that I'd wife.

Over the next few weeks, Inez did everything but rob and kill to get back in my good graces. Since she was being so generous and placating, I taxed her purse excessively. To cement my title as the nigga who was now holding Inez down, I took her to the clubs and other spots where most hustlers and playaz flossed.

Street mafuckaz recognized Inez as Fat Stan's lady and probably shook their heads at her disloyalty. Most were just hatin', wishing they were knockin' Inez' ass outta socket while Fat Stan was away.

Real niggaz knew and respected the rules of the game. Few niggaz could hold a bitch down from prison, especially one as fine and as game tight as Inez.

The bitches who peeped us together knew the deally, too. Shit, most of them probably had a nigga doing time and another one holding them down in his absence, too. Any street nigga who didn't understand that was in for a cold surprise when he blew trial and went to prison, as happened more often than not.

Fat Stan was being introduced to the truth about a bitch's loyalty, or lack of it, when a nigga was on lock.

Inez let the answering machine deflect his calls instead of her refusing them, but it amounted to the same. She didn't want to talk to him. If she accepted anymore of Fat Stan's calls or wrote him letters, she did so when I wasn't present, afraid to piss me off. I knew before long Inez would stop visiting him, too.

Now that I look back on it, I realized that a street nigga had to train his girl to love him with her mind, not her body or heart. 'Cause when he was on lock or just in the streets too much, another nigga could always penetrate his girl's pussy or her emotions. But it was much harder for a nigga to erase what had been engraved in a bitch's mind.

Anyway, Fat Stan was assed out. Inez was now under my spell.

CHAPTER 25

Baby mamas always find a way to 'cause drama and disruption in a nigga's life when he didn't fuck with them no more. Them hos thought having a nigga's child gave them a lifetime claim on their baby's daddy. At all times, they felt like a nigga owed them something. In that regard, Cheryl was no different from Shan and a whole world of bitches.

My pager went off back to back to back to back, with the same number displaying across the pager's tiny screen, along with this one-word message: *EMERGENCY.*

I was already in the process of going to handle one emergency. My sister had called me crying, saying her man had beaten her up. I was on my way to her crib, packin' heat, to see what the fuck was going down. Now Cheryl was paging me like crazy, as though something was seriously urgent. I was thinking something could be wrong with Eryka or the baby in Cheryl's belly.

I floored the gas pedal and made it to Toi's crib without getting pulled over for speeding.

Toi opened the door as soon as I knocked, and the first thing that greeted me was her eye! Her shit was swollen shut, already black and blue.

"Where that bitch nigga at?" I snapped. My sister's whole right side of her face was swollen. She hugged me and started crying.

"You might need to go to the hospital," I told Toi. "Put some ice on your eye and stop crying. I need to call Cheryl right quick."

I was fuming.

"Hello?" Cheryl answered the phone.

"What's the emergency? Is Eryka all right?" I didn't have time for Cheryl's usual babbling.

"You need to come and get us."

"Look, Cheryl, I'm in the middle of something. Is something wrong with my daughter or the baby you're carrying? If not, I'll call you later."

"Dag. You act like we don't matter." I could hear Cheryl crying. "If you can't come and get us now, I don't know where we'll be later. We ain't got nowhere to go!" *Sniffling.*

"Cheryl, what the fuck is you talkin' 'bout?" My patience was zero. *Why had I planted, not one, but two seeds in this dingy-ass bitch?*

"Mama is putting us out," Cheryl cried. "She talkin' 'bout we crowding her space and she want me out of her house tonight." She started crying harder.

"Put your mama on the phone!"

Cheryl's dirty-ass Ma Dukes had the nerve to get on the phone with a funky attitude. I didn't even ask her what the problem was. I could tell by her nasty tone she'd already made up her mind that Cheryl, Eryka, and the baby Cheryl was carrying had to get out. I knew it more than likely had to do with Cheryl letting her mom's house go filthy and not picking up after Eryka. Still, what type of parent would put their own pregnant daughter *and* their only grandchild out on the street?

I said acidly, "Just let them stay there until I finish handling some business. I'll be by to get them in an hour or two."

"You better hurry up!" *Click.*

I didn't bother calling back.

Toi was in her bedroom laying on the bed, crying. She hadn't put any ice to her face and it was swelling more by the minute. I told her she needed to go to the hospital, something might be broken.

"What happened?" I asked. What reason had that bitch nigga, Glen, have for putting his mafuckin' hands on her?

Toi just cried. I couldn't get her to tell me what had gone down.

What was she hiding? Why was she protecting Glen? She had already told me he'd jumped on her. Why wouldn't she tell me the cause?

The sound of the doorbell distracted my thoughts.

I'd gone to the front door, gat in hand, thinking it might be that fuckin' nigga, Glen. When I saw that it wasn't, I'd put my gat in my waistband, under my shirt and opened the door. I'd looked at my mom's like I hadn't been expecting her. She'd returned the look with the exact same stare. I didn't even acknowledge her husband's presence. I just told Ma Dukes Toi was in the bedroom.

Ma Duke saw Toi's battered face and immediately went to the phone to call the police. Toi damn near tackled her.

"I'll go to the hospital, but don't call the police," she said.

Ma Dukes insisted on calling the police, but Toi wasn't having none of that. I interjected my opinion, which was that we do what Toi wanted.

As Ma Duke and Raymond drove my sister to the emergency room, I trailed behind their car, mad as a mafucka. I wanted to find Glen and bust lead in his ass.

My sister was admitted into the hospital, suffering from a fractured cheekbone. Glen must've punched her like he would punch another man. I damn near had tears in my eyes. That fuck nigga was gonna pay for beating my peeps.

A policeman showed up at the emergency room to question Toi.

She refused to drop dime on Glen, which led to my mother telling the police who had jumped on her daughter. Ever since OJ had killed his bitch and got away with it, po-po was hard on domestic violence.

The policeman questioned Toi relentlessly, to no avail. Finally, the doctor told po-po to stop bothering Toi. She was in pain and under medication.

Ma Dukes didn't know jack about Glen, other than his first name. And I didn't have no rap for po-po, regardless to the situation. Besides, I had forgot to leave my heater in the whip. I was just hoping po-po didn't notice the bulge under my shirt.

When Toi was taken to a room and given more pain medication, I waited until she had fallen asleep, then I dipped. Ma Duke and Raymond stayed.

It was close to midnight when I picked Cheryl and Eryka up from Cheryl's mother's house. Their clothes were packed in suitcases and bags. Eryka's crib, playpen and all their things were sitting by the front door when I walked in. I gave Cheryl's mother a look that could kill.

But the bitch just turned her head away. I didn't say a word to Cheryl. I just started loading the things in my truck. Whatever couldn't fit, I told Cheryl's mother I'd be back for another day.

My daughter was asleep across my shoulder as I carried her to my truck.

But before I left, I called Cheryl's mother a dirty, lowdown bitch.

"If I'm a bitch, I'm a good one," she shot back. Her comment surprised the fuck out of me. Still, I let it bounce off of my back.

While driving, I didn't bother to ask Cheryl if she had somewhere to go now that she'd been kicked out.

Who wanted a fat, lazy, pregnant teenager, who already had one baby and no job living with them?

I popped in a Mary J. Blige CD, something mellow so I wouldn't wake Eryka and hoped Mary J's singing would discourage Cheryl from talking.

Over Mary J's lyrics, Cheryl suggested I take her and Eryka to a motel that had cheap weekly rates. I knew she was just frontin'.

The bitch knew that I'd never allow her to take Eryka to live in a cheap motel room, not even for a few days. Cheryl just wanted to front like she didn't need me.

I ignored her and drove on to my crib. Once there, I unloaded the truck and took Cheryl's and my daughter's things inside of my apartment. No kids were allowed to live in the apartments, but I knew the apartment manager would look the other way for a coupla C-notes.

In the meantime, I laid down some rules Cheryl would have to follow: First and foremost, she would *have* to keep the place clean, no excuses! We *weren't* back together and I *wasn't* fucking her. She had no say as to where I went or when I returned. She could not have any company over. And she shouldn't expect to live with me permanently. She needed to call and make up with her bitch-ass mother soon or come up with some other plan. And she could use the Nissan to go to doctor's appointments and the store. That was it!

I didn't know she had dropped out of school 'til that night.

Damn!

I was already a dropout, so was Shan. I'd thought Cheryl would at least be different than Shan and the hood rats from around my way.

I set Cheryl up in the bedroom that Lil' T slept in when he came over and me and Eryka slept on the couch in the living room.

I definitely didn't like the situation, but I'd use it to bond closer with my baby girl. And I was determined not to let Cheryl milk the situation for months. In the meantime, I could always bounce and go stay at Inez' crib when Cheryl's presence agitated me.

Inez understood the situation when I told her how it went down the next morning. Not that she had any other choice but to accept it. I was holding her down, not the other way around.

She hooked me up some French toast and eggs before I dipped to the hospital to check on my sister.

Ma Dukes was there with Toi when I got there. She spoke to me awkwardly. I nodded, walked past where Ma Dukes was sitting and went over to the bed and kissed Toi on the forehead.

I didn't ask her any stupid shit, like how was she feeling or tell her a lie that she looked better than she had the night before. Her mug was fucked up, wasn't no way to sugarcoat that, so I said nothing.

Anyway, Toi was drugged up and half asleep and might not have understood me had I said something.

Seeing my peeps like that had my blood boiling, murder on my mind! I didn't know what made Toi's nigga beat her down like that, but his fuckin' ass was gonna pay whenever I caught up with him.

Toi might've been his woman, but she was my fam'. Wasn't no way I was going for a nigga putting my peeps in the hospital. Toi could protect that bitch nigga from the police, but she'd never be able to protect him from me.

I'd seen a few niggaz beat on my mom's while growing up, wasn't no way I was letting a nigga beat on my sister. It was like Glen was disrespecting me, too. Like he was saying I was pussy, he could beat my peeps to a pulp and I wouldn't straighten it.

Fuck dat.

I was one young'n old heads had to respect on all levels or they'd got found with their heads in their lap, especially about my sister. I had peeped some shit at Toi's crib that gave me a clue to Glen's steelo. I understood the nigga now. Why he kept my sis' on locks and didn't want me to come by her crib.

I would rap with Toi about that later.

As for Glen, I had a clip full of hollow points with his name on them.

I looked around the hospital room. A mirror on the wall was covered with a towel. The same deally when I went in the bathroom. I asked my moms what the deal was on that? She told me the nurses had covered the mirrors so Toi wouldn't look in the mirror and see her own swollen face.

Ma Duke then started crying, maybe recalling going through similar drama herself.

She put her hand on my arm when I sat in the chair next to hers. "Terrence," she said, almost whimpering, "no matter what you may think, I love you and Toi."

I didn't say shit.

"If you had been right, and Raymond was wrong, I never would've taken his side," she continued. "I chose the side of right over wrong. Not Raymond over you. Let's—"

"Save it, Ma! It don't matter, you still let a man come between us," I interrupted. "You made your choice. I don't wanna talk about it." I stood up and walked out of the room.

After I left the hospital that evening, I went to the hood and copped a fifty-dollar sack of raw. I hadn't snorted cocaine in a long time, like way back before I went to prison to serve that nickel, but the stress and anger had me wanting something more than weed.

Murder Mike said, "Nigga, you fuckin' wit' dat raw now, huh?" He took the fifty-dollar bill and handed me a small plastic bag of powder.

"Naw, playa," I lied. "I got a freak bitch at the hotel, she like the raw damn near more than she like the dick."

"Word?"

"Word, dawg."

I stopped at the crib to check on Cheryl and Eryka. To my surprise the crib was in order. I played with my lil' girl for a while and jetted over to Inez'.

I let myself in but Inez wasn't home. So I sat down on the sofa and laid out the cocaine on top of the coffee table. I was gettin' rawed, thinking about Toi, Ma Dukes and the situation with Cheryl.

The cocaine had me contemplating some Eminem shit, thinking about killing Cheryl, after she had the baby. *Fuck it.* I'd raise my seeds myself.

I had to be rawed up, 'cause that was some ill shit to even contemplate. I hadn't needed to snort cocaine to contemplate killing that bitch nigga, Glen, though. That thought was foremost on my mind.

Inez came home while I was snorting the last line. Walked right in on me.

"Whud up?" I said.

"Hey," Inez greeted me, looking fly as usual. She looked down at the cocaine residue on the coffee table.

"What you doing?"

"Gettin' my snort on, a little." *Fuck it.*

"*Hmmpff.* I didn't know you get rawed." She sat down next to me.

"You got a problem with it?" I challenged.

"Not as long as it ain't a habit."

"Naw, shawdy, it ain't no habit. Shit just stressin' a nigga out." Inez stood up and straddled my legs, her arms went around my neck. "What's wrong, baby? You wanna talk about it?" So we did.

I was animated and crunk like a mafucka when telling Inez what that nigga, Glen, had did to my sister's face. She could tell I was wired and thirsty for blood.

Inez didn't interrupt me, she just listened and watched while I animatedly moved around her living room, arms gesturing. Finally, my adrenaline returned to normal and I sat back down on the sofa and explained the beef I had with my Ma Dukes and why I still couldn't forgive her. I didn't have to recount my problems with my baby mamas, Inez already knew those stories.

Later that night, we were lying in bed. I had just dicked Inez down.

"I wanna ask you something, Youngblood," Inez said as if the question had been on her tongue for a while.

"Spit it out, shawdy."

"Have you ever beat up one of your girlfriends?"

I thought about that for a minute. Growing up I had seen men bounce knuckles off of Ma Dukes chin, so I wasn't trying to be no woman beater. On the other hand, I knew that street niggaz sometimes had to chin check their bitch, 'cause we fucked with street bitches who'd run over a nigga if he didn't tap them on the head when they violated. Still, it was more my style to just put a bitch on timeout than to be WWF wrestling with a hard-headed ho all the time.

"So," I concluded. "I'll check a bitch if she gets way outta pocket. But I ain't no woman beater."

"Look at it this way," Inez countered. "Maybe your sister got *way* outta pocket with her man."

"That don't matter, yo. His bitch ass still ain't gettin' away with it, no matter what Toi did!" I wasn't hearing that shit.

"Don't get mad with me," Inez said. "I'm just trying to get you to look at it from all angles. In my opinion, your sister shouldn't have called you and told you her man jumped on her. That's just gonna get somebody killed."

"You right about that!"

"See, that's what I'm saying. If it was me, I would've just stopped fucking wit' him. Why get my brother killed or get him locked up for murder?"

Deep down I knew what Inez was saying made hella sense. But I wasn't hearing it. Fuck what made sense, I was gonna get just as stupid as that nigga got when he put his hands on my peeps. Stupid mafuckaz made you do stupid shit to 'em. I told Inez to shut up and taste my dick.

"Yo' ass be trippin'. Why you come out of left field with some shit like that?"

"Aww, you know I'm just playin', shawdy," I laughed.

Ten minutes later, I had my dick in her mouth, though.

The day my sister was being released from the hospital, I was riding with Rich Kid discussing the situation concerning his ex-lieutenant, King. I assured Rich Kid that although I had a few personal dramas on my mind, I had not pushed the hit on King to the side. I asked him if King was aware there was fatal beef between them? I wanted to know for sure if King would be expecting Rich Kid to send someone after him. If so, I wouldn't be able to go as a friend and then catch King with his guard down whenever I located him.

Rich Kid promised me that he and King didn't have any cross words when King decided to go on his own. In fact, according to Rich Kid, he hadn't wanted King hit until later, when he found out his ex-lieutenant was setting up crews to rival his. Then, Rich Kid had reevaluated everything about his once-trusted henchman. And in hind sight, no longer giving King the benefit of doubt, Rich Kid counted numerous times the mafucka had lied to him or stolen from him. I could believe that. King had stolen from *me* once. I told Rich Kid about it.

He just nodded. I could see the hurt in his eyes. The pain King's betrayal was causing Rich Kid.

It was supposed to be *blood in, blood out.* When partners got bodies with a nigga, major paper with a nigga, flossed and rode with a nigga, one wouldn't ever expect he'd betray him. Especially if he was the one who put the nigga in the game, and the game in the nigga, like the streets said Rich Kid had done with King.

Shit, I hadn't fed Shotgun Pete like Rich Kid had done King, but I'd done major crimes with him. Deep down, Pete's betrayal had burned like six caps to the back. My pride just wouldn't let it show.

Other than what I'd heard from the streets, I only knew Rich Kid and King's story from Rich Kid's perspective, but I could believe it was King who violated their bond.

And for what? Money? Power? Shine? Probably all three.

I knew that none of that bullshit could make me cross my dawg, Lonnie. All of that shit was what we strove for, but it was just like a bitch, a bus and a problem, they all come and go.

Of course, greed and jealously festered inside 99 percent of the mafuckaz I've met. So, the other side po-po always won in the end.

Anyway, I let Rich Kid know that if King didn't show his face in the ATL soon, the murder rate in Kentucky would increase by at least one.

We whipped to the hospital to pick up Toi. She'd had reconstructive surgery on her face. It was still slightly puffy and bandaged.

She was ashamed that I'd brought Rich Kid along.

On the way to the hospital, I had told him the deal, so he'd stopped at the hospital gift shop and bought Toi a teddy bear and *welcome home* balloons. She accepted them with embarrassment, thanked Rich Kid and lowered her head. My pager went off, so I left them in the hospital room and went to the pay phone to answer it.

It was Poochie calling. She asked if I could stop by and bring her a few dollars. I told her I'd stop by later.

"Is Lil' T over there?"

"No. He's with Shan, I guess."

"A'ight. I'll stop by later. You're a'ight, ain't you?"

"Yeah. I'm doing fine," Poochie said.

I hung up from Poochie and called Inez. Her weed connection was over there dropping off some ganja so I told her I'd holla later. I made a few other calls, just wasting away a few minutes 'til I figured Toi was checked out and ready to leave.

Rich Kid pushed Toi toward the elevator in a wheelchair, with a fat nurse right on their heels. I hung up the phone and caught up with them.

"Why is she in a wheelchair?"

"Hospital policy," replied Fatso.

I waited with Toi and the nurse at the main exit while Rich Kid went to get his whip.

A few minutes later, he pulled his Escalade up, got out and helped Toi up into the high sitting SUV as though she were an invalid. Though Toi was clearly uncomfortable by her predicament, I sensed that she was flattered that Rich Kid was showing so much compassion. I was sure he'd never said more than *What's up?* or honked his horn at my sister before.

Toi wasn't a dime, but she was just a penny or two short of being one. At least when she wasn't swollen-faced and bandaged.

Rich Kid's sudden interest could've just been his way of showing love 'cause Toi was my peeps and he wanted to use the situation to help cement my loyalty to him. Or it could've been genuine. There was always a flip side to a coin. Both possibilities flashed through my mental, but I wasn't real concerned about either at the time.

When we got to Toi's condo, it was exactly as it was the last time I'd been there. If Glen had been by there, he'd left no evidence. After Toi assured us she'd be okay alone, me and Rich Kid told her we'd holla later. He gave Toi his cell phone number and told her to call if she needed something and couldn't reach me.

It was a few hours later when I whipped over to Poochie's crib.

Her sons were there babysitting my son, Lil' T and Poochie was nowhere around. Poochie's sons were not yet teenagers and I wondered why Poochie would leave them alone watching Lil' T for the hour-and-a-half I waited there for her to return.

The boys didn't know where she'd gone, only that she'd said she'd be back before dark. It was beginning to get dark out and my patience was wearing thin. I gave the oldest boy some loot and told him to give it to Poochie when she returned.

"Tell her to call me," I said. "Y'all don't open the door for anybody but her."

I had to bounce, but I took Lil' T along with me. I wasn't leaving my lil' man in the care of other kids although Poochie's sons were pretty sharp for their age. The hood bred 'em like that. But I still wasn't comfortable with Poochie's absence.

I stopped at a pay phone and called Shan and ran down the situation to her.

"Zack and 'em can take care of the house for a few hours," she said. "They're not babies."

"Whatever," I shot back. "Lil' T is with me."

"Don't be having him in the streets with you or around all your bitches. I know how—"

"Shut up." I hung up on her ass.

Poochie didn't call me that night.

I kept Lil' T with me the whole weekend, letting him and Eryka get used to each other. It wasn't often I was able to have both of my children over at the same time. With Cheryl and Eryka temporarily staying at my crib, it was now easier to go get Lil' T and enjoy both of my seeds.

Lil' Terrence sort of treated Eryka like a toy, but they enjoyed each other and that made a nigga proud.

Sunday evening, I took Lil' T back over Poochie's crib since Shan hadn't answered my calls.

Poochie opened the door and let me in, looking like I'd seen her look a thousand times back in the past. I knew that popeyed look like I knew none other.

"What's up?" Poochie licked her dry lips. *Damn.*

You a'ight?" I asked, just to hear Poochie's response. I could tell she'd fallen weak and had been out smoking crack.

"I'm cool," Poochie lied weakly, her voice cracking and betraying her.

"C'mon, Poochie. You know you ain't gotta lie to me. I got love for you no matter what."

That was when she broke down in tears and confessed to getting high. I let her cry and hugged her to my chest, like an understanding son/lover/son-in-law/friend.

I told Poochie that one slip-up didn't mean she had to wash all the months of drug-free living down the drain.

By the time I bounced, I was somewhat hopeful that Poochie would pull herself together and not fall weak to the pipe again. Yet, I was only hopeful. The pipe was too formidable a foe to bet against.

CHAPTER 26

It was my good luck, and the beginning of King's bad luck, that he decided to come back to ATL and floss and profile his new come-up. Playa had been seen around the city in all the hot spots hustlers go to mingle and outshine the next mafucka. I had heard he was whippin' a double R, a Rolls Royce. *Damn!*

That nigga had to be stacking major chips to roll like that. Either Kentucky was a dope boy's gold mine or King had stolen mad loot from Rich Kid while he was the muscle for Rich Kid's crew. It was one or the other, 'cause street wisdom had always proven that kingpins like Rich Kid didn't ever paid their workers enough loot for the worker to get rich. I guess they figured if they let the worker get rich, they'd lose their power over 'em.

The vibe got back to Rich Kid and it had to be vexing him real bad 'cause he was talking careless on the phone when I answered my pager.

Rich Kid told me he'd throw in an extra ten G's if I'd slump King while he was in Atlanta playing Big Willie, like his black Warren Sapp-looking-ass was bullet proof.

"Slow down, playboy! You know your cell phone ain't tap-proof, either," I reminded Rich Kid.

"Yeah, you're right, lil' nigga." I told Rich Kid I'd handle business as soon as I could get the drop on King.

"He'll be at the Player's Ball Saturday night," Rich Kid informed me.

"Yeah, but I can't get up in there. That shit be invitation only, don't it? I ain't got juice like that," I cracked.

"I do," Rich Kid boasted. "You can roll with me and my crew."

"That's peace." After getting some info on when, where and how we'd hook up Saturday night, I told Rich Kid I'd holla later and hung up.

I dipped by my sister's crib just to see how she was doing and to pass a few hours away before I'd go by Inez' crib and chill for the rest of the night.

I had no plans to go to my own apartment. Cheryl and my daughter were still staying with me and I wasn't up to even looking at Cheryl's fat pitiful ass. I knew there was food and pampers there and as long as my daughter was okay, I wasn't feeling any rush to go home.

When I got to my sister's crib she was just chillin' around the apartment in old shorts and a big T-shirt, but her hair was fresh.

Two months had passed since Toi had reconstructive surgery on her face. It had healed beautifully except underneath her left eye was a shade or two darker. I guess that was where that fuck nigga's punch had connected with her face. I was still hot about it, but I hadn't yet run into Toi's boyfriend on the half dozen occasions I'd stopped by Toi's crib since that foul shit went down.

Probably Glen knew I was gonna straighten that beat down he put on my sister, so he was ducking the payback, creeping back and forth to her crib when he felt safe.

"Hey, Terrence!" Toi greeted me with genuine affection.

"What up, sis?" I went straight to her fridge and grabbed a Corona.

From the living room, Toi yelled, "You want something to eat?"

"What you working with? I don't see nothing in the fridge and freezer but salad and TV dinners. I ain't no rabbit, and I eat enough TV dinners at my own spot."

By now Toi was in the kitchen nudging me aside, telling me I needed to stop fucking with hoodrats and lazy hos, and find me a woman who could at least cook and put some meat on my skinny ass.

I laughed. "But what if she can cook but the pussy ain't no good?" I could kick it with my sister like that, we kept it trill.

"Fool, you so crazy! I'm sure you can find some girl to do both things good, since you so nasty and sex means so much to you."

I told Toi that Poochie was da bomb with both, but I wasn't up to fighting the pipe, Poochie's guilt and her back-and-forth religion for her affection.

"Don't tell me you been sexin' Shan's mama?" Toi gasped. "Y'all should be ashamed of y'all self!"

"Why? Shan ain't ashamed of having a brat by a nigga who was supposed to be my dawg."

I didn't bother telling Toi that I'd been splacking Poochie's guts long before Shan crossed me out with Shotgun Pete. It didn't make any difference in my eyes. Deep down I didn't blame Shan as much for her betrayal as I did Shotgun Pete for his.

"You want me to warm your trifling ass up some leftover lasagna?" A hint of laughter was in her voice.

"That sounds cool. But don't warm up a lot 'cause I ain't that hungry. Plus, Inez will probably have something hooked up for me to grub on when I fall through her spot after I leave here."

"Well, you want me to just heat you up one of these soups?"

"Hell naw!" I damn near barked when I saw the Ramen soup Toi pulled from the cabinet. I'd bought those same kinds of soups from the commissary for five mahfuckin' years in the pen. I'd promised myself when I touched freedom I'd never eat another one, I explained to Toi.

"Oh. My bad. I'll heat up the lasagna," Toi said.

We ate lasagna and garlic bread, I guzzled down two Coronas then fired up a spliff. When Toi took a pull of the weed, she started choking and coughing like a new jack. My sister didn't chief on the regular, but she wasn't new to it, either.

"Damn! Ugh—ugh!" she coughed. "I ain't smoked in awhile." She passed the spliff back to me.

It was cool with me, 'cause I could blaze like a Rastafarian. I didn't need Toi to smoke with me if her lungs weren't up to it.

We were watching a rerun of *Martin*, trippin', when Toi asked me if the Inez I had mentioned was the same female that had a daughter by Fat Stan?

"Yeah, that's the shawdy I'm holding down now," I confirmed.

Toi said, "You must be death-struck for real. That fat ass nigga be trying to kill niggas 'bout that girl."

"Since when did I bar another nigga? He got beef about it, he better check Inez. 'Cause I don't owe his fat ass no loyalty. I'll send him to his maker." I popped, seriously, and raised up my shirt.

“Now why you gotta bring that gun in my house?” Toi asked, though she knew the answer.

My heater was like my arms and legs, with me *wherever* I went.

I told my peeps to relax, Fat Stan was on locks for a nickel and time would teach him that when the dog’s away, the cat gon’ play.

Awhile later, we heard keys jingling outside of the apartment door.

“That’s Glen!” Toi sounded panicked. “Don’t start no shit, Terrence! Give me your gun.”

Yeah, right. I ignored the lame request.

Glen stepped through the door carrying a tennis bag. He didn’t speak to Toi or me. He sniffed the air inside of the apartment and asked Toi, in a scolding tone, what she’d been smoking.

“I smoked a blunt with my brother,” Toi’s tone was like a frightened child being fussed at by her father.

“I only hit it once,” she added as if that would diminish Glen’s anger.

“Open some windows or turn on the air conditioner, that shit stinks!” Glen barked. “Then step back here in the bedroom, I need to holla at you.”

“Whoa, mafucka! Where you going so fast?” I got up off of the couch with gat in hand, aimed at his egg-shaped head. “We got some bidness to settle.”

“What?” He was caught off-guard.

“You heard me, fuck-ass nigga! You gotta answer for that shit you did to my sister.”

I couldn’t tell if he was gonna try to make a mad dash for the bedroom or at me. Nor did I know what he was packing inside of that tennis bag, but I felt sure it wasn’t no tennis gear.

“Put that gun up!” Toi cried, hysterically.

“Stay out the way!” I warned her, never taking my aim off her nigga.

Now he was at my mercy, like Toi had been at his that day he beat her down. I was gonna teach him not to fuck with my peeps.

But what really had me heated was the way the nigga had just came in the apartment and walked right past me, like I was pussy and wasn't gon' straighten out that beat down he'd put on my sister a couple of months ago.

Toi was still screaming for me to put the gun down. That shit only made me more determined to light a spark in Glen's ass. He hadn't shown my sister no pity, yet she was trying and crying to save his ass. But in vain. 'Cause once I pulled out the heater, I was

Glen tried to con his way out of getting what he had coming to him.

When he realized I wasn't studyin' that shit, he said, "Put the gun down and we can step outside and settle this man to man".

My gat stared steadily in his face while I said, "It wasn't man to man when you was punching my sister out, nigga!"

"Terrence! That's over with. We talked about it and Glen promised he'd never hit me again," Toi lamely explained.

"Just shut up, and stay out the way!" She was pissing me off even more, trying to save her nigga from a bullet he couldn't avoid.

I didn't know if Glen was strapped or not, for all I knew the nigga could've had a street sweeper in that tennis bag or his own heater tucked in his waist. I couldn't allow my sister to distract me or I could end up back wearing a shit bag. I wasn't having dat.

"It's time to face the music, nigga!" I aimed the gat at Glen's kneecap and squeezed the trigger, the gunshot sounded like an explosion inside of the apartment.

Glen stumbled back and fell to the floor.

Toi screamed and ran and jumped on my back, trying with all her might to stop me from bodying her nigga. I easily brushed her to the side, pointed the gat at *her* silly ass and told her I'd bust a cap in her stupid ass if she tried that dumb shit again. She screamed she was calling the police, so I snatched the phone cord out the wall in the living room and she couldn't get past me to the cordless phone in her bedroom.

Glen was on the floor holding his right knee, cussin' and trying to plug the hole with his hands to slow the blood from pouring out. Still it poured down his pants leg. I aimed at his other knee, the left one and squeezed the trigger again. He yelped. The bitch nigga started begging me not to shoot him again.

I slapped him across the head with the gat a few times 'til blood ran down the side of his face. Each time I slapped him upside the head with the steel, I said, "Put—your—hands—on—my sister again—and—I'ma kill you!" Then I took the tennis bag and looked inside. "When you learn how to treat my sister I'll give you back your shit!" I whipped away from there like a nigga trying to get out of Forsyth County KKK territory before dark.

I didn't dare go to my crib. My stupid, lovesick sister might've called po-po and told them where I rested my head. Nor did I go by Inez' crib as I'd originally planned. I'd told Toi I was boning Inez and though I doubted Toi knew where Inez lived, I wasn't taking any unnecessary chances.

Toi could also describe all of my whips to po-po.

I drove to the airport and paid to park my car in the long-term lot just in case there was an APB out on me. I would push my incognito whip so it would be safe at the airport for a few days. At least long enough to find out if Toi or Glen had put the heat on me.

Niggas in the streets may have thought that it was stupid of me to spark Glen up, especially after the way my sister had tried to defend the nigga. But it was just in me to wet the nigga up for fuckin' my peeps up like he did. I had to let the nigga know that Toi wasn't defenseless. I'd get with his bitch ass no matter how my sister felt about him hitting her. The next time I would dead his ass. If Toi still loved him after that, she could always go visit his grave.

I took a taxi from the airport to a hotel way on the other side of the city. I called Inez and told her where I was at. Then I jumped in the shower to wash the stress away. I had forgotten all about the tennis bag I took from Glen.

Once out the shower, I dried off and went to the phone and ordered some pizza so Inez and I wouldn't have to leave the room to get some grub once she got to the hotel.

Inside the tennis bag was five kilos of cocaine, fifteen G's, two automatic heaters, a .45 and a .9mm. I instantly realized I could've been dead. Why hadn't Glen gone for his heaters when I'd turned to snatch the phone plug out of the wall? Was he pussy? Packing steel but afraid to let the gun speak? Or had he been in so much pain he'd forgotten the heaters were near him, inside the tennis bag?

Damn, I'd almost slipped and ended up on permanent timeout. Now I was mad at Toi, her hysterics could've cost a young nigga his life.

I put the loot and shit back inside of the tennis bag and tossed it inside of the closet. I didn't want Inez to see it, I wasn't gonna hip her to what had gone down. I never told anyone anything they didn't have to know or one day they'd be on that witness stand helping those crackers to send my ass to prison.

"Hey, boo," Inez greeted me when I let her into the room. She was looking fly in a Prada jumpsuit that showed off her curves.

"That outfit is bangin', playgirl," I complimented. Inez did a slow three-sixty degree turn.

"You like it?"

"No doubt, shawdy. But not as much as I like what's underneath it."

"You want me to take it off so you can get some of what's underneath it?" Her tone was seductive.

I was still amped up from blasting Glen's punk ass, so my joint got hard the second Inez touched me.

I'd been holding Inez down for months now and the pussy was still bangin'. For some reason I couldn't explain, capers and gunplay always left a nigga wanting to fuck something. Add to that, Inez' Stacey Dash's looks and mad sex appeal. It took every ounce of a young nigga's resolve not to fuck her right there where we stood in the room. I held my composure, though.

"Don't be starting nothing you don't wanna finish," Inez said playfully.

But I could tell she meant it. She was ready to fuck a nigga's back out and get me out of the crunk-up mode she could tell I was in. Inez was just perceptive like dat. Maybe that was how she was able to play Fat Stan, a lesser nigga than me, into being an all-out fool over her.

Of course, I was too game tight to fall under any bitch's spell.

The pizza arrived and I fucked up the whole pie. Inez said she'd already eaten.

Someone was paging me so much the mafuckin' beeper was damn near vibrating off the nightstand, but I ignored it after I checked the number and saw that it was Ma Duke calling.

"You got some weed with you?" I asked Inez.

"I brought two blunts."

"Damn, playgirl." I handed her a lighter. "Fire one up."

We got blazed and fucked all night.

The next morning, Inez asked me how long I planned to stay at the hotel. I told her she could bounce if she had something to do.

"Well," she said, "I need to at least go home and get a change of clothes. Plus, I need to drop off a few things at my mother's house, stuff for my daughter."

"Go do your thing, shawdy." Inez' daughter was so seldom around while I was kicking it with her; I had almost forgotten she had a child.

"I can come back in a few hours if you want me to," Inez offered.

"That's cool." I told her to bring me some clean gear that I kept over her crib. I gave her some tongue and she bounced.

When the door closed, I finally returned my mother's call. "Yeah, what's up?" I asked when she answered.

"Terrence, have you lost your damn mind?"

"Calm down, Ma! Or I'm just gonna hang up." The momentary silence told me she was fighting her natural need to cuss and fuss, knowing full well that our relationship had already been strained for years, and I wouldn't hesitate to hit her in the ear with a dial tone. It wasn't disrespect that I felt for my Ma Duke, it was bitterness.

"Why did you go over Toi's house and shoot her boyfriend? Are you crazy? You wanna go back to prison? You need to learn to let the police handle stuff like that."

"Look, Ma", I said. "I did what I felt I had to do. Now if Glen or Toi wanna run to the police on me, I'll do what I gotta do then, too."

"And what is that, Terrence?"

"I ain't going back to prison."

"So you'll make the police find you and kill you?"

Without hesitation I countered, "The police ass ain't immune to dying. They gotta bring some to get some!" A few seconds later, I heard a dial tone.

While I was at the pay phone, Lonnie paged me so I hit him up asap.

Recognizing my voice, he said, "Damn, dawg. Your sister called me talking all crazy, saying something about you wet up her nigga and took a lot of money from him."

"It ain't go down exactly like that," I countered.

"Whatever, dawg. I knew you was gonna step to dude sooner or later," Lonnie said, not asking for details. "You all right?"

"Yeah, I'm cool," I assured him.

"Come holla at me when you think it's cool," he shot back.

"You know I will, main man. Peace."

I left the payphone and went back to the hotel room. Since I didn't have any weed to burn, I thought about busting one of the kilos I'd taken from that chump, Glen, and gettin' rawed-up. But I wasn't trying to turn into no powder head, so I cancelled the thought and just laid back and chilled.

I had come down off that mad rush a nigga be feelin' when he pulled a caper or let that pistol bark, and now I was weighing the repurcussions of what I'd done, but I wasn't regretting my acts. But I knew not to take shit for granted, or I could end up in a grave behind this shit.

I knew very little about Glen or his business, but common sense told me that a nigga holding that much yayo could retaliate against me. Hell, a nigga just pushing a few rocks was capable of mad revenge, especially if he felt a nigga's acts had violated some principle. More niggaz done got deaded over principle in the streets than anything else. So I wasn't about to take it for granted that Glen wasn't gonna try to straighten his business.

On the other hand, I wasn't shaking in my Timbs, either. I knew one indisputable fact, he would have to bring ass to get some. Unless he'd send another nigga at me.

Still, I planned to be on-point 24/7. What was really on my mental was the five bricks and the fifteen G's, plus those two heaters in the tennis bag.

My plan was to give that sucka, Glen, back the dope if he hadn't already dropped dime on me to po-po. If he had, I'd use the dope to strengthen my bank while I was on the run. No matter if Glen had dropped dime on me or not, I wasn't returning the money or the heaters.

The way I saw it, the fifteen G's was payment for stressing me when he beat down Toi. As for the heaters, wasn't no goddamn way I was gonna give a nigga a gun back that he might later use to clap me. Shit, the nigga was blessed that I planned to return his dope. *I'm a robber, I never giveth, I taketh.*

But since this wasn't 'bout no jack moves and was strictly personal beef, the code was different, which was also why I didn't body the nigga. I'd just wanted to teach the nigga a lesson: *that there was a severe penalty for putting his nut scratchers on my peeps*. He had put my sister in the hospital, now I'd done the same to him. That was street justice. Ghetto style.

My pager started ringing. I checked the number and walked back to the pay phone a few blocks from the hotel.

"Yo. This is Youngblood," I said into the phone as soon as I heard the familiar voice on the other end.

"What's up, lil' nigga?" It was Rich Kid.

"Same old, same old," I rapped. "What's up with you, playboy?"

Rich Kid asked if I was still gonna handle that business with King for him. I told him that my word was bond, I'd meet him at the Player's Ball Saturday, but I didn't want King to see us kicking it. I was thinking I could play my way up under King by telling him I had some type of beef with Rich Kid. If King took the bait, I'd ask him to put me down with his crew. Then I'd soon get the opportunity to dead him.

Besides, with the heat I anticipated being on me for that Glen shit, a few weeks of being in Kentucky to play up under King would be right on time. It wouldn't be easy to hook up with King, though. I knew the nigga didn't like me, and I suppose he felt the same vibe from me.

I told Rich Kid I was in a predicament which didn't allow me to get to any real money for a minute and I needed some cash flow to buy some boss gear for me and a shawdy to rock at The Ball. Plus, I needed floss money. Fuck it, Rich Kid had to cover the expenses since he wanted the hit done in such a rush.

Not that I was foolish enough to try to hit King at The Player's Ball. I knew nothing about the set-up of the club, nor how crew-deep King would be rolling. Unless the opportunity to body King unexpectedly presented itself Saturday night, I would have to use that night as a linkage to touch King a little later

Rich Kid came right over to the hotel and dropped a fat roll of dough in my grip. He didn't ask me why I was holed up in a hotel, and I didn't volunteer an explanation. It wasn't his biz.

Before leaving he gave me invitations to The Player's Ball for Inez and me.

Inez showed back up at the room about 3 p.m. She must've heard a nigga's stomach growling from way over wherever she had came from, 'cause she brought a nigga some soft tacos and chicken fajitas and fries. I attacked the food like I hadn't eaten in days.

Inez smiled. "Damn, slow down before you choke."

I told her she was a lifesaver and kissed her before eating the last of six tacos and the remainder of a large order of fries.

Even though I told her she didn't owe me no rundown, she told me what she'd done between leaving the hotel early that morning and now. Fat Stan's jealous ass probably had questioned Inez so thoroughly about her whereabouts whenever she left the crib that it had become habit for her to justify any period of absence to a nigga. I didn't check no ho for hints of unfaithfulness every time she stepped out of my sight and returned.

Fuck smelling their panties for another nigga's scent and shit. If a ho couldn't be trusted, a nigga had to either let her go or just serve her booty calls.

"I'm just letting you know what my day been like," Inez corrected, sounding hurt that I wasn't really interested.

I didn't try to placate her feelings, though. Shit, once I started catering to a bitch's every emotion, it was just a matter of time before a nigga found himself vulnerable to all types of shit.

I changed subjects and asked Inez if she wanted to be the lucky one I sported on my arm to The Player's Ball Saturday.

"You're serious?" she beamed. "How you get an invitation? I thought only major hustlers get invited to that shit? Not to sound like I'm dissin' you, boo," Inez polished up her response.

I told her that she was indeed right, only major niggaz were invited to The Player's Ball, which meant she was underestimating my clout. I let her know that sometimes a nigga had power through the mafuckaz he knew.

I was thinking it would be good for my pockets if I could clap King real soon and get the bonus Rich Kid had added as a sweetner. But even better for my pockets would be if I could play up under King or tail him to Kentucky and relieve him of his stash money after I deaded him.

That was the plan that appealed to me most because it would probably mean more loot in my grip.

I'd probably need Lonnie and someone else's help to do it like that, though. I wasn't gonna lie, Shotgun Pete would have been perfect to take along with me and Lonnie. But I couldn't forgive his betrayal, it hinted of other flaws in that ugly ass nigga's character. I didn't trust my life and freedom to his shady ass. I treated him like I'd treat a grimey bitch, I stopped fucking with him and there was no going back.

Inez' voice interrupted my thoughts.

"... plus I'll have to get my hair and my nails done. And how am I gonna find something to wear? I don't know? Saturday ain't but three days away." Inez was saying.

I broke her off a thick wad from the money Rich Kid had given me and told her to go buy the flyest, sexiest dress she could find, regardless of the cost.

"And while you're at it," I added another stack of benjamins to the wad I'd just given her. "Buy me some fly thug gear. Not no tuxedo or shit like that. Nah mean?"

"Why can't you go shopping with me?" she whined.

"Nah, shawdy. I'm keepin' a low profile for a few days."

But I didn't bother to explain, and Inez didn't press me any further, which was one of the things that I liked about shawdy. Inez' understanding on how to treat a hustler was far more advanced than my babies' mamas.

Inez just knew when to be up under a nigga and when to give him space. Maybe she'd gained that wisdom through trial and error. Or maybe being a hustler herself she understood that a mafucka couldn't stack love and sex in a safe, like you could money.

Despite Inez' many attributes I still wasn't on any love shit with her. Like I said, five years in prison had killed whatever it was in a nigga that allowed him to love a bitch. I'd already told Inez those exact words, no cut on'em.

"All women aren't bitches," she had argued.

"Name one that's not," I challenged her.

"*I'm* not a bitch." Her tone was defiant.

"I bet Fat Stan thinks you're a bitch right about now." My tone was matter of fact.

"Yeah, he might feel that way right now because he's jealous and locked up," Inez conceded. "But whenever he sits down and analyzes the situation, unemotionally, he'll respect the choices I've made, and he'll respect me as a woman."

I was laid back across the bed recalling that conversation now.

Inez had put the bankroll I'd just given her on the nightstand, and she was laying her head on my stomach, her hand rubbing the scars from where I'd been shot. I saw a quick smile come across her face, as it always did each time she saw the tat'—Hard 2 Kill—encircling the scar. But like always, she offered no comment.

Her touch was arousing a nigga, while her tongue ran traces across my chest.

But other shit was on my mental.

While Inez was trying to seduce me, I interrupted her. "Say, playgirl. When Fatboy comes home, what you gon' do if me and you are still kickin' it?"

"Why we gotta go there?" Inez started. "I must not be turning you on?"

"Just answer the quesiton."

Inez propped up on her elbow and looked me in the eyes. She said, "How do you expect me to tell you what I'm gonna do five years from now? I ain't Miss Cleo. And I know you ain't the type of nigga who needs to be lied to."

I didn't say shit.

Inez sat up and leaned back against the headboard, her eyes still locked with mine. She let out a sound of exasperation, as if it was taking away her strength to have to respond to the question.

"Boo," she continued, sounding sincere, "I know that you think all females are trife, and I can understand why you feel that way, 'cause of the stuff Shan and 'em be taking you through. But I'm not Shan or Cheryl and whoever else got you scarred like that." She told me that she would be all the way down with me until our time ran out, whenever that day came.

"See, Youngblood," Inez went on, "one day I'm gonna want to get married and get away from the streets and hustlers. I don't see you as the type of man who'll ever get married and leave hustling alone. Therefore, it's only inevitable the day will come when we'll go our separate ways. But I hope, whenever that day comes, we'll part as friends."

As soon as Inez made that comment, I was thinking: *Cool, bitch. But yo' ass won't* be parting with no gear I bought on your back!

"... and to answer your question, I don't plan on gettin' back with Stan when he gets out, no matter who I'm with at that time."

"Why not?" I asked.

"'Cause I don't ever want a jealous man again," Inez answered with conviction. "I don't know why you feel intimidated by Stan. Just 'cause he's my baby's daddy don't mean I belong to him forever. You don't belong to none of your baby's mamas, do you?"

I told Inez I wasn't really trippin' the situation, I just wanted to see what type of flava she'd spit.

Inez said, "Here, boo." She handed me the wad of money back. "I guess you're trippin' 'cause of *this*, but I can buy my own outfit. I'm a hustler just like you."

"What? You mad?" I said, not really giving a fuck.

"Ain't nothing to be mad about," said Inez.

A little while later, I was dicking her down, making her slob my knob and prove that she didn't have an attitude about the shit.

I offered to pay for the outfit Inez would cop to wear to The Player's Ball since she wasn't trippin' it, but shawdy insisted on paying for it herself. I wasn't about to force the loot on her, so I just gave her a few G-notes and told her my sizes.

After we both had showered and dressed, Inez dropped me off at Lonnie's crib and she bounced to Lenox Mall.

Lonnie was glad to see a young nigga, just to know that I was all right and up on myself since my fiasco with Glen.

We smoked some bomb-ass dro and sipped Henny. My dawg told me that my sister had been blowing up his pager every hour, on the hour. She'd told Lonnie that Glen hadn't told the police I wet him up and took his shit.

Lonnie said Toi was stressing that all Glen wanted was his stuff back, his money, yayo and the heaters. I told Lonnie what I felt about that proposal and he said I was a better man than him 'cause once he took a nigga's shit, he wouldn't give them a crumb back.

"But I understand why you're giving the fool the dope back. Besides," Lonnie added, "Toi says the nigga is blaming her, screaming she set him up for you to lick him."

I didn't see how the fool could think something like that, especially the way Toi was going bananas when I put that steel in his face.

Shit, she'd have had to be an Academy Award-winning actress to fake the emotions she'd shown that day. I was betting that her nigga knew better then that. He was just using that to get her to try her damdest to convince me to return his shit. Now I was contemplating keeping it all.

"Ain't no warrants out on you, dawg. I had Delina call and check it out," Lonnie told me.

"You sure?" I asked.

Lonnie looked at me reproachfully, reminding me that his word was bond.

"True dat," I said.

Knowing there wasn't any warrants out for my arrest allowed me to move around and not have to be holed up in the motel. Lonnie dropped me off at my crib and I told him I'd get back with him later.

I hadn't filled him in on my business with Rich Kid, yet. I wanted to wait and see if I'd need his help before I ran it down to him.

At the crib, Eryka crawled to me, smiling like the little princess she was. She wasn't walking yet, and her vocabulary was some real gibberish, but she recognized her pops and loved to crawl up in my lap.

Cheryl was looking like she was due to drop my next seed soon. The crib was clean and her appearance was better than what had become usual. I asked her a few questions concerning Eryka, and what they'd been up to while I was ghost. She responded that they'd just been chillin', but they'd gone to visit Cheryl's mother earlier in the day. I didn't ask about her stankass Ma Dukes.

"Are you going back out tonight?" Cheryl asked.

"Yeah," I said, dashing out any hopes she may have had of me staying home with her ass.

When she went to the bathroom, I quickly checked the freezer to make sure the crazy bitch hadn't been dabbling in my stash.

It was all there or her role in life would've ended right here.

I played with my lil' girl for a minute until she got tired and fell asleep, then I changed into some new gear, baggie jeans, McNabb Tshirt, Timbs and green bandana. I then dipped out of the door and jumped in my Lex' truck. I then whipped over to the hood to see what was poppin'.

Like always, niggaz were on the block and on the grind from lil' bad ass shorties and all the way up to old school hustlers still slangin' break down sacks.

It was dusk dark outside, but a gang of hos were still outside sitting on their porch or on top of a nigga's whip, gossiping and watching out for po-po so their man wouldn't get bagged.

I parked my whip and got out and flashed my platinum smile at a group of hos I knew. They were all choosing but I wasn't on the come up. Stank pussy Fiona was in the bunch, eyeing me like her looks could kill. I walked over to where she was posted up and served her some game.

"Hey, fly girl," I popped. "You be looking so good, a boss hustler gon' marry you and move you out the hood one day." That had her so off balance she forgot she was mad at me for driving off and leaving her at the store the last time I'd seen her.

All she said was, "I hope it's you." Smiling like the gullible rat that she was.

I'd rather stick my dick in a pitbull's mouth than marry her ass. But I was playing the ho up in front of her girls, making peace, 'cause a nigga don't need no unnecessary enemies.

Murder Mike was moving up a notch in the dope game. He was no longer out on the block slangin' his own sacks. Now, he had two young niggaz trapping for him.

He pulled up on the set in a tricked-out bowling-ball blue Acura Legend, Eve bumpin' out of the system.

When Murder Mike stepped out of his whip and the dome light came on, I saw Cita profiling in the passenger seat like she had stacked the cheddar to buy the whip sun was pushing.

I just shook my head.

Cita had something that made Murder Mike keep fucking with her or else Murder Mike was really just a trick nigga. But trick or not, he was a'ight with me.

"Whud up, playboy?" I said and gave him some dap. "I see you been on the grind."

He tried not to smile, like his coming up wasn't a big deal. But a nigga who came from the gutter and made any progress had to be proud.

"Just trying to get my piece of the pie," Murder Mike said with a tight grin.

"I see you and Cita still tight like thieves." I cut my eyes toward his Acura.

Murder Mike hunched his shoulders. "You know how it is, dawg, convenient pussy," he rapped. "Still, it's M.O.B., nigga."

"Always." And I meant it, whether he did or not.

I dapped him and jetted down to the Ribs Lady spot and copped some grub.

On the way back to my whip, I saw this shawdy who be hooking up a nigga's braids in some real fly styles. I made an appointment for Friday night, paid her in advance to cement the deal.

From there I jetted over to Poochie's, hoping Lil' T would be over there. He was, but so was Shan and ugly ass Pete and their crumb snatcher. I spoke to Poochie, snatched up my lil' man and dipped before Shan could say two words.

"I'll bring him back tomorrow," I said over my shoulder.

"Wait! He—" Shan yelled.

I was ghost before she could spit it out.

I stopped at a pay phone and called Inez on her cell. She was still late-night shopping at the mall, excited about the gear she had picked out for us to wear Saturday to The Ball.

"We gon' be tight, boo," she said.

"I'ma see. You better not have me looking like no prep or no pimp."

"Nigga, I copped you some gear that'll have you thugged-out and fly," she promised.

"A'ight, I'll see. Look, I got my son with me. Is it cool if we all just chill at your crib tonight?"

"Yeah. I'll be there in an hour."

CHAPTER 27

Saturday morning came before I knew it and found me at the crib asleep with Eryka on my chest, drooling slob on my face, trying to wake me up. I opened my eyes and turned my head away from her sloppy kisses.

"Yuk!" I exclaimed. Eryka giggled.

A while later, I showered, dressed and dipped out of the door. I whipped over to Inez' crib so that we could take care of a few last minute things before the big event later that night. Inez still had to go get her hair fixed and her nails done. My hair was already freshly braided in a zig-zag style. My ice was already on Inez' dresser, so with those things handled, all I had to do was take the truck to the detail shop for a wash and wax.

By 9 p.m. we were back at Inez' crib getting ready. I let Inez get dressed first because all females took forever to get dressed and made-up, and I didn't want to be sitting around dressed while she was stuck in the mirror.

By ten, we were both ready to step out of the door. Inez was rockin' a skin-tight, blue mini-dress, made of satin and sequin by Dolce' & Gabbana, with one strap over her right shoulder. The left shoulder was bare and exposed her left breast. A blue sequined satin star was pasted over the left breast nipple, ala' Lil' Kim.

I wondered how her left tittie stood up so straight. She was rockin' alligator stiletto heals with a matching clutch purse. Her hair was tinted with streaks of gold and fell to her shoulders. She sported some big movie-star glasses with alligator print frames. Her neck, fingers and wrists were iced-out. Shawdy was a dime plus some tonight.

I was thugged-out supreme in a baggy Gucci jean suit, with a matching platinum-studded sun visor cocked to the side to allow my braid design to show. I had on some fresh blue Timbs that Inez had gotten customized with the Gucci jean material on the sides and heels of the Timbs. I was rockin' a platinum cuban-link necklace, with a crystal coffin medallion. On my left wrist was a Gucci watch platinum face, jean band. On my right wrist I sported a pair of handcuffs, one cuff dangling. A fat blunt was behind my left ear and in my left earlobe was a platinum bullet. I was thugged-out to the max.

When we fell up in The Player's Ball, mafuckaz was eyeing Inez like she was J-Lo. While they were eyeing the eye candy on my arm a few of their bitches was eyeing me. I believed I was one of the youngest niggas on the set. The only nigga in thug gear and jeans. The other niggas were sporting expensive gear, but more formal.

I spotted major hustlers that were seldom seen. In a different set of circumstances, I would've been casing them for a lick.

Rich Kid came through the door with two dimes on his arm. Fly bitches that looked like he cut 'em out of a magazine. Playboy had mad taste. I had to give him props on that.

Hannibal was there, too. So were many of the major hustlers in the city. I was thinking of a way to rob all them mafuckaz.

I was a little vexed when I saw this one dude show up with a white bitch whom I undoubtedly recognized on his arm. It was Blondie from The Passion Palace. *Damn!*

I rushed over to Rich Kid and whispered some game in his ear since he was really the only nigga on the set who knew me. I also knew that he and Blondie knew each other, and I didn't want him telling her I was the same dude he'd told her was in the music industry that night at the club.

Rich Kid laughed, remembering the lie he'd helped me perpetrate, though he was still blind to what he'd really helped me pull off. He told me not to sweat it. He'd tell Blondie I wasn't the same dude if she asked.

"Just keep your eyes open for King," Rich Kid said.

"I'ma do that."

They had a fool-ass comedian for entertainment. Then a local R&B group crooned the top twenty-five R&B songs regularly played on the radio.

But King still hadn't showed up.

Inez and me sipped on bubbly and enjoyed the show. She knew a few of the hustlers in attendance and gave me a quick rundown on 'em. The ones she knew, so she said, had stepped to her in the past, but she wasn't interested in being put in one of their stables. Pimps, major dope boys and other street hustlers were all representin'.

When I went to the men's room, I walked right past Blondie and the nigga who was sporting her. I didn't know him but I knew that if he wasn't a pimp, he had to be a trick. 'Cause he had a trick ass bitch on his arm.

On the way back to my table, playboy stopped me, but it was Blondie who spoke.

"How're you doing, Popeye?" the white bitch said. Her eyes were locked on me, studying my every feature.

"What'd you call me?" I changed my voice to throw her off and made the question sound as if I was offended.

"Your name *is* Popeye, isn't it? Don't you remember me?" Blondie responded with certainty.

I told her she had me fucked up and did I look like a nigga who'd be named after some cartoon character? And wouldn't she feel disrespected if I called her Snow White?

"My name *is* Youngblood," I said with mad 'tude. "I guess you think all black people look alike!" I balled my face up. feigning anger. and then I turned and walked off.

A short while later, I saw Blondie and her nigga 'versing with Rich Kid. I assumed she was asking him if I was the same dude he'd told her was in the music industry that night at the strip club. All I could do was trust that Rich Kid wouldn't reveal my identity to her.

But if he did, I was strapped. I kept my eyes on Blondie and her nigga, in case he wanted drama. Inez must've been following my stares because she asked me if everything was a'ight.

"Yeah, I'm cool." So she let it ride at that.

A few minutes later, a big black nigga came through the entrance followed by a slew of young soldiers.

King!

He was dressed to the T, wearing mad bling. While the ten young soldiers wore army fatigues. King's entrance was climatic. Even from across the club, I could see the look of disdain that was plastered on Rich Kid's face. His ex-lieutenant's shine was hard for him to swallow, for some reason. As if King had stolen loot from him, used it to blow up and was now flaunting it in Rich Kid's face.

Whatever their true beef was wasn't my concern. I had the scope on King for monetary and personal reasons. So, in essence, he was just a dead man walking, like a mafucka sentenced to death row. His end had already been written.

I turned my attention back to Inez and the bubbly, but I kept one eye on Blondie and dude with her. I'd wait for the right opportunity to approach King. From the looks of his crew, the lay-out of the club and the fact that Inez was with me, I knew I wouldn't be hittin' King just yet.

Now the party was in full swing. Hustlers relaxed their code and hit the dance floor with their ladies or one of the many dimes who'd been invited in case a nigga came without one. Fly honeys like Halle Berry and Vanessa Williams would've gotten overlooked amongst the honeys in attendance, that was how fly most of them were.

Even though Inez was looking as fine as J-Lo, she still wasn't one of the top ten at the Ball; however, her sexy outfit was definitely top three. Still, I sweetened her cup, telling her that she was the flyest female on the set.

"You mean that?"

"No doubt, shawdy."

She gave me a wide smile, which I returned with a wink.

"Nigga, you're so smooth it ain't even funny," she said over the music that had begun to play.

We continued to talk as the band played a handful of oldies but goldies, shit my Ma Dukes used to jam to before she soldout and got with Raymond.

Inez talked me into slow dancing to a song or two. And on the way back from the dance floor, I saw niggaz eyeing her like she belonged on *their* arm. I wasn't peeved, though. Not only did I have confidence in my ability to hold any bitch down, I also knew that a bitch was replaceable. And if Inez was to choose one of those niggaz over me, I knew where she laid her head and how she got her money. I could always rob her ass.

"What's up, Youngblood? You mind if I dance with your girl?" King stood over our table, his soldiers right on his heels.

Not only had he stolen some of Rich Kid's money and his clientele in Kentucky, he'd also stolen his steelo.

"She's a big girl," I said with an even tone, "ask her." I didn't trip it, either, when Inez got up and went to the dance floor with King.

The band had stopped playing and the dee-jay was spinning up-to-date rap music. I watched with a casual eye as Inez shook what her mama gave her, and King moved fluidly for a man of his size. I noted that he was up close on Inez, obviously doing as much talking as dancing. Whatever King was saying it had Inez blushing.

King's army-clad soldiers stood at the edge of the dance floor, at attention, like well trained GIs. To me, they looked like fools, jock riders. There was nothing wrong with being down with a nigga, but those niggas had to be ass kissers, willing to play toy soldier to gloss another nigga's shine. I wasn't built like dat.

King was definitely making an impression, letting niggaz know he would soon be a force to reckon with in the game. Though he got his cheddar in Kentucky, it was obvious that ATL was still in his blood.

It shouldn't have been hard for the dope boys in attendance to prophesize that one day, soon, King would return to Atlanta and make a play for Big Dog status in the city's dope trade.

Little did King know, I had a far bleaker prophecy in mind for him. Now I was even more certain I'd soon serve King his demise.

Like I said, it was mad dime pieces at The Ball, many had the ups on Inez and had come unescorted. I had no doubt King could've had his pick of any one of them, yet, he was glued to my bitch.

What the arrogant nigga was doing was trying to flex his weight, letting me know that I was such a minor figure in his eyes that he could pull my shawdy right off of my arm. It had to be that because I didn't see him disrespecting none of the other hustlers by shootin' game at the bitches on their arm.

King might not have considered me a major nigga, but he definitely knew I was a killer. So, he had to be bored with life.

While King was all up in Inez' ear, I was content to sit back and just take in the whole scenery. This wasn't really my kind of set, but I reminded myself I was there on business. The music stopped and an emcee grabbed the mic and announced it was time to present the yearly hustling awards.

Pimp of the Year went to some perm-wearing fool named Diamond Rick. The award for *Player of the Year* went to a dude whose name I couldn't recall. Hannibal won *Hustler of the Year*, which seemed appropriate to his rep on the streets. Rich Kid was runner-up.

"The final award for tonight," the emcee announced. "The prestigious award for the city's most *Up-and-Coming Hustler* goes to Little Gotti!"

A round of applause filled the ballroom and I watched the dude Blondie was with go up onstage and accept the award.

Okay, I said to myself, *now I would have to take the threat of him finding out my identity seriously.*

Still, since he was showcasing a trick bitch like Blondie on his arm, I had to question Little Gotti's wisdom in the game. Any bitch that was for sale could always be bought. Meaning, for the right price, Blondie would sell Little Gotti out.

I was ready to dip, come back in a bucket and try to follow King and his crew to wherever they were laying their heads in the city. Rich Kid had bounced soon after receiving his award. I hadn't seen him and King 'verse with one another at all. So apparently, King knew beef existed between them. I did see King talking to Blondie for a minute, but they hadn't seemed to be paying any attention to me. Or maybe she was asking him about me, on the sly.

I excused myself from Inez and went to the men's room again.

Coming back to the booth, I caught a glimpse of Inez and King exchanging something, probably phone numbers. Cool. I pretended I hadn't seen a thing. King and Inez pretended they hadn't done a thing.

A short while later, Inez and me dipped and went back to her crib.

I didn't return to The Player's Ball to get a drop on King that night because I had another idea of how I'd get to touch him. Me and Inez just went back to her crib and got our freak on. Shawdy was on some real passionate shit, giving a nigga wet, sloppy head and a private strip tease. I couldn’t help but to taste her. I licked her from head to toe. I had her body shaking like electro-shock, begging for the dick.

CHAPTER 28

A couple of weeks after wetting Toi's nigga up, I finally returned my sister's call.

"What's up?" I said, as if everything was good.

"Don't play dumb, Terrence. You know what I'm calling about." Her voice reflected a tone of tiredness, as if she had no will to argue.

I told Toi I had no beef with her other than her being stupid and still trying to defend that nigga of hers.

"Well, if you care 'bout me you'll give Glen his stuff back," my sister said. "You know he thinks I helped you plan this."

"No, he don't. The nigga just using that as leverage to get you to do everything you can to get his shit back." I don't know why she couldn't see through Glen's bullshit, it wasn't like Toi grew up in the 'burbs.

All around her, growing up in the hood, niggaz had mad game. I guess females let emotions overrule common sense and wisdom 'cause Toi definitely should've been able to peep Glen's rap.

Whatever. It didn't change my intentions and I let Toi know that there was no way I was returning the money or the guns.

"Tell your nigga he gotta charge it to the game. Shit, he's lucky I'm givin' him the coke back. Really, I should've domed his bitch ass!"

I told Toi the situation wasn't negotiable. I wasn't returning nothing but the yayo and if her nigga wasn't satisfied with that, he might not get nothing back. Toi started crying.

"Terrence, you're going to get me killed."

"I wish that fuck nigga would put his mafuckin' hands on you again! You tell dat nigga he's not getting shit back until we meet face-to-face! Holla at me when he gets out the hospital and can meet with me, face-to-face. I love you. Bye." I hung up, vexed that Glen was still trying to run that shit on my sister.

I knew I'd be hearing from Glen soon. Even though I wouldn't relinquish the loot and guns, he'd definitely want his dope back. And if Glen never called to get his shit back, then I'd fo' sho' have to dome him. 'Cause a nigga would have to either be straight pussy or planning my death to let it ride like that. I was gonna stay on my Ps and Qs until Glen showed his hand.

Meanwhile, Rich Kid was pressing me to bag King. It seemed that King's appearance at The Player's Ball had only infuriated Rich Kid more than before.

Street niggaz and all the bitches were talkin' about how King had come to The Player's Ball dressed to the nines, surrounded by fatigue-clad soldiers. Rumor had it that he'd been surrounded by one hundred SKS-packing soldiers, which wasn't true. I'd been at The Player's Ball and had peeped King and his entourage up close, but I didn't try to set the record straight. In the hood, just like in the pen, rumors were stronger than fact.

Most niggaz had no idea I'd even gone to The Ball. Like I said, it was invitation only, and Rich Kid was the only hustler from our block who had enough juice to get invited.

However, my block bred dimes like none other. So, a few females from around my way had been at The Ball and had spread the word of my presence. Now, mafuckaz were thinking I had mad clout in the game but I was playing my hand close to the vest trying to keep muthafuckaz out of my business.

No matter how hard I denied pushing weight, niggaz kept asking me to put them on. And the few fly bitches from my hood who'd been selecselective enough with which playa they'd give the pussy to, now considered prize hos, were all on my dick. Normally them bitches wouldna given me the time of day.

Some trick dope boys had moved them out the hood and went to prison trying to keep them bitches in luxury. Now those hos were either looking for a nigga with a cape to save 'em, or they'd gotten desperate and put on a G-string and went to work at a strip club, where tricks are in abundance.

One or two had their gold-digging eyes on me, falsely believing the rumors that I was large in the game. I didn't tell them yay or nay, I just capitalized on the hype.

I was whippin' through the hood, on my way to see what Murder Mike was up to. The Lex truck was sparkling, bumpin' mad sound out of the system.

As soon as I pulled to the curb, where Murder Mike was sitting on the hood of his Navigator talking to a couple of his workers, a purple Viper whipped up next to me.

Damn! Who in da hood whippin' like dat?

A quick look over my left shoulder and down rerevealed a head of long blond weave. I hopped down from my whip and saw that it was this bitch named Juanita pushing the Viper. Shawdy was a few years older than me, but I knew her and her story well.

Juanita grew up a block from where we were now parked. Her Ma Dukes was Miss Pearl, a nice woman who was rarely seen completely sober.

I could tell Miss Pearl had been a dime in her day, now she was barely a penny.

Her oldest son was killed while I was in juvenile. Another son was serving life-and thirty for dome calling a fool during a botched robbery. A third son, two years older than Juanita was in the Army, escaping family tragedy and hood pains. Juanita had an older sister who'd been missing for years, assumed dead. Their family album was mostly tragic, but not so unlike many from the hood.

Juanita was the baby of the family, pretty and fine like Miss Pearl must've been in her youth. Juanita had been a quiet and book loving girl in school, never hanging out with the fast crowd or dating dudes from around our way.

Every hood had seen the type females who didn't just wanna rise above poverty, they acted like they were too good for niggaz on the block. They either married a white boy or some nigga who impersonated one. Which was where Juanita's story differed, yet remained typical. She didn't marry a white boy or some fake brother from the 'burbs, nor did academics release her from the ghetto's grip.

Though Juanita's early teenaged years promised a different script than the norm, hood niggaz came in so many sizes, shapes and colors and with so much game, it was damn near pre-destined that Juanita would fall into one hustler's grip. Better than being snagged by a lazy nigga, with boss game, who'd tie her down with baby after baby. But really, Juanita had found no reprieve, at all.

Juanita's first taste of ghetto fame came at the age of sixteen when she got snagged by the super, supreme hustler in the city, a nigga known as Godd.

I was in and out of YDC back then, but like I said, word from the streets traveled into the pen, and vice versa. None of us in juvenile lockup knew Godd personally, but we all knew his rep. He was large back then, bigger than life now. In fact, I had never seen playa.

Anyway, about eight years ago, Godd had plucked Juanita right out of the ghetto and high school classrooms. They say the nigga was whippin' double R's back then. So how could high school allure compete with a skilled playa pushin' a Rolls Royce to a green shawdy from the hood? It couldn't.

Like poof! Juanita was living in a plushed-out crib, pushing fly whips and rockin' the ultimate fly girl gear. It was escape from the hood nine thousand! It might not have followed her *blueprint,* but like all things, the end justifies the means.

Only, Juanita couldn't handle the fame, or probably she wasn't prepared for the other things that come with being a big-time dopeboy's bitch: the other women, the loneliness and isolation from family and friends, the trips out of town dropping off dope and the beatdowns to keep her in line, intimidated. The same shit I suspected Toi was experiencing.

Juanita was young and emotional when Godd had introduced her to the highs and lows of that lifestyle, and she hadn't been able to handle the lows, mostly the other women. Godd hadn't tried to break Juanita's will and force her to remain on his team, instead, he returned her to the hood, back to grim reality.

But Juanita didn't just return to the hood empty handed. She still had the shine and gear Godd had given her in exchange for her teenage dreams. But more importantly, she still had the attitude of class she'd enhanced while being in his company.

In no time, she snagged a Big Willie from Miami who was doing his thing in Atlanta.

Like most niggaz I knew from The Bottom, Miami dude was a resthaven for a broad. He kept Juanita laced and fly, rocked her grill and had her believing her pussy was *one of a kind.*

Life was bliss for Juanita for a handful of years, until last year when the feds sntached away her meal ticket. They hit Miami dude with the RICO Act and sent him away for 360 months, thirty years!

So now, word in the hood was, Juanita was shake-dancing to maintain a life of luxury she'd gotten too used to *to* surrender.

"Hey, Terrence," she spoke out the driver's window.

"Whud up, ma?" I said, going up to her whip. "You ain't been gone from the hood too long to know they don't call me Terrence no more."

"Excuse me?" Juanita said, feigning apology. "What do they call you now?"

"Youngblood."

She smiled. "Yeah, I knew that."

"How did you know that?" I flirted.

"Word gets around."

We bullshitted each other back and forth, Juanita claiming to have heard I was ruling the streets.

Yeah, right.

I told her the real word was that she was a star in the strip clubs and had all the major niggaz feindin' for her.

"Nah, it's not like that," Juanita said with pride, nevertheless. "I don't even date men I meet at work. Matter-of-fact, I haven't dated *anyone* in months. Really, other than work, I'm a homebody."

Whatever.

"Why didn't you speak to me at The Player's Ball? I saw you there with Inez; I know you saw me."

"Naw, I didn't see you," I lied. Let her swallow that and, for once, not take it for granted that every nigga had to notice *her.*

I didn't really dig Juanita's kind, hos who chose a nigga according to the depths of the nigga's pockets and rarely even spoke to a nigga who didn't have major juice. She was just like the chickens I'd usually see in the whip with Rich Kid, acting like they owned the world just because their looks had snagged a Big Willie.

Most people from our hood disliked Juanita, especially the females who were probably a bit jealous of her. Juanita acted like hood mafuckaz were beneath her. Plus, she did nothing, any of us could see, for Miss Pearl.

"So, Inez is your girl?" she asked.

"I be holding her down," was all the info I allowed.

"In other words, she ain't got no papers on you?" Juanita asked for clarification.

"I ain't a slave, ma. Don't nobody got papers on me. In other words," I added before she took my words out of context, "It's cool for us to hook up if you get too lonely."

"Oh, is that the only way we can hook up? 'Cause I don't do the booty call thing," Her Highness stated.

"Sex has never been a priority to an ambitious man. You've been with a few boss hustlers, you ought to know that," I checked the bitch.

Her response was, "I just want you to know I'm not anyone's booty call."

Yeah, right. We'd see.

I watched her write down my pager number with delicate hands, Gucci nails and blinding bling on her fingers and wrists. Then she went in her Gucci purse and produced a business card with her digits imprinted on it. The card claimed Goldie, Juanita, was a model/private dancer. Her pager and cell phone number was inscribed across the bottom of the card. Juanita wrote her home number on the back of the card and told me to call anytime after 9 p.m. because she worked the 12 to 8 p.m. shift at the strip club.

"Goldie, huh?"

"My stage name," she said. "You can call me Juanita." Of course I'd call her Juanita, that's what her mother named her.

She whipped off, leaving the scent of *Obsession for Women* in my nostrils and her business card in my clutch. She hadn't as much as nodded hello to Murder Mike, proving that *rumor* was stronger than fact. The gold digging bitch was all in my grill because she'd seen me at The Player's Ball and had assumed I was major in the game unless I wouldn't have been invited. Which was way off.

I stuffed Juanita's card in the back pocket of my Phat Farm khakis and pushed her to the back of my mental. Murder Mike kidded me about being the *ladies' choice* these days and asked me to toss Juanita his way whenever I was finished with her.

Just then, Cita whipped up in a drop Mazda, looking like a cheaper version of Juanita.

"You can't afford Cita *and* Juanita, playboy." I said it playfully so Murder Mike wouldn't feel like I was trying to disrespect.

I liked Murder Mike, though I didn't like his free-heartedness with Cita. But it wasn't my place to tell playa how to spend his loot, though.

I watched through narrow eyes, like slits, as Murder Mike handed Cita a roll of money and she drove off. I guessed Murder must've read my expression.

"It ain't like dat, dawg. She's about to go pay for some new rims I'm copping for one of my other whips," he explained defensively.

I told him it was his hand, he didn't owe me an explanation on how he chose to play it.

"True dat," he said, and we let it ride at that.

I whipped over to Shan's crib just in time to catch Lil' T walking home from school. He was now in the second grade. He dropped his book bag and ran and jumped in my arms like he hadn't seen me in years. Of course I'd just seen him a week ago, but his excitement still made a nigga proud.

I asked him a few questions about school, but he was too hyper to answer coherently. He was more interested in getting me to take him to McDonald's, as we stood on Shan's front steps.

"Hi, Lil' Terrence," some fine shawdy waved from across the street. He waved back to her.

"Who is that?" I asked my son.

"My girlfriend," he answered, blushing. Okay, now I'd finally seen the mysterious girlfriend, shawdy who had my son love-struck.

"Penny?" I called out to her, remembering the name Lil' Terrence had mentioned many months ago.

She came over to where we stood outside Shan's unit.

"You must be Big Terrence?"

"Yeah. But call me Youngblood."

The bitch was showing all thirty-two of her teeth, giving off mad sexual vibes. Of course, I wasn't responding to that because, as far as I was concerned, Penny was my son's bitch, even if it was just in his fantasy. No matter, I wouldn't fuck my son's girl. Besides, Shan came outside cockblocking and frontin' like she was still on my team.

I stiff-armed Shan, said goodbye to Penny, and took my lil' man to McDonald's.

Later, I was at Inez' crib chilling when she got a phone call from that nigga, King. I know because I was listening on the extension in her bedroom while she was on the one in the living room.

King started off by telling Inez he would only be in Atlanta another day or two, and he hoped they could hookup before he had to return to Kentucky and Check his traps, he boasted.

Inez responded by reminding him that she was involved with me and I might not approve of her hooking up with him.

"Afterall, why would I mess up my thing here in Atlanta for a man who'll soon return to Kentucky and who knows who?" she wisely questioned King.

He came back with, "I feel where you're coming from, but it's not like I can't send for you to come up to Kentucky. Anyway, you're wasting your time with that loser you were with at The Ball." Inez didn't swallow that salt, she half-assed defended me, leaving herself enough wiggle room not to turn-off King.

Still, he continued to drop salt about my age, my hustle potential and my lack of ability to be the type nigga Inez needed in her life.

I replaced the receiver quietly back on the hook when I heard them set a date for lunch the following day. I didn't let King's salt vex me. If Inez was foolish enough to sell-out to a hater like King, then she would share his fate.

The nigga just didn't know, while he was dropping salt, he was making my job a lot easier, plotting his own death.

Besides, dropping salt on a nigga to his bitch don't do shit but make the bitch cling tighter to her nigga. If King's game was on point, he could've trusted his rap to pull Inez from me, instead of trying to salt a nigga's name. I never did shit like that, but then again, I kept it trill.

CHAPTER 29

I was on my way to Applebee's restaurant to meet Juanita for a simple dinner. She had suggested a much more formal place when we had made the date earlier in the week, but I told her I was a jeans and Timbs-type nigga and since we were both from the hood, wasn't no use in either of us putting on a phony face. She had a comment about there being nothing wrong with eating at a fancy restaurant once in a while, but she didn't argue about it.

Two weeks had passed since Juanita had hit me with her digits, and had she not called me, we probably wouldn't be hooking up for this first date. 'Cause I had no plans to call her.

Juanita was waiting for me in the foyer of the restaurant, drawing the attention of every male's eye, black and white. She was wearing hip-hugging Pelle Pelle jeans that showed off her perfect curves and her sweet-looking belly button and a silk blouse tied in a knot about that gorgeous navel. A floppy hat gave style to her causal outfit, long blond tinted tresses hung down to her shoulders. Red lipstick accentuated her breathtaking smile when she greeted me.

I was rockin' a Sean Jean denim outfit, wearing a matching-colored stocking cap over my braids and bling on my neck and both wrists.

Seated at a cozy booth inside of the restaurant, we shared a basket of hot wings and fries. Juanita had some type of fruity cocktail-mixed drink, while I ordered two Coronas.

I wasn't trying to *pull* Juanita, so I did very little talking and a whole lot of listening.

She told me her story, which didn't differ much from the story the hood told of her. Afterwards, claiming that she had promised herself she'd never get involved with another dope boy, I asked her why not, just to remind her I *could* talk. She said that dope boys didn't really appreciate *any* woman 'cause women came plentiful and easy to them.

"Every dope boy I've met, deep down they view females as possessions, like their cars," Juanita said somewhat solemnly.

"Most females view niggaz as assets, like their credit cards," I countered for the sake of conversation.

Juanita claimed it wasn't that type of party with her. She freely admitted she didn't want a nigga who had little to offer, but neither was a nigga'z bank the most important concern for her when choosing whom she'd get involved with.

But I couldn't tell. The two niggaz I'd known her to be involved with were certainly big money niggaz, and I was sure that wasn't by accident.

I didn't know her whole profile, but Juanita didn't strike me as the type of female who'd kick it with an average, everyday nigga. The strip club had sharpened her game, just listening to her was obvious she was no longer the bookworm shawdy I'd observed from a distance while growing up. The strip club and the fast life had taught Juanita's tongue how to deliver what sounded real to a nigga.

Juanita was saying, "I want a man who wants me for more than my looks. Somebody I can share everything with, start a family and settle down with."

"You don't ask for much," I said sarcastically, and Juanita laughed. A real feminine laugh. Her sexuality was powerful and probably intentional.

We were both young, and in our early twenties, but neither of us were new jacks to the cat-and-mouse game played between players and bitches, Gs and hos. I'd learned the ways of women through observation and personal pain. I was sure Juanita's realistic view of men came from not only her past relationships but the ill shit she witnessed on the daily working at strip clubs.

She went on to tell me that she hadn't been with a man in six months and was thinking about remaining celibate until she got married.

So here was what I was thinking: Her Miami nigga had got popped by the feds sometime last year, but she'd only gone without sex the past six months. So she hadn't remained faithful long after dude got popped. Also, I'd have to marry her to get what other niggaz had gotten on-the-strength.

Fuck dat!

I was also thinking maybe Juanita was doing the girl-girl thing these past months, mostly all strip hos dibbled and dabbed like that.

I spat it to her in the raw, no cut.

Juanita seemed to be letting my words register before responding.

She flashed that cryptonite smile at me, acknowledging my straight forwardness.

"I'm not going to lie," she finally said. "I'm not ashamed of anything I do. I met a friend a few months after Trent went to the feds, but it wasn't anything serious. He was a lot older than I am and he's married, so it was just somebody I could call when I got lonely. See, I don't have a lot of female friends. They're too jealous and petty. But I realized my male friend was getting too serious about me, so I stopped seeing him. I haven't slept with anyone since." She paused to sip her margarita, leaving red lipstick around the edge of the cocktail glass.

"As far as having sex with women," she continued, "I tried that once when I used to be with this dude named Godd. Well, he talked me into trying it with another girl. But it wasn't my cup of tea. So now, I'm either strictly dickly or I please myself."

"True dat. What about playboy in the feds, you still in touch with him?"

"Who? Trent?"

"Whatever playboy's name is from Miami?"

"Trent. Naw, we're no longer in touch," Juanita admitted with no visible regret. "He told me, as soon as he got sentenced, that he wouldn't be home for a long time and to go on with my life. I tried to write him when he first got sent away, but he wouldn't write back."

Her expression saddened for a few seconds, maybe she was reminiscing about better times, when life with Trent was all bling and shopping sprees. Before he had to pay the piper.

"Enough about me, though," her expression quickly brightened. "What's been up with you since we both left the neighborhood?"

"I lay my head elsewhere, but I'm still in da hood, shawdy." I wanted Juanita to understand I was still all hood. That way, she wouldn't be expecting me to open no car doors for her or none of that gentleman shit.

"Anyway, I've just been tryin' to maintain and stay a step ahead of my enemies. You know how the street is, on top today, obituary page tomorrow."

Juanita acknowledged my doomsical outlook of the streets and seconded my opinion with an observation from a females' view.

She said life wasn't all bliss from their end, either. The ups and downs, joys and pains made them old before they reached thirty.

I could feel where she was coming from but I disagreed that their pain was comparable to a hustler's ultimate fate. A female's loss was mostly emotional or material when her nigga took a fall. A few hos bit dirt with their nigga if they happened to be with him when the enemy came. But, for the most part, they only suffered until they hooked another hustler to replace the fallen one. While a nigga usually fell hard, mad years in the pen or faced-up in a box, nothing could replace what he lost.

Juanita and I rapped for another hour, then she paid our tab and we went our separate ways, promising we'd hook up again, soon.

Inez went out of town for the weekend, so I picked up Lil' T from Shan and we chilled at the crib with Eryka and Cheryl.

Cheryl was due to have the baby in a matter of days, so I'd promised to hang close to the crib, in case she went into labor and needed to be taken to the hospital right way.

It was hard to do the family bonding thing while not feeling any affection toward Cheryl. I knew my disinterest in Cheryl pained her heart and made her life miserable.

It was obvious things would never be the same between us,and that Cheryl couldn't remain living with me much longer. Other residents had begun complaining to the manager. Cheryl's days in my crib were numbered.

Still, I enjoyed three days with Lil' T and Eryka. Around them I was a clown, not a G. It was funny how I forgot all about murder, money and bitches when I was with my seeds. Nothing else mattered but their laughter.

Of course, it was just a matter of time before I'd put that ski mask on and pick up that heater and *take* what I wanted from this world. I was a robber/killer-for-hire, out to get enough bread to provide a good life for me and mine.

Watching me at home with Lil' T and Eryka, no one would ever have guessed the life I lived, the way I got my loot. But, then again, that was the way to play it.

CHAPTER 30

My dawg, Lonnie, was with me riding shotgun. I was on my way to meet with Glen to return his dope and lay down the law, just in case the silly nigga had any idea of punishing my sister for what I'd done to him.

We agreed to meet in the food court of Greenbriar Mall where the open space would provide us both a little sense of security.

Lonnie and I arrived an hour earlier than I'd agreed to meet Glen so we could checkout the scene and make sure I wasn't being lured into a trap. I had told Lonnie if Glen showed up with po-po at his side, get out of the way 'cause I was going out like a G, guns blazing.

Wasn't no sense in Lonnie catching a murder on a cop, this wasn't his beef. Still, he said he had my back, true nigga that he was.

Glen rolled up not long after Lonnie and me. He, too, must've wanted to checkout the scene, leery of an ambush.

My sister was pushing the nigga in a wheelchair; one leg was heavily bandaged, the other was in some type of plastic cast.

"We came to get the stuff you said ya'll have for Glen," my sister said blandly.

I looked at her, showing no sign of the love. This was business.

"No disrespect, sis, but I wanna holla at Glen without your interference. Why don't you and Lonnie give us a little privacy?"

Lonnie went and sat at a table ten feet away. Only after Glen nodded his consent did Toi follow Lonnie.

"Look, playboy," I was mean-mugging the nigga as I spoke. "I'm not gonna make this speech any longer than it has to be. I'm sure Toi already told you what I said I'll return." Glen nodded, mean-mugging me back.

"That's the price you pay for putting your hands on my folks." I didn't take my eyes off his. I wanted him to know that if he retaliated against my sister for my decision not to return the money and guns, he would be in a box next time instead of a wheelchair. I didn't have to verbalize it, my stare said it all.

There was nothing else to say besides letting Glen know that I'd have someone to drop the dope off at my sister's crib later.

On the way out, I told Toi she needed to start keeping better company, my sarcasm obvious.

Inez had got back in town the day before, so I got her to drop off the dope at my sister's crib. She told me the drop went smooth, no hitch.

We were chillin' at Inez' crib, just passing time before we went to the movies. She'd told me yesterday all about her trip out of town, at least, as much as she wanted me to know. I'd questioned her relentlessly, not that I was a jealous nigga, but it was important that I got the full scoop. I was confident Inez revealed all.

The movie was some weak love-story shit, but Inez was loving it so I gritted my teeth and endured a boring two hours.

Back at Inez' crib, I dicked her down and we both slept like babies. Well, until I got a persistent page and learned that Cheryl was at the hospital in labor.

"Shawdy, I gotta bounce," I told Inez without any explanation.

I hopped up and was dressed and out of the door in minutes. When I reached the hospital, I was surprised to see Cheryl's mother in the waiting room. She was holding Eryka like the perfect grandmother, which the bitch isn't, wasn't, probably won't ever be. I swooped Eryka up out of her arms and sat down a few seats from her.

"Are you going in the delivery room with Cheryl when she's ready?" Cheryl's mother asked.

"Naw."

"Why not?" Her tone was distasteful.

I didn't even answer the bitch. Fuck her! I didn't owe her no explanation.

I hated long waits in hospitals, so I'd come prepared. Eryka was asleep across my lap when I put on the headphones to the walkman I'd brought along with me. Cash Money Millionaires was pumpin' in my ears. Big Tymer was spitting a verse about flossing in the hood when a nurse came out into the waiting room and announced something. I couldn't hear her, obviously, so I took off the headphones. The nurse repeated her announcement.

Without saying a word, I handed Eryka to Cheryl's mother, then I followed the nurse to Cheryl's room. Cheryl was in the middle of a painful contraction, yet she tried to smile when she noticed me.

I rubbed her shoulder, trying to comfort her.

"Hey, fat girl," I half-joked.

"Shut—up!" Cheryl cried.

I kissed her on the forehead and told her to be strong. I didn't hate Cheryl like I did Shan. The only things I had against Cheryl was that she had grown lazy and fat, and she was crowding a young nigga's space. But I put all that to the side and went into the delivery room with Cheryl and held her hand as she gave birth to another baby girl.

"So what did y'all name the new baby?" Inez asked while rolling a blunt.

"Chante Sierre," I said, "and, of course, my last name."

"That's a pretty name," Inez complimented. "Who thought of it, you or Cheryl?"

"Me," I boasted.

"Well, you better start thinking of another name for a child because my period is two weeks late."

"What?"

"I wasn't going to say anything until I was sure, 'cause you already have enough baby mama drama. Don't worry, I'm gonna get an abortion if I am pregnant," Inez switched up.

"C'mon, ma!" I was instantly pissed. "I thought you were on birth control?"

"Don't worry, nigga, I said I'm getting an abortion. You already got enough kids." She sounded pissed. Like her situation was all *my* fault.

Shit! Everywhere I turned bitches were popping up pregnant. As if a nigga didn't have enough responsibilities already. I was so mad I just got up and left.

About forty-five minutes later, I was seated by myself at a table inside of the Gentleman's Escape, the strip club where Juanita worked as Goldie.

I was in the back of the club tossing down Henny and Cokes, wondering why every shawdy I fucked had to get pregnant?

I was *feeling* Inez, and we were in deeper than I've led on, but I wasn't trying to see Stan's baby mama become my baby mama, too.

On the other hand, it could work to my advantage, assuring Inez' loyalty, to an extent. Plus, if Inez didn't get an abortion it would prove that she had no plans of getting back with Fat Stan when he got out.

I was sure his pussy-whipped ass wasn't beyond forgiving such a transgression.

I was weighing the pros and the cons, gettin' my buzz on, not really paying attention to the dancers in the club. I shooed a few snow whites away, but paid attention to the golden brown honey onstage working the pole like a human slinky, Goldie.

White men were lined up at the edge of the stage, with fists full of dollars. The few black men in attendance seemed more occupied by the snow white beauties in thongs.

Juanita was working the stage like a porn star. She'd leave the stage and return in different costumes, strip down to skin and collect another garter belt full of cash. It was easy to understand how she could afford the Viper she owned. Even from a distance, her curves were spellbinding. If I had any trick blood in my veins I would've been jostling with the white men, begging Goldie to hurry and take my fist full of money next.

As it was, I was a thugged-out young nigga with natural playa skills. So I just chilled in the back with my Henny and thoughts, still shooing bitches away from my table.

An hour after Goldie came off of stage and had completed her tour around the club, flirting with white men, she finally strutted over to my table.

"Hi. You look like you could use some company. Do you mind if—Youngblood? What are you doing here?" She was surprised and startled by my presence.

"Hey, you never know when I might pop up."

She smiled genuinely and leaned down to hug my neck. But I leaned away from the attempt.

"Naw, ma, not in here. I don't wanna be mistaken for one of your tricks."

"Fans," Juanita clarified. "In order for them to be my tricks I'd have to be a ho. And *that* I'm not. They pay to *look*, no amount of money allows them to touch."

I quickly retorted, "Don't get so defensive."

"Oh, I'm not," Juanita stated. "Just don't label me as the typical dancer. It's a job, not *who* I am."

I told shawdy not to trip it. It was just the way I talked. Then I attended to my drink and advised her to go attend to her fans.

"I see you're in a good mood," she said sarcastically. Then she walked away, trying to be dignified in a mafuckin' G-string. I laughed like a crazy man. The strobe lights were probably reflecting off of my platinum teeth.

I had barely stopped laughing when Juanita came back to my table fully dressed, a clothes bag slung over her shoulder.

"Let's go." She said it like there was no doubt I'd leave with her.

So, shit, I did.

I pulled beside Juanita's whip and parked when we reached her crib. She lived in a one-level house, on a cul-de-sac, in a new subdivision in the suburb of Union City. The inside of Juanita's crib was immaculate and furnished in good taste. Gucci-print sofas and loveseats, smoked-glass cocktail tables with Gucci-printed base, porcelin oriented statues and other whatnots.

She told me to have a seat and relax while she took a quick shower.

"Oh, I'm sorry," she said on second thought. "Would you like a drink or something to snack on?"

"Nah, I'm good." Juanita turned on the stereo and then disappeared into another part of the house, leaving Maxwell crooning throughout the room.

Now dude can blow with the best of singers, but I wasn't be on no slow, romantic shit. So, by the time Juanita had showered and returned wearing a black leotard, I had replaced Maxwell with a Big Pun CD.

I was bobbing my head to the beat, watching Juanita move around in the kitchen. Shawdy was all dat and some more. I mean, the ATL was home to some of the finest, prettiest females on earth, so beauty wasn't new to me. But Juanita was flawless, above any other female I'd ever laid eyes on. She had to know she was most nigga's dream. I wasn't drooling at the mouth, though, 'cause I already knew that despite Juanita's perfect figure and looks, the bitch had to have some type of flaw. There was no such thing as a perfect bitch.

She came back into the living room with a bottle of lime water and some fruit sticks and sat next to me on the couch, Indian-style.

Her pussy print poked out of the leotards like a ripe cantaloupe.

"Your crib is nice," I said. I didn't know what else to say. I couldn't lie, shawdy had a nigga tonguetied. I'd have to watch my step or I'd fall hard for this close-to-perfect bitch.

"Thanks." She sipped her water through a straw.

"You mind if I put on some less aggressive music?" she asked, rubbing my arm.

"Hey, it's your crib. Do what you feel," I shot back.

"Yeah, but you're company." She got up and turned the music off.

"How about we just talk?"

I asked her why women always wanted to talk? Didn't they know how to just chill?

Juanita laughed. Even her laugh was perfect.

"How do we get to know one another if we don't talk, ask each other questions?"

I told her we couldn't get to know each other by talking and asking questions, 'cause both of us were gonna lie about the things we felt the other wouldn't like.

"Like, would you tell me the truth if I asked how many niggaz you done fucked? Or if you've ever fucked a cracker?"

"Yeah, I'd be honest about it. Or else I wouldn't answer the question," Juanita admitted. That was why I wouldn't ask it, I told her.

Because either I wouldn't believe her answer or I'd get mad at the truth, like if she were to admit she'd fucked a cracker.

"And, really I'd be wrong. 'Cause, number one, I ain't your man. And if I was, it still would be ill for me to get mad about some shit you done before we hooked up."

"Are you the jealous type?" she asked calmly.

"Not at all, shawdy," I said truthfully. "I live and let live. I don't *own* nobody but myself."

Juanita was feeling me on that, but she disagreed that talking, to get to know each other, was fruitless. She felt that what a person said gave you something to hold them to and when their actions contradicted their words, then it was time to move on. I could understand her point of view, I told her, but I preferred to just kick it and let things settle into its own rhythm.

"When you're just kickin' it with a woman, does that involve sex?"

"Usually."

"Well, baby, I'm afraid you're going to find me unusual."

"Yeah, how's that?" I pressed.

Juanita claimed that she no longer had sex with any man that she wasn't seriously involved with or one that wasn't monogamously involved with her.

"In other words, I don't sleep with other women's men," she clarified. "I did that once upon a time, but not now."

"A nigga can always lie," I reminded her.

"Of course, but the truth will eventually reveal itself."

"By then you could be too deep in to turn around and let go."

"Ain't no such thing," she firmly stated.

I liked Juanita's mature, no nonsense reply. If true, it meant she had principles she lived by.

We rapped way past midnight and then I told her I had to bounce before I got too sleepy to drive home.

"You could stay overnight in the guest room," she offerred. But I declined the invitation, telling her that when the time came for me to spend the night at her crib, I wouldn't be sleeping in no guest room.

"That time will come when you decide that I'm the one and only woman you need and want. Believe me, I'm enough woman for you, and I'll be true to you in return. Think about that," Juanita said, and gave me mad tongue at the door.

On the way home, I tossed Juanita around in my head, comparing the things we had in common with the ways we were totally opposite from one another. Of course the things we had in common were of little worry, except that I sensed she had game, like I did. Of concern were those things we didn't share. More so, it was difficult for me to reconcile Juanita's spoken words with her profession.

How many women of strong character stripped for a living?

I was thinking the bitch had boss game. It wasn't that she didn't fuck niggaz who had other bitches, it was probably that she had been there and done that and already knew it was a dead-end street. So now, she was trying to make a nigga, like me, damn near wife her before she would come off the ass.

Well, I was gonna test her resolve. And if that failed, I would lie to get the pussy. How a bitch gon' lay boundaries on me? Shit, shawdy was from the hood, where pussy was cheaper than a blunt or a bottle of wine. She should've realized that if she put those type of stipulations on the pussy, a nigga would lie to get it. Hos be on some dumb shit when they try to regulate like dat.

Why take a nigga through all of that drama when the shit gon' still turn out the same? If it was meant to be, it was gon' be. If it wasn't meant to be, the shit wasn't gonna last even if a nigga wifed 'em. The way I saw it, they might as well give up the pussy the first night. Then they'd avoid all the bullshit a nigga had to tell them to get the booty.

It didn't matter, though, I'd win in the end. I fo' sho wasn't letting Inez go to get with Juanita.

Yeah, Juanita was 100 percent eye-candy, but it wasn't like Inez was hard on the eyes. Plus, Inez was adding to a nigga'z bank and proving that she was down.

I let myself in with the key she'd been given me. It was damn near one o'clock in the morning, but Inez was still awake, reading a magazine, when I got up to her bedroom.

"Hey," I spoke.

"Hey back," she said, no hint of anger in her voice or expression.

I asked if she felt like getting up and fixing me some tacos. She immediately put the magazine away and went down to the kitchen.

She stood behind me, twenty minutes later, messaging my neck while I ate. I asked if she was mad at me.

"For what?"

"Look, shawdy," I began, "don't think a nigga don't want you to carry his seed. It ain't that. The shit just caught me off guard."

"I'm gonna have an abortion," she reiterated.

"What if I don't want you to kill my seed?"

She told me to eat my food and we could discuss it after we both had a few days to consider all the consequences.

"You gon' give me some loving tonight?" I was testing her, to see if she was mad, deep down.

She said "You don't have to ask for that, I'm still your lady, ain't I?"

CHAPTER 31

I was expecting Cheryl to go home and stay with her Ma Dukes again when she was released from the hospital with the new baby. But obviously, her mother's act of concern didn't extend that far.

So, once again, I found myself with the responsibility of having to provide a home for Cheryl and the kids. The situation was stressing me out. *A young nigga shouldn't have so much weight on his back.*

My life was fast becoming one big drama and most of the conflicts centered around bitches. I wasn't tryin' to roll like that, though. I guessed shit just happened.

Still, my priority was building up my bank. Regardless to the drama, money still made the world go around. Yet, I was learning, firsthand, that more money didn't only bring more bitches, it also brought more problems. And it wasn't like I was sitting on riches.

Compared to the major hustlers, like Rich Kid and Hannibal and 'em, I was a minor figure. Yet, honeys were all on my dick, trying to carry my seeds and lay permanent claim in a nigga'z life. Even a choice shawdy, like Juanita, wanted to put a young G on lock.

I couldn't front, the shit had a nigga's chest swole. But I was determined not to lose my focus. I still had to deal with King.

Inez and I rapped about her situation and decided that she would give birth to my seed.

I got with Rich Kid to assure him that moves were being formulated to eliminate his nemesis, King. I just needed him to understand that we'd both have to show some patience, 'cause haste could be severe and catastrophic.

Deading a nigga was as simple and easy as pulling a trigger, but it took either luck or meticulous planning to avoid being bagged for the murder. And I wasn't placing my life and freedom in the hands of Lady Luck.

A nigga'z plate was full. I would have to help Cheryl find a place for her and the kids to live, and soon. 'Cause mafuckaz in my apartment complex were sure to start complaining loudly to management.

Besides, Cheryl's presence was cramping my style. On the other hand, I didn't want to be responsible for supporting Cheryl. I had no qualms about taking care of my seeds, but I had no intentions of being Cheryl's meal ticket.

I guessed the bitch was trying to follow her stankass mother's blue print: find a man to take care of her. But I wasn't playing that part. The bitch would have to sign-up for welfare and apply for a Section 8 apartment. There were some decent Section 8 apartments around the city. And if push came to shove, my kids weren't too good to live in the hood.

Cheryl wasn't feelin' that shit, though. When I mentioned it to her, she responded like her fat ass was too good to live in the hood. Which was some ill shit, 'cause when I had first started fucking Cheryl she was going out of her way, trying to be a down-the-way bitch. Now she was trying to act like that bitch, Hillary, on the *Fresh Prince of Belair*, like anything but a mansion was beneath her.

Well, if the bitch expected to live in luxury, she would have to get off of her fat ass and find a job or get a hustle that paid like that! I spit it to her just like that, in the raw. Her 'tude turned bitchy, as though what I was stressing was stupid.

"Look, fat bitch!" I swore. "I ain't no rest haven for your lazy ass! In the two years I've known you, you've gone from sugar to shit. I can't even stand to look at you. I'm gonna take care of my kids but I'm not taking care of you no more! By the time Chante' turns three months old you better have found a job and somewhere to live, 'cause I'm puttin' yo' ass out of here!"

I grabbed some gear and jetted, leaving Cheryl crying like a red Miss Piggy.

Later, I got with Lonnie to discuss a home invasion he had planned for us. I didn't know dude whose house we were to invade, but I trusted Lonnie wouldn't put me down on a lick he hadn't thoroughly cased-out.

A couple nights later, a few hours after midnight, Lonnie parked around the corner from our intended victim's crib and we both got out of the nondescript car. We were in the customary robber's gear, all black. We'd wait 'til we were at the vic's back door before pulling on our ski masks.

The one-block hike seemed much further to me. I had an AK-47 down the pants leg of the black over-all jumpsuit I was wearing, which made me walk like my whole leg was in a cast.

Lonnie was packing two automatic handguns. Though we weren't expecting a confrontation, we both wore vests underneath our clothes.

We'd just stopped by a nightclub and Lonnie verified that the dopeboy whose house we were about to invade was indeed partying at the club.

It only took two powerful kicks for the cheap wooden backdoor to give in. I was upstairs faster than a computer comic villian. The assault rifle warned the half-asleep, startled woman that this wasn't any computer game. Still, she couldn't help but to scream. It was reflexive. So was my reaction.

I smashed her across the face with the end of the AK-47, and she crumbled across the bed. I ignored the brown ass hanging out the white panties. I put the tip of the AK-47 to her temple.

"Scream again, you'll die!"

I hollered downstairs to Lonnie that everything was under control upstairs. Then, at gunpoint, I led the bitch to a bedroom window where I could watch the driveway while Lonnie searched the crib.

Five minutes later, we were on our way back to Lonnie's crib.

The next day, I put fifteen G's inside of a frozen chicken box and placed it in the freezer where I kept my stash. I gave Cheryl fifteen hundred to go shopping for Eryka and Chanté, and permission to use the Maxima. She wanted me to come along, but I wasn't hearing that.

I dipped by Poochie's crib to see if Lil' T was over there, he wasn't. But Poochie seemed to be maintaining. Her appearance was up to par and her crib was clean and her sons were in their room playing video games.

I told Poochie the truth, she was looking good, and asked her what she'd been up to.

"Just going to work and to church, and trying to raise my sons right," she said.

"Do you miss me?" I flirted.

Poochie flashed a smile, I guess she was reminiscing.

"Sometimes," she admitted. "But what we were doing wasn't right."

"In whose eyes?"

"In the eyes of the Lord."

How could I argue that?

I gave her eight hundred for Lil' T and five hundred for her and her sons, and told her to go shopping for Lil' T.

"Don't give Shan the money."

"I won't," she promised.

I hugged her goodbye and could've sworn I felt more than a little heat in her embrace. It had been awhile since I'd hit it. I wanted to fuck Poochie real bad, but not as bad as I wanted to see her prosper and maintain her self-respect. So I dipped without comment.

I whipped over to the hood to see what I could get into, some hoodrat would end up in the motel with me.

When I got to Englewood, it seemed like the whole projects were under siege. Police cruisers were everywhere! A helicopter came hovering over. News station vans, with sattelite dishes atop, lined the horseshoe where most of the drug activity in the projects took place.

I swiftly parked the Lex, stuck my heater in the secret compartment and hopped out before po-po noticed a young nigga pushin' a ghetto-fabulous whip and wanted to harass me.

From all the activity, I knew that something major had gone down.

But what?

Immediately I thought of Murder Mike. He was beginning to make his presence felt. More money in his pockets meant less in someone else's. The type of shit that fueled turf wars. And Englewood was predominantly Rich Kid's turf. Though Rich kid was now a nigga pushing weight, Englewood traps were his steady, like a pimp's bottom ho.

For years Murder Mike had toiled, small time, in the project, clockin' lil' boy figgas, and not a threat to Rich Kid's pockets. Now Murder Mike had a hookup. He had plugged in to somebody in power, and was fast on-the-rise. No doubt, his rise was subtracting dollars from Rich Kid. But Rich Kid was major paid, why would he trip trap money? It wasn't like Rich Kid's and King's beef. Murder Mike had never been down with Rich Kid, he owed him no loyalty.

Maybe Rich Kid's Englewood crew had rode on Murder Mike's boys, but the beef wasn't ordered by Rich Kid?

Perhaps it had been spontaneous?

I had love for Murder Mike and a certain degree of loyalty to Rich Kid. Where did that place me in their beef? Murder Mike was my dawg, closer to me than Freddie had been when Rich Kid took him off the shelf. Damn!

I doubted Murder had the power to win a war against Rich Kid, few niggaz in the city did. Which put me in a fucked up position 'cause I didn't wanna see Murder Mike extinct. Yet, it wasn't my biz.

Mafuckaz were everywhere. On porches. Parked cars. In yards.

Nappy headed, nosey bitches with babies cradled on their hips.

Junkies still trying to buy a rock, on the down low, with po-po not even ten feet away. I saw Fiona and her crew posted up near the dumpster. Cita would've been around, too, except Murder Mike had moved her out of the hood, I'd heard.

Had Cita's man been killed? Or just some of his soldiers?

I spotted him out the corner of my eye leaning against his black Navigator, tricked-out, parked on the front lawn of a basehead named Mildred. My nigga was ghetto fabulous. He was rockin' black, baggy denim pants, sagging. A black, Falcons jersey, and a fitted black leather Falcons cap, brim turned to the left side, dreadlocks sticking out. Even from across the street, the platinum and ice around his neck was blinging. So were both his wrists. Up close I saw his new platinum grill. The top row of teeth spelled M-U-R-D-E-R in platinum, the bottom spelled, M-I-K-E. I saw that he had two platinum fingernails cut in the design of a .9mm. I knew that the platinum fingernails represented two bodies, indicating that Murder Mike had sent two people to their graves. He had a cell phone to his ear and one clipped to his waist.

The newest ghetto king.

I wasn't hatin' on my nigga, though. When a nigga rose from nothing, he couldn't help but to floss.

Cita was glued to Murder Mike's side, like a third arm. She rocked a short, black mini and a black and red cashmere sweater that hugged her shoulders and breasts, but left her navel exposed. A diamond cross hung from her pierced navel. She wore mad bling, too neck, ears, wrists, and fingers. Hair bangin', frosted blond at the tips. Red lipstick. No need for make-up, just a dab of eye shadow. Cell phone clipped to her waist, like the one clipped to Murder's. Alligator purse and high heeled alligator stilettos.

The newest ghetto queen.

I wasn't mad at her, either. She had wandering eyes, but she'd been *mostly* loyal to Murder Mike, even when he was only clockin' McDonald's loochie. She'd excused him fucking her friends, beefing with them hos instead of with him, and endured the occasional beatdown whenever Murder Mike felt like Iron Mike Tyson. It was only natural that she'd want to floss, proving to the hood that her humiliations hadn't been in vain. Mad hos had put up with the same and didn't have shit to show for it.

At least for now, mafuckaz had to respect Cita's shine.

Murder Mike ended his phone call and noticed my approach.

"Whud up, main man?" I said, and dapped hands.

"It's your world, whoady," Murder popped back.

"What's the deal with all the police and news people?"

"Somebody robbed and killed the Ribs Lady. They just discovered her body in her apartment a little while ago."

"Damn! No more rib dinners." I shook my head, disgusted at the thought, hungry now.

"Yeah, that's fucked up!" Murder agreed.

Cita butted in. "That's all y'all thinking about? Rib dinners? That lady is dead! And that lil' girl she adopted is damn near dead!" Her face wore a scowl. Murder Mike told her to shut up before he slapped her lipstick crooked.

"Matter of fact," he added, "go sit in the car until you learn to be quiet when grown folks talkin'!"

"I'm going over there with Fiona and 'em," Cita said defiantly.

She took one step but froze when Murder said, "I'll break your jaw if you don't get in the car. I don't care how many police are around!"

Cita gave me the mean mug, as if it was my fault her nigga put her ass in check. Like she didn't know there was a steep price to pay to be a ghetto king's ghetto queen. The bitch hadn't seen the half of it. Let her stick around while Murder continued to rise in the game. Eventually, she'd surrender all of her pride for the bling.

Like a chastised child, Cita obediently went and sat inside of the truck.

"I'm still training her," Murder Mike half-joked. "Anyway, let me tell you what the business is."

"Run it down to me, my nigga," I said, and then I listened intensely as he told me what was up.

When he was done, I assured him I would handle his problem for him, right away.

Later that week, I drove Inez to Kentucky in a rental car. She was down with helping me clap King. I'd enlisted her help the minute King had showed interest in her at The Player's Ball.

At first Inez had balked, not wanting to get involved with a murderous plot. But I'd given her an ultimatum—prove she was truly down with me or find another nigga to hold her down. Of course, I also threatened that she now knew too much for me to let her live if she wouldn't cooperate. I also promised her my love, blah, blah, blah.

So, King's arrogant ass was put in the cross the minute he'd approached my shawdy. His own arrogance, mixed with his underestimation of me, didn't even allow him to consider the possibility that Inez' receptiveness wasn't genuine.

King picked Inez up from the motel that night, believing she had caught an airplane in, like on her first visit. He was pushing a black whip, with dark tinted windows. I was relieved to see that he'd come alone to pick up Inez.

I followed in the rental car at a safe distance until King and Inez pulled into the driveway of a large white house.

I drove on by, looking for a nice, quiet place to park and wait.

It was a long, nervous, hour wait that seemed like four hours. I got rawed-up a little on powder, to put myself in that indestructale mode.

This setup was a dangerous one. I'd have no one to watch my back.

Plus, I'd be depending on Inez to execute her end properly. A lot of trust to put in a novice. If one thing went wrong, I could end up in a box. I'd drilled it in Inez that she couldn't allow King to leave the bedroom once she'd made the call.

"You'll have to call me again if he does," I'd lectured her. "And if he has music in his bedroom, turn it on so he won't hear me climbing the stairs, not loud, though. I need to be able to hear. Make sure you swipe his door keys and drop them out the bathroom window. Wrap 'em in a white towel so they'll be easy to find." I had told her.

My cell phone twerped.

"Yeah?"

"It's *all good,*" she whispered.

"You're sure?"

"Yeah. Wait about fifteen minutes before you come."

"Don't forget to drop the keys. Is there an alarm?"

"I've already dropped them. The alarm is off." The anxiety had her on edge.

"Are you sure the alarm is off?"

"Yeah! It's inside the front door. I turned it off when he went to the kitchen to fix our drinks. I gotta go!"

"Wait! Where's the bedroom, when I come upstairs?" Inez hurriedly whispered directions. I could hear tap water running in the background.

"Call back if he leaves the bedroom," I reminded her.

"I will!" she assured me before disconnecting.

Finding the white towel in the dark of night was no problem.

Figuring out which key opened the front door took a few seconds. But I was inside fast. No alarm blaring.

I tiptoed up the stairs, street sweeper in hand, ready to blast away anything that moved. Anything!

Soft lamp-light illuminated the bed on which they laid, under covers.

Inez saw me first.

I put a finger to my lips. Still, she screamed.

King rolled off of her, butt ass naked, and faced the masked gunman. Me.

"Move and you die!" I barked.

The nigga surprised the hell out of me when he grabbed Inez and covered his body with hers, simultaneously choking her from behind.

"Fool! This will shoot through your bitch!" I bluffed.

"Ahhh!" he suddenly yelped. Inez had bitten a plug out of his forearm. He let her go and she scrambled out of bed and then hurried into her clothes.

I made King lie on his stomach and put his hands behind his back.

I took a pair of handcuffs from my pocket and told Inez to cuff him.

Shawdy wasn't nervous.

I then duct-taped his ankles together and removed the mask from over my face. I wanted to see his expression when he realized he had seriously underestimated me.

But that was a mistake. 'Cause now he *knew* he was gonna die and refused to tell me where his stash was at.

It didn't matter, I'd find it if it was there at the house.

I taped King's mouth and told Inez to go find a bottle of rubbing alcohol.

She could only find Peroxide. That was cool. I poured the peroxide over the bite mark on King's arm to wash away Inez' saliva and DNA. Then I told her to take the peroxide and go wipe down everything she'd touched in the house, plus the inside of King's car.

"When you're finished, wait for me downstairs."

"Rich Kid says hello!" I antagonized my prey. I taped his feet to his hands behind his back. It had to be painful, King was a big man.

Then I searched his house, room by room, looking for a safe, or money hid in closets, drawers, shoes, behind pictures, everywhere.

As I half-expected, I found rolls of money inside of suit jackets and stuffed in the toe of shoes. But the big prize was the safe in the attic.

The problem was, I couldn't lift the safe by myself and King wasn't giving up the combination. Not even after I rammed the muzzle of the street sweeper up his ass! So I had to send Inez up the street to get the car.

There was no way I was leaving the safe behind. Together, it still took Inez and me thirty minutes to get the safe down the stairs and loaded into the rental car.

I had her go back and wipe down the house again 'cause she hadn't worn gloves as I had. She also had to pick up her broken fingernails. Though the neighboring homes were spaced a good distance apart, we worked quietly. When we were finished I told Inez to go wait in the car.

I went back upstairs to say *goodbye* to King.

CHAPTER 32

Back in Atlanta, I met with Rich Kid and collected the twenty-five G's he had promised me for completing the hit.

With Lonnie's help I found someone to blow torch the door off of the safe I'd taken from King. But I didn't allow the welder to look inside the safe after his job was executed. I paid him and hurried him along.

Then, alone at Inez' crib I tallied up the loot. Adding the money from the safe with all the loot I'd found hidden inside of closets at King's house, the total came to $890,075.00! When I added the eight kilos I'd also found at King's house, plus the twenty-five grand Rich Kid had just paid me, plus the loot I'd already had stashed at home in the freezer, I was a young millionaire!

I had hit the fuckin' stickup kid's lottery!

I was so excited, my dick got hard.

"Yeah!" I ran around Inez' crib screaming like a crazy man, beating my chest and high-fiving the air.

If hos thought I was hard on 'em before, how would they like me now?

What could they do with a young, rich nigga? Nothing!

I calmed down long enough to pack the loot in garbage bags and put the bags inside of my whip. There was no way I was letting Inez see how much had been inside of the safe. The bitch might have wanted half.

I drove the money and dope to my crib, nervous as a mafucka, praying po-po wouldn't get behind me and pull me over.

Thankfully, I felt at the time, I made it home without incident.

Cheryl was in the living room with the kids, feeding Chanté milk from a plastic bottle. Eryka crawled ran to me as soon as I stepped through the door. "Da Da! Da! Da!" she cried with excitement.

I dropped the two heavy garbage bags and scooped my lil' princess up in my arms. I rained kisses all over her fat, chubby cheeks. Then I sat her back down on the floor, dashed back to the whip to retrieve the other bags.

When I got back inside of the apartment, curious Eryka was pulling stacks of money out of one of the garbage bags I'd left on the living room floor and putting the roll of money to her mouth.

"Why the fuck you lettin' her put that nasty money in her mouth?" I shouted at Cheryl.

"You're the one who left it where she can reach it!" Cheryl shouted back and got up to haul Eryka over to the couch.

Eryka cried at the top of her little lungs. "Leave my lil' princess alone." I snatched my daughter from Cheryl's clutch. "C'mon, honey bunny. Help daddy count his riches."

Later, I went out and bought two medium-sized safes to stash the money in. Of course, I'd waited 'til dark to carry the safes into my apartment.

All of the money wouldn't fit inside the two safes, so I stored some inside of the freezer with my other stash.

I gave Lonnie fifty Gs and a whole kilo. Just 'cause he was my tightman. Inez got fifty G's, too. She never asked how much was inside of the safe. I sold the other seven kilos to Murder Mike for one hundred grand. It sort of surprised me that he was sitting on that much cash.

I had been prepared to have to wait until he flipped the dope to get paid in full. But Murder had all the loot, up front. Playboy was definitely on-the-rise. He asked if I was pushing weight for Rich Kid. Said he had heard me and Rich Kid was airtight.

"We're cool," I admitted, "but I ain't on his team like dat." After a pause, I asked, "Why? You and Rich Kid got beef?"

"Naw, main man. I was just wondering," he said. But I didn't believe him. Whatever. It wasn't my concern.

CHAPTER 33

Now that I was sitting on grown-up money, I could afford to relax a while and ponder my options: How could I make the mil' grow and last a lifetime?

First and foremost, I wanted Cheryl out of my crib and able to support herself. I decided I'd rush her into applying for Section 8 housing. Once she was awarded it, I'd furnish her crib and let her have the Maxima. I'd also pay for her to attend beauty school since she liked to do hair. That way, once she completed school, she could get a job and support herself.

I felt that was more than I owed the lazy bitch. She seemed to embrace my plans for her, but wanted to wait until Chanté was a few months older before going to beauty school. By then, her Section 8 application would be approved.

I gave my apartment manager a thousand dollars, under the table, to allow Cheryl and the kids to remain living with me for three more months.

Once they were settled in good, I took Inez and her daughter on a weekend cruise to the Bahamas.

We had a nice time, though it would've been better if Inez and I had gone alone. 'Cause her daughter definitely wasn't feeling me! I guess she was a daddy's girl and disliked the fact that some man other than Fat Stan was dicking her mama. I wasn't trying to play step-pop, though. So I just made it through the weekend, ignoring the little brat as much as possible. There was no sense in trying to get the little girl to like me, shortie wasn't having that! Her mom was carrying my seed and my secrets, so I'd have to deal with Fat Stan's daughter, from time to time. No problem.

Still I was glad when the cruise was over.

Not long after returning from the Bahamas, I whipped up to Shan's front door in the brand new SL-500 Benz drop that I'd just recently purchased. The exterior was bowling ball black, chrome trimmings, light gray, pillow-soft interior, DVD players in the dash and in the back of both front seat headrests.

I was rocking blue denim Phat Farm, matching jersey and beige Timbs. Mad bling hanging from my left ear, neck and both wrists. My grill was polished and my braids were fresh.

Lil' T was dressed in Phat Farm gear that matched mine, his hair was braided, too. A small diamond in his left earlobe, riding shotgun with his pops.

Inez was in the backseat, alone, having surrendered the front passenger seat to my son. She was fly in tight, hip-hugging jeans, cut at the navel jacket and a lace bra. She was iced-to-the-max, too.

Lil' Terrence had spent the past few days with us, but now I was returning him to Shan after a day at the carnival.

I honked the horn so I wouldn't have to knock on Shan's door.

The door swung open and ugly ass Shotgun Pete, who was home from doing county time, stood in the doorway. He recognized it was me, stepped back into the apartment and then Shan came outside to meet Lil' T and help him take the prizes he had won inside of the crib.

Inez got out the backseat and into the front, letting Shan peep her profile. I guessed it was a girl thing.

Shan lived in a hood spot so mad mafuckaz was outside, doing nothing. Hos were eating me up with their eyes. Niggaz were doing the same to Inez.

When I took the dirt bike I'd bought for Lil' T out of the trunk, my jersey rose up, revealing the heater on my waist. I purposely left it uncovered in case niggaz were sizing me up for a jack, letting them know I stayed strapped.

I dropped Inez off at her crib and whipped over to Englewood to cop some weed since Inez hadn't any. Too bad the Ribs Lady had been killed, I could've gone for a couple of her dinners.

I bought an ounce of 'dro from the niggaz by the b-ball court and whiped back through the horseshoe, profilin' in my drop. Fiona and 'em waved me over.

They came up to the whip in a cluster.

"I like your new car," one of them said.

"Thanks." I nodded at her.

"You heard about junkie Blue, didn't you?" Fiona asked me.

I told her naw, I'd been out of town.

"They arrested him for killing the Ribs Lady, and for almost killing her adopted daughter."

"Word?"

"Un-huh," they all said in unison.

"Damn!" I was shaking my head.

"They also found Hannibal's body floating in a lake. He had been missing for weeks," Fiona reported. "I got the newspaper article right here," one of her friends chimed in and then handed me the article from her purse.

I turned off the ignition and quickly read the article. All the article really said was that Hannibal DeFabio and his alleged righthand man, Shawn Price, bodies were discovered floating faced-down in a lake in North Georgia.

Damn! Hannibal had got caught slippin'.

He'd pissed somebody off or else he'd been in the way of somebody's come-up. I handed shawdy the news article back and let them all fawn over my drop for awhile.

"Which two of y'all wanna go with me to the motel, get high and get our freak on—menagé trois-style?"

Fiona said, "Hmmph!" But four of her friends were with it.

I chose the finest two and dipped.

At the Embassy Suites hotel, out by Atlanta's Hartsfield Airport, Keisha, Angel, and me smoked 'dro and drank E&J. We all got nice and mellow, not too high. I turned the radio to a station playing love music and told them to get naked and dance with each other.

Angel hestitated, but got on with the program when she saw Keisha coming out of her clothes.

Keisha was five-seven and weighed about 125 pounds. Her skin was dark, like molasses, smooth like satin. She had a mouthful of titties with dark brown nipples. The hair on her pussy was a neat mass of silk. If I had to compare her to anyone, I would say she closely resembled the rapper Foxy Brown.

Angel was a Charli Baltimore clone, red hair and all, even the small patch of hair over her plump pussy mound was red. Her titties were small but perky, with long nipples that stayed hard. She had a handful of freckles scattered about her light skin, adding uniqueness to her nakedness. An earring hung down from where I guessed her clit would be.

I stripped down to my Phat Farm boxers and sat down to enjoy the amateur show.

Angel appeared to be nervous. Keisha seemed turned on.

"Put on a good show and I might make both of y'all mine." I knew they'd be game for it. They wouldn't care how many women I had, they just wanted their slice of the pie. Once they got in, they could always play for the whole thing, even if they had to cross one another out.

They were breast to breast, belly to belly, arms around each other's shoudlers.

Outside, it was thundering and lightening as if the sexual electricity in the suite had ignited the skies. Keisha gyrated her pelvis against Angel's and stared her in the eyes. She was clearly the aggressor. But Angel didn't retreat. Instead, she closed her eyes.

Maybe savoring the female contact. Maybe wondering how in the hell did she get herself in such a predicament.

"Kiss her Keisha," I instructed.

Keisha complied with my instructions, but Angel didn't reciprocate. The station went to a commercial and the girls broke their embrace.

I said, "Look, Angel, you're with a big-time nigga. If you wanna be down, you're gonna have to do big girl things. If you got a problem with it, I can call you a cab."

She seemed to think it over for a minute.

Then she said, nervously, "I ain't ever done anything like this before."

"I haven't either," Keisha proclaimed. "But, girl, there's a first time for everything." She took the words right out of my mouth.

I had Angel sit on my lap when the music came back on and told Keisha to give us a private dance. Keisha moved slow and seductive, rubbing her nipples against Angel's then her steaming body against her friend's nose. All the while, I was rubbing Angel's thighs. I soon felt her juices flood my fingers.

After the sexual fury simmered, I watched both girls to see how they would react to the aftermath of lesbian sex. As I expected, Angel averted her eyes away from both Keisha and me.

I could see that Keisha was still excited, her passion not yet relieved. I told her to get on top of Angel and fuck her.

"Oh!" Angel gasped, spreading her legs wide apart.

Keisha was on her faster than the thought. She quickly rubbed her body against her friends', all the while kissing Angel's lips. The contact caused an involuntary spasm to run throughout Angel's body.

"Ah—Keisha!" she moaned. Then she began thrusting her body upwards to meet Keisha's thrusts.

Angel must have came five times, back to back. She came once so violently her head lashed from side to side and her body went into convulsions. All I could see were the whites of her eyes. Then Keisha gripped her strongly and began furiously rubbing her body against Angel's, until they both screamed in sexual release.

Finally, they were spent. They looked at each other and laughed.

"What's so funny?" I asked either of them.

"Nothing," said Keisha

"I never thought I'd do something like that," Angel said, "especially not with her!" They looked at one another and giggled like schoolgirls.

We lounged around, naked, smoking blunts and waiting on the Philly steak and cheese sandwiches to be delivered by the late-night deli near the airport.

After we had eaten, the three of us showered together and retired to the bedroom to resume our threesome.

"I wanna get on top and fuck her, this time," Angel whispered in my ear. No longer the shy girl.

I told Keisha to lie down. It was Angel's turn to please her.

Angel attacked Keisha's nakedness, without hestitation. She touched and licked her friend in the most delicate places, behind the ear, the side of the neck, the shoulders, nipples, navel, thighs and finally, she kissed the center of Keisha's wetness.

"Aww—shit!" Keisha panted. "Eat all of me!"

Angel brought her to a climax. My dick was stiff as a board! I put on a rubber and crawled in bed between them.

CHAPTER 34

The next morning, I was awakened by the sound of my pager vibrating on the nightstand. I crawled from between my two naked freaks, sat at the foot of the bed and used the telephone on the nightstand to call Juanita back.

"Whud up, Miss Thang?"

She answered, "I was calling to invite you to breakfast. I'm cooking."

I told her I was tied up at the moment, but I could probably come by around noon.

"That's cool. I won't go to work, then."

"Don't let me stop your hustle," I said.

Juanita ignored my remark. "What time can I expect you?" she asked.

"Twelve, twelve-thirty."

"I'll see you, then.

"Peace."

I dropped Keisha and Angel off in Englewood, promising I'd come through and holla in a few days. Then I dipped to my spot to shower and change gear.

Some nigga was standing outside of my door, knocking, when I pulled up. I got out of my whip and pounced up the steps in two strides.

"Who you looking for, my man?" I asked dude.

With a Hatian accent, he said he'd just recently moved into the complex and was wondering if there was any chance he could use my telephone. I told him I didn't have a phone inside and directed him to the pay phone near the manager's office.

Cheryl was at the door as soon as I opened it. "You know that fool?" I questioned her.

"Naw," she swore, "I saw him moving in a few weeks ago. I don't know nobody in this complex. I rarely come out of the house."

"Yeah, well, don't let nobody in here, to use the phone or nothing!"

"I ain't," she promised.

The crib was clean and none of my shit appeared to have been disturbed. The safes were locked and too heavy for Cheryl to move around. My freezer stash was proper, though. I could tell she had come across it while searching the freezer for food to cook. Boxes and freezer bags had been rearranged but my dough was straight.

Cool. Because if it wasn't I would twist her goddam wig, I said to myself as I closed the door and walked out of the kitchen into the bedroom.

I showered and changed into some fresh gear. Before I bounced, Cheryl told me she had put in an application for Section 8, and she showed me a brochure from a beauty school.

I told her to let me know when everything was set and how much it all would cost.

"I'll take you furniture shopping once they give you an apartment."

"I'm gonna try to find a Section 8 house," she said.

"That's cool." I then dipped before Eryka woke up and starting having a fit when I tried to leave.

I zipped over to Inez' to see what was shaking. She was weighing up ounces of dro and then separate ounces of regular weed. I grabbed an ounce of 'dro and put it in the inside pocket of the jacket I was wearing.

"Touch up my braids for me."

"So, I can assume you're just making a pit stop you ain't staying long?" she assumed correctly.

"True. But I'll be back later," I promised.

I was again pushing the Benz drop, decked out in MECCA gear, head to toe. Not much bling on but an earring and a watch. A young, thug millionaire with nothing to do all day but shine and figure out which bitch to fuck with.

Soon I would start looking for a condo to rent, somewhere on the outskirts of the city, where my whips wouldn't cost more than my crib. But that could wait until Cheryl was out of my hair.

I was also contemplating opening a nightclub or a restaurant. Too bad Blue had killed the Ribs Lady, she and I could've opened a chain of Rib Shacks.

Speaking of Blue, Keisha and Angel had told me the fool had been buying bundles of crack from niggaz in da hood. He'd been seen with wads of money, only hours after the Ribs Lady body had been discovered. Somebody dropped dime on him, and the police picked him up and questioned him. They matched his fingerprints to those discovered on the bloody aluminum bat found next to the Ribs Lady body.

The police interrogated Blue until he confessed. Then they charged him with armed robbery, murder and attempted murder.

They hinted if the little girl recovered well enough to identify Blue as the perpertrator, they would seek the death penalty. I figured if the girl died, they would surely seek it.

Juanita must've heard me whip into her driveway 'cause she was standing with the door open as soon as I reached her porch. We spoke, then I handed her the teddy bear I had hidden behind my back. Most women love stuffed animals. I guessed it played into their desire to always be daddy's little girl.

Juanita squealed with genuine delight and hugged the teddy bear to her bosom.

"Lunch is ready," she said, escorting me into the dining room. "I hope you're ready to eat."

We ate grilled chicken strips and pasta, cucumber and lettuce salad and nibbled on low-fat cheese crackers. Juanita drank bottled water, but served me imported beer that was the best I'd ever tasted.

I had fresh peaches and French ice-cream for dessert, Juanita had frozen yogurt. I guessed that was how she kept a perfect figure.

I watched her as she cleared the table. The cotton sweatpants couldn't hide her perfect ass, plus her walk was jaw-dropping! She wore a T-shirt, tied in a knot above her sexy navel, with the words *Good Girl* emblazoned across the front. Her hair was in feathers down past her shoulders and her nails were painted rainbow.

She flashed me a smile that was accentuated by the two open-faced crowns in the top of her grill. A diamond centered both crowns.

Pressed to make a comparison, I'd have to say that Juanita resembled a younger Lisa Raye.

We moved into the den and I fired up a blunt. Juanita didn't mind, so she said she just turned on the ceiling fan and busied herself until I was finished blazing. Then she snuggled into my arms and put her lips up to be kissed. One kiss leads to another and then another. But she drew back before things got too hot. I wasn't trippin' it, I was fucked out!

"How long do you plan to be in the streets?" Juanita suddendly asked.

I told her I really couldn't say. Shit, the streets were in me.

Juanita began telling me her goals and dreams, stating that she had no more time to waste. She planned to quit her job at The Gentlemen's Escape, sell her house and move away. She said she had some money saved up, enough to live off of while she went to college and pursued her dream of becoming a surgical doctor.

"If my student grants run out, I may eventually have to get a part-time job to help pay for classes." Juanita had it all planned out.

She told me that she could see herself falling in love with me, even spending a lifetime with me. But not if I stayed connected to the streets.

"The streets is all I know, shawdy."

"But it's not all you can learn. Don't limit yourself like that. Why be one more hustler, when you can be so much more?" she challenged.

She told me I could go back to school and then on to college. Or I could open my own business, she'd help me every step of the way.

She said we could get married and be a team, legitimately, no crime.

"I'll love you and *only you,* forever," Juanita claimed. "Just say yes. Really, I'm a good girl, you'll see. I ain't ever cheated on no man I ever had."

She said the streets were killing brothers and sending a record number of them to prison, leaving behind broken-hearted, lonely young women.

Tears were in her eyes.

She said, "I'm—not—gonna let the streets claim me by proxy and they do, every time they claim someone I love or care about. And they'll claim you, too, if you don't let go."

I reminded Juanita that she couldn't love me, we had no history together. Her response was that she liked me a lot and would grow to love me if I chose to move away with her. She claimed she didn't want just any man, she wanted me. It made a nigga feel good 'cause I knew Juanita had plenty suitors.

Like the time before, all types of thoughts were jostling in my head when I left Juanita's crib. She'd given me one month to reach a decision. After that, she'd be moving away and starting her life over.

How could she expect me to just up and leave my seeds, even if they could visit me wherever we moved to. Didn't Juanita know the streets had just as strong a pull as she did? She didn't know I was sitting on a mil', enjoying my ghetto fame. If she had, maybe she wouldn't have suggested I walk away from the shine. Shit, I had been down too long, not to enjoy my sudden wealth and fame.

CHAPTER 35

I hadn't talked to or seen Toi since that day at the food court in Greenbriar's Mall.

It was Saturday morning and pouring down raining as I waited impatiently inside of the Waffle House for my sister to show. She was already a half hour late. I'd wait another few minutes, though. I played with a patty melt and hash browns while I watched the parking lot for her car.

A Cadillac SUV drove up and I saw Toi hurry out the driver's door and dash inside of the small restaurant. She shook the rain off of her umbrella, closed it and walked briskly over to the booth where I waited.

"Sorry I'm late," she said, out of breath. "I had to drop Glen off at his physical therapist. I can't stay long. I told him I had mistakenly left something cooking in the oven."

"This won't take long," I assured her.

She began drinking my cup of coffee, warming herself. I told her I missed her and it was too bad we weren't as close as we used to be.

Toi said we were still close in her heart, we just couldn't see each other often. For obvious reasons.

We talked for twenty minutes, catching each other up on what was going on in our separate lives. She told me she'd page me when she could get away for a few hours, 'cause she wanted to see my kids, especially the new baby.

She wanted to know if I planned on taking Chanté by Mama's.

"You know I ain't got no mama, as far as I'm concerned. But let's not go there." I reminded her.

A few minutes later, Toi said she had to go. I walked her out to the truck, both of us under her umbrella and slipped a wad of money in her lap.

"What's this?" she asked, surprised.

I told her it was ten grand. "Don't tell Glen about it," I cautioned her. "Put it away, in case you ever decide you're tired of his shit. And I've got plenty more where that came from." Toi hugged me and promised she'd put the money some place Glen couldn't find it. Then she tried to tell me that he was really a decent man. I didn't wanna hear it, though.

"Why didn't you ever ask me what I'd did to make Glen hit me?"

"'Cause it didn't matter," I simply said, and meant it.

"I gotta get going. Bye. I love you." A tear rolled down her face.

"I love you, too."

My heart ached as I watched her walk outside in the rain, climb in her ride and drive off.

Why did things have to be so murky? I asked myself.

I placed a tip on the table for the waitress and then walked out in the rain, not even bothering to shelter myself from the downpour.

My mood was somber when I reached Inez' crib, and it remained that way until I feel asleep next to her in bed that night.

Sometime in the middle of the night, Inez awakened screaming and sweating like she'd just ran the one-hundred-meter dash. I sat up in bed and wrapped my arms around her until she came out of the nightmare.

She'd been having nightmares since our ordeal in Kentucky. I'd taken her to a doctor, but he couldn't help much since she lied about the 'cause of the bad dreams. Nor could the doctor prescribe valium or any other medicine to help her sleep through the night, for fear that the medicine might harm the baby inside Inez' womb.

She would have to tough the nightmares out. I constantly reassured her that they'd soon cease.

"You okay?" I wiped her forehead with a cold towel.

"Mmm-hmmm," she mumbled, leaning back against my chest.

"I keep seeing his face," she said after a while.

"Let's not talk about it, boo."

I massaged her shoulders, all the while wondering if she was gonna nut up and leave me no choice but to plant her in dirt. I didn't wanna have to do that, but I'd do so before I'd let her send me back to prison. I wasn't letting anything separate me from the million dollars I had stashed away. I had caught lightning in a bottle. I planned to keep it trapped.

For the next couple of weeks, I spent an equal number of nights at my apartment as I did at Inez'.

At home, I enjoyed my two little princesses, but mostly ignored their mother. Eryka was crawling around, getting into everything! I was loving every minute of it. At night I'd usually fall asleep with Chanté on my chest and Eryka hugged to my side. Cheryl slept on the couch whenever I was there all night.

At Inez', I slept light, not because of her nightmares, but due to the fact she still sold weed to a select clientele. I was a robber, paranoid by trade. I decided that once I moved into a condo, I would not spend nights at Inez', she'd have to come spend the night with me.

I went by Juanita's house to visit a few times, and even stopped by the club once as a surprise. She was always happy to see me and stopped whatever she was doing to pay attention to me.

Shawdy was working on my resistance, something serious! I could see the wisdom of her plans and goals. I just couldn't see how they were compatible with mine. She probably didn't know it, but I was thirsty for her.

Maybe I wanted what I couldn't have? At least, I couldn't have Juanita without giving up the streets, Inez, and all that I felt comfortable with. I wasn't ready to do that.

On one occasion I was over Juanita's house watching her do aerobics. She quickly concluded her workout, then she took a quick shower, returning to me in nothing but a silk wrap-around robe and a towel wrapped high around her head. She looked like an Egyptian Queen, beautiful, sexy and divine. Damn! Away from the club I would've never guessed she was a stripper.

I proposed, "Let's make love *one* time, to see if our attraction to each other is real or just lust."

She fed me a slice of apple and kissed me softly on the lips. "It's real, you just gotta give it a chance," she said confidently.

But at the time, the streets were in me too deep.

During the day, I would whip around the city in my drop or my Lex, occasionally being harassed by the cops. But all of my papers were in order, and I kept my gat hidden in the secret compartment of the Lex' or the Benz, so po-po had no choice but to let me drive on. Jay-Z said it best: *"Can I live!"*

I got with Keisha and Angel again a few weeks after our threesome, but the second time didn't produce the same fire as our first menage-a-trois. I got the feeling those freak hos were more into each other than they were into me. Fuck it! At least I'd helped them realize they could be more than friends.

I was at a sports bar when I ran into Blondie, the stripper I had robbed along with her friends. She was working behind the counter, sweating me like crazy.

A young nigga, braided up, came from a back room and joined her at the register. A few minutes later, he came over to my table and introduced himself.

"I'm Little Gotti," he said. "Welcome to my establishment. Don't I know you from somewhere?" Seeing if I'd lie.

"Yeah. We were both at The Player's Ball," I acknowledged, "I'm Terrence." Knowing that it would be more difficult for him to find street niggaz who knew Terrence than it would be to find those who knew Youngblood.

"Can I send you over something to drink?" Little Gotti offered.

"Naw, I just stopped in for a minute to check out the scenery."

"Be sure to come back, and bring some friends." He sounded like he'd fallen for my nonchalance.

I said, "I will." I stuck around for twenty minutes just to play my hand right. Then I dipped.

CHAPTER 36

Poochie greeted me with a hug. “James, this is my son-in-law Terrence,” she introduced me to her company, an older cat who struck me as a deacon of a church.

“Terrence?” he said, extending his hand.

I shook it and then made small talk until a pause in the boring conversation afforded me the opportunity to say I had to get going.

Poochie walked me outside, complimented me on my drop and laughed when I teased her about trading me in for an old fossil.

“Boy, you’re the devil!” she kidded back.

After leaving there, I would’ve went by Lonnie’s and smoked some weed while kicking his ass at John Madden Bowl, but I remembered he was up in New York visiting family. So, instead, I drove by the game room to see what was poppin’.

A couple of Rich Kid’s workers were amongst those shooting pool. I nodded at them. I had spoken to Rich Kid a few days ago, he’d said he was just checking on me and would holla again later.

Bitches were in the game room, dressed to attract ballers as usual.

A few of them were sexy, in comparison to the others, but none were dimes and none were eatable. I bounced from the game room and headed down to Englewood.

Murder Mike appeared to be putting one of his workers in check when I pulled up in the horseshoe. The young soldier bowed down under the barrage of his bossman’s tirade. I parked the drop and got out andaited for the storm coming from Murder’s mouth to cease. When it did he came over to where I’d parked.

“Whud up, main man?” I greeted him.

“You own the world, whoady,” he shot back, eyeing my whip for the first time. “Business must be good. I didn’t know Rich Kid paid his lieutenant so well,” he cracked.

“What?” I asked, a little peeved. That was the second time he’d tried to connect me with Rich Kid.

He laughed, but it was forced. “C’mon, dawg, you think I can’t tell those kilos you sold me was the same type yayo his crew be slangin’ by the basketball court?”

Damn! That was news to me. The seven keys I'd sold Murder Mike had come from King's safe. How could it be the same dope Rich Kid's crew was pushing? Unless King had stolen it from Rich Kid?

Or, more likely, they'd had the same supplier. I couldn't figure the shit out. I did *know* that my man, Murder, was interrogating me.

And I didn't like it.

I told him that he and I go way back, like roaches in the projects.

It wasn't my style to reveal my hand to him, but I assured him I wasn't selling dope for Rich Kid or anyone. "You know I don't get down like that," I said.

"Bet dat." Murder Mike dapped hands with me, letting me know he believed me.

I wondered how long it would be before he made his move on Rich Kid.

Fiona came up and interrupted us.

"Don't you see us talking?" My tone checked the bitch.

"I'm sorry. I—"

"It's cool," Murder said. "I gotta make a quick call, anyways" He walked off a few paces and called someone on his cellphone.

Fiona wasn't talking about shit. She was still peeved that I'd taken her friends to the hotel, like I had violated *her* by doing so.

"Ho, please!" I snapped. "When you start making me some money, then you can have an attitude about who I fuck."

"Yo' ass gon' catch AIDS!"

I pulled out a pack of Magnums. "Never! Leave! Home! Without! 'Em!" I barked, one word at a time. Then I tossed a pack at her, hitting her in the face. The young hustlers around cracked the fuck up!

Fiona walked away warning: "What goes up, must come down!" Like the jealous-hearted hoodrat she was.

I bullshitted the day away in the hood—shooting dice by the basketball court, puffing on a stogie filled with 'dro, listening to lil' niggaz bustin' ryhmes, freestyled and rehearsed.

When I got hungry I copped some hot dogs and chips from the rolling store, a truck/van that drove through the hoods selling groceries and other items at high prices to mafuckaz too lazy to walk to the store.

Juanita's mother, Miss Pearl, had come up to the rolling store wanting a pint of Mad Dog while I was waiting on my hot dogs. She was thirty-five cents short so the man wouldn't let her have the cheap wine. I told him to give her two bottles and put it on my tab. Then I squeezed a hundred-dollar bill into the palm of her swollen hand. She looked at the money for a long while and then looked at me like I was Heaven sent.

"Thank you, son," Miss Pearl said and hurried down the hill.

She hadn't recalled my face as one of the lil' boys who used to rip and run all over the projects. And I was sure she didn't know her daughter was trying hard to pull me away from the streets.

By the time I left Englewood, it was just turning dark. I saw Murder Mike's whip still parked in the horseshoe, but he wasn't around. A red Mercedes E-Class was parked in front of Cita's mama's unit. I'd heard earlier that day that Murder had blessed Cita with a Benz. I didn't know what Cita's grip was on my homeboy, but, whatever it was, it had to be strong.

I stopped at a music store a few blocks from I-20 Expressway to cop the latest edition of *Jay-Z's Hard Knocks* and that white boy, Eminem's, latest CD, plus, anything that was hot by ATL niggaz.

A half hour later, I came out of the store with a box of incense and five CDs.

A van was parked so close to my drop, I had to turn side-ways to get to the driver's door. I was at the car door, digging in my jeans pocket for my car keys when I heard the van's side door slide open. I should've jetted, on foot, or at least pulled the gat that was at my waist. Instead, instinct made me turn to face the sound of the sliding van door.

That was a big mistake!

I was staring at a Dread holding a sawed-off shotgun aimed at my chest. "Don't be stoopid, mon!" the Dread barked.

I would've still tried the mafucka, fuck going out without a fight!

Fuck being a hostage or the victim of a kidnapping, eventually found with my dick in the dirt! I was going for my gat, half-turning away from the sawed-off when some strong mafucka grabbed me from behind, pinning my arms to my sides. My gat hit the pavement and skidded under my whip. A third mafucka bent down and scooped it up.

I yelled at the top of my lungs! Not like a bitch, but to attract a crowd. Then I was thrown inside of the van, choked by the strong ass nigga, threatened with the sawed-off and whisked away.

They drove around, beating me with a lead pipe, cussin' and threatening me in Jamaican accents, saying *I was fuckin' wit' da wrong people, mon!*

I pretended to be dead and the beating stopped. I was tossed out of the van while it was still going about twenty miles per hour. They didn't rob me or hold me for ransom. Maybe they didn't know I was worth a million and some change?

I scrambled to my feet, my entire body in pain, blood running down my face and the back of my head. So much blood was in my eyes and I was so weak and dizzy that I couldn't make out where I was, but it seemed very familiar.

I stumbled up on the closest porch and rang the bell. The person on the other side of the door said something, but I was too disoriented to comprehend.

"I—need you—to call an—ambulance." I mumbled.

The door yanked open and I fell face-first into the doorway. The last thing I remembered hearing before I blacked out from my pain was a woman's scream.

I didn't find out until I woke up in the hospital the next day that it was Inez' crib I'd stumbled into. It was she who'd called an ambulance to rush me to the emergency room. Whoever had kidnapped and beaten me, obviously *intended* to toss me out the van in front of her crib, which meant they had to be someone who'd knew I was holding her down.

My face was hideously swollen from a broken jaw. I'd suffered two cracked ribs, a concussion and several gashes to the back of my head. But I was still alive and somebody would have to pay!

My mouth was wired shut, but I could talk through clenched teeth after a few days. I told Inez to go down to the music store and check on my whip.

The next day she informed me that the store's owner said the police had towed it away the same night I'd gotten snatched inside of the van. He'd seen the altercation and had called the police but wanted nothing else to do with the matter.

I could understand that.

Mafuckaz in the hood had heard that I got snatched up in a van, but they didn't know my whereabouts until a bitch from Englewood, who worked as a cleaning woman in the emergency room, started running her mouth. Then, mad mafuckaz from the hood came to the hospital to visit me: Keisha and Angel. A couple of lil' niggaz who worked the traps for Rich Kid. Poochie and Shan. Bitches whose names I didn't even know. And, of course, my main man, Murder Mike.

I didn't like them seeing me banged up and shit. Yet I appreciated the love shown. And I would definitely hunt down my enemies and let the streets know that I was not to be fucked with!

Murder Mike said, "How you feelin', main main?"

"Ready to go to war." I mumbled.

He said he'd keep his ear to the streets and if he found out who had banged me up, he'd ride down on 'em with me when I was well enough. I appreciated his concern and knew it was genuine.

Lonnie was still up in New York and had no way of knowing I was laid up in a hospital. I asked Inez if I'd been wearing my pager that night.

"No, boo. You must've lost it before those cowards pushed you out of the van." She was being concerned and sweet, staying at the hospital with me all day, until visiting hours ended.

My sister came to visit me the fourth day I was in the hospital.

She'd just heard about it. She said that Glen hadn't even tried to stop her from visiting me. He knew where to draw the line, she said.

"Terrence," she said, "Glen didn't have anything to do with this. He just got back from Florida yesterday, and he's still on crutches. I questioned him about—" She hushed when a nurse came in to check my vital signs. When the nurse was gone, Toi said, "Trust me. Glen's my man, I would be able to tell if he were lying."

Then without any prompting, Toi told me the whole story of why Glen had jumped on her that day. It fucked me up. I would've never suspected it. Glen had jumped on Toi after catching her creepin' with Rich Kid! Not once, but twice! It also should've embedded in me that you never know anybody like you thought you did. But I wouldn't come to that unbending conclusion until much, much later.

Juanita showed up in my hospital room looking so beautiful I forgot about all my pain. She was carrying a get-well card so huge it came up past her shoulders when sat on the floor. She let me read it and then sat the huge card in a corner of the room.

"How're you feeling, baby?" Her eyes were sad for me.

"I've had better days," I admitted, mumbling the words.

"Say what?" she moved closer to my bed so she could hear me more clearly.

"I'm a'ight," I said. "How did you find out I was in the hospital?" She said she'd been paging me for the past week, with no reply.

Worried, she'd driven over to Englewood and asked of my whereabouts. Some fool had told her I was dead and my body had been found in a dumpster. Others said they hadn't seen me but had heard I'd been kidnapped out of my Benz in front of the music shop near I-20.

Finally, in near hysterics, she ran into Cita, who told her where to find me.

"You look so helpless lying there," Juanita cried. "When you get out of the hospital, I'm taking you home with me." She leaned over and kissed my forehead just as Inez returned from calling to check on her daughter.

Juanita spoke first.

"Hi," Inez returned the greeting, with no sincerity.

She then turned to me and said, "I gotta go take my daughter some cough medicine and soup. Mama says she's coming down with the flu. I'll be back in a few hours."

If I had a response, Inez didn't wait to hear it.

Juanita didn't comment on Inez' thinly disguised attitude.

For the next two hours, she just kept me company, bringing me up to date on her plans to move away and pursue her goals.

"I found a buyer for my house, we're supposed to close the deal in a few weeks," she said expectantly.

She told me to think about moving away with her and to consider coming to stay at her house when I got out the hospital in a few days.

"I will," I promised.

She said, "I'll come back to see you if you want me to. But I don't want to 'cause a problem between you and Inez."

"I'll be getting released in a few days," I mumbled.

"Please think about what I said." She kissed me softly before saying goodbye.

Rich Kid came to see me later that same evening. He showed concern, offered any help that I might need and asked if I needed anything until I could get back on my feet. He couldn't tell that I was now seeing him through slightly different eyes. I told him I was straight and kept what I now knew about him and Toi to myself.

So, everyone I would've expected to visit me in the hospital had now shown up. Some sooner than others, but all just the same. I knew Lonnie and Delina were still in New York, and he didn't know what had happened or he'd been the first at my bedside.

Cheryl was at my crib, just a twenty-minute drive away, but she might as well have been on the moon, for all she knew about what was happening with me. She didn't know my niggaz from Englewood. She knew Lonnie and Rich Kid, but she had no way of contacting either of them. She'd probably tried to page me over the past few days, but undoubtedly figured I had gone out of town, or just hadn't wanted to call her back.

If something was seriously wrong with one of my daughters, I guessed Cheryl would still have Toi's number.

I imagined what her dingy ass would say once she found out I had been in the hospital. She'd probably say, *"Boy, you could've had someone come by and tell me you were hurt. Dag!"*

CHAPTER 37

The last night before I was to be released from the hospital, I laid in bed all night trying to figure out who had wanted me beat down, but not dead?

Number One on my list was Big G, Glen. Despite what my sister believed, I didn't believe she could tell when he was lying. Love blinded her from the truth. *But why would Glen have me beaten up instead of killed?* I had shot him in the knees and kept his money and guns. A beatdown hardly revenged that.

Number Two on my list was Little Gotti, Blondie's man. Maybe she had convinced him that Terrence and Popeye was one and the same? For what I'd done to her, a beatdown might have seemed sufficient.

I moved Little Gotti to the top of the list, ahead of Glen.

Who else would want to see me hurt? And would know I fucked with Inez? And where she lived? Rich Kid, maybe? But he had no beef with me. Plus, he hired out killers, not mafuckaz who'd roughed you up.

I was also thinking: *This was the second time somebody had done me bodily harm and both times, I'd just got finished dissin' Fiona.*

Could she be behind this shit? I wondered

Naw, that po' bitch don't have the juice to have me touched. The bitch just provokes bad karma.

Now, who did I know with affiliations to Dreads? The shit had me vexed! But I had a brave heart, a few loyal friends and mad loot to help me find out who my enemies were.

Why did niggaz have to bring the drama, just when I was trying to chill and enjoy my mil'?

I closed my eyes and tried to sleep, thinking about Juanita's offer, knowing I couldn't walk away from Inez or my unfinished business in the streets.

Inez arrived at the hospital to take me home early the next day. It didn't take too long for the day nurse to do all the things she needed to do in order for me to be discharged and sent on my way. While the nurse was doing those things, Inez went down to the hospital pharmacy and had my prescriptions filled.

Armed with gauze rolls to wrap around my cracked ribs, clean dressings for the gash in the back of my head and plenty of prescription pain pills, Inez wheeled me down the hall onto the elevator, and, finally, to the hospital exit.

We drove straight to the police impound to get my whip. My shit was mad filthy, inside and out. I told Inez to go on home, I'd be over there later after I got my car washed and cleaned and went to Decatur to check on Cheryl and my things.

"Be careful," she said.

"Naw, mafuckaz better beware!"

A READING GROUP GUIDE
TRUST NO MAN
CA$H
ABOUT THIS GUIDE

The suggested questions are intended to enhance your group's reading of this book.

DISCUSSION QUESTIONS

1. Why do you think Shan hooked up with Youngblood's partner, Shotgun Pete, when Youngblood went to prison?
2. Is Youngblood justified in being salty with them both? Why?
3. Is Youngblood's anger towards his mother justified?
4. Who do you think shot Youngblood?
5. Was Youngblood right to check his sister Toi's boyfriend, Glen, for jumping on her? Or did Toi's reaction show that Youngblood should stay out of their business?
6. Was Youngblood wrong for his treatment of Cheryl?
7. What do you think of Youngblood messing around with Poochie? Is it just sexual?
8. Is Inez truly a ride-or-die chick?
9. Do you think Juanita will steal Youngblood away from Inez?
10. Who is Youngblood's trusted friend: Lonnie, Rich Kid, or Murder Mike?

Excerpt from Trust No Man II

After my whip was spotless, shining and smelling brand new, I paid and tipped the boys who had detailed my ride. Then I drove out to Decatur to my crib to check on Cheryl, my daughters and my bank. I knew Cheryl would be mad because I hadn't told her I was in the hospital, banged up, but that was the least of my concerns.

I'ma find those niggaz that banged me up and show 'em how the fuck I get down! I was thinking as I pulled into my apartment complex, parked, got out of my ride and headed up to my apartment.

As soon as I opened the door and stepped inside, I knew something wasn't right. The only sound in the apartment was of water dripping from the faucet in the kitchen sink.

I followed the sound. When I reached the kitchen, the freezer door was ajar and a puddle of water was on the floor. The chicken boxes in which I kept some of my stash were scattered about the kitchen counter, empty as fuck!

My safes! My million-dollar stash!

In a panic, I dashed to the bedroom to check the closet. The closet door stood wide open. I held my breath and peeked inside.

Both safes were gone! *Oh, hell naw!*

So was my small cache of guns.

My clothes were cut up and strewn all over the bedroom.

That lowdown bitch! Some nigga put her up to this! My million-dollar stash was gone! I screamed like a madman through my wired mouth.

Then the pain from my cracked ribs hit me so hard I crumpled to the floor. After the pain lessened a bit, I was able to get to my feet, stumble back into the kitchen where I noticed a letter in Cheryl's handwriting stuck on the refrigerator door, held in place with one of those small, plastic smiley faces with a magnetized back.

I snatched the letter off the door and began reading.

Youngblood,

Don't bother trying to find us, nigga, 'cause you never will! You didn't want me in your life, so now I'm out, me and your daughters!

See, we are a package deal—you can't have them and not me! I give you credit for loving Chanté and Eryka, but you treated me like shit.

Nigga, you made me stop loving you, after money made you stop loving me. Money changed you, nigga! That's why I'm taking all of your dough. Maybe without riches you'll treat women nicer.

Oh, just so you know, I have a man who loves me now. He's the Haitian nigga you caught knocking on the door that time. Yep, caught your ass slippin', not up on your game. I may have gotten fat, but your ass got dumb! Again, don't try to find us, we're moving out of the country and never coming back. Dag, motherfucker, I hate you! But who's crying now? It sho' ain't me. Thanks to you, I'm a rich, fat bitch!

Later nigga,

Cheryl, Chante and Eryka

Cheryl's letter smashed me! I fell to my knees in the puddle of water and cried like a baby. The bitch had run off with my two little princesses and all my bank.

Bitch, you think stealing my dough is gonna make me nicer? Hell the fuck naw! It's gonna make me even more of a killa—startin' with your fam.

Coming Soon from Lock Down Publications/Ca$h Presents

TORN BETWEEN TWO

By **Coffee**

LAY IT DOWN **III**

By **Jamaica**

BLOOD OF A BOSS **IV**

By **Askari**

BRIDE OF A HUSTLA **III**

By **Destiny Skai**

WHEN A GOOD GIRL GOES BAD **II**

By **Adrienne**

LOVE & CHASIN' PAPER

By **Qay Crockett**

I RIDE FOR MY HITTA **II**

By **Misty Holt**

THE HEART OF A GANGSTA **II**

By **Jerry Jackson**

Available Now

RESTRAING ORDER **I & II**

By **CA$H & Coffee**

LOVE KNOWS NO BOUNDARIES **I II & III**

By **Coffee**

LAY IT DOWN **I & II**

By **Jamaica**

PUSH IT TO THE LIMIT

By **Bre' Hayes**

BLOOD OF A BOSS **I II & III**

By **Askari**

THE STREETS BLEED MURDER **I, II & III**

By **Jerry Jackson**

CUM FOR ME

An **LDP Erotica Collaboration**

BRIDE OF A HUSTLA **I & II**

By **Destiny Skai**

WHEN A GOOD GIRL GOES BAD

By **Adrienne**

A GANGSTER'S REVENGE **I II III & IV**

A SAVAGE LOVE 1

By **Aryanna**

WHAT ABOUT US **I & II**

NEVER LOVE AGAIN

THUG ADDICTION

By **Kim Kaye**

THE KING CARTEL **I, II & III**

By **Frank Gresham**

THESE NIGGAS AIN'T LOYAL **I, II & III**

By **Nikki Tee**

GANGSTA SHYT **I II & III**

By **CATO**

THE ULTIMATE BETRAYAL

By **Phoenix**

DON'T FU#K WITH MY HEART **I & II**

By **Linnea**

BOSS'N UP **I & II**

By **Royal Nicole**

I LOVE YOU TO DEATH

By Destiny J

I RIDE FOR MY HITTA

By **Misty Holt**

Stay Connected with Us!

Text **LOCKDOWN** to 22828 to stay up-to-date with new releases, sneak peaks, contests and more…

Made in the USA
Middletown, DE
13 September 2024

60917635R00186